Henry Home Kames

Elements of criticism

With the author's last corrections and additions. Vol. 1

Henry Home Kames

Elements of criticism
With the author's last corrections and additions. Vol. 1

ISBN/EAN: 9783337113155

Printed in Europe, USA, Canada, Australia, Japan

Cover: Foto ©Andreas Hilbeck / pixelio.de

More available books at **www.hansebooks.com**

ELEMENTS

OF

CRITICISM.

WITH THE

AUTHOR's LAST CORRECTIONS AND ADDITIONS.

First 𝔄merican *from the Seventh* London Edition.

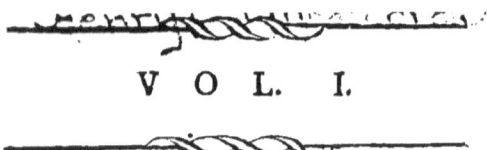

V O L. I.

Boston:

From the Press

OF SAMUEL ETHERIDGE,

For J. WHITE, THOMAS & ANDREWS, W. SPOTSWOOD,
D. WEST, W. P. BLAKE, E. LARKIN, & J. WEST.

M DCC XCVI.

PREFACE.

PRINTING, by multiplying copies at will, affords to writers great opportunity of receiving inftruction from every quarter. The author of this treatife, having always been of opinion that the general tafte is feldom wrong, was refolved from the beginning to fubmit to it with entire refignation : its fevereft difapprobation might have incited him to do better, but never to complain. Finding now the judgment of the public to be favourable, ought he not to draw fatisfaction from it ? He would be devoid of fenfibility were he not greatly fatisfied. Many criticifms have indeed reached his ear; but they are candid and benevolent, if not always juft. Gratitude, therefore, had there been no other motive, muft have roufed his utmoft induftry to clear this edition from all the defects of the former, fo far as fuggefted by others, or difcov-
cred

ered by himfelf. In a work containing many particulars, both new and abftrufe, it was difficult to exprefs every article with fufficient perfpicuity; and, after all the pains beftowed, there remained certain paffages which are generally thought obfcure. The author, giving an attentive ear to every cenfure of that kind, has, in the prefent edition, renewed his efforts to correct every defect; and he would gladly hope that he has not been altogether unfuccefsful. The truth is, that a writer, who muft be poffefied of the thought before he can put it into words, is but ill qualified to judge whether the expreffion be fufficiently clear to others : in that particular, he cannot avoid the taking on him to judge for the reader, who can much better judge for himfelf.

June 1763.

CONTENTS.

CONTENTS.

VOLUME I.

INTRODUCTION.

INTRODUCTION.

THAT nothing external is perceived till firſt it makes an impreſſion upon the organ of ſenſe, is an obſervation that holds equally in every one of the external ſenſes. But there is a difference as to our knowledge of that impreſſion : in touching, taſting, and ſmelling, we are ſenſible of the impreſſion ; that, for example, which is made upon the hand by a ſtone, upon the palate by an apricot, and upon the noſtrils by a roſe : it is otherwiſe in ſeeing and hearing ; for I am not ſenſible of the impreſſion made upon my eye, when I behold a tree ; nor of the impreſſion made upon my ear, when I liſten to a ſong.* That difference in the manner of perceiving external objects, diſtinguiſheth remarkably hearing and ſeeing from the other ſenſes ; and I am ready to ſhow, that it diſtinguiſheth ſtill more remarkably the feelings of the former from that of the latter ; every feeling, pleaſant or painful, muſt be in the mind ; and yet, becauſe in taſting, touching, and ſmelling, we are ſenſible of the impreſſion
made

* See the Appendix, § 13.

made upon the organ, we are led to place there alſo the pleaſant or painful feeling cauſed by that impreſſion ;* but, with reſpect to ſeeing and hearing, being inſenſible of the organic impreſſion, we are not miſled to aſſign a wrong place to the pleaſant or painful feelings cauſed by that impreſſion ; and therefore we naturally place them in the mind, where they really are : upon that account, they are conceived to be more refined and ſpiritual, than what are derived from taſting, touching, and ſmelling ; for the latter feelings, ſeeming to exiſt externally at the organ of ſenſe, are conceived to be merely corporeal.

The pleaſures of the eye and the ear, being thus elevated above thoſe of the other external ſenſes, acquire ſo much dignity as to become a laudable entertainment. They are not, however, ſet on a level with the purely intellectual ; being no leſs inferior in dignity to intellectual pleaſures,

---

* After the utmoſt efforts, we find it beyond our power to conceive the flavour of a roſe to exiſt in the mind : we are neceſſarily ed to conceive that pleaſure as exiſting in the noſtrils along with he impreſſion made by the roſe upon that organ. And the ſame ill be the reſult of experiments with reſpect to every feeling of aſte, touch, and ſmell. Touch affords the moſt ſatisfactory experiments. Were it not that the deluſion is detected by philoſophy, no perſon would heſitate to pronounce, that the pleaſure ariſing from touching a ſmooth, ſoft, and velvet ſurface, has its exiſtence at the ends of the fingers, without once dreaming of its exiſting any where elſe.

pleafures, than fuperior to the organic or corporeal : they indeed refemble the latter, being,
like them, produced by external objects ; but
they alfo refemble the former, being, like them,
produced without any fenfible organic impreffion. Their mixt nature and middle place between organic and intellectual pleafures, qualify
them to affociate with both ; beauty heightens
all the organic feelings, as well as the intellectual : harmony, though it afpires to inflame
devotion, difdains not to improve the relifh of a
banquet.

The pleafures of the eye and the ear have
other valuable properties befide thofe of dignity
and elevation : being fweet and moderately exhilarating, they are in their tone equally diftant
from the turbulence of paffion, and the langour
of indolence ; and by that tone are perfectly
well qualified, not only to revive the fpirits
when funk by fenfual gratification, but alfo to
relax them when overftrained in any violent
purfuit. Here is a remedy provided for many
diftreffes ; and, to be convinced of its falutary
effects, it will be fufficient to run over the following particulars. Organic pleafures have
naturally a fhort duration ; when prolonged,
they lofe their relifh ; when indulged to excefs,
they beget fatiety and difguft : and, to reftore

a proper·

a proper tone of mind, nothing can be more
happily contrived than the exhilarating pleafures of the eye and ear. On the other hand,
any intenfe exercife of intellectual powers,
becomes painful by overftraining the mind :
ceffation from fuch exercife gives not inftant
relief ; it is neceffary that the void be filled
with fome amufement, gently relaxing the
fpirits :* organic pleafure, which hath no relifh
but while we are in vigour, is ill qualified for
that office ; but the finer pleafures of fenfe,
which occupy without exhaufting the mind, are
finely qualified to reftore its ufual tone after
fevere application to ftudy or bufinefs, as well,
as after fatiety from fenfual gratification.

　Our firft perceptions are of external objects,
and our firft attachments are to them. Organic
pleafures take the lead ; but the mind, gradually
ripening, relifheth more and more the pleafures
of the eye and ear ; which approach the purely
mental, without exhaufting the fpirits ; and exceed the purely fenfual, without danger of fatiety. The pleafures of the eye and ear have
accordingly a natural aptitude to draw us from
the immoderate gratification of fenfual appetite ;
and the mind, once accuftomed to enjoy a variety of external objects without being fenfible
　　　　　　　　　　　　　　　　　　　of

---

　* Du Bos judicioufly obferves, that filence doth not tend to calm
an agitated mind ; but that foft and flow mufic hath a fine effect.

of the organic impreſſion, is prepared for enjoying internal objects where there cannot be
an organic impreſſion. Thus the author of nature, by qualifying the human mind for a ſucceſſion of enjoyments from low to high, leads
it by gentle ſteps from the moſt grovelling corporeal pleaſures, for which only it is fitted in
the beginning of life, to thoſe refined and ſublime pleaſures that are ſuited to its maturity.

But we are not bound down to this ſucceſſion by any law of neceſſity : the God of Nature offers it to us in order to advance our happineſs ; and it is ſufficient, that he hath enabled
us to carry it on in a natural courſe. Nor has
he made our taſk either diſagreeable or difficult :
on the contrary, the tranſition is ſweet and eaſy,
from corporeal pleaſures to the more refined
pleaſures of ſenſe ; and no leſs ſo, from theſe to
the exalted pleaſures of morality and religion.
We ſtand therefore engaged in honour, as well
as intereſt to ſecond the purpoſes of nature, by
cultivating the pleaſures of the eye and ear, thoſe
eſpecially that require extraordinary culture ;*
such

* A taſte for natural objects is born with us in perfection ; for rel-
iſhing a fine countenance, a rich landſcape, or a vivid colour, culture is unneceſſary. The obſervation holds equally in natural founds,
ſuch as the ſinging of birds, or the murmuring of a brook. Nature
here, the artificer of the object as well as of the percipient, hath
accurately ſuited them to each other. But of a poem, a cantata, a
picture, or other artificial production, a true reliſh is not commonly attained, without ſome ſtudy and much practice.

B 3

fuch as arife from poetry, painting, fculpture, mufic, gardening, and architecture. This efpecially is the duty of the opulent, who have leifure to improve their minds and their feelings. The fine arts are contrived to give pleafure to the eye and the ear, difregarding the inferior fenfes. A tafte for thefe arts is a plant that grows naturally in many foils; but, without culture, fcarce to perfection in any foil: it is fufceptible of much refinement; and is, by proper care, greatly improved. In this refpect, a tafte in the fine arts goes hand in hand with the moral fenfe, to which indeed it is nearly allied: both of them difcover what is right and what is wrong: fafhion, temper, and education, have an influence to vitiate both, or to preferve them pure and untainted: neither of them are arbitrary nor local; being rooted in human nature, and governed by principles common to all men. The defign of the prefent undertaking, which afpires not to morality, is, to examine the fenfitive branch of human nature, to trace the objects that are naturally agreeable as well as thofe that are naturally difagreeable; and by thefe means to difcover, if we can, what are the genuine principles of the fine arts. The man who afpires to be a critic in thefe arts muft pierce ftill deeper: he muft

acquire

acquire a clear perception of what objects are lofty, what low, what proper or improper, what manly, and what mean or trivial. Hence a foundation for reafoning upon the tafte of any individual, and for paffing fentence upon it ; where it is conformable to principles, we can pronounce with certainty that it is correct; otherwife, that it is incorrect, and perhaps whimfical. Thus the fine arts, like morals, become a rational fcience ; and, like morals, may be cultivated to a high degree of refinement.

Manifold are the advantages of criticifm, when thus ftudied as a rational fcience. In the firft place, a thorough acquaintance with the principles of the fine arts, redoubles the pleafure we derive from them. To the man who refigns himfelf to feeling without interpofing any judgment, poetry, mufic, painting, are mere paftime. In the prime of life, indeed, they are delightful, being fupported by the force of novelty, and the heat of imagination : but in time they lofe their relifh ; and are generally neglected in the maturity of life, which difpofes to more ferious and more important occupations. To thofe who deal in criticifm as a regular fciecnc, governed by juft principles, and giving fcope to judgment as well as to fancy, the fine arts are a favourite entertainment ;

and

and in old age maintain that relifh which they produce in the morning of life.*\

In the next place, a philofophic inquiry into the principles of the fine arts, inures the reflect-ing mind to the moft enticing fort of logic : the practice of reafoning upon fubjects fo agree-able, tends to a habit, and a habit ftrengthening the reafoning faculties, prepares the mind for en-tering into fubjects more intricate and abftract. To have in that refpect, a juft conception of the importance of criticifm, we need but reflect upon the ordinary method of education ; which, after fome years fpent in acquiring languages, hur-ries us, without the leaft preparatory difcipline, into the moft profound philofophy. A more effectual method to alienate the tender mind from abftract fcience, is beyond the reach of invention : and accordingly, with refpect to fuch fpeculations, our youth generally contract a fort of hobgoblin terror, feldom if ever fub-dued. Thofe who apply to the arts are train-ed in a very different manner : they are led, ftep by ftep, from the eafier parts of the operation, to what are more difficult ; and are not permitted to make a new motion, till
they

* " Though logic may fubfift without rhetoric or poetry, yet fo neceffary to thefe laft is a found and correct logic, that without it they are ⁊ better than warbling trifles." *Hermes, p.* 6.

they are perfected in thofe which go before. Thus the fcience of criticifm may be confidered as a middle link, connecting the different parts of education into a regular chain. This fcience furnifheth an inviting opportunity to exercife the judgment : we delight to reafon upon fub-jects that are equally pleafant and familiar : we proceed gradually from the fimpler to the more involved cafes ; and in a due courfe of difcipline, cuftom, which improves all our fac-ulties, beftows acutenefs on that of reafon, fuffi-cient to unravel all the intricacies of philofophy.

Nor ought it to be overlooked, that the rea-fonings employed on the fine arts are of the fame kind with thofe which regulate our con-duct. Mathematical and metaphyfical reafon-ings have no tendency to improve our knowl-edge of man ; nor are they applicable to the common affairs of life : but a juft tafte of the fine arts, derived from rational principles, fur-nifhes elegant fubjects for converfation, and pre-pares us for acting in the focial ftate with dig-nity and propriety.

The fcience of rational criticifm tends to im-prove the heart no lefs than the underftanding. It tends, in the firft place, to moderate the felf-ifh affections : by fweetening and harmoniz-ing the temper, it is a ftrong antidote to the turbulence of paffion, and violence of purfuit : it procures to a man fo much mental enjoyment, that, in order to be occupied, he is not tempted to deliver up his youth to hunting, gaming, drinking ;* nor his middle age to ambition ; nor his old age to avarice. Pride and envy, two difguftful paffions, find in the conftitution no enemy more formidable than a delicate and difcerning tafte : the man upon whom nature and culture have beftowed this blefling, delights in the virtuous difpofitions and actions of others : he loves to cherifh them, and to publifh them to the world : faults and failings, it is true, are to him no lefs obvious ; but thefe he avoids, or removes out of fight, becaufe they give him pain. On the other hand, a man void of tafte, upon whom even ftriking beauties make but a faint impreffion, indulges pride or envy without control, and loves to brood over errors and blemifhes. In a word, there are other paffions, that upon occafion, may difturb the peace of fociety more than thofe mentioned ; but not another paffion is fo unwearied an antagonift to the fweets of focial intercourfe :

pride

---

* If any youth of a fplendid fortune and Englifh education ftumble perchance upon this book and this paffage, he will pronounce the latter to be empty declamation. But if he can be prevailed upon to make the experiment, he will find much to his fatisfaction every article well founded.

pride and envy put a man perpetually in oppofition to others ; and difpofe him to relifh bad
more than good qualities, even in a companion.
How different that difpofition of mind, where
every virtue in a companion or neighbour is,
by refinement of tafte, fet in its ftrongeft light ;
and defects or blemifhes, natural to all, are
fupprefled, or kept out of view !

In the next place, delicacy of tafte tends no
lefs to invigorate the focial affections, than to
moderate thofe that are felfifh. To be convinced of that tendency, we need only reflect,
that delicacy of tafte neceffarily heightens our
feeling of pain and pleafure ; and of courfe our
fympathy, which is the capital branch of every
focial paffion. Sympathy invites a communication of joys and forrows, hopes and fears :
fuch exercife, foothing and fatisfactory in itfelf, is neceffarily productive of mutual good-
will and affection.

One other advantage of rational criticifm is
referved to the laft place, being of all
the moft important ; which is, that it is a
great fupport to morality. I infift on it with
entire fatisfaction, that no occupation attaches
a man more to his duty, than that of cultivating a tafte in the fine arts : a juft relifh of what
is beautiful, proper, elegant, and ornamental,

in

in writing or painting, in architecture or gardening, is a fine preparation for the fame juft
relifh of thefe qualities in character and behaviour. To the man who has acquired a tafte
fo acute and accomplifhed, every action wrong
or improper muft be highly difguftful : if, in
any inftance, the overbearing power of paffion
fway him from his duty, he returns to it with
redoubled refolution never to be fwayed a fecond time : he has now an additional motive to
virtue, a conviction derived from experience,
that happinefs depends on regularity and order,
and that difregard to juftice or propriety never
fails to be punifhed with fhame and remorfe.*

Rude ages exhibit the triumph of authority
over reafon : Philofophers anciently were divided into fects, being Epicureans, Platonifts,
Stoics, Pythagoreans, or Sceptics : the fpecu-
lative relied no farther on their own judgment
but to choofe a leader, whom they implicitly followed. In later times, happily, reafon hath obtained the afcendant : men now affert their native privilege of thinking for themfelves : and
difdain to be ranked in any fect, whatever be
                                                    the

* Genius is allied to a warm and inflammable conftitution, delicacy of tafte to calmnefs and fedatenefs.   Hence it is common to
find genius in one who is a prey to every paffion ; but feldom delicacy of tafte.   Upon a man poffeffed of that bleffing, the moral
duties, no lefs than the fine arts, make a deep impreffion, and counterbalance every irregular defire : at the fame time, a temper calm
and fedate is not eafily moved, even by a ftrong temptation.

the fcience. I am forced to except criticifm,
which, by what fatality I know not, continues to
be no lefs flavifh in its principles, nor lefs fub-
miffive to authority, than it was originally.
Boffu, a celebrated French 'critic, gives many
rules ; but can difcover no better foundation for
any of them, than the practice merely of Homer and Virgil, fupported by the authority of
Ariftotle ; Strange ! that in fo long a work,
he fhould never once have ftumbled upon the
queftion, Whether, and how far, do thefe rules
agree with human nature. It could not furely
be his opinion, that thefe poets, however eminent for genius, were entitled to give law to
mankind ; and that nothing now remains, but
blind obedience to their arbitrary will: if in
writing they followed no rule, why fhould
they be imitated ? If they ftudied nature, and
were obfequious to rational principles, why
fhould thefe be concealed from us ?

With refpect to the prefent undertaking, it
is not the author's intention to compofe a regular treatife upon each of the fine arts ; but only, in general, to exhibit their fundamental principles, drawn from human nature, the true
fource of criticifm. The fine arts are intended to
entertain us, by making pleafant impreffions ;
and, by that circumftance, are diftinguifhed

from

from the ufeful arts : but, in order to make
pleafant impreffions, we ought, as above hinted, to know what objects are naturally agreeable, and what naturally difagreeable. That
fubject is here attempted, as far as neceffary for
unfolding the genuine principles of the fine arts ;
and the author affumes no merit from his performance, but that of evincing, perhaps more
diftinctly than hitherto has been done, that
thefe principles, as well as every juft rule of
criticifm, are founded upon the fenfitive part
of our nature. What the author hath difcovered or collected upon that fubject, he choofes
to impart in the gay and agreeable form of criticifm ; imagining that this form will be more
relifhed, and perhaps be no lefs inftructive, than
a regular and laboured difquifition. His plan is,
to afcend gradually to principles, from facts and
experiments ; inftead of beginning with the
former, handled abftractedly, and defcending
to the latter. But, though criticifm is thus
his only declared aim, he will not difown, that
all along it has been his view, to explain the
nature of man, confidered as a fenfitive being
capable of pleafure and pain : and, though he
flatters himfelf with having made fome progrefs
in that important fcience, he is, however, too
fenfible of its extent and difficulty, to undertake

take it profeffedly, or to avow it as the chief purpofe of the prefent work.

To cenfure works, not men, is the juft prerogative of criticifm ; and accordingly all perfonal cenfure is here avoided, unlefs where neceffary to illuftrate fome general propofition. No praife is claimed on that account ; becaufe cenfuring with a view merely to find fault, cannot be entertaining to any perfon of humanity. Writers, one fhould imagine, ought, above all others, to be referved on that article, when they lie fo open to retaliation. The author of this treatife, far from being confident of meriting no cenfure, entertains not even the flighteft hope of fuch perfection. Amufement was at firft the fole aim of his inquiries : proceeding from one particular to another, the fubject grew under his hand ; and he was far advanced before the thought ftruck him, that his private meditations might be publicly ufeful. In public, however, he would not appear in a flovenly drefs ; and therefore he pretends not otherwife to apologife for his errors, than by obferving, that in a new fubject no lefs nice than extenfive, errors are in fome meafure unavoidable. Neither pretends he to juftify his tafte in every particular : that point muft be extremely clear, which admits not variety of opinion ; and in

fome

fome matters fufceptible of great refinement, time is perhaps the only infallible touchftone of tafte : to that he appeals, and to that he cheerfully fubmits.

N. B. The Elements of Criticism, meaning the whole, is a title too affuming for this work. A number of thefe elements or principles are here unfolded : but, as the author is far from imagining that he has completed the lift, a more humble title is proper, fuch as may exprefs any number of parts lefs than the whole. This he thinks is fignified by the title he has chofen, viz. Elements of Criticism.

ELEMENTS

ELEMENTS

OF

CRITICISM.

CHAPTER I.

Perceptions and Ideas in a Train.

A MAN, while awake, is confcious of a continued train of perceptions and ideas paffing in his mind.
It requires no activity on his part to carry on the train :
nor can he at will add any idea to the train*. At the
fame time, we learn from daily experience, that the train
of our thoughts is not regulated by chance : and if it depend not upon will, nor upon chance, by what law is it
governed? The queftion is of importance in the fcience
of human nature ; and I promife beforehand, that it will
be found of great importance in the fine arts.

It appears, that the relations by which things are linked together, have a great influence in directing the train
of thought. Taking a view of external objects, their inherent

* For how fhould this be done ? what idea is it that we are to add ? If we
can fpecify the idea, that idea is already in the mind, and there is no occafion for
any act of the will. If we cannot fpecify any idea, I next demand, how
can a perfon will, or to what purpofe, if there be nothing in view? We cannot form a conception of fuch a thing. If this argument need confirmation,
I urge experience : whoever makes a trial will find, that ideas are linked together in the mind, forming a connected chain ; and that we have not the command of any idea independent of the chain.

herent properties are not more remarkable than the various relations that conneƈt them together : Caufe and
effeƈt, contiguity in time or in place, high and low, prior
and pofterior, refemblance, contraft, and a thoufand other
relations, conneƈt things together without end. Not a
fingle thing appears folitary and altogether devoid of
conneƈtion ; the only difference is, that fome are intimately conneƈted, fome more flightly ; fome near, fome
at a diftance.

Experience will fatisfy us of what reafon makes probable, that the train of our thoughts is in a great meafure regulated by the foregoing relations : an external
objeƈt is no fooner prefented to us in idea, than it fuggefts to the mind other objeƈts to which it is related ; and
in that manner is a train of thoughts compofed. Such
is the law of fucceffion ; which muft be natural, becaufe
it governs all human beings. The law, however, feems
not to be inviolable : it fometimes happens that an idea
arifes in the mind without any perceived conneƈtion ; as,
for example, after a profound fleep.

But, though we cannot add to the train an unconneƈt-
ed idea, yet in a meafure we can attend to fome ideas,
and difmifs others. There are few things but what are
conneƈted with many others ; and, when a thing thus
conneƈted becomes a fubjeƈt of thought, it commonly
fuggefts many of its conneƈtions : among thefe a choice
is afforded ; we can infift upon one, rejeƈting others ;
and fometimes we infift on what is commonly held the
flighter conneƈtion. Where ideas are left to their natural courfe, they are continued through the ftriƈteft
conneƈtions : the mind extends its view to a fon more
readily than to a fervant ; and more readily to a neighbour than to one living at a diftance. This order, as obferved, may be varied by will, but ftill within the limits
of related objeƈts ; for though we can vary the order of
a natural train, we cannot diffolve the train altogether,
by carrying on our thoughts in a loofe manner without
                                                        any

any connection. So far doth our power extend; and that power is fufficient for all ufeful purpofes: to have more power, would probably be hurtful inftead of be‑ ing falutary.

Will is not the only caufe that prevents a train of thought from being continued through the ftrifteft con‑ nections: much depends on the prefent tone of mind: for a fubjeft that accords with that tone is always wel‑ come. Thus, in good fpirits, a cheerful fubjeft will be introduced by the flighteft connection; and one that is melancholy, no lefs readily in low fpirits: an inter‑ efting fubjeft is recalled, from time to time, by any con‑ nection indifferently, ftrong or weak; which is finely touched by Shakefpear, with relation to a rich cargo at fea.

> My wind, cooling my broth,
> Would blow me to an ague, when I thought
> What harm a wind too great might do at fea.
> I fhould not fee the fandy hour-glafs run,
> But I fhould think of fhallows and of flats;
> And fee my wealthy Andrew dock'd in fand,
> Vailing her high top lower than her ribs,
> To kifs her burial. Should I go to church,
> And fee the holy edifice of ftone,
> And not bethink me ftrait of dangerous rocks?
> Which touching but my gentle veffel's fide,
> Would fcatter all the fpices on the ftream,
> Enrobe the roaring waters with my filks;
> And, in a word, but now worth this,
> And now worth nothing.
>
> *Merchant of Venice, act* 1. *fc.* 1.

Another caufe clearly diftinguifhable from that now mentioned, hath alfo a confiderable influence to vary the natural train of ideas; which is, that, in the minds of fome perfons, thoughts and circumftances crowd upon each other by the flighteft connections. I afcribe this to a bluntnefs in the difcerning faculty; for a perfon who cannot accurately diftinguifh between a flight con‑ nection and one that is more intimate, is equally affected

by

by each : fuch a perfon muft neceffarily have a great
flow of ideas, becaufe they are introduced by any relation indifferently ; and the flighter relations, being without number, furnifh ideas without end. This doctrine
is, in a lively manner, illuftrated by Shakefpear.

Falftaff. What is the grofs fum that I owe thee ?
Hoftefs. Marry, if thou wert an honeft man, thyfelf and thy money too.
Thou didft fwear to me on a parcel-gilt-goblet, fitting in my Dolphin-
chamber, at the round table, by a fea-coal fire, on Wednefday in Whit-
fun-week, when the Prince broke thy head for likening him to a finging man of Windfor, thou didft fwear to me then, as I was wafhing
thy wound, to marry me, and make me my Lady thy wife. Canft thou
deny it ? Did not Goodwife Keech, the butcher's wife, come in then,
and call me Goffip Quickly ? coming in to borrow a mefs of vinegar ;
telling us fhe had a good difh of prawns ; whereby thou didft defire to eat fome ; whereby I told thee they were ill for a green wound.
And didft not thou, when fhe was gone down ftairs, defire me to be no
more fo familiar with fuch poor people, faying, that ere long they
fhould call me Madam ? And didft thou not kifs me, and bid me fetch
thee thirty fhillings ? I put thee now to thy book-oath, deny it if thou
canft ?   *Second Part, Henry IV. act 2. fc. 2.*

On the other hand, a man of accurate judgment cannot have a great flow of ideas ; becaufe the flighter relations, making no figure in his mind, have no power
to introduce ideas. And hence it is, that accurate judgment is not friendly to declamation or copious eloquence. This reafoning is confirmed by experience ; for
it is a noted obfervation, That a great or comprehenfive
memory is feldom connected with a good judgment.
As an additional confirmation, I appeal to another
noted obfervation, That wit and judgment are feldom
united. Wit confifts chiefly in joining things by diftant
and fanciful relations, which furprife becaufe they are unexpected : fuch relations, being of the flighteft kind,
readily occur to thofe only who make every relation equally
welcome. Wit, upon that account, is in a good meafure incompatible with folid judgment ; which, neglecting trivial relations, adheres to what are fubftantial and
permanent.

permanent. Thus memory and wit are often conjoined: folid judgment feldom with either.

Every man who attends to his own ideas, will dif-cover order as well as connection in their fucceffion. There is implanted in the breaft of every man a princi-ple of order, which governs the arrangement of his per-ceptions, of his ideas, and of his actions. With re-gard to perceptions, I obferve that, in things of equal rank, fuch as fheep in a fold, or trees in a wood, it muft be indifferent in what order they be furveyed. But, in things of unequal rank, our tendency is, to view the principal fubject before we defcend to its acceffories or ornaments, and the fuperior before the inferior or de-pendent; we are equally averfe to enter into a minute confideration of conftituent parts, till the thing be firft furveyed as a whole. It need fcarce be added, that our ideas are governed by the fame principle; and that, in thinking or reflecting upon a number of objects, we nat-urally follow the fame order as when we actually furvey them.

The principle of order is confpicuous with refpect to natural operations; for it always directs our ideas in the order of nature: thinking upon a body in motion, we follow its natural courfe; the mind falls with a heavy body, defcends with a river, and afcends with flame and fmoke: in tracing out a family, we incline to begin at the founder, and to defcend gradually to his lateft pof-terity; on the contrary, mufing on a lofty oak, we be-gin at the trunk, and mount from it to the branches: as to hiftorical facts, we love to proceed in the order of time; or, which comes to the fame, to proceed along the chain of caufes and effects.

But though, in following out an hiftorical chain, our bent is to proceed orderly from caufes to their effects, we find not the fame bent in matters of fcience: there we feem rather difpofed to proceed from effects to their caufes, and from particular propofitions to thofe which

C 3

are more general. Why this difference in matters that appear fo nearly related? I anfwer, The cafes are fimilar in appearance only, not in reality. In an hiftorical chain every event is particular, the effect of fome former event, and the caufe of others that follow : in fuch a chain there is nothing to bias the mind from the order of nature. Widely different is fcience, when we endeavour to trace out caufes and their effects : many experiments are commonly reduced under one caufe ; and again, many of thefe caufes under one ftill more general and comprehenfive : in our progrefs from particular effects to general caufes, and from particular propofitions to the more comprehenfive, we feel a gradual dilatation or expanfion of mind, like what is felt in an afcending feries, which is extremely pleafing : the pleafure here exceeds what arifes from following the courfe of nature ; and it is that pleafure which regulates our train of thought in the cafe now mentioned, and in others that are fimilar. Thefe obfervations, by the way, furnifh materials for inftituting a comparifon between the fynthetic and analytic methods of reafoning : the fynthetic method, defcending regularly from principles to their confequences, is more agreeable to the ftrictnefs of order ; but in following the oppofite courfe in the analytic method, we have a fenfible pleafure like mounting upward, which is not felt in the other: the analytic method is more agreeable to the imagination ; the other method will be preferred by thofe only who with rigidity adhere to. order, and give no indulgence to natural emotions*.

It now appears that we are framed by nature to relifh order and connection. When an object is introduced by a proper connection, we are confcious of a certain pleafure arifing from that circumftance. Among objects of equal rank, the pleafure is proportioned to the degree of connection : but among unequal objects, where we

* A train of perceptions or ideas, with refpect to its uniformity and variety, is handled afterwards, chap. 9.

we require a certain order, the pleafure arifes chiefly from an orderly arrangement; of which one is fenfible, in tracing objects contrary to the courfe of nature, or contrary to our fenfe of order : the mind proceeds with alacrity down a flowing river, and with the fame alacrity from a whole to its parts, or from a principal to its acceffories; but in the contrary direction, it is fenfible of a fort of retrograde motion, which is unpleafant. And here may be remarked the great influence of order upon the mind of man : grandeur, which makes a deep impreffion, inclines us, in running over any feries, to proceed from fmall to great, rather than from great to fmall ; but order prevails over that tendency, and affords pleafure as well as facility in paffing from a whole to its parts, and from a fubject to its ornaments, which are not felt in the oppofite courfe. Elevation touches the mind no lefs than grandeur doth ; and in raifing the mind to elevated objects, there is a fenfible pleafure : the courfe of nature, however, hath ftill a greater influence than elevation; and therefore, the pleafure of falling with rain, and defcending gradually with a river, prevails over that of mounting upward. But where the courfe of nature is joined with elevation, the effect muft be delightful : and hence the fingular beauty of fmoke afcending in a calm morning.

I am extremely fenfible of the difguft men generally have to abftract fpeculation ; and I would avoid it altogether, if it could be done in a work that profeffes to draw the rules of criticifm from human nature, their true fource. We have but a fingle choice, which is, to continue a little longer in the fame train, or to abandon the undertaking altogether. Candour obliges me to notify this to my readers, that fuch of them as have an invincible averfion to abftract fpeculation, may ftop fhort here ; for till principles be unfolded, I can promife no entertainment to thofe who fhun thinking. But I flatter myfelf with a different bent in the generality of readers :

C 4

fome

fome few, I imagine, will relifh the abftract part for its own fake; and many for the ufeful purpofes to which it may be applied. For encouraging the latter to proceed with alacrity, I affure them beforehand, that the foregoing fpeculation leads to many important rules of criticifm, which fhall be unfolded in the courfe of this work. In the mean time, for inftant fatisfaction in part, they will be pleafed to accept the following fpecimen.

Every work of art, that is conformable to the natural courfe of our ideas, is fo far agreeable; and every work of art that reverfes that courfe, is fo far difagreeable. Hence it is required in every fuch work, that, like an organic fyftem, its parts be orderly arranged and mutually connected, bearing each of them a relation to the whole, fome more intimate, fome lefs, according to their deftination: when due regard is had to thefe particulars, we have a fenfe of juft compofition, and fo far are pleafed with the performance. Homer is defective in order and connection; and Pindar more remarkably. Regularity, order, and connection, are painful reftraints on a bold and fertile imagination; and are not patiently fubmitted to, but after much culture and difcipline. In Horace there is no fault more eminent than want of connection: inftances are without number. In the firft fourteen lines of ode 7. lib. 1. he mentions feveral towns and diftricts, more to the tafte of fome than of others: in the remainder of the ode, Plancus is exhorted to drown his cares in wine. Having narrowly efcaped death by the fall of a tree, this poet* takes occafion to obferve juftly, that while we guard againft fome dangers, we are expofed to others we cannot forefee: he ends with difplaying the power of mufic. The parts of ode 16. lib. 2. are fo loofely connected as to disfigure a poem otherwife extremely beautiful. The 1ft, 2d, 3d, 4th, 11th, 24th, 27th odes of the 3d book, lie open all of them to the fame cenfure. The firft fatire, book 1. is

fo

* Lib. 2. ode 13.

fo deformed by want of connection, as upon the whole to be fcarce agreeable : it commences with an important queftion, How it happens, that people, though much fatisfied with themfelves, are feldom fo with their rank or condition. After illuftrating the obfervation in a fprightly manner by feveral examples, the author, forgetting his fubject, enters upon a declamation againft avarice, which he purfues till the line 108. there he makes an apology for wandering, and promifes to return to his fubject ; but avarice having got poffeffion of his mind, he follows out that theme to the end, and never returns to the queftion propofed in the beginning.

Of Virgil's Georgics, though efteemed the moft complete work of that author, the parts are ill connected, and the tranfitions far from being fweet and eafy. In the firft book * he deviates from his fubject to give a defcription of the five zones : the want of connection here, as well as in the defcription of the prodigies that accompanied the death of Cæfar, are fcarce pardonable. A digreffion on the praifes of Italy in the fecond book,† is not more happily introduced : and in the midft of a declamation upon the pleafures of hufbandry, which makes part of the fame book,‡ the author introduces himfelf into the poem without the flighteft connection. In the Lutrin the Goddefs of Difcord is introduced without any connection : fhe is of no confequence in the poem ; and acts no part except that of lavifhing praife upon Lewis the Fourteenth. The two prefaces of Salluft look as if by fome blunder they had been prefixed to his two hiftories ; they will fuit any other hiftory as well, or any fubject as well as hiftory. Even the members of thefe prefaces are but loofely connected : they look more like a number of maxims or obfervations than a connected difcourfe.

An epifode in a narrative poem, being in effect an acceffory, demands not that ftrict union with the principal

* Lin. 231. † Lin. 136. ‡ Lin. 475.

cipal fubject, which is requifite between a whole and its conftituent parts : it demands, however, a degree of union, fuch as ought to fubfift between a principal and acceffory ; and therefore will not be graceful if it be loofely connected with the principal fubject. I give for an example the defcent of Æneas into hell, which employs the fixth book of the Æneid : the reader is not prepared for that important event : no caufe is affigned that can make it appear neceffary, or even natural, to fufpend for fo long a time the principal action in its moft interefting period : the poet can find no pretext for an adventure fo extraordinary, but the hero's longing to vifit the ghoft of his father recently dead : in the mean time the ftory is interrupted, and the reader lofes his ardour. Pity it is that an epifode fo extremely beautiful were not more happily introduced. I muft obferve at the fame time, that full juftice is done to this incident, by confidering it to be an epifode ; for if it be a conftituent part of the principal action, the connection ought to be ftill more intimate. The fame objection lies againft that elaborate defcription of Fame in the Æneid :* any other book of that heroic poem, or of any heroic poem, has as good a title to that defcription as the book where it is placed.

In a natural landfcape we every day perceive a multitude of objects connected by contiguity folely ; which is not unpleafant, becaufe objects of fight make an impreffion fo lively, as that a relation even of the flighteft kind is relifhed. This however ought not to be imitated in defcription : words are fo far fhort of the eye in livelinefs of impreffion, that in a defcription, connection ought to be carefully ftudied ; for new objects introduced in defcription, are made more or lefs welcome in proportion to the degree of their connection with the principal fubject. In the following paffage different things are brought together without the flighteft connection,

nection,

---

* Lib. 4. lin. 173.

nection, if it be not what may be called verbal, *i. e.* taking the fame word in different meanings.

> Surgamus : folet effe gravis cantantibus umbra.
> Juniperi gravis umbra : nocent et frugibus umbræ.
> Ite domum faturæ, venit Hefperus, ite capellæ.
> *Virg. Buc.* x. 75.

The introduction of an object metaphorically or figuratively, will not juftify the introduction of it in its natural appearance : a relation fo flight can never be relifhed.

> Diftruft in lovers is too warm a fun ;
> But yet 'tis night in love when that is gone.
> And in thofe climes which moft his fcorching know,
> He makes the nobleft fruits and metals grow.
> *Part* 2. *Conqueft of Granada,* act 3.

The relations among objects have a confidcrable influence in the gratification of our paffions, and even in their production. But that fubject is referved to be treated in the chapter of emotions and paffions*.

There is not perhaps another inftance of a building fo great erected upon a foundation fo flight in appearance, as the relations of objects and their arrangement. Relations make no capital figure in the mind, the bulk of them being tranfitory, and fome extremely trivial : they are, however, the links that, by uniting our perceptions into one connected chain, produce connection of action, becaufe perception and action have an intimate correfpondence. But it is not fufficient for the conduct of life, that our actions be linked together, however intimately : it is befide neceffary that they proceed in a certain order ; and this alfo is provided for by an original propenfity. Thus order and connection, while they admit fufficient variety, introduce a method in the management of affairs : without them our conduct would be fluctuating and defultory ; and we fhould be hurried from thought to thought, and from action to action, entirely at the mercy of chance.

CHAP.

C H A P. II.

Emotions and Passions.

OF all the feelings raifed in us by external objects, thofe only of the eye and the ear are honoured
with the name of *passion* or *emotion :* the moft pleafing
feelings of tafte, or touch, or fmell, afpire not to that
honour. From this obfervation appears the connection
of emotions and paffions with the fine arts, which, as
obferved in the introduction, are all of them calculated
to give pleafure to the eye or the ear ; never once con-
defcending to gratify any of the inferior fenfes. The
defign accordingly of this chapter is to delineate that
connection, with the view chiefly to afcertain what power
the fine arts have to raife emotions and paffions. To
thofe who would excel in the fine arts, that branch of
knowledge is indifpenfible; for without it the critic, as well
as the undertaker, ignorant of any rule, have nothing left
but to abandon themfelves to chance. Deftitute of that
branch of knowledge, in vain will either pretend to fore-
tel what effect his work will have upon the heart.

The principles of the fine arts, appear in this view to
open a direct avenue to the heart of man. The inquif-
itive mind beginning with criticifm, the moft agreeable
of all amufements, and finding no obftruction in its progrefs, advances far into the fenfitive part of our nature ;
and gains imperceptibly a thorough knowledge of the human heart, of its defires, and of every motive to action ; a
fcience, which of all that can be reached by man, is to
him of the greateft importance.

Upon a fubject fo comprehenfive, all that can be expected in this chapter, is a general or flight furvey : and
to fhorten that furvey, I propofe to handle feparately
fome emotions more peculiarly connected with the fine
arts.

arts. Even after that circumſcription, ſo much matter comes under the preſent chapter, that, to avoid confuſion, I find it neceſſary to divide it into many parts : and though the firſt of theſe is confined to ſuch cauſes of emotion or paſſion as are the moſt common and the moſt general ;˙ yet upon examination I find this ſingle part ſo extenſive, as to require a ſubdiviſion into ſeveral ſections. Human nature is a complicate machine, and is unavoidably ſo in order to anſwer its various purpoſes. The public indeed have been entertained with many ſyſtems of human nature that flatter the mind by their ſimplicity : according to ſome writers, man is entirely a ſelfiſh being ; according to others, univerſal benevolence is his duty : one founds morality upon ſympathy ſolely, and one upon utility. If any of theſe ſyſtems were copied from nature, the preſent ſubject might be ſoon diſcuſſed. But the variety of nature is not ſo eaſily reached : and for confuting ſuch Utopian ſyſtems without the fatigue of reaſoning, it appears the beſt method to take a ſurvey of human nature, and to ſet before the eye, plainly and candidly, facts as they really exiſt.

PART I.

Cauſes unfolded of the Emotions and Paſſions.

SECT. I.

Difference between Emotion and Paſſion.—Cauſes that are the moſt common and the moſt general.—Paſſion conſidered as productive of Action.

THESE branches are ſo interwoven, that they cannot be handled ſeparately. It is a fact univerſally admitted, that no emotion or paſſion ever ſtarts up in the mind without a cauſe : if I love a perſon, it is for good

qualities

qualities or good offices : if I have refentment againſt a man, it muſt be for ſome injury he has done me : and I cannot pity any one who is under no diſtreſs of body nor of mind.

The circumſtances now mentioned, if they raiſe an emotion or paſſion, cannot be entirely indifferent ; for if ſo, they could not make any impreſſion. And we find upon examination, that they are not indifferent : looĸing back upon the foregoing examples, the good qualities or good offices that attraĉt my love, are antecedently agreeable ; if an injury did not give uneaſineſs, it would not occaſion reſentment againſt the author : nor would the paſſion of pity be raiſed by an objeĉt in diſtreſs, if that objeĉt did not give pain.

What is now ſaid about the produĉtion of emotion or paſſion, reſolves into a very ſimple propoſition, That we love what is agreeable, and hate what is diſagreeable. And indeed it is evident, that a thing muſt be agreeable or diſagreeable, before it can be the objeĉt either of love or of hatred.

This ſhort hint about the cauſes of paſſion and emotion, leads to a more extenſive view of the ſubjeĉt. Such is our nature, that upon perceiving certain external objeĉts, we are inſtantaneouſly conſcious of pleaſure or pain : a gently-flowing river, a ſmooth extended plain, a ſpreading oak, a towering hill, are objeĉts of ſight that raiſe pleaſant emotions : a barren heath, a dirty marſh, a rotten carcaſe, raiſe painful emotions. Of the emotions thus produced we inquire for no other cauſe but merely the preſence of the objeĉt.

The things now mentioned raiſe emotions by means of their properties and qualities : to the emotion raiſed by a large river, its ſize, its force, and its fluency, contributes each a ſhare : the regularity, propriety, and convenience, of a fine building, contribute each to the emotion raiſed by the building.

If

If external properties be agreeable, we have reaſon to expect the ſame from thoſe which are internal ; and accordingly power, diſcernment, wit, mildneſs, ſympathy, courage, benevolence, are agreeable in a high degree : upon perceiving theſe qualities in others, we inſtantaneouſly feel pleaſant emotions, without the ſlighteſt act of reflection, or of attention to conſequences. It is almoſt unneceſſary to add, that certain qualities oppoſite to the former, ſuch as dulneſs, peeviſhneſs, inhumanity, cowardice, occaſion in the ſame manner painful emotions.

'ı Senſible beings affect us remarkably by their actions. Some actions raiſe pleaſant emotions in the ſpectator, without the leaſt reflection ; ſuch as graceful motion, and genteel behaviour. But as *intention*, a capital circumſtance in human actions, is not viſible, it requires reflection to diſcover their true character : I ſee one delivering a purſe of money to another, but I can make nothing of that action, till I learn with what intention the money is given ; if it be given to diſcharge a debt, the action pleaſes me in a ſlight degree ; if it be a grateful return, I feel a ſtronger emotion ; and the pleaſant emotion riſes to a greater height, when it is the intention of the giver to relieve a virtuous family from want. Thus actions are qualified by intention : but they are not qualified by the event ;. for an action well intended gives pleaſure, whatever the event be. Further, human actions are perceived to be *right* or *wrong ;* and that perception qualifies the pleaſure or pain that reſults from them.*

Emotions

* In tracing our emotions and paſſions to their origin, my firſt thought was, that qualities and actions are the primary cauſes of emotions ; and that theſe emotions are afterward expanded upon the being to which theſe qualities and actions belong. But I am now convinced that this opinion is erroneous. An attribute is not, even in imagination, ſeparable from the being to which it belongs ; and, for that reaſon, cannot of itſelf be the cauſe of any emotion. We have, it is true, no knowledge of any being or ſubſtance but by means of its attributes ; and therefore no being can be agreeable to us otherwiſe than by their means. But ſtill, when an emotion is raiſed, it is the being itſelf, as we apprehend the matter, that raiſes the emotion ; and it raiſes it by means of one or other of its attributes. If it be urged, That we can in idea abſtract

a quality

Emotions are raifed in us, not only by the qualities and actions of others, but alfo by their feelings : I cannot behold a man in diftrefs, without partaking of his pain ; nor in joy, without partaking of his pleafure. The beings or things above defcribed occafion emotions in us, not only in the original furvey, but alfo when recalled to the memory in idea : a field laid out with tafte, is pleafant in the recollection, as well as when under our eye : a generous action defcribed in words or colours, occafions a fenfible emotion, as well as when we fee it perfomed ; and when we reflect upon the diftrefs of any perfon, our pain is of the fame kind with what we felt when eye-witneffes. In a word, an agreeable or difagreeable object recalled to the mind in idea, is the occafion of a pleafant or painful emotion, of the fame kind with that produced when the object was prefent : the only difference is, that an idea being fainter than an original perception, the pleafure or pain produced by the former, is proportionably fainter than that produced by the latter.

Having explained the nature of an emotion, and mentioned feveral caufes by which it is produced, we proceed to an obfervation of confiderable importance in the fcience of human nature ; which is, That defire follows fome emotions, and not others. The emotion raifed by a beautiful garden, a magnificent building, or a number of fine faces in a crowded affembly, is feldom accompanied

a quality from the thing to which it belongs ; it might be anfwered, That fuch abftraction may ferve the purpofes of reafoning, but is too faint to produce any fort of emotion. But it is fufficient for the prefent purpofe to anfwer, That the eye never abftracts : by that organ we perceive things as they really exift, and never perceive a quality as feparated from the fubject. Hence it muft be evident, that emotions are raifed, not by qualities abftractly confidered, but by the fubftance or body fo and fo qualified. Thus, a fpreading oak raifes a pleafant emotion, by means of its colour, figure, umbrage, &c. it is not the colour, ftrictly fpeaking, that produces the emotion, but the tree colcured : it is not the figure abftractly confidered that produces the emotion, but the tree of a certain figure. And hence, by the way, it appears, that the beauty of fuch an object is complex, refolvable into feveral beauties more fimple.

accompanied with defire. Other emotions are accompanied with defire ; emotions, for example, raifed by
human actions and qualities : a virtuous action raifeth
in every fpectator a pleafant emotion, which is commonly attended with defire to reward the author of
the action : a vicious action, on the contrary, produceth
a painful emotion, attended with defire to punifh the delinquent. Even things inanimate often raife emotions
accompanied with defire : witnefs the goods of fortune,
which are objects of defire almoft univerfally ; and the
defire, when immoderate, obtains the name of *avarice.*
The pleafant emotion produced in a fpectator by a capital picture in the poffeffion of a prince, is feldom accompanied with defire ; but if fuch a picture be expofed to
fale, defire of having or poffeffing is the natural confequence of a ftrong emotion.

It is a truth verified by induction, that every paffion is
accompanied with defire ; and if an emotion be fometimes accompanied with defire, fometimes not, it comes
to be a material inquiry, in what refpect a paffion differs
from an emotion. Is paffion in its nature or feeling diftinguifhable from emotion ? I have been apt to think that
there muft be fuch a diftinction ; but, after the ftricteft
examination, I cannot perceive any : what is love, for example, but a pleafant emotion raifed by a fight or idea of
the beloved female, joined with defire of enjoyment ?
In what elfe confifts the paffion of refentment, but in a
painful emotion occafioned by the injury, accompanied
with defire to chaftife the guilty perfon ? In general, as
to paffion of every kind, we find no more in its compofition, but the particulars now mentioned, an emotion
pleafant or painful, accompanied with defire. What then
fhall we fay ? are *paffion* and *emotion* fynonymous terms ?
That cannot be averred ; becaufe no feeling nor agitation of the mind void of defire, is termed a paffion; and
we have difcovered, that there are many emotions which
pafs away without raifing defire of any kind. How is

the difficulty to be folved ? There appears to me but one folution, which I relifh the more, as it renders the doctrine of the paffions and emotions fimple and per- fpicuous. The folution follows. An internal motion or agitation of the mind, when it paffeth away without defire, is denominated *an emotion* : when defire follows, the motion or agitation is denominated *a paffion*. A fine face, for example, raifeth in me a pleafant feeling : if that feeling vanifh without producing any effect, it is in proper language an emotion ; but if the feeling, by reiterated views of the object, become fufficiently ftrong to occafion defire, it lofes its name of emotion, and ac- quires that of paffion. The fame holds in all the other paffions : the painful feeling raifed in a fpectator by a flight injury done to a ftranger, being accompanied with no defire of revenge, is termed an emotion ; but that injury raifeth in the ftranger a ftronger emotion, which being accompanied with defire of revenge, is a paffion : external expreffions of diftrefs produce in the fpectator a painful feeling, which being fometimes fo flight as to pafs away without any effect, is an emotion ; but if the feeling be fo ftrong as to prompt defire of affording re- lief, it is a paffion, and is termed *pity :* envy is emula- tion in excefs; if the exaltation of a competitor be barely difagreeable, the painful feeling is an emotion ; if it produce defire to deprefs him, it is a paffion.

To prevent miftakes, it muft be obferved, that defire here is taken in its proper fenfe, namely, that internal act, which, by influencing the will, makes us proceed to action. Defire in a lax fenfe refpects alfo actions and events that depend not on us, as when I defire that my friend may have a fon to reprefent him, or that my coun- try may flourifh in arts and fciences: but fuch internal act is more properly termed a *wifh* than a *defire*.

Having diftinguifhed paffion from emotion, we pro- ceed to confider paffion more at large, with refpect efpecially to its power of producing action.

We

We have daily and conſtant experience for our authority, that no man ever proceeds to action but by means of an antecedent deſire or impulſe. So well eſtabliſhed is this obſervation, and ſo deeply rooted in the mind, that we can ſcarce imagine a different ſyſtem of action : even a child will ſay familiarly, What ſhould make me do this or that, when I have no deſire to do it ? Taking it then for granted, that the exiſtence of action depends on antecedent deſire ; it follows, that where there is no deſire, there can be no action. This opens another ſhining diſtinction between emotions and paſſions. The former, being without deſire, are in their nature quieſcent: the deſire included in the latter, prompts one to act in order to fulfil that deſire, or, in other words, to gratify the paſſion.

The cauſe of a paſſion is ſufficiently explained above : it is that being or thing, which, by raiſing deſire, converts an emotion into a paſſion. When we conſider a paſſion with reſpect to its power of prompting action, that ſame being or thing is termed its *object :* a fine woman, for example, raiſes the paſſion of love, which is directed to her as its object : a man, by injuring me, raiſes my reſentment, and becomes thereby the object of my reſentment. Thus the cauſe of a paſſion, and its object, are the ſame in different reſpects. An emotion, on the other hand, being in its nature quieſcent, and merely a paſſive feeling, muſt have a cauſe ; but cannot be ſaid, properly ſpeaking, to have an object.

The objects of our paſſions may be diſtinguiſhed into two kinds, general and particular. A man, a houſe, a garden, is a particular object : fame, eſteem, opulence, honour, are general objects, becauſe each of them comprehends many particulars. The paſſions directed to general objects are commonly termed *appetites*, in contradiſtinction to paſſions directed to particular objects, which retain their proper name : thus we ſay an appetite for fame, for glory, for conqueſt, for riches ; but we fay the paſſion of friendſhip, of love, of gratitude, of envy, of refentment. And there is a material difference between appetites and paſſions, which makes it proper to diſtinguiſh them by different names : the latter have no exiſtence till a proper object be prefented ; whereas the former exiſt firſt, and then are directed to an object : a paſſion comes after its object ; an appetite goes before it, which is obvious in the appetites of hunger, thirſt, and animal love, and is the fame in the other appetites above mentioned.

By an object fo powerful as to make a deep impreſſion, the mind is inflamed, and hurried to action with a ſtrong impulfe. Where the object is lefs powerful, fo as not to inflame the mind, nothing is felt but defire without any fenfible perturbation. The principle of duty affords one inſtance : the defire generated by an object of duty, being commonly moderate, moves us to act calmly, without any violent impulfe ; but if the mind happen to be inflamed with the importance of the object, in that cafe defire of doing our duty becomes a warm paſſion.

The actions of brute creatures are generally directed by inſtinct, meaning blind impulfe or defire, without any view to confequences. Man is framed to be governed by reafon : he commonly acts with deliberation, in order to bring about fome defirable end ; and in that cafe his actions are means employed to bring about the end defired : thus I give charity in order to relieve a perfon from want : I perform a grateful action as a duty incumbent on me : and I fight for my country in order to repel its enemies. At the fame time, there are human actions that are not governed by reafon, nor are done with any view to confequences. Infants, like brutes, are moſtly governed by inſtinct, without the leaſt view to any end, good or ill. And even adult perfons act fometimes inſtinctively : thus one in extreme hunger fnatches at food, without the flighteſt confideration

whether

whether it be falutary: avarice prompts to accumulate wealth, without the leaft view of ufe; and thereby abfurdly converts means into an end : and animal love often hurries to fruition, without a thought even of gratification.

A paffion when it flames fo high as to impel us to act blindly without any view to confequences, good or ill, may in that ftate be termed *inftinctive ;* and when it is fo moderate as to admit reafon, and to prompt actions with a view to an end, it may in that ftate be termed *deliberative.*

With refpect to actions exerted as means to an end, defire to bring about the end is what determines one to exert the action ; and defire confidered in that view is termed a *motive :* thus the fame mental act that is termed *defire* with refpect to an end in view, is termed a *motive* with refpect to its power of determining one to act. Inftinctive actions have a caufe, namely, the impulfe of the paffion ; but they cannot be faid to have a motive, becaufe they are not done with any view to confequences.

We learn from experience that the gratification of defire is pleafant ; and the forefight of that pleafure becomes often an additional motive for acting. Thus a a child eats by the mere impulfe of hunger : a young man thinks of the pleafure of gratification, which being a motive for him to eat, fortifies the original impulfe : and a man farther advanced in life, hath the additional motive, that it will contribute to his health.*

From thefe premifes, it is eafy to determine with accuracy, what paffions and actions are felfifh, what focial. It is the end in view that afcertains the clafs to which they belong : where the end in view is my own good, they are felfifh ; where the end in view is the good of another, they are focial. Hence it follows, that inftinctive

---

* One exception there is, and that is remorfe, when it is fo violent as to make a man defire to punifh himfelf. The gratification here is far from being pleafant. See p. 188. of this volume. But a fingle exception, inftead of overturning a general rule, is rather a confirmation of it.

tive actions, where we act blindly and merely by impulfe, cannot be reckoned either focial or felfifh : thus eating, when prompted by an impulfe merely of nature, is neither focial nor felfifh ; but add a motive, that it will contribute to my pleafure or my health, and it becomes in a meafure felfifh. On the other hand, when affection moves me to exert an action to the end folely of advancing my friend's happinefs, without regard to my own gratification, the action is juftly denominated *focial*, and fo is alfo the affection that is its caufe ; if another motive be added, that gratifying the affection will alfo contribute to my own happinefs, the action becomes partly felfifh. If charity be given with the fingle view of relieving a' perfon from diftrefs, the action is purely focial ; but if it be partly in view to enjoy the pleafure of a virtuous act, the action is fo far felfifh.* Animal love when carried into action by natural impulfe fingly, is neither focial nor felfifh : when exerted with a view to gratification, it is felfifh : when the motive of giving pleafure to its object is fuperadded, it is partly focial, partly felfifh. A juft action, when prompted by the principle of duty folely, is neither focial nor felfifh. When I perform an act of juftice with a view to the pleafure of gratification, the action is felfifh : I pay a debt for my own fake, not with a view to benefit my creditor. But fuppofe the money has been advanced by a friend without intereft, purely to oblige me : in that cafe, together with the motive of gratification, there arifes a motive of gratitude, which refpects the creditor folely, and prompts me to act in order to do him good ; and the action is partly focial, partly felfifh. Suppofe again I meet with a furprifing and

---

* A felfifh motive proceeding from a focial principle, fuch as that mentioned, is the moft refpectable of all felfifh motives. To enjoy the pleafure of a virtuous action, one muft be virtuous ; and to enjoy the pleafure of a charitable action, one muft think charity laudable at leaft, if not a duty. It is otherwife where a man gives charity merely for the fake of oftentation ; for this he may do without having any pity or benevolence in his temper.

and unexpected act of generofity, that infpires me with love to my benefactor, and the utmoft gratitude : I burn to do him good : he is the fole object of my defire ; and my own pleafure in gratifying the defire vanifheth out of fight : in this cafe, the action I perform is purely focial. Thus it happens, that when a focial motive becomes ftrong, the action is exerted with a view fingly to the object of the paffion, and felf never comes in view. The fame effect of ftifling felfifh motives, is equally remarkable in other paffions that are in no view focial. An action for example, done to gratify my ambitious views, is felf-ifh : but if my ambition become headftrong, and blindly impel me to action, the action is neither felfifh nor focial. A flight degree of refentment, where my chief view in acting is the pleafure arifing to myfelf from gratifying the paffion, is juftly denominated *felfifh :* where revenge flames fo high as to have no other aim but the deftruction of its object, it is no longer felfifh ; but, in oppofition to a focial paffion, may be termed *diffocial.**

When this analyfis of human nature is confidered, not one article of which can with truth be controverted, there is reafon to be furprifed at the blindnefs of fome philofophers, who, by dark and confufed notions, are led to deny all motives to action but what arife from felf-love. Man, for aught appears, might poffibly have been fo framed, as to be fufceptible of no paffions but what have felf for their object : but man thus framed, would be ill fitted for fociety : his conftitution, partly felfifh, partly focial, fits him much better for his prefent fituation.†

Of

* This word, hitherto not in ufe, feems to fulfil all that is required by Demetrius Phalereus *(Of elocution, ∫ El.* 96.) in coining a new word : firft, that it be perfpicuous ; and next, that it be in the tone of the language ; that we may not, fays our author, introduce among the Grecian vocables, words that found like thofe of Phrygia or Scythia.

† As the benevolence of many human actions is beyond the poffibility of doubt, the argument commonly infifted on for reconciling fuch actions to the

felfifh

Of ſelf, every one hath a direct perception ; of other things we have no knowledge but by means of their attributes : and hence it is, that of ſelf the perception is more lively than of any other thing. Self is an agreeable object ; and, for the reaſon now given, muſt be more agreeable than any other object. Is this ſufficient to account for the prevalence of ſelf-love ?

In the foregoing part of this chapter it is ſuggeſted, that ſome circumſtances make beings or things fit objects for deſire, others not. This hint ought to be purſued. It is a truth aſcertained by univerſal experience, that a thing which in our apprehenſion is beyond reach, never is the object of deſire ; no man, in his right ſenſes, deſires to walk on the clouds, or to deſcend to the centre of the earth : we may amuſe ourſelves in · a reverie, with building caſtles in the air, and wiſhing for what can never happen ; but ſuch things never move deſire. And indeed a deſire to do what we are ſenſible is beyond our power, would be altogether abſurd. In the next place, though the difficulty of attainment with reſpect to things within reach, often inflames deſire ; yet, where the proſpect of attainment is faint, and the event extremely uncertain, the object, however agreeable, ſeldom raiſeth any ſtrong deſire ; thus beauty, or any other good quality, in a woman of rank, ſeldom raiſes love in a man greatly her inferior. In the third place, different objects, equally within reach, raiſe emotions in different degrees ; and when deſire accompanies any of theſe emotions, its ſtrength, as is natural, is proportioned to that of its cauſe. Hence the remarkable difference among deſires directed to beings inanimate,

---

ſelfiſh ſyſtem, is, that the only motive I can have to perform a benevolent action, or an action of any kjnd, is the pleaſure that it affords me. So much then is yielded, that we are pleaſed when we do good to others : which is a fair admiſſion of the principle of benevolence ; for without that principle, what pleaſure could one have in doing good to others ? And admitting a principle of benevolence, why may it not be a motive to action, as well as ſelfiſhneſs is, or any other principle ?

mate, animate, and rational : the emotion cauſed by a
rational being, is out of meaſure ſtronger than any cauſed by an animal without reaſon ; and an emotion raiſed by ſuch an animal, is ſtronger than what is cauſed by
any thing inanimate. There is a ſeparate reaſon why
deſire, of which a rational being is the object, ſhould be
the ſtrongeſt : our deſires ſwell by partial gratification;
and the means we have of gratifying deſire, by benefit-
ing or harming a rational being, are without end : deſire directed to an inanimate being, ſuſceptible neither
of pleaſure nor pain, is not capable of a higher gratification than that of acquiring the property. Hence it is,
that though every emotion accompanied with deſire, is
ſtrictly ſpeaking a paſſion ; yet commonly none of theſe
· are denominated paſſions, but where a ſenſible being,
capable of pleaſure and pain, is the object.

S E C T. II.

Power of Sounds to raiſe Emotions and Paſſions.

UPON a review, I find the foregoing ſection
almoſt wholly employed upon emotions and paſſions
raiſed by objects of ſight, though they are alſo raiſed by
objects of hearing. As this happened without intention,
merely becauſe ſuch objects are familiar above others, I
find it proper to add a ſhort ſection upon the power
of ſounds to raiſe emotions and paſſions.

I begin with comparing ſounds and viſible objects with
reſpect to their influence upon the mind. It has already
been obſerved, that of all external objects, rational beings,
eſpecially of our own ſpecies, have the moſt powerful influence in raiſing emotions and paſſions ; and, as ſpeech
is the moſt powerful of all the means by which one human being can diſplay itſelf to another, the objects of
the eye muſt ſo far yield preference to thoſe of the ear.

With

With reſpect to inanimate objects of ſight, ſounds may be ſo contrived as to raiſe both terror and mirth beyond what can be done by any ſuch object. Muſic has a commanding influence over the mind, eſpecially in conjunction with words. Objects of ſight may indeed contribute to the ſame end, but more faintly ; as where a love-poem is rehearſed in a ſhady grove, or on the bank of a purling ſtream. But ſounds which are vaſtly more ductile and various, readily accompany all the ſocial affections expreſſed in a poem, eſpecially emotions of love and pity.

Muſic having at command a great variety of emotions, may, like many objects of ſight, be made to promote luxury and effeminacy ; of which we have inſtances without number, eſpecially in vocal muſic. But, with reſpect to its pure and refined pleaſures, muſic goes hand in hand with gardening and architecture, her ſiſter-arts, in humanizing and poliſhing the mind ;* of which none can doubt who have felt the charms of muſic. But, if authority be required, the following paſſage from a grave hiſtorian, eminent for ſolidity of judgment, muſt have the greateſt weight. Polybius, ſpeaking of the people of Cynætlia, an Arcadian tribe, has the following train of reflections. " As the Arcadians have always been celebrated for their piety, humanity, and hoſpitality, we are naturally led to inquire, how it has happened that the Cynætheans are diſtinguiſhed from the other Arcadians, by ſavage manners, wickedneſs and cruelty. I can attribute this difference to no other cauſe, but a total neglect among the people of Cynætha, of an inſtitution eſtabliſhed among the ancient Arcadians with a nice regard to their manners and their climate : I mean the diſcipline and exerciſe of that genuine and perfect muſic, which is uſeful in every ſtate, but neceſſary to the Arcadians ; whoſe manners, originally rigid

and

* See Chapter 24.

and auftere, made it of the greateft importance to incorporate this art into the very effence of their government. All men know that, in Arcadia, the children are early taught to perform hymns and fongs compofed in honour of their gods and heroes; and that, when they have learned the mufic of Timotheus and Philoxenus, they affemble yearly in the public theatres, dancing with emulation to the found of flutes, and acting in games adapted to their tender years. The Arcadians, even in their private feafts, never employ hirelings, but each man fings in his turn. They are alfo taught all the military fteps and motions to the found of inftruments, which they perform yearly in the theatres, at the public charge. To me it is evident, that thefe folemnities were introduced, not for idle pleafure, but to foften the rough and ftubborn temper of the Arcadians, occafioned by the coldnefs of a high country. But the Cynætheans, neglecting thefe arts, have become fo fierce and favage, that there is not another city in Greece fo remarkable for frequent and great enormities. This confideration ought. to engage the Arcadians never to relax in any degree, their mufical difcipline; and it ought to open the eyes of the Cynætheans, and make them fenfible of what importance it would be to reftore mufic to their city, and every difcipline that may foften their manners; for otherwife they can never hope to fubdue their brutal ferocity.*"

No one will be furprifed to hear fuch influence attributed to mufic, when, with refpect to another of the fine arts, he finds a living inftance of an influence no lefs powerful. It is unhappily indeed the reverfe of the former; for it has done more mifchief by corrupting Britifh manners, than mufic ever did good by purifying thofe of Arcadia.

The licentious court of Charles II. among its many diforders, engendered a peft, the virulence of which fubfifts

to

* Polybius, lib. 4. cap. 3.

to this day. The Englifh comedy, copying the manners
of the court, became abominably licentious ; and continues fo with very little foftening. It is there an eftablifhed
rule, to deck out the chief charaƈters with every vice in
fafhion, howevcr grofs. But, as fuch charaƈters viewed
in a true light would be difguftful, care is taken to difguife their deformity under the embellifhments of wit,
fprightlinefs, and good humour, which in mixed company makes a capital figure. It requires not much thought
to difcover the poifonous influenceof fuch plays. A young
man of figure, emancipated at laft from the feverity and
reftraint of a college education, repairs to the capital difpofed to every fort of excefs. The playhoufe becomes
his favourite amufement ; and he is enchanted with the
gaiety and fplendour of the chief perfonages. The difguft which vice gives him at firft, foon wears off, to
make way for new notions, more liberal in his opinion ;
by which a fovereign contempt of religion, and a declared war upon the chaftity of wives, maids, and wid-
ows, are converted from being infamous vices to be
fafhionable virtues. The infeƈtion fpreads gradually
through all ranks, and becomes univerfal. How gladly
would I liften to any one who fhould undertake to prove,
that what I have been defcribing is chimerical ! but the
diffolutenefs of our young men of birth will not fuffer
me to doubt of its reality. Sir Harry Wildair has completed many a rake; and in the *Sufpicious Hufband*, Ran-
ger, the humble imitator of Sir Harry, has had no flight
influence in fpreading that charaƈter. What woman
tinƈtured with the playhoufe-morals, would not be the
fprightly, the witty, though diffolute Lady Townly,
rather than the cold, the fober, though virtuous Lady
Grace ? How odious ought writers to be who thus employ the talents they have from their Maker moft traitor-
oufly againft himfelf, by endeavouring to corrupt and
disfigure his creatures! If the comedies of Congreve did
not rack him with remorfe in his laft moments, he muft
                                                    have

have been loft to all fenfe of virtue. Nor will it afford
any excufe to fuch writers, that their comedies are entertaining ; unlefs it could be maintained, that wit and
fprightlinefs are better fuited to a vicious than a virtuous
character. It would grieve me to think fo ; and the direct contrary is exemplified in the *Merry Wives of Windfor*, where we are highly entertained with the conduct of
two ladies, not more remarkable for mirth and fpirit than
for the ftricteft purity of manners.

S E C T. III.

Caufes of the Emotions of Joy and Sorrow.

THIS fubject was purpofely referved for a
feparate fection, becaufe it could not, with perfpicuity,
be handled under the general head. An emotion accompanied with defire is termed *a paffion ;* and when
the defire is fulfilled, the paffion is faid to be gratified.
Now, the gratification of every paffion muft be pleafant ; for nothing can be more natural than that the
accomplifhment of any wifh or defire fhould affect us
with joy : I know of no exception but when a man ftung
with remorfe defires to chaftife and punifh himfelf.
The joy of gratification is properly called *an emotion ;* becaufe it makes us happy in our prefent fituation, and is
ultimate in its nature, not having a tendency to any thing
beyond. On the other hand, forrow muft be the refult
of an event contrary to what we defire ; for if the accomplifhment of defire produce joy, it is equally natural
that difappointment fhould produce forrow. ·
 An event, fortunate or unfortunate, that falls out by
accident, without being forefeen or thought of, and which
therefore could not be the object of defire, raifeth an
emotion of the fame kind with that now mentioned ; but
the caufe muft be different ; for there can be no gratification

cation where there is no defire. We have not however far to feek for a caufe : it is involved in the nature of man, that he cannot be indifferent to an event that concerns him or any of his connections ; if it be fortunate, it gives him joy ; if unfortunate, it gives him forrow. .

In no fituation doth joy rife to a greater height than upon the removal of any violent diftrefs of mind or body ; and in no fituation doth forrow rife to a greater height, than upon the removal of what makes us happy. The fenfibility of our nature ferves in part to account for thefe effects. Other caufes concur. One is, that violent diftrefs always raifes an anxious defire to be free from it ; and therefore its removal is a high gratification : nor can we be poffeffed of any thing that makes us happy, without wifhing its continuance ; and therefore its removal, by croffing our wifhes, muft create forrow. The principle of contraft is another caufe : an emotion of joy arifing upon the removal of pain, is increafed by contraft when we reflect upon our former diftrefs : an emotion of forrow, upon being deprived of any good, is increafed by contraft when we reflect upon our former happinefs :

> *Jaffer.* There's not a wretch that lives on common charity,
> But's happier than me. For I have known
> The lufcious fweets of plenty : every night
> Have flept with foft content about my head,
> And never wak'd but to a joyful morning.
> Yet now muft fall like a full ear of corn,
> Whofe bloffom 'fcap'd, yet's withered in the ripening.
>
> *Venice Preferv'd, act* 1. *fc.* 1.

It hath always been reckoned difficult to account for the extreme pleafure that follows a ceffation of bodily pain ; as when one is relieved from the rack, or from a violent fit of the ftone. What is faid explains this difficulty, in the eafieft and fimpleft manner: ceffation of bodily pain is not of itfelf a pleafure, for a *non ens* or a negative can neither give pleafure nor pain ; but a man is fo framed by nature as to rejoice when he is eafed of pain,

· as

as well as to be forrowful when deprived of any enjoyment. This branch of our conftitution is chiefly the caufe
of the pleafure. The gratification of defire comes in as
an acceffory caufe : and contraft joins its force, by increafing the fenfe of our prefent happinefs. In the cafe
of an acute pain, a peculiar circumftance contributes its
part : the brifk circulation of the animal fpirits occafioned
by acute pain, continues after the pain is gone, and produceth a very pleafant emotion. Sicknefs hath not that
effeft, becaufe it is always attended' with a depreffion of
fpirits.

Hence it is, that the gradual diminution of acute
pain, occafions a mixt emotion, partly pleafant, partly
painful : the partial diminution produceth joy in proportion : but the remaining pain balanceth the joy.
This mixt emotion, however, hath no long endurance ;
for the joy that arifeth upon the diminution of pain,
foon vanifheth, and leaveth in the undifturbed poffeffion,
that degree of pain which remains.

What is above obferved about bodily pain, is equally
applicable to the diftreffes of the mind ; and accordingly
it is a common artifice to prepare us for the reception of
good news by alarming our fears.

S E C T. IV.

Sympathetic Emotion of Virtue, and its caufe.

ONE feeling there is that merits a deliberate
view, for its fingularity as well as utility. Whether to
call it an emotion or a paffion, feems uncertain : the
former it can fcarce be becaufe it involves defire ; the
latter it can fcarce be becaufe it has no objeft. But this
feeling, and its nature, will be beft underftood from examples. A fignal aft of gratitude produceth in the fpeftator or reader, not only love or efteem for the author,
but

but alfo a feparate feeling, being a vague feeling of gratitude without an object ; a feeling, however, that difpofes the fpectator or reader to acts of gratitude, more
than upon an ordinary' occafion. This feeling is overlooked by writers upon ethics ; but a man may be convinced of its reality, by attentively watching his own
heart when he thinks warmly of any fignal act of gratitude ; he will be confcious of the feeling, as diftinct
from the efteem or admiration he has for the grateful
perfon. The feeling is fingular in the following refpect,
that it is accompanied with a defire to perform acts of
gratitude, without having any object ; though in that
ftate, the mind, wonderfully bent on an object, neglects
no opportunity to vent itfelf : any act of kindnefs or
good-will that would pafs unregarded upon another occafion, is greedily feized ; and the vague feeling is converted into a real paffion of gratitude : in fuch a ftate,
favours are returned double.

In like manner, a courageous action produceth in a
fpectator the paffion of admiration directed to the author : and befide this well known paffion, a feparate
feeling is raifed in the fpectator ; which may be called *an
emotion of courage ;* becaufe, while under its influence, he
is confcious of a boldnefs and intrepidity beyond what is
ufual, and longs for proper objects upon which to exert
this emotion :

Spumantemque dari, pecora inter inertia, votis
Optat aprum, aut fulvum defcendere monte leonem.
Æneid. iv. 158.

Non altramente il tauro, one l'irriti
Gelofo amor con ftimoli pungenti,
Horribilmente mugge, e co'muggiti
Gli fpirti in fe rifueglia, e l'ire ardenti :
E'l corno aguzza a i tronchi, e par ch'inuiti
Con vani colpi a'la battaglia i venti.
Taffo, canto 7. *ſ.* 55.

So

So full of valour that they ſmote the air
For breathing in their faces.

Tempeſt, act 4. ſc. 4.

The emotions raiſed by muſic independent of words, muſt be all of this nature: courage rouſed by martial muſic performed upon inſtruments without a voice, cannot be directed to any object; nor can grief or pity raiſed by melancholy muſic of the ſame kind have an object.

For another example, let us figure ſome grand and heroic action, highly agreeable to the ſpectator: be-ſide veneration for the author, the ſpectator feels in himſelf an unuſual dignity of character, which diſpoſ-eth him to great and noble actions: and herein chief-ly conſiſts the extreme delight every one hath in the hiſtories of conquerors and heroes.

This ſingular feeling, which may be termed *the ſym-pathetic emotion of virtue,* reſembles, in one reſpect, the well known appetites that lead to the propagation and preſervation of the ſpecies. The appetites of hunger, thirſt, and animal love, ariſe in the mind before they are directed to any object; and in no caſe whatever is the mind more ſolicitous for a proper object, than when under the influence of any of theſe appetites.

The feeling I have endeavoured to unfold, may well be termed *the ſympathetic emotion of virtue;* for it is raiſed in a ſpectator, or in a reader, by virtuous actions of every kind, and by no other ſort. When we con-template a virtuous action, which fails not to prompt our love for the author, our propenſity at the ſame time to ſuch actions is ſo much enlivened, as to become for a time an actual emotion. But no man hath a pro-penſity to vice as ſuch: on the contrary, a wicked deed diſguſts him, and makes him abhor the author; and this abhorrence is a ſtrong antidote againſt vice, as long as any impreſſion remains of the wicked action.

In a rough road, a halt to view a fine country is refrefhing; and here a delightful profpect opens upon us. It is indeed wonderful to obferve what incitements there are to virtue in the human frame: juftice is perceived to be our duty; and it is guarded by natural punifhments, from which the guilty never efcape: to perform noble and generous actions, a warm fenfe of their dignity and fuperior excellence is a moft efficacious incitement.* And to leave virtue in no quarter unfupported, here is unfolded an admirable contrivance, by which good example commands the heart, and adds to virtue the force of habit. We approve every virtuous action, and beftow our affection on the author; but if virtuous actions produced no other effect upon us, good example would not have great influence: the fympathetic emotion under confideration beftows upon good example the utmoft influence, by prompting us to imitate what we admire. This fingular emotion will readily find an object to exert itfelf upon: and at any rate, it never exifts without producing fome effect; becaufe virtuous emotions of that fort, are in fome degree an exercife of virtue; they are a mental exercife at leaft, if they appear not externally. And every exercife of virtue, internal and external, leads to habit; for a difpofition or propenfity of the mind, like a limb of the body, becomes ftronger by exercife. Proper means at the fame time, being ever at hand to raife this fympathetic emotion, its frequent reiteration may, in a good meafure, fupply the want of a more complete exercife. Thus, by proper difcipline, every perfon may acquire a fettled habit of virtue: intercourfe with men of worth, hiftories of generous and difinterefted actions, and frequent meditation upon them, keep the fympathetic emotion in conftant exercife, which by degrees introduceth

---

* See Effays on morality and natural religion, part 1. eff. 2. ch. 4.

duceth a habit, and confirms the authority of virtue : with reſpeƈt to education in particular, what a ſpacious and commodious avenue to the heart of a young perſon is here opened !

SECT. V.

In many inſtances one Emotion is produƈtive of another.
The ſame of Paſſions.

IN the firſt chapter it is obſerved, that the relations by which things are conneƈted, have a remarkable influence on the train of our ideas. I here add, that they have an influence, no leſs remarkable, in the produƈtion of emotions and paſſions. Beginning with the former, an agreeable objeƈt makes every thing conneƈted with it appear ⸱ agreeable ; for the mind gliding ſweetly and eaſily through related objeƈts, carries along the agreeable properties it meets with in its paſſage, and beſtows them on the preſent objeƈt, which thereby appears more agreeable than when conſidered apart.* This reaſon may appear obſcure and metaphyſical, but the faƈt is beyond all diſpute. No relation

---

* Such proneneſs has the mind to this communication of properties, that we often find a property aſcribed to a related objeƈt, of which naturally it is not ſuſceptible. Sir Richaid Grenville in a ſingle ſhip, being ſurpriſed by the Spaniſh fleet, was adviſed to retire. He utterly refuſed to turn from the enemy ; declaring, " he would rather die, than diſhonour himſelf, his country, and her Majeſty's ſhip." *Hakluyt, vol.* 2. *part* 2. *p.* 169. To aid the communication of properties in inſtances like the preſent, there always muſt be a momentary perſonification : a ſhip muſt be imagined a ſenſible being, to make it ſuſceptible of honour or diſhonour. In the battle of Mantinea, Epaminondas being moitally wounded, was carried to his tent in a manner dead : recovering his ſenſes, the firſt thing he inquired about was his ſhield ; which being brought, he kiſſed it as the companion of his valour and glory. It muſt be remaiked, that among the Greeks and Romans it was deemed infamous for a ſoldier to return from battle without his ſhield.

E 2

tion is more intimate than that between a being and its qualities : and accordingly, every quality in a hero, even the flighteft, makes a greater figure than more fub- ftantial qualities in others. The propenfity of carrying along agreeable properties from one object to another, is fometimes fo vigorous, as to convert defects into properties : the wry neck of Alexander was imitated by his courtiers as a real beauty, without intention to flatter: Lady Piercy, fpeaking of her hufband Hotfpur,

> —————————————————By his light
> Did all the chivalry of England move,
> To do brave acts. He was indeed the glafs,
> Wherein the noble youths did drefs themfelves.
> He had no legs that practis'd not his gait :
> And fpeaking thick, which Nature made his blemifh,
> Became the accents of the valiant :
> For thofe who could fpeak flow and tardily,
> Would turn their own perfection to abufe,
> To feem like him.   *Second part, Henry* IV. *act* 2. *fc.* 6,

The fame communication of paffion obtains in the relation of principal and acceffory. Pride, of which felf is the object, expands itfelf upon a houfe, a gar- den, fervants, equipage, and every acceffory. A lover addreffeth his miftrefs' glove in the following terms :

> Sweet ornament that decks a thing divine.

Veneration for relics has the fame natural founda- tion ; and that foundation with the fuperftructure of fuperftition, has occafioned much blind devotion to the moft ridiculous objects, to the fuppofed milk, for ex- ample, of the Virgin Mary, or the fuppofed blood of St. Januarius.* A temple is in a proper fenfe an ac- ceffory

---

* But why worfhip the crofs which is fuppofed to be that upon which our Saviour fuffered ? That crofs ought to be the object of hatred, not of veneration. If it be urged, that as an inftrument of Chrift's fuffering it was falutary to mankind, I anfwer, Why is not alfo Pontius Pilate rever- enced, Caiaphas the high prieft, and Judas Ifcariot ?

ceffory of the deity to which it is dedicated : Diana is chafte, and not only her temple, but the very ificle which hangs on it, muft partake of that property :

> The noble fifter of Poplicola,
> The moon of Rome ; chafte as the ificle
> That's curdled by the froft from pureft fnow,
> And hangs on Dian's temple.
>
> *Coriolanus, act* 5. *fc.* 3.

Thus it is, that the refpect and efteem, which the great, the powerful, the opulent, naturally command, are in fome meafure communicated to their drefs, to their manners, and to all their connections : and it is this communication of properties, which, prevailing even over the natural tafte of beauty, helps to give currency to what is called *the fafhion.*

By means of the fame eafinefs of communication, every bad quality in an enemy is fpread upon all his connections. The fentence pronounced againft Ravaillac for the affaffination of Henry IV. of France, ordains, that the houfe in which he was born fhould be razed to the ground, and that no other building fhould ever be erected on that fpot. Enmity will extend paffion to objects ftill lefs connected. The Swifs fuffer no peacocks to live, becaufe the Duke of Auftria, their ancient enemy, wears a peacock's tail in his creft. A relation more flight and tranfitory than that of enmity, may have the fame effect : thus the bearer of bad tidings becomes an object of averfion :

> Fellow, begone ; I cannot brook thy fight ;
> This news hath made thee a moft ugly man.
>
> *King John, act* 3. *fc.* 1.

> Yet the firft bringer of unwelcome news
> Hath but a lofing office : and his tongue
> Sounds ever after as a fullen bell
> Remember'd, tolling a departed friend.
>
> *Second part, Henry* IV. *act* 1. *fc.* 3.

E 3   In

In borrowing thus properties from one object to beftow them on another, it is not any object indifferently
that will anfwer. The object from which properties
are borrowed, muft be fuch as to warm the mind and
enliven the imagination. Thus the beauty of a miftrefs, which inflames the imagination, is readily communicated to a glove, as above mentioned ; but the
greateft beauty a glove is fufceptible of, touches the
mind fo little, as to be entirely dropped in paffing from
it to the owner. In general, it may be obferved, that
any drefs upon a fine woman is becoming : but that
ornaments upon one who is homely, muft be elegant
indeed to have any remarkable effect in mending her
appearance.*

· The emotions produced as above may properly be
termed *fecondary*, being occafioned either by antecedent emotions or antecedent paffions, which in
that refpect may be termed *primary*. And to complete the prefent theory, I muft add, that a fecondary emotion may readily fwell into a paffion
for the acceffory object, provided the acceffory be
a proper object for defire. Thus it happens that
one paffion is often productive of another : examples
are without number ; the fole difficulty is a proper
choice. ‣ I begin with felf-love, and the power it hath
to generate love to children. Every man, befide making part of a greater fyftem, like a comet, a planet,
or fatellite only, hath a lefs fyftem of his own, in the
centre of which he reprefents the fun darting his fire
and heat all around ; efpecially upon his neareft connections : the connection between a man and his chil-
                                                dren,

---

* A houfe and gardens furrounded with pleafant fields, all in good order, beftow greater luftre upon the owner than at firft will be imagined.
The beauties of the former are, by intimacy of connection, readily communicated to the latter ; and if it have been done at the expenfe of the
owner himfelf, we naturally transfer to him whatever of defign, art, or
tafte appears in the performance. Should not this be a ftrong motive with
proprietors to embellifh and improve their fields ?

dren, fundamentally that of cauſe and effect, becomes, by the addition of other circumſtances, the completeſt that can be among individuals ; and therefore ſelf-love, the moſt vigorous of all paſſions, is readily expanded upon children. The ſecondary emotion they produce by means of their connection, is ſufficiently ſtrong to move deſire even from the beginning ; and the new paſſion ſwells by degrees, till it rivals in ſome meaſure ſelf-love, the primary paſſion. To demonſtrate the truth of this theory, I urge the following argument. Re-morſe for betraying a friend, or murdering an enemy in cold blood, makes a man even hate himſelf : in that ſtate, he is not conſcious of affection to his children, but rather of diſguſt or ill-will. What cauſe can be aſſigned for that change, other than the hatred he has to himſelf, which is expanded upon his children ? And if ſo, may we not with equal reaſon derive from ſelf-love, ſome part at leaſt of the affection a man generally has to them ?

The affection a man bears to his blood relations, de-pends partly on the ſame principle : ſelf-love is alſo ex-panded upon them ; and the communicated paſſion is more or leſs vigorous in proportion to the degree of connection. Nor doth ſelf-love reſt here : it is, by the force of connection, communicated even to things inanimate : and hence the affection a man bears to his property, and to every thing he calls his own.

Friendſhip, leſs vigorous than ſelf-love, is, for that reaſon, leſs apt to communicate itſelf to the friend's children, or other relations. Inſtances however are not wanting of ſuch communicated paſſion, ariſing from friendſhip when it is ſtrong. Friendſhip may go higher in the matrimonial ſtate than in any other con-dition : and Otway, in *Venice preſerved*, takes advan-tage of that circumſtance : in the ſcene where Belvi-dera ſues to her father for pardon, ſhe is repreſented as

pleading

pleading her mother's merit, and the refemblance fhe
bore to her mother :

> *Priuli.* My daughter!
> *Belvidera.* Yes, your daughter, by a mother
> Virtuous and noble, faithful to your honour,
> Obedient to your will, kind to your wifhes,
> Dear to your arms. By all the joys fhe gave you
> When in her blooming years fhe was your treafure,
> Look kindly on me ; in my face behold
> The lineaments of her's y'have kifs'd fo often,
> Pleading the caufe of your poor caft-off child.

And again,

> *Belvidera.* Lay me, I beg you, lay me
> By the dear afhes of my tender mother :
> She would have pitied me, had fate yet fpar'd her.
>
> *Act 5. fc. 1.*

This explains why any meritorious action, or any illuftrious qualification, in my fon or my friend, is apt to
make me over-value myfelf : if I value my friend's wife
or fon upon account of their connection with him, it is
ftill more natural that I fhould value myfelf upon account of my connection with him.

Friendfhip, or any other focial affection, may, by
changing the object, produce oppofite effects. Pity,
by interefting us ftrongly for the perfon in diftrefs,
muft of confequence inflame our refentment againft the
author of the diftrefs : for, in general, the affection we
have for any man, generates in us good-will to his
friends, and ill-will to his enemies. Shakefpear fhows
great art in the funeral oration pronounced by Antony
over the body of Cæfar. He firft endeavours to excite grief in the hearers, by dwelling upon the deplorable lofs of fo great a man : this paffion, interefting
them ftrongly in Cæfar's fate, could not fail to produce a lively fenfe of the treachery and cruelty of the
confpirators ;

conspirators ; an infallible method to inflame the resentment of the people beyond all bounds :

> *Antony.* If you have tears, prepare to shed them now,
> You all do know this mantle. I remember
> The first time ever Cæsar put it on ;
> 'Twas on a summer's evening, in his tent,
> That day he overcame the Nervii———
> Look ! in this place ran Cassius' dagger through ;———
> See what a rent the envious Casca made.———
> Through this the well-beloved Brutus stabb'd ;
> And, as he pluck'd his cursed steel away,
> Mark how the blood of Cæsar follow'd it !
> As rushing out of doors, to be resolv'd,
> If Brutus so unkindly knock'd or no :
> For Brutus, as you know, was Cæsar's angel.
> Judge, oh you God's ! how dearly Cæsar lov'd him !
> This, this, was the unkindest cut of all ;
> For when the noble Cæsar saw him stab,
> Ingratitude, more strong than traitor's arms,
> Quite vanquish'd him ; then burst his mighty heart ;
> And, in his mantle muffling up his face,
> Which all the while ran blood, great Cæsar fell,
> Even at the base of Pompey's statue.
> O what a fall was there, my countrymen !
> Then I and you, and all of us, fell down,
> Whilst bloody treason flourish'd over us.
> O, now you weep ; and I perceive you feel
> The dint of pity ; these are gracious drops.
> Kind souls ! what ! weep you when you but behold
> Our Cæsar's vesture wounded ? look you here !
> Here is himself, marr'd, as you see, by traitors.
>
> *Julius Cæsar, act* 3. *sc.* 6.

Had Antony endeavoured to excite his audience to
vengeance, without paving the way by raising their
grief, his speech would not have made the same impression.

Hatred, and other dissocial passions, produce effects
directly opposite to those above mentioned. If I hate a
man, his children, his relations, nay his property, become to me objects of aversion : his enemies on the
other hand, I am disposed to esteem.

The

The more ſlight and tranſitory relations are not favourable to the communication of paſſion. Anger, when ſudden and violent, is one exception ; for, if the perſon, who did the injury be removed out of reach, that paſſion will vent itſelf againſt any related object, however ſlight the relation be. Another exception makes a greater figure : a group of beings or things, becomes often the object of a communicated paſſion, even where the relation of the individuals to the percipient is but ſlight. Thus, though I put no value upon a ſingle man for living in the ſame town with myſelf ; my townſmen, however, conſidered in a body, are preferred before others. This is ſtill more remarkable with reſpect to my countrymen in general : the grandeur of the complex objects ſwells the paſſion of ſelf-love by the relation I have to my native country ; and every paſſion, when it ſwells beyond its ordinary bounds, hath a peculiar tendency to expand itſelf along related objects. In fact, inſtances are not rare, of perſons, who upon all occaſions are willing to ſacrifice their lives and fortunes for their country. Such influence upon the mind of man hath a complex object, or, more properly ſpeaking, a general term*.

, The ſenſe of order hath influence in the communication of paſſion. It is a common obſervation, that a man's affection to his parents is leſs vigorous than to his children : the order of nature in deſcending to children, aids the tranſition of the affection : the aſcent to a parent, contrary to that order, makes the tranſition more difficult. Gratitude to a benefactor is readily extended to his children ; but not ſo readily to his parents. The difference, however, between the natural and inverted order, is not ſo conſiderable, but that it may be balanced by other circumſtances. Pliny† gives

an

---

* See Eſſays on morality and natural religion, part 1. eſſ. 2. ch. 5.

† Lib. 7. cap. 36.

an account of a woman of rank condemned to die for
a crime ; and, to avoid public fhame, detained in pri-
fon to die of hunger : her life being prolonged beyond
expectation, it was difcovered, that fhe was nourifhed
by fucking milk from the breafts of her daughter.
This inftance of filial piety, which aided the tranfition,
and made afcent no lefs eafy than defcent is commonly, procured a pardon to the mother, and a penfion to
both. The ftory of Androcles and the lion* may be accounted for in the fame manner : the admiration, of
which the lion was the object for his kindnefs and gratitude to Androcles, produced good will to Androcles,
and a pardon of his crime.

And this leads to other obfervations upon communicated paffions. I love my daughter lefs after fhe
is married, and my mother lefs after a fecond marriage: the marriage of my fon or of my father diminifhes
not my affection fo remarkably. The fame obfervation
holds with refpect to friendfhip, gratitude, and other
paffions : the love I bear my friend is but faintly
extended to his married daughter : the refentment I
have againft a man is readily extended againft children
who make part of his family ; not fo readily againft
children who are foris-familiated, efpecially by marriage. This difference is alfo more remarkable in daughters than in fons. Thefe are curious facts; and, in order to difcover the caufe, we muft examine minutely
that operation of the mind by which a paffion is extended to a related object. In confidering two things
as related, the mind is not ftationary, but paffeth and
repaffeth from the one to the other, viewing the relation from each of them perhaps oftener than once;
which holds more efpecially in confidering a relation
between things of unequal rank, as between the caufe
and

* Aulus Gellius, lib. 5. cap. 14.

and the effect, or between a principal and an accessory,
in contemplating, for example, the relation between a
building and its ornaments, the mind is not satisfied
with a single transition from the former to the latter ;
it must also view the relation, beginning at the latter,
and passing from it to the former.   This vibration of
the mind in passing and repassing between things related, explains the facts above mentioned : the mind pass-
eth easily from the father to the daughter ; but where
the daughter is married, this new relation attracts the
mind, and obstructs, in some measure, the return from
the daughter to the father ; and any circumstance that
obstructs the mind in passing and repassing between its
objects, occasions a like obstruction in the communication of passion.   The marriage of a male obstructs
less the easiness of transition : because a male is less
sunk by the relation of marriage than a female.

The foregoing instances are of passion communicated from one object to another 'But one passion may
be generated by another, without change of object,
It in general is observable, that a passion paves the way
to others similar in their tone, whether directed to the
same or to a different object ; for the mind, heat-
ed by any passion, is, in that state, more susceptible of
a new impression in a similar tone, than when cool and
quiescent.   It is a common observation, that pity generally produceth friendship for a person in distress.   One
reason is, that pity interests us in its object, and recommends all its virtuous qualities : female beauty accordingly shows best in distress ; being more apt to inspire love, than upon an ordinary occasion.   But the
chief reason is, that pity, warming and melting the
spectator, prepares him for the reception of other tender affections ; and pity is readily improved into love
or friendship, by a certain tenderness and concern for
the object, which is the tone of both passions.   The
                                        aptitude

aptitude of pity to produce love, is beautifully illuſtrated by Shakeſpear :

> *Othello.* Her father lov'd me ; oft invited me ;
> Still queſtion'd me the ſtory of my life,
> From year to year ; the battles, ſieges, fortunes,
> That I have paſt.
> I ran it through e'en from my boyiſh days,
> To th' very moment that he bade me tell it :
> Wherein I ſpoke of moſt diſaſtrous chances,
> Of moving accidents by flood and field ;
> Of hair-breadth 'ſcapes in th' imminent deadly breach;
> Of being taken by the inſolent foe,
> And ſold to ſlavery ; of my redemption thence,
> And with it all my travel's hiſtory.
> ———————— All theſe to hear
> Would Deſdemona ſeriouſly incline ;
> But ſtill the houſe-affairs would draw her thence
> Which, ever as ſhe could with haſte diſpatch,
> She'd come again, and with a greedy ear
> Devour up my diſcourſe : Which I obſerving,
> Took once a pliant hour, and found good means
> To draw from her a prayer of earneſt heart,
> That I would all my pilgrimage dilate,
> Whereof by parcels ſhe had ſomething heard,
> But not diſtinctively. I did conſent,
> And often did beguile her of her tears,
> When I did ſpeak of ſome diſtreſsful ſtroke
> That my youth ſuffer'd. My ſtory being done,
> She gave me for my pains a world of ſighs :
> She ſwore, in faith, 'twas ſtrange, 'twas paſſing ſtrange—
> 'Twas pitiful, 'twas wondrous pitiful—
> She wiſh'd ſhe had not heard it :—yet ſhe wiſh'd
> That Heaven had made her ſuch a man : ſhe thank'd me,
> And bade me, if I had a friend that lov'd her,
> I ſhould but teach him how to tell my ſtory,
> And that would woo her. On this hint I ſpake :
> She lov'd me for the dangers I had paſt,
> And I lov'd her, that ſhe did pity them :
> This only is the witchcraft I have us'd.
>
> *Othello, act 1. ſc.* 8.

In this inſtance it will be obſerved that admiration concurred with pity to produce love.

SECT.

SECT. VI.

Caufes of the Paffions of Fear and Anger.

FEAR and anger, to anfwer the purpofes of nature, are happily fo contrived as to operate fometimes inftinctively, fometimes deliberately, according to circumftances. As far as deliberate, they fall in with the general fyftem, and require no particular explanation : if any object have a threatening appearance, reafon fuggefts means to avoid the danger : if a man be injured, the firft thing he thinks of, is what revenge he fhall take, and what means he fhall employ. Thefe particulars are no lefs obvious than natural. But, as the paffions of fear and anger, in their inftinctive ftate, are lefs familiar to us, it may be acceptable to the reader to have them accurately delineated. He may alfo poffibly be glad of an opportunity to have the nature of inftinctive paffions more fully explained, than there was formerly opportunity to do. I begin with fear.

Self-prefervation is a matter of too great importance to be left entirely to the conduct of reafon. Nature hath acted here with her ufual forefight. Fear and anger are paffions that move us to act, fometimes deliberately, fometimes inftinctively, according to circumftances ; and by operating in the latter manner, they frequently afford fecurity when the flower operations of deliberate reafon would be too late : we take nourifhment commonly, not by the direction of reafon, but by the impulfe of hunger and thirft ; and in the fame manner, we avoid danger by the impulfe of fear, which often, before there is time for reflection, placeth us in fafety. Here we have an illuftrious inftance of wifdom in the formation of

man ;

man ; for it is not within the reach of fancy, to conceive any thing more artfully contrived to anſwer its
purpoſe, than the inſtinctive paſſion of fear, which; upon the firſt ſurmiſe of danger, operates inſtantaneouſly.
So little doth the paſſion, in ſuch inſtances, depend on
reaſon, that it frequently operates in contradiction to it :
a man who is not upon his guard cannot avoid ſhrink-
ing at a blow though he knows it to be aimed in ſport ;
nor avoid cloſing his eyes at the approach of what may
hurt them, though conſcious that he is in no danger.
And it alſo operates by impelling us to act even where
we are conſcious that our interpoſition can be of no
ſervice : if a paſſage-boat, in a briſk gale, bear much
to one ſide, I cannot avoid applying the whole force of
my ſhoulders to ſet it upright ; and, if my horſe ſtum-
ble, my hands and knees are inſtantly at work to prevent him from falling.

Fear provides for ſelf-preſervation by flying from
harm ; anger, by repelling it. Nothing, indeed, can
be better contrived to repel or prevent injury, than
anger or reſentment : deſtitute of that paſſion, men,
like defenceleſs lambs, would lie conſtantly open to
miſchief.* Deliberate anger cauſed by a voluntary injury, is too well known to require any explanation :
if my deſire be to reſent an affront I muſt uſe means ;
and theſe means muſt be diſcovered by reflection : deliberation is here requiſite ; and in that caſe the paſſion ſeldom exceeds juſt bounds. But, where anger
impels one ſuddenly to return a blow, even without
thinking of doing miſchief, the paſſion is inſtinctive ;
and it is chiefly in ſuch a caſe that it is raſh and ungovernable, becauſe it operates blindly, without affording time for deliberation or foreſight.

Inſtinctive

---

* Braſidas being bit by a mouſe he had catched, let it ſlip out of his fingers : " No creature (ſays he) is ſo contemptible, but what may provide
for its own ſafety, if it have courage." *Plutarch, Apothegmata.*

Inſtinctive anger is frequently raiſed by bodily pain, by a ſtroke, for example, on a tender part, which, ruffling the temper, and unhinging the mind, is in its tone ſimilar to anger : and when a man is thus beforehand diſpoſed to anger, he is not nice nor ſcrupulous about an object; the perſon who gave the ſtroke, however accidentally, is by an inflammable temper held a proper object, merely for having occaſioned the pain. It is ſtill more remarkable, that a ſtock or a ſtone by which I am hurt, becomes an object for my reſentment: I am violently excited to cruſh it to atoms. The paſſion, indeed, in that caſe, can be but a ſingle flaſh ; for being entirely irrational, it muſt vaniſh with the firſt reflection. Nor is that irrational effect confined to bodily pain : internal diſtreſs, when exceſſive, may be the occaſion of effects equally irrational : perturbation of mind occaſioned by the apprehenſion of having loſt a dear friend, will, in a fiery temper, produce momentary ſparks of anger againſt that very friend, however innocent : Thus Shakeſpear, in the *Tempeſt*,

> *Alonzo.*————————Sit down and reſt.
> Ev'n here I will put off my hope, and keep it
> No longer for my flatterer ; he is drown'd
> Whom thus we ſtray to find, and the ſea mocks
> Our fruſtrate ſearch on land. Well, let him go.
>   *Act 3. ſc. 3.*

The final words, *Well, let him go,* are an expreſſion of impatience and anger at Ferdinand, whoſe abſence greatly diſtreſſed his father, dreading that he was loſt in the ſtorm. This nice operation of the human mind, is by Shakeſpear exhibited upon another occaſion, and finely painted in the tragedy of *Othello :* Iago, by dark hints and ſuſpicious circumſtances, had rouſed Othello's jealouſy; which, however, appeared too ſlightly founded to be vented upon Deſdemona, its proper object. The perturbation and diſtreſs of mind thereby occaſioned,

produced

produced a momentary reſentment againſt Iago, conſidered as occaſioning the jealouſy, though innocent :

> *Othello.* Villain, be ſure thou prove my love a whore ;
> Be ſure of it : give me the ocular proof,
> Or by the wrath of man's eternal ſoul
> Thou hadſt better have been born a dog,
> Than anſwer my wak'd wrath.
> *Iago.* Is't come to this ?
> *Othello.* Make me ſee't ; or, at the leaſt, ſo prove it,
> That the probation bear no hinge or loop
> To hang a doubt on : or wo upon thy life !
> *Iago.* My noble Lord——
> *Othello.* If thou doſt ſlander her and torture me,
> Never pray more ; abandon all remorſe ;
> On horror's head horrors accumulate ;
> Do deeds to make heav'n weep, all earth amaz'd :
> For nothing canſt thou to damnation add
> Greater than that. *Othello, act 2. ſc. 8.*

This blind and abſurd effect of anger is more gaily illuſtrated by Addiſon, in a ſtory, the *dramatis perſonae* of
which are, a cardinal, and a ſpy retained in pay for intelligence. The cardinal is repreſented as minuting
down the particulars. The ſpy begins with a low
voice, " Such an one the advocate whiſpered to one of
his friends within my hearing, that your Eminence was
a very great poltroon ;" and after having given his
patron time to take it down, adds, " That another called him a mercenary raſcal in a public converſation."
The cardinal replies, " Very well," and bids him go on.
The ſpy proceeds, and loads him with reports of the
ſame nature, till the cardinal riſes in a fury, calls him an
impudent ſcoundrel, and kicks him out of the room.*

We meet with inſtances every day of reſentment
raiſed by loſs at play, and wreaked on the cards or
dice. But anger, a furious paſſion, is ſatisfied with a
connection ſtill ſlighter than that of cauſe and effect :
of

* Spectator, No. 439.

of which Congreve, in the *Mourning Bride*, gives one
beautiful example :

Gonfalez.   Have comfort.
Almeria.   Curs'd be that tongue that bids me be of
comfort,
Curs'd my own tongue that could not move his pity,
Curs'd thefe weak hands that could not hold him here,
For he is gone to doom Alphonfo's death.

Act 4. *fc.* 8.

I have chofen to exhibit anger in its more rare appearances, for in thefe we can beft trace its nature and
extent.   In the examples above given, it appears to be
an abfurd paffion, and altogether irrational.   But we
ought to confider, that it is not the intention of nature
to fubject this paffion, in every inftance, to reafon and
reflection : it was given us to prevent or to repel inju-
ries; and, like fear, it often operates blindly and inftinctively, without the leaft view to confequences : the very
firft apprehenfion of harm fets it in motion to repel
injury by punifhment.   Were it more cool and deliberate, it would lofe its threatening appearance, and be
infufficient to guard us againft violence.   When fuch
is and ought to be the nature of the paffion, it is not
wonderful to find it exerted irregularly and capriciouf-
ly, as it fometimes is where the mifchief is fudden and
unforefeen.   All the harm that can be done by the
paffion in that ftate is inftantaneous; for the fhorteft
delay fets all to rights ; and circumftances are feldom
fo unlucky as to put it in the power of a paffionate
man to do much harm in an inftant.

Social paffions, like the felfifh, fometimes drop their
character, and become inftinctive.   It is not unufual to
find anger and fear refpecting others fo exceffive, as to
operate blindly and impetuoufly, precifely as where
they are felfifh.

SECT.

THE attentive reader will obferve, that hitherto no fiction hath been affigned as the caufe of any
paffion or emotion : whether it be a being, action, or
quality, that moveth us, it is fuppofed to be really exifting. This obfervation fhows that we have not yet
completed our tafk ; becaufe paffions, as all the world
know, are moved by fiction as well as by truth. In
judging beforehand of man, fo remarkably addicted
to truth and reality, one fhould little dream that fiction can have any effect upon him ; but man's intellectual faculties are not fufficiently perfect to dive far
even into his own nature. I fhall take occafion afterward to fhow, that the power of fiction to generate
paffion is an admirable contrivance, fubfervient to excellent purpofes : in the mean time, we muft try to
unfold the means that give fiction fuch influence over
the mind.

That the objects of our external fenfes really exift in
the way and manner we perceive, is a branch of in-
tuitive knowledge : when I fee a man walking, a tree
growing, or cattle grazing, I cannot doubt but that
thefe objects are really what they appear to be : if I
be a fpectator of any tranfaction or event, I have a
conviction of the real exiftence of the perfons engaged, of their words and of their actions. Nature determines us to rely on the veracity of our fenfes ; for
otherwife they could not in any degree anfwer their
end, that of laying open things exifting and paffing
around us.

By

By the power of memory, a thing formerly ſeen may be recalled to the mind with different degrees of accuracy. We commonly are ſatisfied with a ſlight recollection of the capital circumſtances; and, in ſuch recollection, the thing is not figured as in our view, nor any image formed: we retain the conſciouſneſs of our preſent ſituation, and barely remember that formerly we ſaw that thing. ‘ But with reſpect to an intereſting object or event that made a ſtrong impreſſion, I am not ſatisfied with a curſory review, but muſt dwell upon every circumſtance. I am imperceptibly converted into a ſpectator, and perceive every particular paſſing in my preſence, as when I was in reality a ſpectator. —For example, I ſaw yeſterday a beautiful woman in tears for the loſs of an only child, and was greatly moved with her diſtreſs: not ſatisfied with a ſlight recollection or bare remembrance, I ponder upon the melancholy ſcene: conceiving myſelf to be in the place where I was an eye-witneſs, every circumſtance appears to me as at firſt: I think I ſee the woman in tears, and hear her moans. Hence it may be juſtly ſaid, that in a complete idea of memory there is no paſt nor future: a thing recalled to the mind with the accuracy I have been deſcribing, is perceived as in our view, and conſequently as exiſting at preſent. Paſt time makes part of an incomplete idea only: I remember or reflect, that ſome years ago I was at Oxford, and ſaw the firſt ſtone laid of the Ratcliff library; and I remember that, at a ſtill greater diſtance of time, I heard a debate in the Houſe of Commons about a ſtanding army.

Lamentable is the imperfection of language, almoſt in every particular that falls not under external ſenſe. I am talking of a matter exceedingly clear in the perception: and yet I find no ſmall difficulty to expreſs it clearly in words; for it is not accurate to talk of incidents

cidents long paſt as paſſing in our ſight, nor of hearing at preſent what we really heard yeſterday or at a
more diſtant time. And yet the want of proper words
to deſcribe ideal preſence, and to diſtinguiſh it from
real preſence, makes this inaccuracy unavoidable.—
When I recal any thing to my mind in a manner ſo
diſtinct as to form an idea or image of it as preſent,
I have not words to deſcribe that act, but that I perceive the thing as a ſpectator, and as exiſting in my
preſence ; which means not that I am really a ſpectator, but only that I conceive myſelf to be a ſpectator,
and have a perception of the object ſimilar to what a
real ſpectator hath.

As many rules of criticiſm depend on ideal preſence,
the reader, it is hoped, will take ſome pains to form an
exact notion of it, as diſtinguiſhed on the one hand
from real preſence, and on the other from a ſuperficial
or reflective remembrance. In contradiſtinction to real
preſence, ideal preſence may properly be termed *a
waking dream ;* becauſe, like a dream, it vaniſheth the
moment we reflect upon our preſent ſituation : real
preſence, on the contrary, vouched by eye-ſight, commands our belief, not only during the direct perception, but in reflecting afterward on the object. To
diſtinguiſh ideal preſence from reflective remembrance,
I give the following illuſtration : when I think of an
event as paſt, without forming any image, it is barely
reflecting or remembering that I was an eye-witneſs :
but when I recal the event ſo diſtinctly as to form a
complete image of it, I perceive it as paſſing in my
preſence ; and this perception is an act of intuition, into which reflection enters not, more than into an act of
ſight.

Though ideal preſence is thus diſtinguiſhed from real
preſence on the one ſide, and from reflective remembrance on the other, it is however variable without

any

any preciſe limits ; riſing ſometimes toward the former, and often ſinking toward the latter. In a vigorous exertion of memory, ideal preſence is extremely diſtinct ; thus, when a man, entirely occupied with ſome event that made a deep impreſſion, forgets himſelf, he perceives every thing as paſſing before him, and hath a conſciouſneſs of preſence ſimilar to that of a ſpectator ; with no difference but that in the former the perception of preſence is leſs firm and clear than in the latter. But ſuch vigorous exertion of memory is rare : ideal preſence is oftener faint, and the image ſo obſcure as not to differ widely from reflective remembrance.

Hitherto of an idea of memory, I proceed to conſider the idea of a thing I never ſaw, raiſed in me by ſpeech, by writing or by painting. That idea with reſpect to the preſent ſubject, is of the ſame nature with an idea of memory, being either complete or incomplete. A lively and accurate deſcription of an important event, raiſes in me ideas no leſs diſtinct than if I had been originally an eye-witneſs : I am inſenſibly transformed into a ſpectator ; and have an impreſſion that every incident is paſſing in my preſence. On the other hand, a ſlight or ſuperficial narrative produceth but a faint and incomplete idea, of which ideal preſence makes no part. Paſt time is a circumſtance that enters into this idea, as it doth into an incomplete idea of memory ; I believe that Scipio exiſted about 2000 years ago, and that he overcame Hannibal in the famous battle of Zama. When I reflect ſo ſlightly upon that memorable event, conſider it as long paſt ; but let it be ſpread out in a lively and beautiful deſcription, I am inſenſibly transformed into a ſpectator : I perceive theſe two heroes in act to engage : I perceive them brandiſhing their ſwords, and cheering their troops ; and in that manner I attend them through

the

the battle, every incident of which appears to be paſſing in my fight.'

I have had occaſion to obſerve,* that ideas both of memory and of ſpeech, produce emotions of the fame kind with what are produced by an immediate view of the object ; only fainter, in proportion as an idea is fainter than an original perception. The infight we now have, unfolds that myſtery : ideal preſence ſupplies the want of real preſence ; and in idea we perceive perſons acting and ſuffering, preciſely as in an original ſurvey : if our ſympathy be engaged by the latter, it muſt alſo in ſome degree be engaged by the former, eſpecially if the diſtinctneſs of ideal preſence approach to that of real preſence. Hence the pleaſure of a reverie, where a man, forgetting himſelf, is totally occupied with the ideas paſſing in his mind, the objects of which he conceives to be really exiſting in his preſence. The power of language to raiſe emotions, depends entirely on the raiſing ſuch lively and diſtinct images as are here deſcribed : the reader's paſ-ſions are never ſenſibly moved, till he be thrown into a kind of reverie : in which ſtate, forgetting that he is reading, he conceives every incident as paſſing in his preſence preciſely as if he were an eye-witneſs. A general or reflective remembrance cannot warm us in-to any emotion : it may be agreeable in ſome flight de-gree ; but its ideas are too faint and obſcure to raiſe any thing like an emotion ; and were they ever ſo live-ly, they paſs with too much precipitation to have that effect : our emotions are never inſtantaneous ; even ſuch as come the ſooneſt to their height, have differ-ent periods of birth and increment ; and to give oppor-tunity for theſe different periods, it is neceſſary that the cauſe of every emotion be preſent to the mind a due

time ;

* Part 1. ſect. 1. of the preſent chapter.

F 4

time ; for an emotion is not carried to its height but by reiterated impreſſions. ; We know that to be the caſe with emotions ariſing from objects of ſight : a quick ſucceſſion, even of the moſt beautiful objects, ſcarce making any impreſſion ; and if this hold in the ſucceſſion of original perceptions, how much more in the ſucceſſion of ideas ?

Though all this while I have been only deſcribing what paſſeth in the mind of every one, and what every one muſt be conſcious of, it was neceſſary to enlarge upon the ſubject ; becauſe, however clear in the internal conception, it is far from being ſo when deſcribed in words. Ideal preſence, though of general importance, hath ſcarce ever been touched by any writer ; and how-ever difficult the explication, it could not be avoided in accounting for the effects produced by fiction. Upon that point, the reader, I gueſs, has prevented me : it already muſt have occurred to him, that if, in reading, ideal preſence be the means by which our paſſions are moved, it makes no difference whether the ſubject be a fable or a true hiſtory : when ideal preſence is com-plete, we perceive every object as in our ſight ; and the mind totally occupied with an intereſting event, finds no leiſure for reflection. This reaſoning is confirmed by conſtant and univerſal experience. Let us take un-der conſideration the meeting of Hector and Andro-mache, in the ſixth book of the Iliad, or ſome of the paſſionate ſcenes in King Lear : theſe pictures of hu-man life, when we are ſufficiently engaged, give an im-preſſion of reality not leſs diſtinct than that given by Tacitus deſcribing the death of Otho : we never once reflect whether the ſtory be true or feigned ; reflection comes afterward, when we have the ſcene no longer before our eyes. This reaſoning will appear in a ſtill clearer light, by oppoſing ideal preſence to ideas raiſed by a curſory narrative ; which ideas being faint, ob-

ſcure,

fcure, and imperfect, leave a vacuity in the mind, which folicits reflection. And accordingly a curt narrative of feigned incidents is never relifhed : any flight pleafure it affords, is more than counterbalanced by the difguft it infpires for want of truth.

To fupport the foregoing theory, I add what I reckon a decifive argument ; which is, that even genuine hiftory has no command over our paffions but by ideal prefence only ; and confequently, that in this refpect it ftands upon the fame footing with fable. To me it appears clear, that in neither can our fympathy hold firm againft reflection : for if the reflection that a ftory is a pure fiction prevent our fympathy, fo will equally the reflection that the perfons defcribed are no longer exifting. What effect, for example, can the belief of the rape of Lucretia have to raife our fpmpathy, when fhe died above 2000 years ago, and hath at prefent no painful feeling of the injury done her ? The effect of hiftory, in point of inftruction, depends in fome meafure upon its veracity. But hiftory cannot reach the heart, while we indulge any reflection upon the facts : fuch reflection, if it engage our belief, never fails at the fame time to poifon our pleafure, by convincing us that our fympathy for thofe who are dead and gone is abfurd. And if reflection be laid afide, hiftory ftands upon the fame footing with fable : what effect either may have to raife our fympathy, depends on the vivacity of the ideas they raife ; and, with refpect to that circumftance, fable is generally more fuccefsful than hiftory.

Of all the means for making an impreffion of ideal prefence, theatrical reprefentation is the moft powerful. That words, independent of action, have the fame power in a lefs degree, every one of fenfibility muft have felt : a good tragedy will extort tears in private, though not fo forcibly as upon the ftage. That power belongs

belongs alſo to painting : a good hiſtorical picture makes a deeper impreſſion than words can, though not equal to that of theatrical action. Painting ſeems to poſſeſs a middle place between reading and acting : in making an impreſſion of ideal preſence, it is not leſs ſuperior to the former, than inferior to the latter.

, It muſt not however be thought, that our paſſions can be raiſed by painting to ſuch a height as by words : a picture is confined to a ſingle inſtant of time, and cannot take in a ſucceſſion of incidents : its impreſſion indeed is the deepeſt that can be made inſtantaneouſly ; but ſeldom is a paſſion raiſed to any height in an inſtant, or by a ſingle impreſſion : it was obſerved above, that our paſſions, thoſe eſpecially of the ſympathetic kind, require a ſucceſſion of impreſſions : and for that reaſon, reading and acting have greatly the advantage, by reiterating impreſſions without end.

Upon the whole, it is by means of ideal preſence that our paſſions are excited ; and till words produce that charm, they avail nothing : even real events entitled to our belief, muſt be conceived preſent and paſſing in our ſight, before they can move us. And this theory ſerves to explain ſeveral phenomena otherwiſe unaccountable. A misfortune happening to a ſtranger, makes a leſs impreſſion than happening to a man we know, even where we are no way intereſted in him : our acquaintance with this man, however ſlight, aids the conception of his ſuffering in our preſence. For the ſame reaſon, we are little moved by any diſtant event ; becauſe we have more difficulty to conceive it preſent, than an event that happened in our neighbourhood.

Every one is ſenſible, that deſcribing a paſt event as preſent, has a fine effect in language : for what other reaſon than that it aids the conception of ideal preſence ? Take the following example.

And

And now with fhouts the fhocking armies clos'd,
To lances lances, fhields to fhields oppos'd ;
Hoft againft hoft their fhadowy legions drew,
The founding darts, in iron tempefts flew ;
Victors and vanquifh'd join promifcuous cries,
Triumphant fhouts and dying groans arife,
With ftreaming blood the flippery field is dy'd,
And flaughter'd heroes fwell the dreadful tide.

In this paffage we may obferve how the writer, inflamed with the fubject, infenfibly advances from the paft time to the prefent ; led to that form of narration by conceiving every circumftance as paffing in his own fight : which at the fame time has a fine effect upon the reader, by prefenting things to him as a fpectator.

But change from the paft to the prefent requires fome preparation ; and is not fweet where there is no ftop in the fenfe : witnefs the following paffage.

Thy fate was next, O Phæftus ! doom'd to feel
The great Idomeneus' protended fteel ;
Whom Borus fent (his fon and only joy)
From fruitful Tarne to the fields of Troy.
The Cretan jav'lin reach'd him from afar,
And pierc'd his fhoulder as he *mounts* his car.
Iliad, v. 57.

It is ftill worfe to fall back to the paft in the fame period ; for that is an anticlimax in defcription :

Through breaking ranks his furious courfe he bends,
And at the goddefs his broad lance extends ;
Through her bright veil the daring weapon drove,
Th' ambrofial veil, which all the graces wove :
Her fnowy hand the razing fteel profan'd,
And the tranfparent fkin with crimfon ftain'd.
Iliad, v. 415.

Again, defcribing the fhield of Jupiter,

Here

Here all the terrors of grim War appear,
Here rages Force, here tremble Flight and Fear,
Here ſtorm'd Contention, and here Fury frown'd,
And the dire orb portentous Gorgon crown'd.

Iliad, v. 914.

Nor is it pleaſant to be carried backward and forward
alternately in a rapid ſucceſſion :

Then dy'd Scamandrius, expert in the chace,
In woods and wilds to wound the ſavage race ;
Diana taught him all her ſylvan arts,
To bend the bow and aim unerring darts :
But vainly here Diana's arts he tries,
The fatal lance arreſts him as he flies ;
From Menelaus' arm the weapon ſent,
Through his broad back and heaving boſom went :
Down ſinks the warrior with a thund'ring ſound,
His brazen armour rings againſt the ground.

Iliad, v. 65.

It is wonderful to obſerve, upon what ſlight foundations nature erects ſome of her moſt ſolid and magnificent works. In appearance at leaſt, what can be
more ſlight than ideal preſence ; and yet, from it is derived that extenſive influence which language hath over
the heart ; an influence, which, more than any other
means, ſtrengthens the bond of ſociety, and attracts individuals from their private ſyſtem to perform acts of
generoſity and benevolence. Matters of fact, it is true,
and truth in general, may be inculcated without taking
advantage of ideal preſence ; but without it, the fineſt
ſpeaker or writer would in vain attempt to move any
paſſion : our ſympathy would be confined to objects
that are really preſent ; and language would loſe entirely its ſignal power of making us ſympathize with
beings removed at the greateſt diſtance of time as well
as of place. Nor is the influence of language by means
of ideal preſence, confined to the heart : it reacheth
alſo

alfo the underftanding, and contributes to belief. For
when events are related in a lively manner, and every
circumftance appears as paffing before us, we fuffer not
patiently the truth of the facts to be queftioned. An
hiftorian, accordingly, who hath a genius for narration,
feldom fails to engage our belief. The fame facts related in a manner cold and indiftinct, are not fuffered
to pafs without examination : a thing ill defcribed is
like an object feen at a diftance, or through a mift ; we
doubt whether it be a reality or a fiction. Cicero fays,
that to relate the manner in which an event paffed, not
only enlivens the ftory, but makes it appear more cred-
ible.*   For that reafon, a poet who can warm and
animate his reader, may employ bolder fictions than
ought to be ventured by an inferior genius : the reader,
once thoroughly engaged, is fufceptible of the ftrongeft
impreffions :

> Veraque conftituunt, quae belle tangere poffunt
> Aureis, et lepido quae funt fucata fonore.
>   *Lucretius, lib.* 1. *l.* 644.

A mafterly painting has the fame effect : Le Brun is
no fmall fupport to Quintus Curtius : and among the
vulgar in Italy, the belief of fcripture-hiftory is perhaps founded as much upon the authority of Raphael,
Michael Angelo, and other celebrated painters, as upon that of the facred writers. †

The foregoing theory muft have fatigued the reader
with much dry reafoning ; but his labour will not be
                                                  fruitlefs ;

---

* De Oratore, lib. 2. fect. 81.

† At quae Polycleto defuerunt, Phidiae atque Alcameni dantur. Phidias tamen diis quam hominibus efficiendis melior artifex traditur : in ebore
vero longe citra aemulum. vel fi nihil nifi Minervam Athenis, aut Olym-
pium in Elide Jovem feciffet, cujus pulchritudo adjeciffe aliquid etiam re-
ceptae religioni videtur ; adeo majeftas operis Deum aequavit. · *Quintilian,*
lib. 12. *cap.* 10. § 1.

fruitlefs.; becaufe from that theory are derived many
ufeful rules in criticifm, which fhall be mentioned in
their proper places. One fpecimcn fhall be our prefent
entertainment. Events that furprife by being unexpected, and yet are natural, enliven greatly an epic poem : but in fuch a poem, if it 'pretend to copy human
manners and actions, no improbable incident ought to
be admitted : that is, no incident contrary to the order
and courfe of nature. A chain of imagined incidents
linked together according to the order of nature, finds
eafy admittance into the mind ; and a lively narrative
of fuch incidents occafions complete images, or, in
other words, ideal prefence : but our judgment revolts
againft an improbable incident ; and, if we once begin
to doubt of its reality, farewell relifh and concern—an
unhappy effect ; for it will require more than ordinary
effort, to reftore the waking dream, and to make the
reader conceive even the more probable incidents as
paffing in his prefence.

I never was an admirer of machinery in an epic
poem, and I now find my tafte juftified by reafon ; the
foregoing argument concluding ftill more ftrongly
againft imaginary beings, than againft improbable
facts : fictions of that nature may amufe by their novelty and fingularity ; but they never move the fympathetic paffions, becaufe they cannot impofe on the
mind any perception of reality. I appeal to the difcerning reader, whether that obfervation be not applicable
to the machinery of Taffo and of Voltaire : fuch machinery is not only in itfelf cold and uninterefting, but
gives an air of fiction to the whole compofition. A
burlefque poem, fuch as the Lutrin or the Difpenfary,
may employ machinery with fuccefs ; for thefe poems,
though they affume the air of hiftory, give entertainment chiefly by their pleafant and ludicrous pictures,
to which machinery contributes : it is not the aim of
                                                        fuch

fuch a poem, to raife our fympathy : and for that reafon a ftrict imitation of nature is not required. A
poem profeffedly ludicrous, may employ machinery to
great advantage ; and the more extravagant the better.

Having affigned the means by which fiction commands our paffions ; what only remains for accom-
plifhing our prefent tafk, is to affign the final caufe. I
have already mentioned, that fiction, by means of language, has the command of our fympathy for the good
of others. By the fame means, our fympathy may
alfo be raifed for our own good. In the fourth fection
of the prefent chapter, it is obferved, that examples
both of virtue and of vice raife virtuous emotions ;
which becoming ftronger by exercife, tend to make us
virtuous by habit, as well as by principle. I now
further obferve, that examples confined to real events
are not fo frequent as without other means to produce
a habit of virtue : if they be, they are not recorded by
hiftorians. It therefore fhows great wifdom to form
us in fuch a manner, as to be fufceptible of the fame
improvement from fable that we receive from genuine
hiftory. By that contrivance, examples to improve
us in virtue may be multiplied without end : no other
fort of difcipline contributes more to make virtue habitual, and no other fort is fo agreeable in the application.
I add another final caufe with thorough fatisfaction : becaufe it fhows, that the author of our nature is not lefs
kindly provident for the happinefs of his creatures, than
for the regularity of their conduct : the power that fiction hath over the mind affords an endlefs variety of
refined amufements, always at hand to employ a vacant hour : fuch amufements are a fine refource in fol-
itude ; and, by cheering and fweetening the mind,
contribute mightily to focial happinefs.

PART

PART II.

*Emotions and Paffions as pleafant and painful, agreea-
ble and difagreeable. Modifications of
thefe Qualities.*

IT will naturally occur at firft, that a difcourfe upon the paffions ought to commence with explaining the qualities now mentioned : but upon trial,
I found that this explanation could not be made diftinctly, till the difference fhould firft be afcertained between an emotion and a paffion, and their caufes unfolded.

Great obfcurity may be obferved among writers
with regard to the prefent point ; particularly no care
is taken to diftinguifh agreeable from pleafant, dif-
greeable from painful ; or rather thefe terms are deemed fynonymous. This is an error not at all venial in
the fcience of ethics ; as inftances can and fhall be
given, of painful paffions that are agreeable, and of
pleafant paffions that are difagreeable. Thefe terms,
it is true, are ufed indifferently in familiar converfa-
tion, and in compofitions for amufement ; but more
accuracy is required from thofe who profefs to explain
the paffions. In writing upon the critical art, I would
avoid every refinement that may feem more curious
than ufeful : but the proper meaning of the terms under confideration muft be afcertained, in order to un-
derftand the paffions, and fome of their effects that are
intimately connected with criticifm.

I fhall endeavour to explain thefe terms by familiar
examples. Viewing a fine garden, I perceive it to be
beautiful or agreeable ; and I confider the beauty or
agreeablenefs as belonging to the object, or as one of
its qualities. When I turn my attention from the garden

den to what paffes in my mind, I am confcious of a pleafant emotion, of which the garden is the caufe: the pleafure here is felt, as a quality, not of the garden, but of the emotion produced by it. I give an op-pofite example. A rotten carcafs is difagreeable, and raifes in the fpectator a painful emotion : the difagree-ablenefs is a quality of the object; the pain is a qual-ity of the emotion produced by it. In a word, agree-able and difagreeable are qualities of the objects we *perceive ;* pleafant and painful are qualities of the emotions we *feel :* the former qualities are perceived as adhering to objects ; the latter are felt as exifting within us.

But a paffion or emotion, befide being felt, is fre-quently made an object of thought or reflection : we examine it ; we inquire into its nature, its caufe, and its effects. In that view, like other objects, it is either agreeable or difagreeable. Hence clearly appear the different fignifications of the terms under confidera-tion, as applied to paffion : when a paffion is termed *pleafant* or *painful,* we refer to the actual feeling ; when termed *agreeable* or *difagreeable,* we refer to it as an object of thought or reflection ; a paffion is pleaf-ant or painful to the perfon in whom it exifts ; it is agreeable or difagreeable to the perfon who makes it a fubject of contemplation.

In the defcription of emotions and paffions, thefe terms do not always coincide : to make which evident, we muft endeavour to afcertain, firft, what paffions and emotions are pleafant, what painful; and next, what are agreeable, what difagreeable. With refpect to both, there are general rules, which, if I can truft to induction, admit not a fingle exception. The na-ture of an emotion or paffion as pleafant or painful, de-pends entirely on its caufe : the emotion produced by an agreeable object is invariably pleafant ; and the emotion produced by a diſagreeable objeĉt is invariably painful.*   Thus a lofty oak, a generous aĉtion, a valuable diſcovery in art or ſcience, are agreeable objeĉts that invariably produce pleaſant emotions.   A ſtinking puddle, a treacherous aĉtion, an irregular, ill-contrived edifice, being diſagreeable objeĉts, produce painful emotions.   Selfiſh paſſions are pleaſant ; for they ariſe from ſelf, an agreeable objeĉt or cauſe.   A ſocial paſſion direĉted upon an agreeable objeĉt, is always pleaſant ; direĉted upon an objeĉt in diſtreſs, is painful.   Laſtly, all diſſocial paſſions, ſuch as envy, reſentment, malice, being cauſed by diſagreeable objeĉts, cannot fail to be painful.

A general rule for the agreeableneſs or diſagreeableneſs of emotions and paſſions is a more difficult enterpriſe : it muſt be attempted however.   We have a ſenſe of a common nature in every ſpecies of animals, particularly in our own ; and we have a conviĉtion that this common nature is *right*, or *perfeĉt*, and that individuals *ought* to be made conformable to it.†   To every faculty, to every paſſion, and to every bodily member, is aſſigned a proper office and a due proportion : if one limb be longer than the other, or be diſproportioned to the whole, it is wrong and diſagreeable : if a paſſion deviate from the common nature, by being too ſtrong or too weak, it is alſo wrong and diſagreeable : but as far as conformable to common nature, every emotion and every paſſion is perceived by us to be right, and as it ought to be ; and upon that account it muſt appear agreeable.   That this holds true in pleaſant emotions and paſſions, will readily be admitted : but the painful are no leſs natural than the other ; and therefore ought not to be an exception.

Thus

---

* See part 7. of this chapter.

† See this doĉtrine fully explained, chap. 25. Standard of Taſte.

Thus the painful emotion raiſed by a monſtrous birth or brutal action, is no leſs agreeable upon reflection, than the pleaſant emotion raiſed by a flowing river or a lofty dome : and the painful paſſions of grief and pity are agreeable, and applauded by all the world.

Another rule more ſimple and direct for aſcertaining the agreeableneſs or diſagreeableneſs of a paſſion as oppoſed to an emotion, is derived from the deſire that accompanies it. If the deſire be to perform a right action in order to produce a good effect, the paſſion is agreeable : if the deſire be to do a wrong action in order to produce an ill effect, the paſſion is diſagreeable. Thus, paſſions as well as actions are governed by the moral ſenſe. Theſe rules by the wiſdom of Providence coincide : a paſſion that is conformable to our common nature muſt tend to good ; and a paſſion that deviates from our common nature muſt tend to ill.

This deduction may be carried a great way farther : but to avoid intricacy and obſcurity, I make but one other ſtep. A paſſion which, as aforeſaid, becomes an object of thought to a ſpectator, may have the effect to produce a paſſion or emotion in him ; for it is natural, that a ſocial being ſhould be affected with the paſſions of others. Paſſions or emotions thus generated, ſubmit, in common with others, to the general law above mentioned, namely, that an agreeable object produces a pleaſant emotion, and a diſagreeable object a painful emotion. Thus the paſſion of gratitude, being to a ſpectator an agreeable object, produceth in him the pleaſant paſſion of love to the grateful perſon : and malice, being to a ſpectator a diſagreeable object, produceth in him the painful paſſion of hatred to the malicious perſon.

We are now prepared for examples of pleaſant paſſions that are diſagreeable, and of painful paſſions that

are

are agreeable. Self-love, as long as confined within
juſt bounds, is a paſſion both pleaſant and agreeable :
in exceſs it is diſagreeable, though it continues to be
ſtill pleaſant. Our appetites are preciſely in the ſame
condition. Reſentment, on the other hand, is, in every
ſtage of the paſſion, painful ; but is not diſagreeable
unleſs in exceſs. Pity is always painful, yet always agreeable. Vanity, on the contrary, is always
pleaſant, yet always diſagreeable. But however diſtinct theſe qualities are, they coincide, I acknowledge,
in one claſs of paſſions : all vicious paſſions tending to
the hurt of others, are equally painful and diſagreeable.

The foregoing qualities of pleaſant and painful, may
be ſufficient for ordinary ſubjects : but with reſpect to
the ſcience of criticiſm, it is neceſſary, that we alſo be
made acquainted with the ſeveral modifications of theſe
qualities, with the modifications at leaſt that make the
greateſt figure. Even at firſt view one is ſenſible, that
the pleaſure or pain of one paſſion differs from that of
another : how diſtant the pleaſure of revenge gratified
from that of love ? ſo diſtant, as that we cannot without reluctance admit them to be any way related. That
the ſame quality of pleaſure ſhould be ſo differently
modified in different paſſions, will not be ſurpriſing,
when we reflect on the boundleſs variety of agreeable
ſounds, taſtes, and ſmells, daily perceived. Our diſcernment reaches differences ſtill more minute, in objects even of the ſame ſenſe : we have no difficulty to
diſtinguiſh different ſweets, different ſours, and different bitters ; honey is ſweet, ſo is ſugar, and yet the
one never is miſtaken for the other : our ſenſe of
ſmelling is ſufficiently acute, to diſtinguiſh varieties in
ſweet-ſmelling flowers without end. With reſpect to
paſſions and emotions, their differences as to pleaſant
and painful have no limits ; though we want acuteneſs
of feeling for the more delicate modifications. There
is

is here an analogy between our internal and external fenfes : the latter are fufficiently acute for all the ufeful purpofes of life, and fo are the former. Some perfons indeed, Nature's favourites, have a wonderful acutenefs of fenfe, which to them unfolds many a delightful fcene totally hid from vulgar eyes. But if fuch refined pleafure be confined to a fmall number, it is however wifely ordered that others are not fenfible of the defect ; nor detracts it from their happinefs that others fecretly are more happy. With relation to the fine arts only, that qualification feems effential ; and there it is termed *delicacy of tafte.*

Should an author of fuch a tafte attempt to defcribe all thofe varieties in pleafant and painful emotions which he himfelf feels, he would foon meet an invincible obftacle in the poverty of language : a people muft be thoroughly refined, before they invent words for expreffing the more delicate feelings ; and for that reafon, no known tongue hitherto has reached that perfection. We muft therefore reft fatisfied with an explanation of the more obvious modifications.

In forming a comparifon between pleafant paffions of different kinds, we conceive fome of them to be *grofs,* fome refined. Thofe pleafures of external fenfe that are felt as at the organ of fenfe, are conceived to be corporeal, or grofs :* the pleafures of the eye and the ear are felt to be internal ; and for that reafon are conceived to be more pure and refined.

The focial affections are conceived by all to be more refined than the felfifh. Sympathy and humanity are univerfally efteemed the fineft temper of mind ; and for that reafon, the prevalence of the focial affections in the progrefs of fociety, is held to be a refinement in our nature. A favage knows little of focial affection,

and

* See the Introduction.

and therefore is not qualified to compare felfifh and focial pleafure ; but a man after acquiring a high relifh
for the latter, lofes not thereby a tafte for the former :
he is qualified to judge, and he will give preference to
focial pleafures as more fweet and refined.   In fact they
maintain that character, not only in the direct feeling,
but alfo when we make them the fubject of reflection :
the focial paffions are far more agreeable than the
felfifh, and rife much higher in our efteem.

There are differences not lefs remarkable among the
painful paffions.   Some are voluntary, fome involuntary : the pain of the gout is an example of the latter ;
grief, of the former, which in fome cafes is fo voluntary as to reject all confolation.   One pain foftens the
temper ; pity is an inftance : one tends to render us favage and cruel, which is the cafe of revenge.   I value
myfelf upon fympathy : I hate and defpife myfelf for
envy.

Social affections have an advantage over the felfifh,
not only with refpect to pleafure, as above explained,
but alfo with refpect to pain.   The pain of an affront,
the pain of want, the pain of difappointment, and a
thoufand other felfifh pains, are cruciating and tor-
menting, and tend to a habit of peevifhnefs and difcon-
tent.   Social pains have a very different tendency : the
pain of fympathy, for example, is not only voluntary,
but foftens my temper, and raifes me in my own
efteem.

Refined manners, and polite behaviour, muft not be
deemed altogether artificial : men who, inured to the
fweets of fociety, cultivate humanity, find an elegant
pleafure in preferring others, and making them happy,
of which the proud, the felfifh, fcarce have a conception.

Ridicule, which chiefly arifes from pride, a felfifh
paffion, is at beft but a grofs pleafure: a people, it is
true,

true, muft have emerged out of barbarity before they can have a tafte for ridicule ; but it is too rough an entertainment for the polifhed and refined. Cicero difcovers in Plautus a happy talent for ridicule, and a peculiar delicacy of wit : but Horace, who made a figure in the court of Auguftus, where tafte was confiderably purified, declares againft the lownefs and roughnefs of that author's raillery. Ridicule is banifhed France, and is lofing ground in England.

Other modifications of pleafant paffions will be occafionally mentioned hereafter. Particularly, the modifications of *high* and *low* are to be handled in the chapter of grandeur and fublimity ; and the modifications of *dignified* and *mean*, in the chapter of dignity and grace.

PART III.

Interrupted Exiftence of Emotions and Paffions.—Their Growth and Decay.

WERE it the nature of an emotion to continue, like colour and figure, in its prefent ftate till varied by fome operating caufe, the condition of man would be deplorable : it is ordered wifely, that emotions fhould more refemble another attribute of matter, namely motion, which requires the conftant exertion of an operating caufe, and ceafes when the caufe is withdrawn. An emotion may fubfift while its caufe is prefent ; and when its caufe is removed, may fubfift by means of an idea, though in a fainter manner : but the moment another thought breaks in and engroffes the mind, the emotion is gone, and is no longer felt : if it return with its caufe, or an idea of

G 4 its

its caufe, it again vanifheth with them when other thoughts crowd in. The reafon is, that an emotion or paffion is connected with the perception or idea of its caufe, fo intimately as not to have any independ-ent exiftence: a ftrong paffion, it is true, hath a mighty influence to detain its caufe in the mind ; but not fo as to detain it for ever, becaufe a fucceffion of perceptions or ideas is unavoidable.* Further, even while a paf-fion fubfifts, it feldom continues long in the fame tone, but is fucceffively vigorous and faint ; the vigour of a paffion depends on the impreffion made by its caufe; and a caufe makes its deepeft impreffion, when, happening to be the fingle interefting object, it attracts our whole attention :† its impreffion is flighter when our attention is divided between it and other objects : and at that time the paffion is fainter in proportion.

When emotions and paffions are felt thus by inter-vals, and have not a continued exiftence, it may be thought a nice problem to determine when they are the fame, when different. In a ftrict philofophic view, every fingle impreffion made even by the fame object is diftinguifhable from what have gone before, and from what fucceed : neither is an emotion raifed by an idea the fame with what is raifed by a fight of the object. But fuch accuracy not being found in com-mon apprehenfion, is not neceffary in common lan-guage : the emotions raifed by a fine landfcape in its fucceffive appearances are not diftinguifhable from each other, nor even from thofe raifed by fucceffive ideas of the object ; all of them being held to be the fame : a paffion alfo is always reckoned the fame as long as it is fixed upon the fame object ; and thus
love

* See this point explained afterwards, chap. 9.

† See the Appendix, containing definitions, and explanation of terms, fect. 33.

love and hatred are faid to continue the fame for life. Nay, fo loofe are we in that way of thinking, that many paffions are reckoned the fame even after a change of object ; which is the cafe of all paffions that proceed from fome peculiar propenfity : envy, for example, is confidered to be the fame paffion, not only while it is directed to the fame perfon, but even where it comprehends many perfons at once : pride and malice are examples of the fame. So much was neceffary to be faid upon the identity of a paffion and emotion, in order to prepare for examining their growth and decay.

The growth and decay of paffions and emotions, traced through all their mazes, is a fubject too extenfive for an undertaking like the prefent : I pretend only to give a curfory view of it, fuch as may be neceffary for the purpofes of criticifm. Some emotions are produced in their utmoft perfection, and have a very fhort endurance ; which is the cafe of furprife, of wonder, and fometimes, of terror. Emotions raifed by inanimate objects, trees, rivers, buildings, pictures arrive at perfection almoft inftantaneoufly; and they have a long endurance, a fecond view producing nearly the fame pleafure with the firft. Love, hatred, and fome other paffions, fwell gradually to a certain pitch ; after which they decay gradually. Envy, malice, pride, fcarce ever decay. Some paffions, fuch as gratitude and revenge, are often exhaufted by a fingle act of gratification : other paffions, fuch as pride, malice, envy, love, hatred, are not fo exhaufted ; but having a long continuance, demand frequent gratification.

To handle every fingle paffion and emotion with a view to thefe differences, would be an endlefs work : we muft be fatisfied at prefent with fome general views. And with refpect to emotions, which are quiefcent becaufe not productive of defire, their growth and decay

are

are eafily explained : an emotion caufed by an inanimate objeft, cannot naturally take longer time to arrive at maturity, than is neceffary for a leifurely furvey :
fuch emotion alfo muft continue long ftationary, without any fenfible decay ; a fecond or third view of the
objeft being nearly as agreeable as the firft : this is
the cafe of an emotion produced by a fine profpeft, an
impetuous river, or a towering hill : while a man
remains the fame, fuch objects ought to have the
fame effeft upon him.   Familiarity, however, hath an
influence here, as it hath every where : frequency of
view, after fhort intervals efpecially, weans the mind
gradually from the objeft, which at laft lofes all relifh :
the nobleft objeft in the material world, a clear and
ferene fky, is quite difregarded, unlefs perhaps after a
courfe of bad weather.   An emotion raifed by human
virtues, qualities, or actions, may, by reiterated views
of the objeft, fwell imperceptibly till it become fo vigorous as to generate defire : in that condition it muft
be handled as a paffion.

As to paffion, I obferve, firft, that when nature requires a paffion to be fudden, it is commonly produced
in perfeftion ; which is the cafe of fear and of anger.
Wonder and furprife are always produced in perfection : reiterated impreffions made by their caufe, exhauft thefe paffions inftead of inflaming them.   This
will be explained afterward.*

In the next place, when a paffion hath for its foundation an original propenfity peculiar to fome men, it
generally comes foon to maturity : the propenfity, upon prefenting a proper objeft, is immediately enlivened
into a paffion ; which is the cafe of pride, of envy, and
of malice.

In the third place, the growth of love and of hatred
is flow or quick according to circumftances : the good
                                        qualities

* Chap. 6.

qualities of a perſon raiſe in me a pleaſant emotion ; which, by reiterated views, is ſwelled into a paſſion in- volving deſire of that perſon's happineſs : this deſire, being freely indulged, works gradually a change in- ternally, and at laſt produceth in me a ſettled habit of affection for that perſon now my friend. Affection thus produced operates preciſely like an original pro- penſity ; for to enliven it into a paſſion, no more is re- quired but the real or ideal preſence of the object. The habit of averſion or of hatred is brought on in the ſame manner. And here I muſt obſerve by the way, that love and hatred ſignify commonly affection and aver- ſion, not paſſion. The bulk of our paſſions are indeed affection or averſion inflamed into a paſſion by differ- ent circumſtances : the affection I bear to my ſon, is inflamed into the paſſion of fear when he is in danger ; becomes hope when he hath a proſpect of good for- tune ; becomes admiration when he performs a laud- able action ; and ſhame when he commits any wrong ; averſion becomes fear when there is a proſpect of good fortune to my enemy ; becomes hope when he is in danger ; becomes joy when he is in diſtreſs ; and ſor- row when a laudable action is performed by him.

Fourthly, paſſions generally have a tendency to ex- ceſs, occaſioned by the following means. The mind affected by any paſſion, is not in a proper ſtate for diſtinct perception, nor for cool reflection : it hath al- ways a ſtrong bias to the object of an agreeable paſ- ſion, and a bias no leſs ſtrong againſt the object of a diſagreeable paſſion. The object of love, for exam- ple, however indifferent to others, is to the lover's conviction a paragon ; and of hatred, is vice itſelf without alloy. What leſs can ſuch deluſion operate, than to ſwell the paſſion beyond what it was at firſt ? for if the ſeeing or converſing with a fine woman, have had the effect to carry me from indifference to

love ;

love ; how much ſtronger muſt her influence be, when now to my conviction ſhe is an angel ? and ha- tred as well as other paſſions muſt run the ſame courſe. Thus between a paſſion and its object there is a natur- al operation, reſembling action and reaction in phyſ- ics : a paſſion acting upon its object, magnifies it greatly in appearance ; and this magnified object re- acting upon the paſſion, ſwells and inflames it mightily.

Fifthly, the growth of ſome paſſion depends often on occaſional circumſtances : obſtacles to gratification, for example, never fail to augment and inflame a paſ- ſion ; becauſe a conſtant endeavour to remove an ob- ſtacle, preſerves the object of the paſſion ever in view, which ſwells the paſſion by impreſſions frequently re- iterated : thus the reſtraint of conſcience, when an obſtacle to love, agitates the mind and inflames the paſſion :

> Quod licet, ingratum eſt : quod non licet, acrius urit.
> Si nunquam Danaën habuiſſet ahenea turris,
> Non eſſet Danaë de Jove facta parens.
> *Ovid, Amor. l.* 2.

At the ſame time, the mind, diſtreſſed with the ob- ſtacles, becomes impatient for gratification, and conſe- quently more deſirous of it. Shakeſpear expreſſes this obſervation finely :

> All impediments in fancy's courſe,
> Are motives of more fancy.

We need no better example than a lover who hath many rivals. Even the caprices of a miſtreſs have the effect to inflame love; theſe occaſioning uncertainty of ſucceſs, tend naturally to make the anxious lover over- value the happineſs of fruition.

So

So much upon the growth of paffions : their continuance and decay come next under confideration.
And, firft, it is a general law of nature, That things
fudden in their growth, are equally fudden in their decay.   This is commonly the cafe of anger.   And, with
refpeft to wonder and furprife, which alfo fuddenly
decay, another reafon concurs, that thcir caufes are of
fhort duration : novelty foon degenerates into familiarity ; and the unexpeftednefs of an objeft is foon funk
in the pleafure that the objeft affords.   Fear, which is
a paffion of greater importance as tending to felf prefervation, is often inftantaneous : and yet is of equal
duration with its caufe : nay, it frequently fubfifts
after the caufe is removed.

In the next place, a paffion founded on a peculiar
propenfity, fubfifts generally for ever ; which is the
cafe of pride, envy, and malice : objefts are never
wanting to inflame the propenfity into a paffion.

Thirdly, it may be laid down as a general law of
nature, That every paffion ceafes upon attaining its ultimate end.   To explain that law, we muft diftinguifh between a particular and a general end.   I call a particular end what may be accomplifhed by a fingle aft : a
general end, on the contrary, admits afts without
number : becaufe it cannot be faid, that a general end
is ever fully accomplifhed, while the objeft of the paffion fubfifts.   Gratitude and revenge are examples of
the firft kind ; the ends they aim at may be accomplifhed by a fingle aft ; and, when that aft is performed, the paffions are neceffarily at an end.   Love
and hatred are examples of the other kind ; defire of
doing good or of doing mifchief to an individual is a general end, which admits afts without number, and which
feldom is fully accomplifhed : therefore thefe paffions
have frequently the fame duration with their objefts.

Laftly,

Laftly, it will afford us another general view, to confider the difference between an original propenfity, and an affection or averfion produced by cuftom. The former adheres too clofe to the conftitution ever to be eradicated ; and for that reafon, the paffions to which it gives birth, continue during life with no remarkable diminution. The latter, which owe their birth and increment to time, owe their decay to the fame caufe: affection and averfion decay gradually as they grow ; and accordingly hatred as well as love are extinguifhed by long abfence. Affection decays more gradually between perfons, who, living together, have daily occafion to teftify mutually their good-will and kindnefs : and, when affection is decayed, habit fupplies its place ; for it makes thefe perfons neceffary to each other, by the pain of feparation.* Affection to children hath a long endurance, longer perhaps than any other affection : its growth keeps pace with that of its objects : they difplay new beauties and qualifications daily, to feed and augment the affection. But whenever the affection becomes ftationary, it muft begin to decay ; with a flow pace indeed, in proportion to its increment. In fhort, man with refpect to this life is a temporary being : he grows, becomes ftationary, decays ; and fo muft all his powers and paffions.

PART IV.

Coexiftent Emotions and Paffions.

FOR a thorough knowledge of the human paffions and emotions, it is not fufficient that they be examined fingly and feparately : as a plurality of them are

* See chap. 14.

are fometimes felt at the fame inftant, the manner of their coexiftence, and the effects thereby produced, ought alfo to be examined. This fubject is extenfive; and it will be difficult to trace all the laws that govern its endlefs variety of cafes : if fuch an undertaking can be brought to perfection, it muft be by degrees. The following hints may fuffice for a firft attempt.

We begin with emotions raifed by different founds, as the fimpleft cafe. Two founds that mix, and, as it were, incorporate before they reach the ear, are faid to be concordant. That each of the two founds, even after their union, produceth an emotion of its own, muft be admitted : but thefe emotions, like the founds that produce them, mix fo intimately, as to be rather one complex emotion than two emotions in conjunction. Two founds that refufe incorporation or mixture, are faid to be difcordant : and when heard at the fame inftant, the emotions produced by them are unpleafant in conjunction, however pleafant feparately.

Similar to the emotion raifed by mixed founds is the emotion raifed by an object of fight with its feveral qualities : a tree, for example, with its qualities of colour, figure, fize, &c. is perceived to be one object; and the emotion it produceth is rather one complex emotion than different emotions combined.

With refpect to coexiftent emotions produced by different objects of fight, it muft be obferved, that however intimately connected fuch objects may be, there cannot be a concordance among them like what is perceived in fome founds. Different objects of fight, meaning objects that can exift each of them independent of the others, never mix nor incorporate in the act of vifion : each object is perceived as it exifts, feparately from others ; and each raifeth an emotion different from that raifed by the other. And the fame holds in all

all the caufes of emotion or paffion that can exift independent of each other, founds only excepted.

To explain the manner in which fuch emotions exift, fimilar emotions muft be diftinguifhed from thofe
that are diffimilar. Two emotions are faid to be fimilar, when they tend each of them to produce the fame
tone of mind : cheerful emotions, however different
their caufes may be, are fimilar : and fo are thofe which
are melancholy. Diffimilar emotions are eafily explained by their oppofition to what are fimilar : pride
and humility, gaiety and gloominefs, are diffimilar emotions.

Emotions perfectly fimilar, readily combine and
unite,* fo as in a manner to become one complex
emotion ; witnefs the emotions produced by a number
of flowers in a parterre, or of trees in a wood. Emotions that are oppofite, or extremely diffimilar, never
combine or unite : the mind cannot fimultaneoufly
take on oppofite tones : it cannot at the fame inftant
be both joyful and fad, angry and fatisfied, proud and
humble : diffimilar emotions may fucceed each other
with rapidity, but they cannot exift fimultaneoufly.

Between thefe two extremes, emotions unite more
or lefs in proportion to the degree of their refemblance,
and the degree in which their caufes are connected.
Thus the emotions produced by a fine landfcape and
the finging of birds, being fimilar in a confiderable
degree, readily unite, though their caufes are little connected. And the fame happens where the caufes are
intimately connected, though the emotions themfelves
have little refemblance to each other : an example of
which

---

* It is eafier to conceive the manner of coexiftence of fimilar emotions,
than to defcribe it. They cannot be faid to mix or incorporate, like concordant founds : their union is rather of agreement or concord ; and therefore I have chofen the words in the text, not as fufficient to exprefs clearly the manner of their coexiftence, but only as lefs liable to exception
than any other I can find.

which is a miſtreſs in diſtreſs, whoſe beauty gives pleaſure, and her diſtreſs pain : theſe two emotions, proceeding from different views of the object, have very
little reſemblance to each other ; and yet ſo intimately
connected are their cauſes, as to force them into a ſort
of complex emotion, partly pleaſant, partly painful.
This clearly explains ſome expreſſions common in poetry, *a ſweet diſtreſs, a pleaſant pain.*

It was neceſſary to deſcribe, with ſome accuracy, in
what manner ſimilar and diſſimilar emotions coexiſt in
the mind, in order to explain their different effects,
both internal and external. This ſubject, though obſcure, is capable to be ſet in a clear light ; and it
merits attention, not only for its extenſive uſe in criticiſm, but for the nobler purpoſe of deciphering many
intricacies in the actions of men. Beginning with internal effects, I diſcover two, clearly diſtinguiſhable
from each other, both of them produced by pleaſant
emotions that are ſimilar ; of which, the one may be
repreſented by addition in numbers, the other by
harmony in ſounds. Two pleaſant emotions that are
ſimilar, readily unite when they are coexiſtent ; and
the pleaſure felt in the union, is the ſum of the two
pleaſures : the ſame emotions in ſucceſſion, are
far from making the ſame figure ; becauſe the mind,
at no inſtant of the ſucceſſion, is conſcious of more
than a ſingle emotion. This doctrine may aptly be
illuſtrated by a landſcape comprehending hills, vallies,
plains, rivers, trees, &c. the emotions produced by
theſe ſeveral objects, being ſimilar in a high degree, as
falling in eaſily and ſweetly with the ſame tone of mind,
are in conjunction extremely pleaſant. This multiplied effect is felt from objects even of different ſenſes,
as where a landſcape is conjoined with the muſic of
birds and odour of flowers ; and reſults partly from
the reſemblance of the emotions and partly from the

connection of their caufes : whence it follows, that the effect muſt be the greateſt, where the caufes are intimately connected and the emotions perfectly fimi-lar. The fame rule is obviouſly applicable to painful emotions that are fimilar and coexiſtent.

The other pleafure ariſing from pleafant emotions fimilar and coexiſtent, cannot be better explained than by the foregoing example of a landſcape, where the fight, hearing, and fmelling, are employed: befide the accumulated pleafure above mentioned, of ſo many different fimilar emotions, a pleafure of a different kind is felt from the concord of thefe emotions. As that pleafure refembles greatly the pleafure of con-cordant founds, it may be termed the *Harmony of Emotions.* This harmony is felt in the different emo-tions occafioned by the vifible objects ; but it is felt ſtill more fenfibly in the emotions occafioned by the objects of different fenfes, as where the emotions of the eye are combined with thofe of the ear. The former pleafure comes under the rule of addition : this comes under a different rule. It is directly in proportion to the degree of refemblance between the emotions, and inverfely in proportion to the degree of connection between the caufes : to feel this pleafure in perfection, the refemblance between the emotions cannot be too ſtrong, nor the connection between their caufes too flight. The former condition is felf-evident ; and the reafon of the latter is, that the pleafure of harmony is felt from various fimilar emotions, diftinct from each other, and yet fweetly combining in the mind ; which excludes caufes intimately connected, for the emotions produced by them are forced into one complex emotion. This pleafure of concord or har-mony, which is the refult of pleafant emotions, and cannot have place with refpect to thofe that are pain-ful, will be further illuſtrated, when the emotions pro-

duced

duced by the found of words and their meaning are taken under confideration.*

The pleafure of concord from conjoined emotions, is felt even where the emotions are not perfectly fimilar. Though love be a pleafant paffion, yet by its foftnefs and tendernefs it refembles in a confiderable degree the painful paffion of pity or of grief ; and for that reafon love accords better with thefe paffions than with what are gay and fprightly. I give the following example from Catullus, where the concord between love and grief has a fine effect even in fo flight a fubject as the death of a fparrow.

> Lugete, ô Veneres, Cupidinefque,
> Et quantum eft hominum venuftiorum !
> Paffer mortuus eft meæ puellæ,
> Quem plus illa oculis fuis amabat.
> Nam mellitus erat, fuamque norat
> Ipfam tam bene, quam puella matrem :
> Nec fefe a gremio illius movebat ;
> Sed circumfiliens modo huc, modo illuc,
> Ad folam dominam ufque pipilabat.
> Qui nunc it per iter tenebrofum,
> Illuc, unde negant redire quemquam.
> At vobis male fit, malæ tenebræ
> Orci, quæ omnia bella devoratis ;
> Tam bellum mihi pafferem abftuliftis.
> O factum male, ô mifelle paffer.
> Tua nunc opera, meæ puellæ
> Flendo turgiduli rubent ocelli.

Next as to the effects of diffimilar emotions, which we may guefs will be oppofite to what are above defcribed. Diffimilar coexiftent emotions, as faid above, never fail to diftrefs the mind by the difference of their tones ; from which fituation a feeling of harmony never can proceed ;

* Chap. 18. fect. 3.

H 2

proceed ; and this holds whether the caufes be connected or not. But it holds more remarkably where
the caufes are connected ; for in that cafe the diffimilar emotions being forced into an unnatural union, produce an actual feeling of difcord. In the next place,
if we would eftimate the force of diffimilar emotions
coexiftent, we muft diftinguifh between their caufes as
connected or unconnected : and in order to compute
their force in the former cafe, fubtraction muft be ufed
inftead of addition ; which will be evident from
what follows. Diffimilar emotions forced into union
by the connection of their caufes, are felt obfcurely and
imperfectly ; for each tends to vary the tone of mind
that is fuited to the other ; and the mind thus diftract-
ed between two objects, is at no inftant in a condition
to receive a deep impreffion from either. Diffimilar
emotions proceeding from unconnected caufes, are in a
very different condition : for as there is nothing to
force them into union, they are never felt but in fucceffion ; by which means, each hath an opportunity to
make a complete impreffion.

This curious theory requires to be illuftrated by examples. In reading the defcription of the difmal wafte,
book 1. of *Paradife Loft*, we are fenfible of a confufed
feeling, arifing from diffimilar emotions forced into
union, to wit, the beauty of the defcription, and the
horror of the object defcribed :

Seeft thou yon dreary plain, forlorn and wild,
The feat of defolation, void of light,
Save what the glimmering of thefe livid flames
Cafts pale and dreadful ?

And with refpect to this and many fimilar paffages
in *Paradife Loft*, we are fenfible, that the emotions being obfcured by each other, make neither of them that
figure

figure they would make ſeparately. For the ſame reaſon, aſcending ſmoke in a calm morning, which inſpires ſtillneſs and tranquillity, is improper in a picture
full of violent action. A parterre, partly ornamented,
partly in diſorder, produces a mixt feeling of the ſame
ſort. Two great armies in act to engage, mix the diſſimilar emotions of grandeur and of terror.

> Sembra d'alberi denſi alta foreſta
> L'um campo, e l'altro ; di tant' aſte abbonda.
> Son teſi gli archi, e ſon le lance in reſta :
> Vibranſi i dardi, e rotaſi ogni ſionda.
> Ogni cavallo in guerra anco s'appreſta,
> Gli odii, e 'l furor del ſuo ſignor feconda :
> Raſpa, batte, nitriſce, e ſi raggira,
> Gonfia le nari ; e fumo, e fuoco ſpira.
> Bello in ſì bella viſta anco è l' orrore :
> E di mezzo la tema eſce il diletto.
> Ne men le trombe orribili e canore,
> Sono a gli orecchi, lieto e fero oggetto.
> Pur il campo fedel, banchè minore,
> Par di ſuon più mirabile, e d' aſpeto.
> E canta in più guerriero e chiaro carme
> Ogni ſua tromba, e maggior luce han l'arme.
> *Gerusalemme liberata, cant.* 20. *ſt.* 29. & 30.

Suppoſe a virtuous man has drawn on himſelf a great
misfortune, by a fault incident to human nature, and
therefore venial : the remorſe he feels aggravates his
diſtreſs, and conſequently raiſes our pity to a high pitch
we at the ſame time blame the man ; and the indignation raiſed by the fault he has committed, is diſſimilar
to pity : theſe two paſſions, however, proceeding from
the ſame object, are forced into a ſort of union ; but
the indignation is ſo ſlight, as ſcarce to be felt in the
mixture with pity. Subjects of this kind are of all the
fitteſt for tragedy ; but of that afterward.*

Oppoſite emotions are ſo diſſimilar as not to admit
any ſort of union, even where they proceed from cauſes
the

---

* Chap. 22.

the moft intimately connected. Love to a miftrefs, and
refentment for her infidelity, are of that nature : they
cannot exift otherwife than in fucceffion, which by the
connection of their caufes is commonly rapid ; and
thefe emotions will govern alternately, till one of them
obtain the afcendant, or both be fpent. A fucceffion
opens to me by the death of a worthy man, who was
my friend as well as my kinfman : when I think of
my friend I am grieved ; but the fucceffion gives me
joy. Thefe two caufes are intimately connected ; for
the fucceffion is the direct confequence of my friend's
death : the emotions however being oppofite, do not
mix ; they prevail alternately, perhaps for a courfe of
time, till grief for my friend's death be banifhed by the
pleafures of opulence. A virtuous man fuffering unjuftly, is an example of the fame kind : I pity him, and
have great indignation at the author of the wrong.
Thefe emotions proceed from caufes nearly connected ;
but being directed to different objects, they are not
forced into union : their oppofition preferves them diftinct : and accordingly they are found to prevail alternately.

I proceed to examples of diffimilar emotions arifing
from unconnected caufes. Good and bad news of
equal importance arriving at the fame inftant from different quarters, produce oppofite emotions, the dif-
cordance of which is not felt, becaufe they are not forced into union : they govern alternately, commonly in
a quick fucceffion, till their force be fpent :

Shylock. How now, Tubal, what news from Genoa ?
haft thou found my daughter ?

Tubal. I often came were I did hear of her, but cannot
find her.

Shy. Why there, there, there, there ! a diamond gone,
coft me two thoufand ducats in Francfort ! the curfe never
fell upon our nation till now ; I never felt it till now : two thoufand ducats in that and other precious, precious jewels ! I
        would

would my daughter were dead at my foot, and the jewels in her ear ; O would ſhe were hers'd at my foot, and the ducats in her coffin. No news of them ; why, ſo! and I know not what's ſpent in the ſearch : why, thou loſs upon loſs ! the thief gone with ſo much, and ſo much to find the thief ; and no ſatisfaction, no revenge, nor no ill luck ſtirring but what lights o' my ſhoulders ; no ſighs but o' my breathing, no tears but o' my ſhedding.

Tub. Yes, other men have ill luck too ; Anthonio, as I heard in Genoa——

Shy. What, what, what ? ill luck, ill luck ?

Tub. Hath an Argoſie caſt away, coming from Tripolis.

Shy. I thank God, I thank God ; is it true ? is it true ?

Tub. I ſpoke with ſome of the ſailors that eſcaped the wreck.

Shy. I thank thee, good Tubal ; good news, good news, ha, ha : where, in Genoa ?

Tub. Your daughter ſpent in Genoa, as I heard, one night, fourſcore ducats.

Shy. Thou ſtick'ſt a dagger in me ; I ſhall never ſee my gold again ; fourſcore ducats at a ſitting, fourſcore ducats !

Tub. There came divers of Anthonio's creditors in my company to Venice, that ſwear he cannot chuſe but break.

Shy. I am glad of it, I'll plague him, I'll torture him ; I am glad of it.

Tub. One of them ſhew'd me a ring, that he had of your daughter for a monkey.

Shy. Out upon her ! thou tortureſt me, Tubal ; it was my Turquoiſe ; I had it of Leah when I was a bachelor ; I would not have given it for a wilderneſs of monkies.

Tub. But Anthonio is certainly undone.

Shy. Nay, that's true, that's very true ; go fee me an officer, beſpeak him a fortnight before. I will have the heart of him, if he forfeit ; for were he out of Venice, I can make what merchandiſe I will. Go, go, Tubal, and meet me at our ſynagogue ; go, good Tubal, at our ſynagogue, Tubal.

Merchant of Venice, act 3. *ſc.* 1.

In the ſame manner, good news arriving to a man labouring under diſtreſs, occaſions a vibration in his mind from the one to the other :

Oſmyn.   By Heav'n thou'ſt rous'd me from my lethargy.
The ſpirit which was deaf to my own wrongs,
And the loud cries of my dead father's blood,
Deaf to revenge—nay, which refus'd to hear
The piercing ſighs and murmurs of my love
Yet unenjoy'd ; what not Almeria could
Revive, or raiſe, my people's voice has waken'd.
O my Antonio, I am all on fire,
My ſoul is up in arms, ready to charge
And bear amidſt the foe with conq'ring troops.
I hear 'em call to lead 'em on to liberty,
To victory ; their ſhouts and clamours rend
My ears, and reach the heav'ns : where is the king ?
Where is Alphonſo ? ha ! where ! where indeed ?
O I could tear and burſt the ſtrings of life,
To break theſe chains.   Off, off, ye ſtains of royalty !
Off, ſlavery ! O curſe, that I alone
Can beat and flutter in my cage, when I
Would ſoar, and ſtoop at victory beneath !

                    Mourning Bride, act 3. ſc. 2.

If the emotions be unequal in force, the ſtronger after a conflict will extinguiſh the weaker.   Thus the
loſs of a houſe by fire, or of a ſum of money by bank-
ruptcy, will make no figure in oppoſition to the birth
of a long-expected ſon, who is to inherit an opulent
fortune : after ſome ſlight vibrations, the mind ſettles in
joy, and the loſs is forgot.

   The foregoing obſervations will be found of great
uſe in the fine arts.   Many practical rules are derived
from them, which ſhall afterward be mentioned ; but
for inſtant gratification in part, the reader will accept
the following ſpecimen, being an application of theſe
obſervations to muſic.   It muſt be premiſed, that no
diſagreeable combination of ſounds is entitled to
the name of muſic : for all muſic is reſolvable
into melody and harmony, which imply agreeable-
                                                        neſs

neſs in their very conception.* Secondly, the agreeableneſs of vocal muſic differs from that of inſtrumental : the former, being intended to accompany words, ought to be expreſſive of the ſentiment that they convey : but the latter having no connection with words, may be agreeable without relation to any ſentiment : harmony, properly ſo called, though delightful when in perfection, hath no relation to ſentiment ; and we often find melody without the leaſt tincture of it.† Thirdly, in vocal muſic, the intimate connection of ſenſe and ſound rejects diſſimilar emotions, thoſe eſpecially that are oppoſite. Similar emotions produced by the ſenſe and the ſound, go naturally into union ; and at the ſame time are concordant or harmonious : but diſſimilar emotions, forced into union by theſe cauſes intimately connected, obſcure each other, and are alſo unpleaſant by diſcordance.

Theſe premiſes make it eaſy to determine what ſort of poetical compoſitions are fitted for muſic. In general, as muſic in all its various tones ought to be agreeable, it never can be concordant with any compoſition in language expreſſing a diſagreeable paſſion, or deſcribing a diſagreeable object : for here the emotions raiſed by the ſenſe and by the ſound, are not only diſſimilar but oppoſite ; and ſuch emotions forced into union produce always an unpleaſant mixture. Muſic accordingly is a very improper companion for ſentiments of malice, cruelty, envy, peeviſhneſs, or of any other

* Sounds may be ſo contrived as to produce horror, and ſeveral other painful feelings, which in a tragedy, or in an opera, may be introduced with advantage to accompany the repreſentation of a diſſocial or diſagreeable paſſion. But ſuch ſounds muſt in themſelves be diſagreeable ; and upon that account cannot be dignified with the name of muſic.

† It is beyond the power of muſic to raiſe a paſſion or a ſentiment : but it is in the power of muſic to raiſe emotions ſimilar to what are raiſed by ſentiment expreſſed in words pronounced with propriety and grace ; and ſuch muſic may juſtly be termed *ſentimental.*

other diſſocial paſſion ; witneſs among a thouſand King
John's ſpeech in Shakeſpear, ſoliciting Hubert to murder Prince Arthur, which even in the moſt curſory
view will appear incompatible with any ſort of muſic.
Muſic is a companion no leſs improper for the deſcription of any diſagreeable object, ſuch as that of Poly-
phemus in the third book of the Æneid, or that of
Sin in the ſecond book of Paradiſe Loſt : the horror
of the object deſcribed and the pleaſure of the muſic,
would be highly diſcordant.

With regard to vocal muſic, there is an additional
reaſon againſt aſſociating it with diſagreeable paſſions.
The external ſigns of ſuch paſſions are painful ; the
looks and geſtures to the eye, and the tone of pronunciation to the ear : ſuch tones therefore can never be
expreſſed muſically, for muſic muſt be pleaſant, or it
is not muſic.

On the other hand, muſic aſſociates finely with poems that tend to inſpire pleaſant emotions : muſic for
example in a cheerful tone, is perfectly concordant
with every motion in the ſame tone ; and hence our
taſte for airs expreſſive of mirth and jollity. Sympathetic joy aſſociates finely with cheerful muſic ; and ſympathetic pain no leſs finely with muſic that is tender
and melancholy. All the different emotions of love,
namely, tenderneſs, concern, anxiety, pain of abſence,
hope, fear, accord delightfully with muſic : and accordingly, a perſon in love, even when unkindly treated, is ſoothed by muſic ; for the tenderneſs of love ſtill
prevailing, accords with a melancholy ſtrain. This
is finely exemplified by Shakeſpear in the fourth act of
Othello, where Deſdemona calls for a ſong expreſſive of
her diſtreſs. Wonderful is the delicacy of that writer's
taſte, which fails him not even in the moſt refined emotions of human nature. Melancholy muſic is ſuited to

ſlight

flight grief, which requires or admits confolation : but deep grief, which refufes all confolation, rejects for that reafon even melancholy mufic.

Where the fame perfon is both the actor and the finger, as in an opera, there is a feparate reafon why mufic fhould not be affociated with the fentiments of any difagreeable paffion, nor the defcription of any difagreeable object; which is, that fuch affociation is altogether unnatural : the pain, for example, that a man feels who is agitated with malice or unjuft revenge, difqualifies him for relifhing mufic, or any thing that is pleafing : and therefore to reprefent fuch a man, contrary to nature, expreffing his fentiments in a fong, cannot be agreeable to any audience of tafte.

For a different reafon, mufic is improper for accompanying pleafant emotions of the more important kind, becaufe thefe totally ingrofs the mind, and leave no place for mufic, nor for any fort of amufement : in a perilous enterprife to dethrone a tyrant, mufic would be impertinent, even where hope prevails, and the profpect of fuccefs is great : Alexander attacking the Indian town, and mounting the wall, had certainly no impulfe to exert his prowefs in a fong.

It is true, that not the leaft regard is paid to thefe rules either in the French or Italian opera : and the attachment we have to operas, may at firft be confidered as an argument againft the foregoing doctrine. But the general tafte for operas is no argument : in thefe compofitions the paffions are fo imperfectly expreffed, as to leave the mind free for relifhing mufic of any fort indifferently ; and it cannot be difguifed, that the pleafure of an opera is derived chiefly from the mufic, and fcarce at all from the fentiments : a happy concordance of the emotions raifed by the fong and by the mufic, is extremely rare : and I venture to affirm, that there is no example of it, unlefs where the

emotion

emotion raiſed by the former is agreeable as well as that raiſed by the latter.*

The ſubject we have run through appears not a little entertaining. It is extremely curious to obſerve, in many inſtances, a plurality of cauſes producing in conjunction a great pleaſure : in other inſtances, no leſs frequent, no conjunction, but each cauſe acting in oppoſition. To enter bluntly upon a ſubject of ſuch intricacy, might gravel an acute philoſopher ; but taking matters in a train, the intricacy vaniſheth.

Next in order, according to the method propoſed, come external effects ; which lead us to paſſions as the cauſes of external effects. Two coexiſtent paſſions that have the ſame tendency, muſt be ſimilar : they accordingly readily unite, and in conjunction have double force. This is verified by experience ; from which we learn, that the mind receives not impulſes alternately from ſuch paſſions, but one ſtrong impulſe from the whole in conjunction ; and indeed it is not eaſy to conceive what ſhould bar the union of paſſions that have all of them the ſame tendency.

Two paſſions having oppoſite tendencies, may proceed from the ſame cauſe conſidered in different views. Thus a miſtreſs may at once be the cauſe both of love and of reſentment : her beauty inflames the paſſion of love ; her cruelty or inconſtancy cauſes reſentment. When two ſuch paſſions coexiſt in the ſame breaſt, the oppoſition of their aim prevents any ſort of union ; and accordingly, they are not felt otherwiſe than in ſucceſſion : the conſequence of which muſt be, either that

* A cenſure of the ſame kind is pleaſantly applied to the French ballettes by a celebrated writer ; " Si le Prince eſt joyeux, on prend part à ſa joye, et l'on danſe : s'il eſt triſte, on veut l'égayer, et l'on danſe. Mais il y a bien d'autres ſujets de danſes ; les plus graves actions de la vie ſe font en danſant. Les prêtres danſent, les ſoldats danſent, les dieux danſent, les diables danſent, on danſe juſques dans les enterremens, et tout danſe à propos de tout."

that the paſſions will balance each other and prevent
external action, or that one of them will prevail and
accompliſh its end.	Guarini, in his *Paſtor Fido,* de-
ſcribes beautifully the ſtruggle between love and reſentment directed to the ſame object :

Coriſca. Chi vide mai, chi mai udi più ſtrana
E più folle, e più fera, e più importuna
Paſſione amoroſa ? amore, ed odio
Con sì mirabil tempre in un cor miſti,
Che l'un par l'altro (e non ſo ben dir come)
E ſi ſtrugge, e s'avanza, e naſce, e more.
S' i' miro alle bellezze di Mirtillo
Dal piè leggiadro al grazioſo volto,
Il vago portamento, il bel ſembiante,
Gli atti, i coſtumi, e le parole, e 'l guardo ;
M'aſſale Amore con sì poſſente foco
Ch' i' ardo tutta, e par, ch'ogn' altro affetto
Da queſto ſol ſia ſuperato, e vinto :
Ma ſe poi penſo all' oſtinato amore,
Ch' ei porta ad altra donna, e che per lei
Di me non cura, e ſpiezza (il vo' pur dire)
La mia famoſa, e da mill' alme, e mille,
Inchinata beltà, bramata grazia ;
L' odio così, così l'aborro, e ſchivo,
Che impoſſibil mi par, ch'unqua per lui
Mi s'accendeſſe al cor fiamma amoroſa.
Tallor meco ragiono : o s'io poteſſi
Gioir del mio dol dolciſſimo Mirtillo,
Sicche foſſe mio tutto, e ch'altra mai
Poſſeder no 'l poteſſe, o più d' ogn' altra
Beata, e feliciſſima Coriſca !
Ed in quel punto in me ſorge un talento
Verſo di lui sì dolce, e sì gentile,
Che di ſeguirlo, e di pregarlo ancora,
E di ſcoprirgli il cor prendo conſiglio.
Che più ? così mi ſtimola il deſio,
Che ſe poteſſi allor l'adorerei.
Dall' altra parte i' mi riſento, e dico,
Un ritroſo ? uno ſchifo ? un che non degna ?
Un, che può d'altra donna eſſer amante ?

Un,

Un, ch'ardifce mirarmi, e non m'adora ?
E dal mio volto fi difende in guifa,
Che per amor non more ? ed io, che lui
Dovrei veder, come molti altri i' veggio
Supplice, e lagrimofo a' piedi miei,
Supplice, e lagrimofo a piedi fuoi
Softerro di cadere ? ah non fia mai.
Ed in quefto penfier tant' ira accoglio ,
Contra di lui, contra di me, che volfi
A feguirlo il penfier, gli occhi a mirarlo,
Che 'l nome di Mirtillo, e l' amor mio
Odio più che la morte ; e lui vorrei
Veder il più dolente, il più infelice
Paftor, che viva ; e fe poteffi allora,
Con le mie proprie man l'anciderei.
Così fdegno, defire, odio, ed amore
Mi fanno guerra, ed io, che ftata fono
Sempre fin qui di mille cor la fiamma,
Di mill' alme il tormento, ardo, e languifco :
E provo nel mio mal le pene altrui.

Act, 1. *fc.* 3.

Ovid paints in lively colours the vibration of mind between two oppofite paffions directed to the fame object. Althæa had two brothers much beloved, who
were unjuftly put to death by her fon Meleager in a
fit of paffion : fhe was ftrongly impelled to revenge ;
but the criminal was her own fon. This ought to
have with-held her hand ; but the ftory is more interefting, by the violence of the ftruggle between refentment and maternal love :

Dona Deûm templis nato victore ferebat ;
Cum videt extinctos fratres Althæa referri.
Quæ plangore dato, mœftis ululatibus urbem
Implet ; et auratis mutavit veftibus atras.
At fimul eft auctor necis editus ; excidit omnis
Luctus : et a lacrymis in pœnæ verfus amorem eft.
Stipes erat, quem, cum partus enixa jaceret
Theftias, in flammam triplices pofuêre forores ;
Staminaque

Staminaque impreſſo fatalia pollici nentes,
Tempora, dixerunt, eadem lignoque, tibique,
O modo nate, damus. Quo poſtquam carmine dicto
Exceſſere dex ; flagrantem mater ab igne
Eripuit torrem : ſparſitque liquentibus undis.
Ille diu fuerat penetralibus abditus imis ;
Servatuſque, tuos, juvenis, ſervaverat annos.
Protulit hunc genitrix, tædaſque in fragmina poni
Imperat ; et poſitis inimicos admovet ignes.
Tum conata quater flammis imponere ramum,
Cœpta quater tenuit. Pugnat materque, ſororque,
Et diverſa trahunt unum duo nomina pectus.
Sæpe metu ſceleris pallebant ora futuri :
Sæpe ſuum fervens oculis dabat ira ruborem,
Et modo neſcio quid ſimilis crudele minanti
Vultus erat ; modo quem miſereri credere poſſes :
Cumque ferus lacrymas animi ſiccaverat ardor ;
Inveniebantur lacrymæ tamen. Utque carina,
Quam ventus, ventoque rapit contrarius æſtus,
Vim geminam ſentit, paretque incerta duobus :
Theſtius haud aliter dubiis affectibus errat,
Inque vices ponit, poſitamque refuſcitat iram.
Incipit eſſe tamen melior germana parente ;
Et, conſanguineas ut ſanguine leniat umbras,
Impietate pia eſt. Nam poſtquam peſtifer ignis
Convaluit ; Rogus iſte cremet mea viſcera, dixit.
Utque manu dirà lignum fatale tenebat ;
Ante ſepulchrales infelix adſtitit aras.
Pœnarumque dex triplices, furialibus, inquit,
Eumenides, ſacris, vultus advertite veſtros.
Ulciſcor, facioque nefas. Mors morte pianda eſt ;
In ſcelus addendum ſcelus eſt, in funera funus :
Per coacervatos pereat domus impia luctus.
An felix Oeneus nato victore fructur,
Theſtius orbus erit ? melius lugebitis ambo.
Vos modo, fraterni manes, animæque recentes,
Officium ſentite meum ; magnoque paratas
Accipite inferias, uteri mala pignora noſtri.
Hei mihi ! quo rapior ? fratres ignoſcite matri.
Deficiunt ad cœpta manus. Meruiſſe fatemur
Illum, cur pereat : mortis mihi diſplicet auctor.
Ergo impune feret ; vivuſque, et victor, et ipſo

Succeſſu

Succeffu tumidus regnum Calydonis habebit ?
Vos cinis exiguus, gelidæque jacebitis umbræ ?
Haud equidem patiar. Pereat fceleratus ; et ille
Spemque patris, regnique trahat, patriæque ruinam,
Mens ubi materna eft ; ubi funt pia jura parentum ?
Et, quos fuftinui, bis menfûm quinque labores ?
O utinam primis arfilles ignibus infans ;
Idque ego paiſa forem ! vixifti munere noftro :
Nunc merito moriere tuo. Cape præmia facti ;
Bifque datam, primum partu, mox ftipite rapto,
Redde animam ; vel me fraternis adde fepulchris.
Et cupio, et nequeo. Quid agam ? modo vulnera
      fratrum
Ante oculos mihi funt, et tantæ cædis imago ;
Nunc animum pietas, maternaque nomina frangunt.
Me miferam ! male vincetis, fed vincite, fratres ;
Dummodo, quæ dedero vobis folatia, vofque
Ipfa fequar, dixit : dextraque averfa trementi
Funereum torrem medios conjecit in ignes.
Aut dedit, aut vifus gemitus eft ill edediffe,
Stipes ; et inviis correptus ab ignibus arfit.
                    Metamorph. lib. 8. l. 445.

In cafes of this kind, one circumftance always augments the fluctuation : after balancing between two actions, a refolution to prefer one of them is an inchoated
gratification of the prevailing paffion, which moderates
it in fome degree ; and that circumftance tends to give
a fuperiority to the oppofite paffion : another circumftance alfo concurs, that this oppofite paffion has, by
reftraint, acquired in the interim fome additional force.

Love and jealoufy connected by a common object,
occupy the mind alternately : when the object is confidered as beautiful, love prevails ; when confidered as
poffibly unfaithful, jealoufy prevails. A fituation of
that kind affords great fcope for fluctuation of paffion ;
which is painted to the life by feveral mafterly hands
in words as well as in colours. Shakefpear handles the
fame fubject, but in a manner uncommon, and pecu-
                                          liar

liar to himfelf : in Othello's foliloquy before putting
his wife to death, love and jealoufy are reprefented,
each exerting its whole force, but without any ftruggle : Othello was naturally inflexible ; and the ten-
dereft love could not divert him from a purpofe he
approved as right, not even for a moment : but every
thing confiftent with fuch a character is done to rec-
oncile the two oppofite paffions ; he is refolved to
put her to death, but he will not fhed her blood, nor
fo much as ruffle her fkin :

> *Othello.* It is the caufe, it is the caufe, my foul ;—
> Let me not name it to you, you chafte ftars !
> It is the caufe———Yet I'll not fhed her blood,
> Nor fcar that whiter fkin of her's than fnow,
> And fmooth as monumental alabafter.
> [*Lays down the fword.*
> Yet fhe muft die ; elfe fhe'll betray more men.
> Put out the light, and then—Put out the light !—
> If I quench thee, thou flaming minifter,
> I can again thy former light reftore,
> Should I repent : but once put out *thy* light.
> Thou cunning'ft pattern of excelling nature,
> I know not where is that Promethean heat
> That can thy light relumine.—(*Sets down the taper.*
> When I have pluck'd thy rofe,
> I cannot give it vital growth again ;
> It needs muft wither.—I'll fmell thee on the tree :
> [*Kiffing her.*
> Oh balmy breath, that doft almoft perfuade
> Juftice to break her fword !—One more ; one more ;
> Be thus when thou art dead, and I will kill thee,
> And love thee after.—One more, that's the laft ;
> So fweet was near fo fatal ! I muft weep,
> But they are cruel tears ! this forrow's heavenly ;
> It ftrikes where it doth love.—   *Act* 5. *fc.* 6.

In Otway's *Orphan*, we have an illuftrious example of
the addrefs employed to gratify oppofite paffions di-

rected to the fame object. Caftalio and Polydore, brothers and rivals, had fworn mutual confidence : Caftalio broke his faith by a private marriage ; which unwarily betrayed Polydore into a difmal deed, that of polluting his brother's bed. Thus he had injured his brother, and was injured by him : juftice prompt- ed him to make full atonement by his own death ; re- fentment againft his brother, required a full atone- ment to be made to himfelf. In coexiftent paffions fo contradictory, one of them commonly prevails af- ter a ftruggle : but here happily an expedient occur- red to Polydore for gratifying both ; which was, that he fhould provoke his brother to put him to death. Polydore's crime in his own opinion, merited that punifhment ; and juftice was fatisfied when he fell by the hand of the man he had injured : he wanted at the fame time to punifh his brother for breach of faith : and he could not punifh more effectually than by betraying his brother to be his executioner.

If difference of aim prevent the union of two paf- fions, though having the fame object ; much more will it prevent their union, when their objects are al- fo different : in both cafes there is a fluctuation ; but in the latter the fluctuation is flower than in the former. A beautiful fituation of that kind is ex- hibited in the *Cid* of Corneille. Don Diegue, an old foldier worn out with age, having received a mortal affront from the Count, father to Chimene, employs his fon Don Rodrigue, Chimene's lover, to demand fatisfaction. This fituation occafions in the breaft of Don Rodrigue a cruel ftruggle between love and honour, one of which muft be facrificed. The fcene is finely conducted, chiefly by making love in fome degree take part with honour, Don Rodrigue reflecting, that if he loft his honour he could not de- ferve his miftrefs : honour triumphs ; and the Count

provoked

provoked to a fingle combat, falls by the hand of Don Rodrigue.

This produceth another beautiful fituation refpect-ing Chimene, which making part of the fame ftory is placed here, though it properly belongs to the fore-going head.   It became the duty of that lady to de-mand juftice againft her lover, for whofe prefervation, in other circumftances, fhe cheerfully would have fac-rificed her own life.   The ftruggle between thefe oppofite paffions directed to the fame object is finely expreffed in the third fcene of the third act :

> *Elvire.* Il vous prive d'un pére, et vous l'aimez
> encore !
> *Chimene.* C'ft peu de dire aimer, Elvire, je l'adore ;
> Ma paffion s'oppofe à mon refentiment,
> Dedans mon ennemi je trouve mon amant,
> Et je fens qu'en depit de toute ma colere,
> Rodrigue dans mon cœur combat encore mon pére.
> Il l'attaque, il le preffe, il céde, il fe défend,
> Tantôt fort, tantôt foible, et tantôt triomphant ;
> Mais en ce dur combat de colére et de flame,
> Il déchire mon cœur fans partager mon ame, ·
> Et quoique mon amour ait fur moi de pouvoir,
> Je ne confulte point pour fuivre mon devoir.
> Je cours fans balancer où mon honneur m'oblige ;
> Rodrigue m'eft bien cher, fon interêt m'afflige,
> Mon cœur prend fon parti ; mais malgré fon effort,
> Je fai que je fuis, et que mon pére eft mort.

Not lefs when the objects are different than when the fame, are means fometimes afforded to gratify both paffions ; and fuch means are greedily embraced. In Taffo's *Gerufalemme*, Edward and Gildippe, hufband and wife, are introduced fighting gallantly againft the Saracens : Gildippe receives a mortal wound by the hand of Soliman : Edward inflamed with revenge, as well as concern for Gildippe, is agitated between the

two different objects. The poet* describes him endeavouring to gratify both at once, applying his right
hand against Soliman, the object of his resentment,
and his left hand to support his wife, the object of
his love.

PART V.

*Influence of Passion with respect to our Perceptions,
Opinions, and Belief.*

CONSIDERING how intimately our
perceptions, passions, and actions, are mutually connected, it would be wonderful if they should have no
mutual influence. That our actions are too much
influenced by passion, is a known truth: but it is not
less certain, though not so well known, that passion
hath also an influence upon our perceptions, opinions, and belief. For example, the opinions we form
of men and things, are generally directed by affection: an advice given by a man of figure, hath great
weight; the same advice from one in a low condition, is despised or neglected: a man of courage
under-rates danger; and to the indolent, the slightest
obstacle appears insurmountable.

This doctrine is of great use in logic; and of still
greater use in criticism, by serving to explain several
principles of the fine arts that will be unfolded in the
course of this work. A few general observations shall
at present suffice, leaving the subject to be prosecuted
more particularly afterward when occasion offers.

There is no truth more universally known, than
that tranquillity and sedateness are the proper state
of

* Canto 20. ft. 97.

of mind for accurate perception and cool deliberation; and, for that reaſon, we never regard the opinion even of the wiſeſt man, when we diſcover prejudice or paſſion behind the curtain. Paſſion, as obſerved above,* hath ſuch influence over us, as to give
a falſe light to all its objects. Agreeable paſſions
. prepoſſeſs the mind in favour of their objects, and
diſagreeable paſſions, no leſs againſt their objects : a
woman is all perfection in her lover's opinion, while,
in the eye of a rival beauty, ſhe is awkward and diſagreeable ; when the paſſion of love is gone, beauty
vaniſhes with it,—nothing left of that genteel motion, that ſprightly converſation, thoſe numberleſs
graces, which formerly, in the lover's opinion, charm-
ed all hearts. To a zealot every one of his own ſect
is a ſaint, while the moſt upright of a different ſect
are to him children of perdition : the talent of ſpeaking in a friend, is more regarded than prudent conduct in any other. Nor will this ſurpriſe one acquainted with the world ; our opinions, the reſult frequently of various and complicated views, are commonly ſo ſlight and wavering, as readily to be ſuſceptible of a bias from paſſion.

   With that natural bias another circumſtance concurs, to give paſſion an undue influence on our opinions and belief ; and that is a ſtrong tendency in
our nature to juſtify our paſſions as well as our actions, not to others only, but even to ourſelves.
That tendency is peculiarly remarkable with reſpect
to diſagreeable paſſions : by their influence, objects are
magnified or leſſened, circumſtances ſupplied or ſup-
preſſed, every thing coloured and diſguiſed, to anſwer
the end of juſtification. Hence the foundation of
ſelf-deceit, where a man impoſes upon himſelf inno-
cently, and even without ſuſpicion of a bias. There
                                                  are

are fubordinate means that contribute to pervert the
judgment, and to make us form opinions contrary
to truth ; of which I fhall mention two. Firft, it
was formerly obferved,* that though ideas feldom
ftart up in the mind without connection, yet that
ideas fuited to the prefent tone of mind are readily
fuggefted by any flight connection : the arguments
for a favourite opinion are always at hand, while we
often fearch in vain for thofe that crofs our inclination. Second, The mind taking delight in agreeable circumftances or arguments, is deeply impreffed
with them ; while thofe that are difagreeable are hurried over fo as fcarce to make any impreffion : the
fame argument, by being relifhed or not relifhed,
weighs fo differently, as in truth to make conviction
depend more on paffion than on reafoning. This
obfervation is fully juftified by experience : to confine
myfelf to a fingle inftance, the numberlefs abfurd religious tenets that at different times have peftered the
world, would be altogether unaccountable but for
that irregular bias of paffion.

We proceed to a more pleafant tafk, which is to
illuftrate the foregoing obfervations by proper examples. Gratitude, when warm, is often exerted upon
the children of the benefactor ; efpecially where he is
removed out of reach by death or abfence.† The
paffion in this cafe being exerted for the fake of the
benefactor, requires no peculiar excellence in his
children : but the practice of doing good to thefe
children produces affection for them, which never
fails to advance them in our efteem. By fuch means,
ftrong connections of affection are often formed
among

---

* Chap. 1.

† See part 1. fect. 1. of the prefent chapter.

among individuals, upon the slight foundation now mentioned.

Envy is a passion, which, being altogether unjustifiable, cannot be excused but by disguising it under some plausible name. At the same time, no passion is more eager than envy, to give its object a disagreeable appearance : it magnifies every bad quality, and fixes on the most humbling circumstances.

> *Cassius.* I cannot tell what you and other men
> Think of this life ; but for my single self,
> I had as lief not be, as live to be
> In awe of such a thing as I myself.
> I was born free as Cæsar, so were you ;
> We both have fed as well ; and we can both
> Endure the winter's cold as well as he.
> For once, upon a raw and gusty day,
> The troubled Tyber chafing with his shores,
> Cæsar says to me, Dar'st thou, Cassius, now
> Leap in with me into this angry flood,
> And swim to yonder point ?—Upon the word,
> Accoutred as I was, I plunged in,
> And bid him follow : so indeed he did.
> The torrent roar'd, and we did buffet it,
> With lusty sinews ; throwing it aside,
> And stemming it with hearts of controversy.
> But ere we could arrive the point propos'd,
> Cæsar cry'd, help me, Cassius, or I sink.
> I, as Æneas, our great ancestor,
> Did from the flames of Troy upon his shoulder
> The old Anchises bear ; so from the waves of Tyber
> Did I the tired Cæsar : and this man
> Is now become a god, and Cassius is
> A wretched creature ; and must bend his body,
> If Cæsar carelessly but nod on him.
> He had a fever when he was in Spain,
> And when the fit was on him, I did mark
> How he did shake. 'Tis true, this god did shake ;
> His coward lips did from their colour fly,
> And that same eye whose bend doth awe the world,

I 4   Did

Did loſe its luſtre ; I did hear him groan ;
Ay, and that tongue of his, that bade the Romans
Mark him, and write his ſpeeches in their books,
Alas ! it cry'd——Give me ſome drink, Titinius,——
As a ſick girl.   Ye gods, it doth amaze me,
A man of ſuch a feeble temper ſhould
So get a ſtart of the majeſtic world,
And bear the palm alone.
Julius Cæſar, *act* 1. *ſc.* 3.

Glo'ſter inflamed with reſentment againſt his ſon
Edgar, could even force himſelf into a momentary
conviction that they were not related :

> O ſtrange faſten'd villain !
> Would he deny his letter ? I never got him.
> *King Lear*, *act* 2. *ſc.* 3.

When by great ſenſibility of heart, or other means,
grief becomes immoderate, the mind, in order to
juſtify itſelf, is prone to magnify the cauſe : and if
the real cauſe admit not of being magnified, the
mind ſeeks a cauſe for its grief in imagined future
events :

> *Buſhy.*   Madam, your Majeſty is much too ſad :
> You promis'd, when you parted with the King,
> To lay aſide ſelf-haiming heavineſs,
> And entertain a cheerful diſpoſition.
>   *Queen.*   To pleaſe the King, I did ; to pleaſe myſelf,
> I cannot do it.   Yet I know no cauſe
> Why I ſhould welcome ſuch a gueſt as grief ;
> Save bidding farewell to ſo ſweet a gueſt
> As my ſweet Richard : yet again, methinks,
> Some unborn ſorrow, ripe in Fortune's womb,
> Is coming tow'rd me ; and my inward ſoul
> With ſomething trembles, yet at nothing grieves,
> More than with parting from my lord the King.
> *Richard* II. *act* 2. *ſc.* 5.

Reſentment

Refentment at firft is vented on the relations of the offender, in order to punifh him : but as refentment, when fo outrageous, is contrary to confcience, the mind, to juftify its paffion, is difpofed to paint thefe relations in the blackeft colours ; and it comes at laft to be convinced, that they ought to be punifhed for their own demerits.

Anger raifed by an accidental ftroke upon a tender part of the body, is fometimes vented upon the undefigning caufe. But as the paffion in that cafe is abfurd, and as there can be no folid gratification in punifhing the innocent ; the mind, prone to juftify as well as to gratify its paffion, deludes itfelf into a conviction of the action's being voluntary. The conviction, however, is but momentary : the firft reflection fhows it to be erroneous ; and the paffion vanifheth almoft inftantaneoufly with the conviction. But anger, the moft violent of all paffions, has ftill greater influence ; it fometimes forces the mind to perfonify a ftock or a ftone, if it happen to occafion bodily pain, and even to believe it a voluntary agent, in order to be a proper object of refentment. And that we have really a momentary conviction of its being a voluntary agent, muft be evident from confidering, that, without fuch conviction, the paffion can neither be juftified nor gratified ; the imagination can give no aid ; for a ftock or a ftone imagined fenfible, cannot be an object of punifhment, if the mind be confcious that it is an imagination merely without any reality. Of fuch perfonification, involving a conviction of reality, there is one illuftrious inftance : when the firft bridge of boats over the Hellefpont was deftroyed by a ftorm, Xerxes fell into a tranfport of rage, fo exceffive, that he commanded the fea to be punifhed with 300 ftripes ; and a pair of fetters to be thrown into it, enjoining the follow-

ing

ing words to be pronounced : " O thou falt and bitter water ! thy mafter hath condemned thee to this
punifhment for offending him without caufe ; and
is refolved to pafs over thee in defpite of thy info-
lence : with reafon all men neglect to facrifice to thee,
becaufe thou art both difagreeable and treacherous.*"

Shakefpear exhibits beautiful examples of the irregular influence of.paffion in making us believe
things to be otherwife than they are.   King Lear, in
his diftrefs, perfonifies the rain, wind, and thunder ;
and, in order to juftify his refentment, believes them
to be taking part with his daughters :

> *Lear.*   Rumble thy belly-full, fpit fire, fpout rain !
> Nor rain, wind, thunder, fire, are my daughters.
> I tax not you, you elements, with unkindnefs ;
> I never gave you kingdoms, call'd you children ;
> You owe me no fubfcription.   Then let fall
> Your horrible pleafure.——Here I ftand, your brave ;
> A poor, infirm, weak, and defpis'd old man !
> But yet I call you fervile minifters,
> That have with two pernicious daughters join'd
> Your high-engender'd battles, 'gainft a head
> So old and white as this.   Oh ! oh ! 'tis foul !
> *Act* 3. *fc.* 2.

King Richard, full of indignation againft his favourite horfe for carrying Bolingbroke, is led into the conviction of his being rational :

> *Groom.*   O, how it yearn'd my heart, when I beheld
> In London ftreets, that coronation-day,
> When Bolingbroke rode on Roan Barbary,
> That horfe that thou fo often haft beftrid,
> That horfe that I fo carefully have dreffed.
> *K. Rich.*   Rode he on Barbary ? tell me, gentle,
> friend, How went he under him.
> *Groom.*   So proudly as he had difdain'd the ground.
> *K. Rich.*

*. Herodotus, book 7.

K. Rich. So proud that Bolingbroke was on his back!
That jade had eat bread from my royal hand.
This hand hath made him proud with clapping him.
Would he not ftumble ? would he not fall down,
(Since pride muft have a fall,) and break the neck
Of that proud man that did ufurp his back ?
Richard II. *aĉ* 5. *fc.* 11.

Hamlet, fwelled with indignation at his mother's fecond marriage, was ftrongly inclined to leffen the time
of her widowhood, the fhortnefs of the time being a
violent circumftance againft her ; and he deludes
himfelf by degrees into the opinion of an interval
fhorter than the real one :

Hamlet.————That it fhould come to this !
But two months dead ! nay, not fo much ; not two ;—
So excellent a king, that was, to this,
Hypeiion to a fatyr : fo loving to my mother,
That he permitted not the winds of heav'n
Vifit her face too roughly.. Heav'n and earth !
Muft I remember—why, fhe would hang on him,
As if increafe of appetite had grown
By what it fed on ; yet, within a month———
Let me not think—Frailty, thy name is *Woman !*
A little month ! or ere thefe fhoes were old,
With which fhe follow'd my poor father's body.
Like Niobe, all tears———Why fhe, ev'n fhe——
(O heav'n ! a beaft that wants difcourfe of reafon,
Would have mourn'd longer—) married with mine
        uncle,
My father's brother ; but no more like my father,
Than I to Hercules., Within a month !——
Ere yet the falt of moft unrighteous tears
Had left the flufhing in her gauled eyes,
She married——Oh, moft wicked fpeed, to poft
With fuch dexterity to inceftuous fheets !
It is not, nor it cannot come to good.
But break, my heart, for I muft hold my tongue.
Aĉ 1. *fc.* 3..
                                                The

The power of passion to falsify the computation of time is remarkable in this instance ; because time, which hath an accurate measure, is less obsequious to our desires and wishes, than objects which have no precise standard of less or more.

Good news are greedily swallowed upon very slender evidence : our wishes magnify the probability of the event, as well as the veracity of the relater ; and we believe as certain, what at best is doubtful :

> Quel, che l'huom vede, amor li fa invisible
> E l'invisibil fa veder amore
> Questo creduto fu, che 'l miser suole   .
> Dar facile credenza a' quel, che vuole.
> > *Orland. Furiof. cant.* 1. *st.* 56.

For the same reason, bad news gain also credit upon the slightest evidence : fear, if once alarmed, has the same effect with hope, to magnify every circumstance that tends to conviction.   Shakespear, who shows more knowledge of human nature than any of our philosophers, hath in his *Cymbeline** represented this bias of the mind ; for he makes the person who alone was affected with the bad news, yield to evidence that did not convince any of his companions. And Othello† is convinced of his wife's infidelity from circumstances too slight to move any person less interested.

If the news interest us in so low a degree as to give place to reason, the effect will not be altogether the same : judging of the probability or improbability of the story, the mind settles in a rational conviction either that it is true or not.   But, even in that case, the mind is not allowed to rest in that degree of conviction

viction

* Aĝ 2 sc. 6.   † Aĝ 3. sc. 8.

viction which is produced by rational evidence : if the
news be in any degree favourable, our belief is raiſed
by hope to an improper height ; and if unfavourable,
by fear.

This obſervation holds equally with reſpect to future events : if a future event be either much wiſhed
or dreaded, the mind never fails to augment the
probability beyond truth.

That eaſineſs of belief with reſpect to wonders and
prodigies, even the moſt abſurd and ridiculous, is a
ſtrange phenomenon ; becauſe nothing can be more
evident than the following propoſition, that the more
ſingular any event is, the more evidence is required
to produce belief : a familiar event daily occurring,
being in itſelf extremely probable, finds ready credit,
and therefore is vouched by the ſlighteſt evidence ;
but to overcome the improbability of a ſtrange and
rare event, contrary to the courſe of nature, the very
ſtrongeſt evidence is required. It is certain, however,
that wonders and prodigies are ſwallowed by the
vulgar, upon evidence that would not be ſufficient to
aſcertain the moſt familiar occurrence. It has been
reckoned difficult to explain that irregular bias of
mind ; but we are now made acquainted with the influence of paſſion upon opinion and belief : a ſtory of
ghoſts or fairies, told with an air of gravity and
truth, raiſeth an emotion of wonder, and perhaps of
dread ; and theſe emotions impoſing upon a weak
mind, impreſs upon it a thorough conviction contrary to reaſon.

Opinion and belief are influenced by propenſity as
well as by paſſion. An innate propenſity is all we
have to convince us, that the operations of nature
are uniform : influenced by that propenſity, we often
raſhly think, that good or bad weather will never
have an end ; and in natural philoſophy, writers, influ-

enced by the fame propenfity, ftretch commonly their analogical reafonings beyond juft bounds.

Opinion and belief are influenced by affeftion as well as by propenfity. The noted ftory of a fine lady and a curate viewing the moon through a telefcope, is a pleafant illuftration : I perceive, fays the lady, two fhadows inclining to each other ; they are certainly two happy lovers : Not at all, replies the curate, they are two fteeples of a cathedral.

APPENDIX to PART V.

Methods that Nature hath afforded for computing Time and Space.

THIS fubjeft is introduced, becaufe it affords feveral curious examples of the influence of paffion to bias the mind in its conceptions and opinions ; a leffon that cannot be too frequently inculcated, as there is not perhaps another bias in human nature that hath an influence fo univerfal to make us wander from truth as well as from juftice.

I begin with time ; and the queftion is, What was the meafure of time before artificial meafures were invented ; and what is the meafure at prefent when thefe are not 'at hand ? I fpeak not of months and days, which are computed by the moon and fun ; but of hours, or in general of the time that paffes between any two occurrences when there is not accefs to the fun. The only natural meafure is the fucceffion of our thoughts ; for we always judge the time to be long or fhort, in proportion to the number of perceptions and ideas that have paffed during that interval.

val. This meaſure is indeed far from being accurate; becauſe in a quick and in a ſlow ſucceſſion, it muſt evidently produce different computaticns of the ſame time : but, however inaccurate, it is the only meaſure by which we naturally calcuſate time ; and that meaſure is applied on all occaſions, without regard to any caſual variation in the rate of ſucceſſion.

That meaſure would however be tolerable, did it labour under no other imperfection beſide that mentioned : but in many inſtances it is much more fallacious ; in order to explain which diſtinctly, an analyſis will be neceſſary. Time is computed at two different periods ; one while it is paſſing, another after it is paſt : theſe computations ſhall be conſidered ſeparately, with the errors to which each of them is liable. Beginning with computation of time while it is paſſing, it is a common and trite obſervation, That to lovers abſence appears immeaſurably long, every minute an hour, and every day a year : the ſame computation is made in every caſe where we long for a diſtant event ; as where one is in expectation of good news, or where a profligate heir watches for the death of an old rich miſer. Oppoſite to theſe are inſtances not fewer in number : to a criminal the interval between ſentence and execution appears wofully ſhort : and the ſame holds in every caſe where one dreads an approaching event ; of which even a ſchool-boy can bear witneſs : the hour allowed him for play, moves in his apprehenſion, with a very ſwift pace ; before he is thoroughly engaged, the hour is gone. A computation founded on the number of ideas, will never produce eſtimates ſo regularly oppoſite to each other ; for our wiſhes do not produce a ſlow ſucceſſion of ideas, nor our fears a quick ſucceſſion. What then moves nature, in the caſes mentioned, to deſert her ordinary meaſure for one

very

very different? I know not that this queſtion ever
has been refolved ; the falfe eſtimates I have ſuggeſted being ſo common and familiar, that no writer has
thought of their caufe. And, indeed, to enter upon
this matter without preparation, might occaſion ſome
difficulty ; to encounter which, we luckily are prepared, by what is faid upon the power of paſſion to
bias the mind in its perceptions and opinions. Among
the circumſtances that terrify a condemned criminal,
the ſhort time he has to live is one : which time, by
the influence of terror, is made to appear ſtill ſhorter
than it is in reality. In the fame manner, among the
diſtreſſes of an abſent lover, the time of ſeparation is
a capital circumſtance, which for that reafon is greatly
magnified by his anxiety and impatience : he imag-
ines that the time of meeting comes on very ſlow, or
rather that it will never come : every minute is
thought of an intolerable length. Here is a fair,
and, I hope, fatisfactory reafon, why time is thought
to be tedious when we long for a future event, and
not lefs fleet when we dread the event. The reafon
is confirmed by other inſtances. Bodily pain, fixt to
one part, produceth a ſlow train of perceptions,
which, according to the common meafure of time,
ought to make it appear ſhort : yet we know, that,
in ſuch a ſtate, time has the oppoſite appearance ;
and the reafon is, that bodily pain is always attended
with a degree of impatience, which makes us think
every minute to be an hour. The fame holds where
the pain ſhifts from place to place ; but not fo remarkably, becaufe ſuch a pain is not attended with
the fame degree of impatience. The impatience a
man hath in travelling through a barren country, or
in a bad road, makes him think, during the journey,
that time goes on with a very ſlow pace. We ſhall
see

fee afterward, that a very different computation is made when the journey is over.

How ought it to ftand with a perfon who appre-hends bad news ? It will probably be thought, that the cafe of this perfon refembles that of a criminal, who, terrified at his approaching execution, believes every hour to be but a minute : yet the computation is dire&ly oppofite. Refle&ing upon the difficulty, there appears one capital diftinguifhing circumftance : the fate of the criminal is determined ; in the cafe under confideration, the perfon is ftill in fufpenfe. Every one has felt the diftrefs that accompanies fuf-penfe : we wifh to get rid of it at any rate, even at the expenfe of bad news. This cafe, therefore, upon a more narrow infpe&ion, refembles that of bodily pain : the prefent diftrefs, in both cafes, makes the time appear extremely tedious.

The reader probably will not be difpleafed, to have this branch of the fubje& illuftrated, by an author who is acquainted with every maze of the human heart, and who beftows ineffable grace and ornament upon every fubje& he handles :

Rofalinda. I pray you, what is't clock ?
Orlando. You fhould afk me, what time o'day ; there's no clock in the foreft.
Rof. Then there is no true lover in the foreft ; elfe, fighing every minute, and groaning every hour, would de-te&t the lazy foot of Time, as well as a clock.
Orla. Why not the fwift foot of Time ? Had not that been as proper ?
Rof. By no means, Sir. Time travels in diverfe paces with diverfe perfons. I'll tell you who Time ambles withal, who Time trots withal, who Time gallops withal, and who he ftands ftill withal.
Orla. I pr'ythee whom doth he trot withal ?
Rof. Marry, he trots hard with a young maid between the contra& of her marriage and the day it is folemnized :
it

if the interim be but a ſe'enight, Time's pace is ſo hard, that
it ſeems the length of ſeven years.

Orla. Whom ambles Time withal ?

Roſ. With a Prieſt that lacks Latin, and a rich man that
hath not the gout : for the one ſleeps eaſily, becauſe he
cannot ſtudy ; and the other lives merrily, becauſe he feels
no pain : the one lacking the burden of lean and waſteful
learning : the other knowing no burthen of heavy tedious
penury.   Theſe time ambles withal.

Orle. Whom doth he gallop withal !

Roſ. With a thief to the gallows : for, though he go as
ſoftly as foot can fall, he thinks himſelf too ſoon there.

Orla. Whom ſtays it ſtill withal ?

Roſ. With lawyers in the vacation : for they ſleep between term and term, and then they perceive not how Time
moves.

As you like it, act 3. ſc. 8.

The natural method of computing preſent time,
ſhows how far from truth we may be led by the
irregular influence of paſſion : nor are our eyes immediately opened when the ſcene is paſt ; for the deception continues while there remain any traces of
the paſſion.   But looking back upon paſt time when
the joy or diſtreſs is no longer remembered, the computation is very different : in that condition, we coolly and deliberately make uſe of the ordinary meaſure, namely, the courſe of our perceptions.   And I
ſhall now proceed to the errors that this meaſure is
ſubjected to.   Here we muſt diſtinguiſh between a
train of perceptions, and a train of ideas : real objects make a ſtrong impreſſion, and are faithfully remembered : ideas, on the contrary, however entertaining at the time, are apt to eſcape a ſubſequent recollection.   Hence it is, that in retroſpection, the time
that was employed upon real objects, appears longer
than that employed upon ideas : the former are more
accurately recollected than the latter ; and we meaſure

ure the time by the number that is recollected. This
doctrine ſhall be illuſtrated by examples. After finiſhing a journey through a populous country, the frequency of agreeable objects diſtinctly recollected by
the traveller, makes the time ſpent in the journey
appear to him longer than it was in reality; which
is chiefly remarkable in the firſt journey, when every
object is new, and makes a ſtrong impreſſion. On
the other hand, after finiſhing a journey through a
barren country thinly peopled, the time appears ſhort,
being meaſured by the number of objects, which were
few, and far from intereſting. Here in both inſtances
a computation is made, directly oppoſite to that made
during the journey. And this, by the way, ſerves
to account for what may appear ſingular, that, in a
barren country, a computed mile is always longer,
than near the capital, where the country is rich and
populous : the traveller has no natural meaſure of the
miles he has travelled, other than the time beſtowed
upon the journey; nor any natural meaſure of the
time, other than the number of his perceptions : now
theſe, being few from the paucity of objects in a waſte
country, lead him to compute that the time has been
ſhort, and conſequently that the miles have been few :
by the ſame method of computation, the great number
of perceptions, from the quantity of objects in a populous country, make the traveller conjecture that the
time has been long, and the miles many. The laſt
ſtep of the computation is obvious : in eſtimating the
diſtance of one place from another, if the miles be
reckoned few in number, each mile muſt of courſe be
long ; if many in number, each muſt be ſhort.

Again, the travelling with an agreeable companion,
produceth a ſhort computation both of the road and
of time ; eſpecially if there be few objects that demand attention, or if the objects be familiar : and the

K 2   caſe cafe is the fame of young people at a ball, or of a joyous company over a bottle : the ideas with which they have been entertained, being tranfitory, efcape the memory : after the journey and the entertainment are over, they reflect that they have been much diverted, but fcarce can fay about what.

When one is totally occupied with any agreeable work that admits not many objects, time runs on without obfervation : and upon a fubfequent recollection, muft appear fhort, in proportion to the paucity of objects. This is ftill more remarkable in clofe contemplation and in deep thinking, where the train, compofed wholly of ideas, proceeds with an extreme flow pace : not only are the ideas few in number, but are apt to efcape an after reckoning. The like falfe reckoning of time may proceed from an oppofite ftate of mind : in a reverie, where ideas float at random without making any impreffion, time goes on unheeded, and the reckoning is loft. A reverie may be fo profound as to prevent the recollection of any one idea : that the mind was bufied in a train of thinking, may in general be remembered : but what was the fubject, has quite efcaped the memory. In fuch a cafe, we are altogether at a lofs about the time, having no *data* for making a computation. No caufe produceth fo falfe a reckoning of time, as immoderate grief : the mind, in that ftate, is violently attached to a fingle object, and admits not a different thought : any other object breaking in, is inftantly banifhed, fo as fcarce to give an appearance of fucceffion. In a reverie, we are uncertain of the time that is paft ; but, in the example now given, there is an appearance of certainty, that the time muft have been fhort, when the perceptions are fo few in number.

The natural meafure of fpace, appears more obfcure than that of time. I venture, however, to mention

tion it, leaving it to be further profecuted, if it be thought of any importance.

The fpace marked out for a houfe appears confiderably larger after it is divided into its proper parts. A piece of ground appears larger after it is furrounded with a fence : and ftill larger when it is made a garden and divided into different compartments.

On the contrary, a large plain looks lefs after it is divided into parts. The fea muft be excepted, which looks lefs from that very circumftance of not being divided into parts.

A room of a moderate fize appears larger when properly furnifhed. But, when a very large room is furnifhed, I doubt whether it be not leffened in appearance.

A room of a moderate fize looks lefs by having a ceiling lower than in proportion. The fame low ceiling makes a very large room look larger than it is in reality.

Thefe experiments are by far too fmall a ftock for a general theory : but they are all that occur at prefent ; and, inftead of a regular fyftem, I have nothing for the reader's inftruction but a few conjectures.

The largeft angle of vifion feems to be the natural meafure of fpace : the eye is the only judge ; and in examining with it the fize of any plain, or the length of any line, the moft accurate method that can be taken is, to run over the object in parts : the largeft part that can be feen with one ftedfaft look, determines the largeft angle of vifion ; and, when that angle is given, one may inftitute a calculation, by trying with the eye how many of thefe parts are in the whole.

Whether this angle be the fame in all men, I know not : the fmalleft angle of vifion is afcertained ; and to afcertain the largeft would not be lefs curious.

K 3   But

But fuppofing it known, it would be a very imperfect meafure; perhaps more fo than the natural
meafure of time: for it requires great fteadinefs of
eye to meafure a line with any accuracy, by applying to it the largeft angle of diftinct vifion. And
fuppofing that fteadinefs to be acquired by practice,
the meafure will be imperfect from other circumftances. The fpace comprehended under this angle
will be different according to the diftance, and
alfo according to the fituation of the object: of
a perpendicular this angle will comprehend the fmalleft fpace; the fpace will be larger in looking upon an
inclined plain; and will be larger or lefs in proportion to the degree of inclination.

This meafure of fpace, like the meafure of time, is
liable to feveral errors, from certain operations of the
mind, which will account for fome of the erroneous
judgments above mentioned. The fpace marked out
for a dwelling-houfe, where the eye is at any reafonable diftance, is feldom greater than can be feen at
once, without moving the head: divide that fpace into
two or three equal parts, and none of thefe parts
will appear much lefs than what can be comprehended at one diftinct look; confequently each of them
will appear equal, or nearly equal, to what the whole
did before the divifion. If, on the other hand, the
whole be very fmall, fo as fcarce to fill the eye at one
look, its divifion into parts will, I conjecture, make it
appear ftill lefs: the minutenefs of the parts is, by
an eafy tranfition of ideas, transferred to the whole;
and we pafs the fame judgment on the latter that we
do on the former.

The fpace marked out for a fmall garden is furveyed
almoft at one view; and requires a motion of the eye
fo flight, as to pafs for an object that can be comprehended under the largeft angle of diftinct vifion: if
not

not divided into too many parts, we are apt to form the ſame judgment of each part, and confequently to magnify the garden in proportion to the number of its parts.

A very large plain without protuberances is an object no leſs rare than beautiful; and in thoſe who ſee it for the firſt time, it muſt produce an emotion of wonder. That emotion, however ſlight, impoſes on the mind, and makes it judge that the plain is larger than it is in reality. Divide the plain into parts, and our wonder ceaſes: it is no longer conſidered as one great plain, but as ſo many different fields or incloſures.

The firſt time one beholds the ſea, it appears to be large beyond all bounds. When it becomes familiar, and ceaſes to raiſe our wonder, it appears leſs than it is in reality. In a ſtorm it appears large, being diſtinguiſhable by the rolling waves into a number of great parts. Iſlands ſcattered at conſiderable diſtances, add in appearance to its ſize : each intercepted part looks extremely large, and we inſenſibly apply arithmetic to increaſe the appearance of the whole. Many iſlands ſcattered at hand, give a diminutive appearance to the ſea, by its connection with its diminutive parts : the Lomond lake would undoubtedly look larger without its iſlands.

Furniture increaſeth in appearance the ſize of a ſmall room, for the ſame reaſon that diviſions increaſe in appearance the ſize of a garden. The emotion of wonder, which is raiſed by a very large room without furniture makes it look larger than it is in reality : if completely furniſhed, we view it in parts, and our wonder is not raiſed.

A low ceiling hath a diminutive appearance, which by an eaſy tranſition of ideas, is communicated to the length and breadth, provided they bear any pro-

K 4   portion

portion to the height. If they be out of all proportion, the oppoſition ſeizes the mind and raiſes
ſome degree·of wonder, which makes the difference
appear greater than it really is.

PART VI.

The Reſemblance of Emotions to their Cauſes.

THAT many emotions have ſome reſem-
blance to their cauſes, is a truth that can be made clear
by induction ; though, as far as I know, the obſervation has not been made by any writer. Motion, in its
different circumſtances, is productive of feelings that
reſemble it : ſluggiſh motion, for example, cauſeth a
languid unpleaſant feeling ; ſlow uniform motion, a
feeling calm and pleaſant ; and briſk motion, a lively
feeling that rouſes the ſpirits, and promotes activity.
A fall of water through rocks, raiſes in the mind a
tumultuous confuſed agitation, extremely ſimilar to its
cauſe. When force is exerted with any effort, the
ſpectator feels a ſimilar effort, as of force exerted
within his mind. A large object ſwells in the heart.
An elevated object makes the ſpectator·ſtand erect.

Sounds alſo produce emotions or feelings that reſemble them. A ſound in a low key brings down the
mind : ſuch a ſound in a full tone hath a certain ſo-
lemnity, which it communicates to the feeling produced by it. A ſound in a high key cheers the mind by
raiſing it : ſuch a ſound in a full tone both elevates
and ſwells the mind.

Again, a wall or a pillar that declines from the perpendicular, produceth a painful feeling as of a tot-
tering

tering and falling within the mind : and a feeling
ſomewhat ſimilar is produced by a tall pillar that
ſtands ſo tickliſh as to look like falling.* A column with a baſe looks more firm and ſtable than
upon the naked ground ; and for that reaſon is
more agreeable ; and though the cylinder is a more
beautiful figure, yet the cube for a baſe is preferred ;
its angles being extended to a greater diſtance from
the centre than the circumference of a cylinder. This
excludes not a different reaſon, that the baſe, the
ſhaft, and the capital, of a pillar, ought, for the ſake
of variety, to differ from each other : if the ſhaft be
round, the baſe and capital ought to be ſquare.

A conſtrained poſture, uneaſy to the man himſelf,
is diſagreeable to the ſpectator ; whence a rule in
painting, that the drapery ought not to adhere to the
body, but hang looſe, that the figures may appear
eaſy and free in their movements. The conſtrained
poſture of a French dancing-maſter in one of Ho-
garth's pieces, is for that reaſon diſagreeable ; and it
is alſo ridiculous, becauſe the conſtraint is aſſumed as
a grace.

The foregoing obſervation is not confined to emotions or feelings raiſed by ſtill life : it holds alſo in
what are raiſed by the qualities, actions, and paſſions,
of a ſenſible being. Love inſpired by a fine woman,
aſſumes her qualities : it is ſublime, ſoft, tender, ſe-
vere, or gay, according to its cauſe. This is ſtill more
remarkable in emotions raiſed by human actions : it
hath already been remarked,† that any ſignal inſtance
of gratitude, beſide procuring eſteem for the author,

raiſeth

---

* Sunt enim Tempe ſaltus tranſitu difficiles : nam præter anguſtias per
quinque millia, qua exiguum jumento onuſto iter eſt, rupes utrinque ita
abſciſſæ ſunt, ut deſpici vix ſine vertigine quadam ſimul oculorum animi-
que poſſit.　*Titus Livius, lib.* 44. *ſect.* 6.

† Part 1. of this chapter, ſect. 4.

raifeth in the fpectator a vague emotion of gratitude,
which difpofeth him to be grateful ; and I now further remark, that this vague emotion hath a ftrong
refemblance to its caufe, namely, the paffion that produced the grateful action : courage exerted infpires
the reader as well as the fpectator with a like emotion of courage, a juft action fortifies our love of
juftice, and a generous action roufes our generofity.
In fhort, with refpect to all virtuous actions, it will be
found by induction, that they lead us to imitation by
infpiring emotions refembling the paffions that produce thefe actions.   And hence the advantage of
choice books and choice company.

Grief as well as joy are infectious : the emotions
they raife in a fpectator, refemble them perfectly.
Fear is equally infectious : and hence in an army, a
few taking fright, even without caufe, fpread the infection till it becomes an univerfal panic. Pity is fimilar to its caufe : a parting fcene between lovers or
friends produceth in the fpectator a fort of pity,
which is tender like the diftrefs : the anguifh of remorfe, produceth pity of a harfh kind ; and if the
remorfe be extreme, the pity hath a mixture of horror.   Anger I think is fingular : for even where it is
moderate, and caufeth no difguft, it difpofes not the
fpectator to anger in any degree.*   Covetoufnefs,
cruelty, treachery, and other vicious paffions, are fo
far from raifing any emotion fimilar to themfelves, to
incite a fpectator to imitation, that they have an oppofite effect : they raife abhorrence, and fortify the
fpectator in his averfion to fuch actions.   When
anger is immoderate, it cannot fail to produce the
fame effect.

PART

---

* Ariftotle, Poet. cap. 18. fect. 3. fays, that anger raifeth in the fpectator a fimilar emotion of anger.

PART VII.

Final Caufes of the more frequent Emotions and Paffions.

IT is a law in our nature, that we never act but by the impulfe of defire ; which in other words is faying, that paffion, by the defire included in it, is what determines the will. Hence in the conduct of life, it is of the utmoft importance, that our paffions be directed to proper objects, tend to juft and rational ends, and with relation to each other, be duly balanced. The beauty of contrivance, fo confpicuous, in the human frame, is not confined to the rational part of our nature, but is vifible over the whole. Concerning the paffions in particular, however irregular, headftrong, and perverfe, in a flight view, they may appear, I hope to demonftrate, that they are by nature modelled and tempered with perfect wifdom, for the good of fociety as well as for private good. The fubject, treated at large, would be too extenfive for the prefent work : all there is room for are a few general obfervations upon the fenfitive part of our nature, without regarding that ftrange irregularity of paffion difcovered in fome individuals. Such topical irregularities, if I may ufe the term, cannot fairly be held an objection to the prefent theory : we are frequently, it is true, mifled by inordinate paffion ; but we are alfo, and perhaps no lefs frequently, mifled by wrong judgment.

In order to fulfil my engagement, it muft be premifed, that an agreeable caufe produceth always a
pleafant

pleafant emotion ; and a difagreeable caufe, a painful
emotion. This is a general law of nature, which admits not a fingle exception : agreeablenefs in the
caufe is indeed fo effentially connected with pleafure
in the emotion, its effect, that an agreeable caufe
cannot be better defined, than by its power of producing a pleafant emotion : and difagreeablenefs in
the caufe has the fame neceffary connection with pain
in the emotion produced by it.

From this preliminary it appears, that in order to
know for what end an emotion is made pleafant or
painful, we muft begin with inquiring for what end
its caufe is made agreeable or difagreeable. And,
with refpect to inanimate objects, confidered as the
caufes of emotions, many of them are made agreeable in order to promote our happinefs ; and it proves
invincibly the benignity of the Deity, that we are
placed in the midft of objects for the moft part agreeable. But that is not all : the bulk of fuch objects,
being of real ufe in life, are made agreeable in order
to excite our induftry ; witnefs a large tree, a well
dreffed fallow, a rich field of grain, and others that
may be named without end. On the other hand, it
is not eafy to fpecify a difagreeable object that is not
at the fame time hurtful : fome things are made difagreeable, fuch as a rotten carcafs, becaufe they are
noxious : others, a dirty marfh, for example, or a
barren heath, are made difagreeable, in order, as
above, to excite our induftry. And, with refpect to
the few things that are neither agreeable nor difagreeable, it will be made evident, that their being left indifferent is not a work of chance, but of wifdom : of
fuch I fhall have occafion to give feveral inftances.

Becaufe inanimate objects that are agreeable fix
our attention, and draw us to them, they in that refpect are termed *attractive* : fuch objects infpire pleafant

ant emotions, which are gratified by adhering to the
objects, and enjoying them. Becaufe difagreeable
objects of the fame kind repel us from them, they in
that refpect are termed *repulſive :* and the painful
emotions raifed by fuch objects are gratified by flying
from them. Thus, in general, with refpect to things
inanimate, the tendency of every pleafant emotion is
to prolong the pleafure ; and the tendency of every
painful emotion is to end the pain.

Senfible beings confidered as objects of paſſion, lead
into a more complex theory. A fenfible being that
is agreeable by its attributes, infpires us with a pleafant emotion accompanied with defire ; and the queftion is, What is naturally the gratification of that defire ? Were man altogether felfifh, his nature would
lead him to indulge the pleafant emotion, without
making any acknowledgment to the perfon who gives
him pleafure, more than to a pure air or temperate
clime : but as man is endued with a principle of benevolence as well as of felfifhnefs, he is prompted by
his nature to defire the good of every fenfible being
that gives him pleafure ; and the happinefs of that
being is the gratification of his defire. The final caufe
of defire fo directed is illuftrious : it contributes to a
man's own happinefs, by affording him means of gratification beyond what felfifhnefs can afford ; and, at
the fame time, it tends eminently to advance the happinefs of others. This lays open a beautiful theory in
the nature of man : a felfifh action can only benefit
myfelf: a benevolent action benefits myfelf as much
as it benefits others. In a word, benevolence may
not improperly be faid to be the moft refined felfifhnefs ; which, by the way, ought to filence certain fhallow philofophers, who ignorant of human nature,
teach a difguftful doctrine, that to ferve others, unlefs
with a view to our own happinefs, is weaknefs and
folly ;

folly ; as if felf-love only, and not benevolence, contributed to our happinefs. The hand of God is too
vifible in the human frame, to permit us to think fe-
rioufly, that there ever can be any jarring or incon-
fiftency among natural principles, thofe efpecially of
felf-love and benevolence, which govern the bulk of
our actions*.

Next in order come fenfible beings that are in diftrefs. A perfon in diftrefs, being fo far a difagreeable object, muft raife in a fpectator a painful paffion ;
and, were man purely a felfifh being, he would defire to be relieved from that pain, by turning from
the object. But the principle of benevolence gives
an oppofite direction to his defire : it makes him defire to afford relief ; and by relieving the perfon from
diftrefs, his paffion is gratified. The painful paffion
thus directed, is termed *fympathy ;* which, though painful, is yet in its nature attractive. And, with refpect
to its final caufe, we can be at no lefs : it not only
tends to relieve a fellow creature from diftrefs, but in
its gratification is greatly more pleafant than if it were
repulfive.

We, in the laft place, bring under confideration
perfons hateful by vice or wickednefs. Imagine a
wretch

---

* With fhallow thinkers the felfifh fyftem naturally prevails in theory,
I do not fay in practice. During infancy, our defires centre moftly in
ourfelves : every one perceives intuitively the comfort of food and rai-
ment, of a fnug dwelling, and of every convenience. But that the doing
good to others will make us happy, is not fo evident ; feeding the hungry,
for example, or clothing the naked. This truth is feen but obfcurely by
the grofs of mankind, if at all feen : the fuperior pleafure that accompanies the exercife of benevolence, of friendfhip, and of every focial principle, is not clearly underftood till it be frequently felt. To perceive
the focial principle in its triumphant ftate, a man muft forget himfelf, and
turn his thoughts upon the character and conduct of his fellow creatures,
he will feel a fecret charm in every paffion that tends to the good of
others, and a fecret averfion againft every unfeeling heart that is indifferent to the happinefs and diftrefs of others. In a word, it is but too common for men to indulge felfifhnefs in themfelves ; but all men abhor
it in others.

wretch who has lately perpetrated fome horrid crime :
he is difagreeable to every fpectator ; and confequently raifeth in every fpectator a painful paffion.   What
is the natural gratification of that paffion ? I muft here
again obferve, that fuppofing man to be entirely a felfifh being, he would be prompted by his nature to relieve himfelf from the pain, by averting his eye, and
banifhing the criminal from his thoughts.   But man
is not fo conftituted : he is compofed of many principles, which, though feemingly contradictory, are perfectly concordant.   His actions are influenced by the
principle of benevolence, as well as by that of felfifhnefs : and in order to anfwer the foregoing queftion,
I muft introduce a third principle, no lefs remarkable
in its influence than either of thefe mentioned ; it is
that principle common to all, which prompts us to
punifh thofe who do wrong.   An envious, a malicious, or a cruel action, being difagreeable, raifeth in
the fpectator the painful emotion of refentment, which
frequently fwells into a paffion ; and the natural gratification of the defire included in that paffion, is to
punifh the guilty perfon : I muft chaftife the wretch
by indignation at leaft and hatred, if not more fevere-
ly.   Here the final caufe is felf-evident.

An injury done to myfelf, touching me more than
when done to others, raifes my refentment to a higher
degree.   The defire, accordingly, included in this
paffion, is not fatisfied with fo flight a punifhment as
indignation or hatred : it is not fully gratified without retaliation ; and the author muft by my hand
fuffer mifchief, as great at leaft as he has done to
me.   Neither can we be at any lofs about the final
caufe of that higher degree of refentment : the whole
vigour of the paffion is required to fecure individuals
from the injuftice and oppreffion of others.*

A wicked

* See Hiftorical Law Tracts, Tract 1.

A wicked or disgraceful action is disagreeable not only to others, but even to the delinquent himself; and raises in both a painful emotion including a desire of punishment. The painful emotion felt by the delinquent, is distinguished by the name of *remorse ;* which naturally excites him to punish himself. There cannot be imagined a better contrivance to deter us from vice ; for remorse itself is a severe punishment. That passion, and the desire of self-punishment derived from it, are touched delicately by Terence :

Menedemus. Ubi comperi ex iis, qui ei fuere confcii,
Domum revorter mœstus, atque animo fere
Perturbato, atque incerto præ ægritudine :
Adfido, adcurrunt fervi, foccos detrahunt :
Video alios feftinare, lectos fternere,
Cœnam adparare : pro fe quifque fedulo
Faciebat, quo illam mihi lenirent miferiam.
Ubi video hæc, cœpi cogitare : Hem ! tot mea
Solius folliciti fint caufa, ut me unum expleant ?
Ancillæ tot me veftiant ? fumptus domi
Tantos ego folus faciam ? fed gnatum unicum,
Quem pariter uti his decuit, aut etiam amplius,
Quod illa ætas magis ad hæc utenda idonea eft,
Eum ego hinc ejici miferum injuftitia mea.
Malo quidem me dignum quovis deputem,
Si id faciam : nam ufque dum ille vitam illam colet
Inopem, carens patria ob meas injurias,
Interea ufque illi de me fupplicium dabo :
Laborans, quærens, parcens, illi ferviens.
Ita facio prorfus : nihil relinquo in ædibus,
Nec vas, nec veftimentum : conrafi omnia,
Ancillas, fervos, nifi eos, qui opere ruftico
Faciundo facile fumptum exercerent fuum :
Omnes produxi ac vendidi : infcripfi illico
Ædes mercede : quafi talenta ad quindecim
Coëgi : agrum hunc mercatus fum : hic me exerceo,
Decrevi tantifper me minus injuriæ,
Chreme, meo gnato tacere, dum fiam mifer :
Nec fas effe ulla me voluptate hic trui,
Nifi ubi ille huc falvos redierit meus particeps.

Heautontimorumenos, act. 1. *fc.* 1.

Otway

Otway reaches the fame fentiment :

> *Monimia.*   Let mifchiefs multiply ! let ev'ry hour
> Of my loath'd life yield me increafe of horror ?
> Oh let the fun to thefe unhappy eyes
> Ne'er fhine again, but be eclips'd for ever !
> May every thing I look on feem a prodigy,
> To fill my foul with terror, till I quite
> Forget I ever had humanity,
> And grow a curfer of the works of nature !
>
> *Orphan,* act 4.

In the cafes mentioned, benevolence alone, or defire of punifhment alone, governs without a rival ;
and it was neceffary to handle thefe cafes feparately,
in order to elucidate a fubject which by writers is left
in great obfcurity.   But neither of thefe principles
operates always without rivalfhip : cafes may be figured, and cafes actually exift, where the fame perfon
is an object both of fympathy and of punifhment.
Thus the fight of a profligate in the venereal difeafe,
overrun with blotches and fores, puts both principles
in motion : while his diftrefs fixes my attention, fympathy prevails ; but as foon as I think of his profli-
gacy, hatred prevails, accompanied fometimes with a
defire to punifh.   This, in general, is the cafe of
diftrefs occafioned by immoral actions that are not
highly criminal : and if the diftrefs and the immoral
action make impreffions equal or nearly fo, fympathy
and hatred counterbalancing each other, will not
fuffer me either to afford relief, or to inflict punifhment.   What then will be the refult ? The principle
of felf-love folves the queftion : abhorring an object
fo loathfome, I naturally avert my eye, and walk off
as faft as I can, in order to be relieved from the pain.

The

The preſent ſubjeƈt gives birth to ſeveral other obſervations, for which I could not find room above,
without relaxing more from the ſtriƈtneſs of order and
conneƈtion, than with ſafety could be indulged in diſ-
courſing upon an intricate ſubjeƈt. Theſe obſervations I ſhall throw out looſely as they occur.

No aƈtion, right nor wrong, is indifferent even to
a mere ſpeƈtator : if right, it inſpires eſteem ; diſguſt,
if wrong. But it is remarkable, that theſe·emotions
ſeldom are accompanied with deſire : the abilities of
man are limited, and he finds ſufficient employment, in relieving the diſtreſſed, in requiting his bene-
faƈtors, and in puniſhing thoſe who wrong him, without moving out of his ſphere for the benefit or chaſ-
tiſement of thoſe with whom he has no conneƈtion.

If the good qualities of others raiſe my eſteem, the
ſame qualities in ·myſelf muſt produce a ſimilar effeƈt
in a ſuperior degree, upon account of the natural
partiality ·every man hath for himſelf : and this increaſes ſelf-love. If theſe qualities be of a high rank,
they produce a conviƈtion of ſuperiority, which excites me to aſſume ſome ſort of government over others. Mean qualities, on the other hand, produce in
me a conviƈtion of inferiority, which makes me ſubmit to others. Theſe conviƈtions, diſtributed among
individuals by meaſure and proportion, may juſtly be eſteemed the ſolid baſis of government; becauſe upon them
depend the natural ſubmiſſion of the many to the few,
without which even the mildeſt government would be
in a violent ſtate, and have a conſtant tendency to
diſſolution.

No other branch of the human conſtitution ſhows
more viſibly our deſtination for ſociety, nor tends
more to our improvement, than appetite for fame or
eſteem : for as the whole conveniencies of life are derived from mutual aid and ſupport in ſociety, it ought

to

to be a capital aim to ſecure theſe conveniencies, by gaining the eſteem and affection of others. Reaſon, indeed, dictates that leſſon : but reaſon alone is not ſufficient in a matter of ſuch importance ; and the appetite mentioned is a motive more powerful than reaſon, to be active in gaining eſteem and affection. That appetite, at the ſame time, is finely adjuſted to the moral branch of our conſtitution, by promoting all the moral virtues : for what means are there to attract love and eſteem ſo effectual as a virtuous courſe of life ? If a man be juſt and beneficent, if he be temperate, modeſt, and prudent, he will infallibly gain the eſteem and love of all who know him.

Communication of paſſion to related objects, is an illuſtrious inſtance of the care of Providence to extend ſocial connections as far as the limited nature of man can admit. That communication is ſo far hurtful, as to ſpread the malevolent paſſions beyond their natural bounds : but let it be remarked, that this unhappy effect regards ſavages only, who give way to malevolent paſſions ; for under the diſcipline of ſociety, theſe paſſions being ſubdued, are in a good meaſure eradicated ; and in their place ſucceed the kindly affections, which, meeting with all encouragement, take poſſeſſion of the mind, and govern all our actions. In that condition, the progreſs of paſſion along related objects, by ſpreading the kindly affections through a multitude of individuals, hath a glorious effect.

Nothing can be more entertaining to a rational mind, than the economy of the human paſſions, of which I have attempted to give ſome faint notion. It muſt however be acknowledged, that our paſſions, when they happen to ſwell beyond proper limits, take on a leſs regular appearance : reaſon may proclaim

our duty, but the will, influenced by paſſion, makes
gratification always welcome. Hence the power of
paſſion, which, when in exceſs, cannot be reſiſted
but by the utmoſt fortitude of mind; it is bent upon
gratification; and where proper objects are wanting,
it clings to any object at hand without diſtinction.
Thus joy inſpired by a fortunate event, is diffuſed
upon every perſon around by acts of benevolence;
and reſentment for an atrocious injury done by one
out of reach, ſeizes the firſt object that occurs to vent
itſelf upon. Thoſe who believe in prophecies, even
wiſh the accompliſhment; and a weak mind is diſpoſed voluntarily to fulfil a prophecy, in order to
gratify its wiſh. Shakeſpear, whom no particle of
human nature hath eſcaped, however remote from
common obſervation, deſcribes that weakneſs:

K. Henry. Doth any name particular belong
Unto that lodging where I firſt did ſwoon?
Warwick. 'Tis call'd *Jeruſalem,* my Noble Lord.
K. Henry. Laud be to God! ev'n there my life muſt end,
It hath been propheſy'd to me many years,
I ſhould not die but in Jeruſalem,
Which vainly I ſuppos'd the holy land.
But bear me to that chamber, there I'll lie;
In that Jeruſalem ſhall Henry die.
Second part, Henry IV. *act* 4. *ſc. laſt.*

I could not deny myſelf the amuſement of the foregoing obſervation, though it doth not properly come
under my plan. The irregularities of paſſion proceeding from peculiar weakneſſes and biaſſes, I do
not undertake to juſtify; and of theſe we have had
many examples.* It is ſufficient that paſſions common to all, are made ſubſervient to beneficent purpoſes. I ſhall only obſerve, that, in a poliſhed ſociety, inſtances of irregular paſſions are rare, and that
their miſchief doth not extend far.

CHAP.

* Part 5. of the preſent chapter.

Beauty.

HAVING difcourfed in general of emotions and paffions, I proceed to a more narrow infpection of fuch of them as ferve to unfold the principles of the fine arts. It is the province of a writer upon eth ics, to give a full enumeration of all the paffions, and of each feparately to affign the nature, the caufe, the gratification, and the effects. But a treatife of ethics is not my province; I carry my view no farther than to the elements of criticifm, in order to fhow, that the fine arts are a fubject of reafoning as well as of tafte. An extenfive work would ill fuit a defign fo limited ; and to confine this work within moderate bounds, the following plan may contribute. The obfervation made above, that things are the caufes of emotions, by means of their properties and attributes,* furnifheth a hint for diftribution. Inftead of a painful and tedious examination of the feveral paffions and emotions, I purpofe to confine my inquiries to fuch attributes, relations, and circumftances, as in the fine arts are chiefly employed to raife agreeable emotions. Attributes of fingle objects, as the moft fimple, fhall take the lead ; to be followed with particulars, which, depending on relations, are not found in fingle objects. Difpatching next fome coincident matters, I proceed to my chief aim ; which is, to eftablifh practical rules for the fine arts, derived from principles previoufly eftablifhed. This is a general view of the intended method : referving however a privilege

L 3

---

* Chap. 2, part 1. fect. 1. firft note.

a privilege to vary it in particular inſtances, where a deviation may be more commodious. I begin with beauty, the moſt noted of all the qualities that be-long to ſingle objeċts.

The term *beauty*, in its native ſignification, is ap-propriated to objeċts of ſight : objeċts of the other ſenſes may be agreeable, ſuch as the ſounds of muſic-al inſtruments, the ſmoothneſs and ſoftneſs of ſome ſurfaces : but the agreeableneſs denominated *beauty* belongs to objeċts of ſight.

Of all the objeċts of external ſenſe, an objeċt of ſight is the moſt complex : in the very ſimpleſt, colour is perceived, figure, and length, breadth, and thick-neſs. A tree is compoſed of a trunk, branches, and leaves ; it has colour, figure, ſize, and ſometimes motion : by means of each of theſe particulars, ſepa-rately conſidered, it appears beautiful ; how much more ſo, when they are all united together ? The beauty of the human figure is extraordinary, being a compoſition of numberleſs beauties ariſing from the parts and qualities of the objeċt, various colours, va-rious motions, figures, ſize, &c. all united in one complex objeċt, and ſtriking the eye with combined force. Hence it is, that beauty, a quality ſo remark-able in viſible objeċts, lends its name to expreſs every thing that is eminently agreeable : thus, by a figure of ſpeech, we ſay a beautiful ſound, a beautiful thought or expreſſion, a beautiful theorem, a beau-tiful event, a beautiful diſcovery in art or ſcience. But, as figurative expreſſion is the ſubjeċt of a follow-ing chapter, this chapter is confined to beauty in its proper ſignification.

It is natural to ſuppoſe, that a perception ſo vari-ous as that of beauty, comprehending ſometimes many particulars, ſometimes few, ſhould occaſion emotions equally various : and yet all the various emotions

of

of beauty maintain one common character, that of fweetnefs and gaiety.

Confidering attentively the beauty of vifible objects, we difcover two kinds. The firft may be termed *intrinfic* beauty, becaufe it is difcovered in a fingle object viewed apart without relation to any other : the examples above given are of that kind. The other may be termed *relative* beauty, being founded on the relation of objects. The purpofed diftribution would lead me to handle thefe beauties feparately; but they are frequently fo intimately connected, that, for the fake of connection, I am forced, in this inftance, to vary from the plan, and to bring them both into the fame chapter. Intrinfic beauty is an object of fenfe merely : to perceive the beauty of a fpreading oak, or of a flowing river, no more is required but fingly an act of vifion. The perception of relative beauty is accompanied with an act of underftanding and reflection : for of a fine inftrument or engine, we perceive not the relative beauty, until we be made acquainted with its ufe and deftination. In a word, intrinfic beauty is ultimate : relative beauty is that of means relating to fome good end or purpofe. Thefe different beauties agree in one capital circumftance, that both are equally perceived as belonging to the object. This is evident with refpect to intrinfic beauty ; but will not be fo readily admitted with refpect to the other : the utility of the plough, for example, may make it an object of admiration or of defire ; but why fhould utility make it appear beautiful ? A natural propenfity mentioned above* will explain that doubt : the beauty of the effect, by an eafy tranfition of ideas, is transferred to the caufe ; and is perceived as one of the qualities of
the

* Chap. 2. part 1. fect. 5.

the caufe. Thus a fubject void of intrinfic beauty appears beautiful from its utility ; an old Gothic tower, that has no beauty in itfelf, appears beautiful, confidered as proper to defend againft an enemy ; a dwelling-houfe void of all regularity, is however beautiful in the view of convenience ; and the want of form or fymmetry in a tree, will not prevent its appearing beautiful, if it be known to produce good fruit.

When thefe two beauties coincide in any object, it ap-pears delightful : every member of the human body poffeffes both in a high degree : the fine proportions and flender make of a horfe deftined for running, pleafe every eye ; partly from fymmetry, and partly from utility.

The beauty of utility, being proportioned accu-rately to the degree of utility, requires no illuftra-tion : but intrinfic beauty, fo complex as I have faid, cannot be handled diftinctly without being analyfed into its conftituent parts. If a tree be beautiful by means of its colour, its figure, its fize, its motion, it is in reality poffeffed of fo many different beauties, which ought to be examined feparately, in order to have a clear notion of them when combined. The beauty of colour is too familiar to need explanation. Do not the bright and cheerful colours of gold and filver contribute to preferve thefe metals in high efti-mation ? The beauty of figure, arifing from various circumftances and different views, is more complex : for example, viewing any body as a whole, the beau-ty of its figure arifes from regularity and fimplicity ; viewing the parts with relation to each other, uni-formity, proportion, and order, contribute to its beauty. The beauty of motion deferves a chapter by itfelf ; and another chapter is deftined for grandeur, being diftinguifhable from beauty in its proper fenfe.

For

For a defcription of regularity, uniformity, proportion, and order, if thought neceffary, I remit my
reader to the Appendix at the end of the book. Upon fimplicity I muft make a few curfory obfervations,
fuch as may be of ufe in examining the beauty of
fingle objects.

A multitude of objects crowding into the mind at
once, difturb the attention, and pafs without making
any impreffion, or any diftinct impreffion ; in a
group, no fingle object makes the figure it would do
apart, when it occupies the whole attention.* For
the fame reafon, the impreffion made by an object
that divides the attention by the multiplicity of its
parts, equals not that of a more fimple object comprehended in a fingle view : parts extremely complex muft be confidered in portions fucceffively ; and
a number of impreffions in fucceffion, which cannot
unite becaufe not fimultaneous, never touch the mind
like one entire impreffion made as it were at one
ftroke. This juftifies fimplicity in works of art, as
oppofed to complicated circumftances and crowded
ornaments. There is an additional reafon for fimplicity, in works of dignity or elevation ; which is,
that the mind attached to beauties of a high rank,
cannot defcend to inferior beauties. The beft artifts
accordingly have in all ages been governed by a tafte
for fimplicity. How comes it then that we find profufe decoration prevailing in works of art ? The reafon plainly is, that authors and architects who cannot reach the higher beauties, endeavour to fupply
want of genius by multiplying thofe that are inferior.

Thefe things premifed, I proceed to examine the
beauty of figure as arifing from the above-mentioned
                                        particulars,

* See the Appendix, containing definitions, and explanation of terms,
fect. 33.

particulars, namely, regularity, uniformity, proportion, order, and fimplicity. To exhauft this fubject
would require a volume ; and I have not even a
whole chapter to fpare. To inquire why an object,
by means of the particulars mentioned, appears beautiful, would, I am afraid, be a vain attempt : it
feems the moft probable opinion, that the nature of
man was originally framed with a relifh for them, in
order to anfwer wife and good purpofes. To explain
thefe purpofes or final caufes, though a fubject of
great importance, has fcarce been attempted by any
writer. One thing is evident, that our relifh for the
particulars mentioned adds much beauty to the objects that furround us ; which of courfe tends to our
happinefs : and the Author of our nature has given
many fignal proofs that this final caufe is not below
his care. We may be confirmed in this thought upon reflecting, that our tafte for thefe particulars is
not accidental, but uniform and univerfal, making a
branch of our nature. At the fame time, it ought
not to be overlooked, that regularity, uniformity,
order, and fimplicity, contribute each of them to
readinefs of apprehenfion ; enabling us to form more
diftinct images of objects, than can be done with the
utmoft attention where thefe particulars are not found.
With refpect to proportion, it is in fome inftances
connected with a ufeful end, as in animals, where
the beft proportioned are the ftrongeft and moft active ; but inftances are ftill more numerous, where
the proportions we relifh have no connection with
utility. Writers on architecture infift much on the
proportions of a column, and affign different proportions to the Doric, Ionic, and Corinthian : but no
architect will maintain, that the moft accurate proportions contribute more to ufe, than feveral that are
lefs accurate and lefs agreeable ; neither will it be
maintained,

maintained, that the length, breadth, and height of. rooms affigned as the moft beautiful proportions, tend alfo to make them the more commodious. With re- fpect then to the final caufe of proportion, I fee not more to be made of it but to reft upon the final caufe firft mentioned, namely, its contributing to our hap- pinefs, by increafing the beauty of vifible objects.

And now with refpect to the beauty of figure as far as it depends on the other circumftances men- tioned ; as to which, having room only for a flight fpecimen, I confine myfelf to the fimpleft figures. A circle and a fquare are each of them perfectly regu- lar, being equally confined to a precife form, which admits not the flighteft variation : a fquare, however, is lefs beautiful than a circle. And the reafon feems to be, that the attention is divided among the fides and angles of a fquare : whereas the circumference of a circle, being a fingle object, makes one entire impreffion. And thus fimplicity contributes to beau- ty : which may be illuftrated by another exam- ple : a fquare, though not more regular than a hexa- gon or octagon, is more beautiful than either ; for what other reafon, but that a fquare is more fimple, and the attention lefs divided ? This reafoning will appear ftill more conclufive, when we confider any regular polygon of very many fides ; for of this figure the mind can never have any diftinct perception.

A fquare is more regular than a parallelogram, and its parts more uniform ; and for thefe reafons it is more beautiful. But that holds with refpect to in- trinfic beauty only ; for in many inftances utility turns the fcale on the fide of the parallelogram : this figure for the doors and windows of a dwelling-houfe is preferred, becaufe of utility ; and here we find the beauty of utility prevailing over that of regularity and uniformity.

A parallelogram

A parallelogram again depends, for its beauty, on the proportion of its fides : a great inequality of fides annihilates its beauty : approximation towards equality hath the fame effect ; for proportion there degenerates into imperfect uniformity, and the figure appears an unfuccefsful attempt toward a fquare. And thus proportion contributes to beauty.

An equilateral triangle yields not to a fquare in regularity, nor in uniformity of parts, and it is more fimple. But an equilateral triangle is lefs beautiful than a fquare ; which muft be owing to inferiority of order in the pofition of its parts : the fides of an equilateral triangle incline to each other in the fame angle, being the moft perfect order they are fufceptible of ; but this order is obfcure, and far from being fo perfect as the parallelifm of the fides of a fquare. Thus order contributes to the beauty of vifible objects, no lefs than fimplicity, regularity, or proportion.

A parallelogram exceeds an equilateral triangle in the orderly difpofition of its parts ; but being inferior in uniformity and fimplicity, it is lefs beautiful.

Uniformity is fingular in one capital circumftance, that it is apt to difguft by excefs ; a number of things deftined for the fame ufe, fuch as windows, chairs, fpoons, buttons, cannot be too uniform ; for fuppofing their figure to be good, utility requires uniformity : but a fcrupulous uniformity of parts in a large garden or field, is far from being agreeable. Uniformity among connected objects belongs not to the prefent fubject : it is handled in the chapter of uniformity and variety.

In all the works of nature, fimplicity makes an illuftrious figure. It alfo makes a figure in works of art : profufe ornament in painting, gardening, or architecture,

chitecture, as well as in drefs or in language, fhows a mean or corrupted tafte :

> Poets, like painters, thus unfkill'd to trace
> The naked nature and the living grace,
> With gold and jewels cover ev'ry part,
> And hide with ornaments their want of art.
>
> *Pope's Effay on Criticifm.*

No fingle property recommends a machine more than its fimplicity ; not folely for better anfwering its pur-pofe, but by appearing in itfelf more beautiful. Sim-plicity in behaviour and manners has an enchanting effect, and never fails to gain our affection : very dif-ferent are the artificial manners of modern times. General theorems, abftracting from their importance, are delightful by their fimplicity, and by the eafinefs of their application to variety of cafes. We take equal delight in the laws of motion, which, with the greateft fimplicity, are boundlefs in their operations.

A gradual progrefs from fimplicity to complex forms and profufe ornament, feems to be the fate of all the fine arts : in that progrefs thefe arts refem-ble behaviour, which, from original candour and fimplicity, has degenerated into artificial refinements. At prefent, literary productions are crowded with words, epithets, figures : in mufic, fentiment is neg-lected for the luxury of harmony, and for difficult movement : in *tafte* properly fo called, poignant fauces, with complicated mixtures of different favours, prevail among people of condition : the French, ac-cuftomed to artificial red on a female cheek, think the modeft colouring of nature altogether infipid.

The fame tendency is difcovered in the progrefs of the fine arts among the ancients. Some veftiges of the old Grecian buildings prove them to be of the Doric order : the Ionic fucceeded, and feems to have

been

been the favourite order, while architecture was in the height of glory : the Corinthian came next in vogue ; and in Greece the buildings of that order appear moſtly to have been erected after the Romans got footing there. At laſt came the Compoſite, with all its extravagancies, where ſimplicity is ſacrificed to finery and crowded ornament.

But what taſte is to prevail next ? for faſhion is a continual flux, and taſte muſt vary with it. After rich and profuſe ornaments become familiar, ſimplicity apears lifeleſs and inſipid ; which would be an inſurmountable obſtruction, ſhould any perſon of genius and taſte endeavour to reſtore ancient ſimplicity.*

The diſtinction between primary and ſecondary qualities in matter, ſeems now fully eſtabliſhed. Heat and cold, ſmell and taſte, though ſeeming to exiſt in bodies, are diſcovered to be effects cauſed by theſe bodies in a ſenſitive being : colour, which appears to the eye as ſpread upon a ſubſtance, has no exiſtence but in the mind of the ſpectator. Qualities of that kind, which owe their exiſtence to the percipient as much as to the object, are termed *ſecondary* qualities, and are diſtinguiſhed from figure, extenſion, ſolidity, which, in contradiſtinction to the former, are termed *primary* qualities, becauſe they inhere in ſubjects whether perceived or not. This diſtinction ſuggeſts a curious inquiry, Whether beauty be a primary or only a ſecondary quality of objects ? The queſtion is eaſily determined with reſpect to the beauty of colour ; for, if colour be a ſecondary quality, exiſting

no

* A ſprightly writer obferves, " that the noble ſimplicity of the Auguſtan age was driven out by falſe taſte ; that the gigantic, the puerile, the quaint, and at laſt the barbarous and the monkiſh, had each their ſucceſſive admirers : that muſic has become a ſcience of tricks and ſlight of hand," &c.

no where but in the mind of the fpectator, its beauty
muft exift there alfo. This conclufion equally holds
with refpect to the beauty of utility, which is plainly
a conception of the mind, arifing not from fight, but
from reflecting that the thing is fitted for fome good
end or purpofe. The queftion is more intricate with
refpect to the beauty of regularity; for, if regularity
be a primary quality, why not alfo its beauty? That
this is not a good inference, will appear from confidering, that beauty, in its very conception, refers to
a percipient; for an object is faid to be beautiful, for
no other reafon but that it appears fo to a fpectator:
the fame piece of matter that to a man appears beautiful, may poffibly appear ugly to a being of a different fpecies. Beauty, therefore, which for its exiftence depends on the percipient as much as on the object perceived, cannot be an inherent property in
either. And hence it is wittily obferved by the poet,
that beauty is not in the perfon beloved, but in the
lover's eye. This reafoning is folid; and the only
caufe of doubt or hefitation is, that we are taught a
different leffon by fenfe: a fingular determination of
nature makes us perceive both beauty and colour as
belonging to the object, and, like figure or extenfion, as
inherent properties. This mechanifm is uncommon;
and, when nature, to fulfil her intention, prefers any
fingular method of operation, we may be certain of
fome final caufe that cannot be reached by ordinary
means. For the beauty of fome objects we are indebted entirely to nature: but, with refpect to the
endlefs variety of objects that owe their beauty to art
and culture, the perception of beauty greatly promotes induftry; being to us a ftrong additional incitement to enrich our fields, and improve our manufactures. Thefe, however, are but flight effects,
compared with the connections that are formed among
individuals

individuals in fociety by means of this fingular me＊chanifm : the qualifications of the head and heart form undoubtedly the moft folid and moft permanent connections ; but external beauty, which lies more in view, has a more extenfive influence in forming thefe connections : at any rate, it concurs in an eminent degree with mental qualifications to produce focial intercourfe, mutual good-will, and confequently mu＊tual aid and fupport, which are the life of fociety.

It muft not, however, be overlooked, that the per＊ception of beauty doth not, when immoderate, tend to advance the interefts of fociety. Love, in particu-lar, arifing from a perception of beauty, lofes, when exceffive, its fociable charaĉter : the appetite for grat＊ification prevailing over affeĉtion for the beloved ob＊ject, is ungovernable ; and tends violently to its end, regardlefs of the mifery that muft follow. Love, in that ſtate, is no longer a ſweet agreeable paffion : it becomes painful, like hunger or thirft ; and produc-eth no happinefs but in the inftant of fruition. This difcovery fuggefts a moft important leffon, That moderation in our defires and appetites, which fits us for doing our duty, contributes at the fame time the moft to happinefs : even focial paffions, when moderate, are more pleafant than when they fwell beyond proper bounds.

CHAP.

CHAP. IV.

Grandeur and Sublimity.

NATURE hath not more remarkably diſtinguiſhed us from other animals by an erect poſture, than by a capacious and aſpiring mind, attaching us to things great and elevated. The ocean, the ſky, ſeize the attention, and make a deep impreſſion:* robes of ſtate are made large and full, to draw reſpect; we admire an elephant for its magnitude, notwithſtanding its unwieldineſs.

The elevation of an object affects us no leſs than its magnitude : a high place is choſen for the ſtatue of a deity or hero : a tree growing on the brink of a precipice looks charming when viewed from the plain below : a throne is erected for the chief magiſtrate ; and a chair with a high ſeat for the preſident of a court. Among all nations, heaven is placed far above us, hell far below us.

In ſome objects, greatneſs and elevation concur to make a complicated impreſſion : the Alps and the Peak of Teneriff are proper examples ; with the following difference, that in the former greatneſs ſeems to prevail, elevation in the latter.

The emotions raiſed by great and by elevated objects, are clearly diſtinguiſhable, not only in internal feeling, but even in their external expreſſions. A great object

* Longinus obſerves, that nature inclines us to admire, not a ſmall rivalet, however clear and tranſparent, but the Nile, the Iſter, the Rhine, or ſtill more the ocean. The ſight of a ſmall fire produceth no emotion ; but we are ſtruck with the boiling furnaces of Ætna, pouring out whole, rivers of liquid flame. *Treatiſe of the Sublime, chap. 29.*

object makes the spectator endeavour to enlarge his
bulk ; which is remarkable in plain people who give
way to nature without referve ; in defcribing a great
object, they naturally expand themfelves by drawing
in air with all their force.   An elevated object produces a different expreffion : it makes the spectator
ftretch upward, and ftand a-tiptoe.

Great and elevated objects confidered with relation to the emotions produced by them, are termed
grand and *fublime*.   *Grandeur* and *fublimity* have a
double fignification : they commonly fignify the
quality or circumftance in objects by which the
emotions of grandeur and fublimity are produced ;
fometimes the emotions themfelves.

In handling the prefent fubject, it is neceffary that
the impreffion made on the mind by the magnitude of
an object, abftracting from its other qualities, fhould
be afcertained.   And becaufe abftraction is a mental
operation of fome difficulty, the fafeft method for
judging is, to choofe a plain object that is neither
beautiful nor deformed, if fuch a one can be found.
The plaineft that occurs, is a huge mafs of rubbifh,
the ruins, perhaps, of fome extenfive building, or a
large heap of ftones, fuch as are collected together .
for keeping in memory a battle or other remarkable
event.   Such an object, which in miniature would be
perfectly indifferent, makes an impreffion by its magnitude, and appears agreeable.   And fuppofing it fo
large, as to fill the eye, and to prevent the attention
from wandering upon other objects, the impreffion it
makes will be fo much the deeper.*

But though a plain object of that kind be agreeable, it is not termed *grand* : it is not entitled to that
character, unlefs, together with its fize, it be poffeffed
                                                        of

---

* See Appendix, Terms defined, fect. 33.

of other qualities that contribute to beauty, fuch as regularity, proportion, order, or colour : and according to the number of fuch qualities combined with magnitude, it is more or lefs grand. Thus, St Peter's church at Rome, the great pyramid of Egypt, the Alps towering above the clouds, a great arm of the fea, and above all, a clear and ferene fky, are grand, becaufe, befide their fize, they are beauti-' ful in an eminent degree. On the other hand, an overgrown whale, having a difagreeable appearance, is not grand. A large building, agreeable by its regularity and proportions, is grand, and yet a much larger building deftitute of regularity, has not the leaft tincture of grandeur. A fingle regiment in battle-array, makes a grand appearance ; which the furrounding croud does not, though perhaps ten for one in number. And a .regiment where the men are all in one livery, and the horfes of one colour, makes a grander appearance, and confequently ftrikes more terror, than where there is confufion of colours and of drefs. Thus greatnefs or magnitude is the circumftance that diftinguifhes grandeur from beauty : agreeablenefs is the genus, of which beauty and grandeur are fpecies.

The emotion of grandeur, duly examined, will be found an additional proof of the foregoing doctrine. That this emotion is pleafant in a high degree, requires no other evidence but once to have feen a grand object ; and if an emotion of grandeur be pleafant, its caufe or object, as obferved above, muft infallibly be agreeable in proportion.

The qualities of grandeur and beauty are not more diftinct, than the emotions are which thefe qualities produce in a fpectator. It is obferved in the chapter immediately foregoing, that all the various emotions

M 2

tions of beauty have one common character, that of fweetnefs and gaiety. The emotion of grandeur has a different character : a large object that is agreeable, occupies the whole attention, and fwells the heart into a vivid emotion, which, though extremely pleafant, is rather ferious than gay. And this affords a good reafon for diftinguifhing in language thefe different emotions. The emotions raifed by colour, by regularity, by proportion, and by order, have fuch a refemblance to each other, as readily to come under one general term, *viz. the emotion of beauty :* but the emotion of grandeur is fo different from thefe mentioned, as to merit a peculiar name.

Though regularity, proportion, order, and colour, contribute to grandeur, as well as to beauty, yet thefe qualities are not by far fo effential to the former as to the latter. To make out that propofition, fome preliminaries are requifite. In the firft place, the mind, not being totally occupied with a fmall object, can give its attention at the fame time to every minute part ; but in a great or extenfive object, the mind being totally occupied with the capital and ftriking parts, has no attention left for thofe that are little or indifferent. In the next place, two fimilar objects appear not fimilar when viewed at different diftances ; the fimilar parts of a very large object cannot be feen but at different diftances ; and for that reafon, its regularity, and the proportion of its parts, are in fome meafure loft to the eye ; neither are the irregularities of a very large object fo confpicuous as of one that is fmall. Hence it is, that a large object is not fo agreeable by its regularity, as a fmall object ; nor fo difagreeable by its irregularities.

Thefe confiderations make it evident, that grandeur is fatisfied with a lefs degree of regularity and of the other qualities mentioned, than is requifite for

beauty ;

beauty ; which may be illuſtrated by the following experiment. Approaching to a ſmall conical hill, we take an accurate ſurvey of every part, and are ſenſible of the ſlighteſt deviation from regularity and proportion. Suppoſing the hill to be conſiderably enlarged, ſo as to make us leſs ſenſible of its regularity, it will, upon that account, appear leſs beautiful. It will not, however, appear leſs agreeable, becauſe ſome ſlight emotion of grandeur, come in place of what is loſt in beauty. And at laſt, when the hill is enlarged to a great mountain, the ſmall degree of beauty that is left, is ſunk in its grandeur. Hence it is, that a towering hill is delightful, if it have but the ſlighteſt reſemblance of a cone ; and a chain of mountains no leſs ſo, though deficient in the accuracy of order and proportion. We require a ſmall ſurface to be ſmooth ; but in an extenſive plain, conſiderable inequalities are overlooked. In a word, regularity, proportion, order, and colour, contribute to grandeur as well as to beauty ; but with a remarkable difference, that in paſſing from ſmall to great, they are not required in the ſame degree of perfection. This remark ſerves to explain the extreme delight we have in viewing the face of nature, when ſufficiently enriched and diverſified with objects. The bulk of the objects in a natural landſcape are beautiful, and ſome of them grand : a flowing river, a ſpreading oak, a round hill, an extended plain, are delightful ; and even a rugged rock or barren heath, though in themſelves diſagreeable, contribute by contraſt to the beauty of the whole : joining to theſe, the verdure of the fields, the mixture of light and ſhade, and the ſublime canopy ſpread over all ; it will not appear wonderful, that ſo extenſive a group of ſplendid objects ſhould ſwell the heart to its utmoſt bounds,

and

M 3

and raife the ftrongeft emotion of grandeur. The fpectator is confcious of an enthufiafm, which cannot bear confinement, nor the ftrictnefs of regularity and order : he loves to range at large ; and is fo enchanted with magnificent objects, as to overlook flight beauties or. deformities.

The fame obfervation is applicable in fome meafure to works of art : in a fmall building, the flighteft irregularity is difagreeable : but, in a magnificent palace, or a large Gothic church, irregularities are lefs regarded : in an epic poem we pardon many negligences that would not be permitted in a fonnet or epigram. Notwithftanding fuch exceptions, it may be juftly laid down for a rule, That in works of art, order and regularity ought to be governing principles : and hence the obfervation of Longinus,* " In works of art we have regard to exact proportion ; in thofe of nature, to grandeur and magnificence."

The fame reflections are in a good meafure applicable to fublimity ; particularly, that, like grandeur, it is a fpecies of agreeablenefs ; that a beautiful object placed high, appearing more agreeable than formerly, produces in the fpectator a new emotion, termed *the emotion of fublimity* ; and that the perfection of order, regularity, and proportion, is lefs required in objects placed high, or at a diftance, than at hand.

The pleafant emotion raifed by large objects, has not efcaped the poets ;

———————He doth beftride the narrow world
Like a Coloffus : and we petty men
Walk under his huge legs.
                                    Julius Cæfar, act 1. *fc.* 3.

  Cleopatra. I dreamt there was an Emp'ror'Antony ;
Oh fuch another fleep, that I might fee
But fuch another man !   His

---

* Chap. 30.

His face was as the heavens : and therein stuck
A sun and moon, which kept their course, and lighted
The little O o' th' earth.
His legs bestrid the ocean, his rear'd arm
Crested the world.

Antony and Cleopatra, act 5. *sc.* 3.

—————·—————————Majesty
Dies not alone, but, like a gulph, doth draw
What's near it with it. It's a massy wheel
Fix'd on the summit of the highest mount ;
To whose huge spokes, ten thousand lesser things
Are mortis'd and adjoin'd, which when it falls,
Each small annexment, petty consequence,
Attends the boist'rous ruin.

Hamlet, act 3. *sc.* 8.

The poets have also made good use of the emotion
produced by the elevated situation of an object :

Quod si me lyricis vatibus inferes,
Sublimi feriam sidera vertice.

Horat. Carm. l. I. *ode* I.

Oh thou ! the earthly author of my blood,
Whose youthful spirit, in me regenerate,
Doth with a twofold vigour lift me up,
To reach at victory above my head.

Richard II. *act* I. *sc.* 4.

Northumberland, thou ladder wherewithal
The mounting Bolingbroke ascends my throne.

Richard II. *act* 5. *sc.* 2.

Anthony. Why was I rais'd the meteor of the world,
Hung in the skies, and blazing as I travell'd,
Till all my fires were spent ; and then cast downward
To be trod out by Cæsar ?

Dryden, All for love, act I.

The

M 4

The defcription of Paradife in the fourth book of *Paradife Loft*, is a fine illuftration of the impreffion made by elevated objects :

> So on he fares, and to the border comes
> Of Eden, where delicious Paradife,
> Now nearer, crowns with her inclofure green,
> As with a rural mound, the champain head
> Of a fteep wildernefs ; whofe hairy fides
> With thicket overgrown, grotefque and wild,
> Accefs deny'd : and over head up grew
> Infuperable height of loftieft fhade,
> Cedar, and pine, and fir, and branching palm,
> A fylvan fcene ; and as the ranks afcend,
> Shade above fhade, a woody theatre
> Of ftatelieft view.   Yet higher than their tops
> The verd'rous wall of Paradife up fprung ;
> Which to our general fire gave profpect large
> Into his nether empire neighb'ring round.
> And higher than that wall a circling row
> Of goodlieft trees, loaden with faireft fruit,
> Bloffoms and fruits at once of golden hue,
> Appear'd with gay enamell'd colours mix'd.
> > *B.* 4. *l.* 131.

Though a grand object is agreeable, we muft not infer that a little object is difagreeable ; which would be unhappy for man, confidering that he is fur-rounded with fo many objects of that kind.   The fame holds with refpect to place : a body placed high is agreeable ; but the fame body placed low, is not by that circumftance rendered difagreeable.   Little-nefs and lownefs of place are precifely fimilar in the following particular, that they neither give pleafure nor pain.   And in this may vifibly be difcovered pe-culiar attention in fitting the internal conftitution of man to his external circumftances : were littlenefs and lownefs of place agreeable, greatnefs and eleva-tion could not be fo : were littlenefs and lownefs of

place

place difagreeable, they would occafion perpetual uneafinefs.

The difference between great and little with re-fpect to agreeablenefs, is remarkably felt in a feries, when we pafs gradually from the one extreme to the other. A mental progrefs from the capital to the kingdom, from that to Europe—to the whole earth—to the planetary fyftem—to the univerfe, is extremely pleafant : the heart fwells, and the mind is dilated, at every ftep. The returning in an oppofite direc-tion is not pofitively painful, though our pleafure leffens at every ftep, till it vanifh into indifference : fuch a progrefs may fometimes produce pleafure of a different fort, which arifes from taking a narrower and narrower infpection. The fame obfervation holds in a progrefs upward and downward. Afcent is pleafant becaufe it elevates us : but defcent is never painful ; it is for the moft part pleafant from a differ-ent caufe, that it is according to the order of na-ture. The fall of a ftone from any height is ex-tremely agreeable by its accelerated motion. I feel it pleafant to defcend from a mountain, becaufe the defcent is natural and eafy. Neither is looking downward painful ; on the contrary, to look down upon objects makes part of the pleafure of elevation : looking down becomes then only painful when the object is fo far below as to create dizzinefs ; and even when that is the cafe, we feel a fort of pleafure mix-ed with the pain, witnefs Shakefpear's defcription of Dover cliffs :

——————————How fearful
And dizzy 'tis, to caft one's eye fo low !
The crows and choughs, that wing the mid-way air,
Shew fcarce fo grofs as beetles. Half-way down
Hangs one that gathers famphire ; dreadful trade !
Methinks he feems no bigger than his head.

The

The fifhermen that walk upon the beach,
Appear like mice ; and yon tall anchoring bark
Diminifh'd to her cock ; her cock, a buoy
Almoft too fmall for fight. The murmuring furge,
That on th' unnumber'd idle pebbles chafes,
Cannot be heard fo high. I'll look no more,
Left my brain turn, and the deficient fight
Topple down headlong.

King Lear, act 4. fc. 6.

A remark is made above, that the emotions of
grandeur and fublimity are nearly allied. And hence
it is, that the one term is frequently· put for the
other : an increafing feries of numbers, for example, producing an emotion fimilar to that of mounting upward, is commonly termed *an afcending feries :*
a feries of numbers gradually decreafing, producing
an emotion fimilar to that of going downward, is
commonly termed *a defcending feries :* we talk familiarly of going *up* to the capital, and of going *down*
to the country : from a leffer kingdom we talk of
going *up* to a greater ; whence the *anabafis* in the
Greek language, when one travels from Greece to
Perfia. We difcover the fame way of fpeaking in
the language even of Japan ;* and its univerfality
proves it the offspring of a natural feeling.

The foregoing obfervation leads us to confider
grandeur and fublimity in a figurative fenfe, and as
applicable to the fine arts. Hitherto thefe terms have
been taken in their proper fenfe, as applicable to objects of fight only : and it was of importance to beftow fome pains upon that article ; becaufe, generally
fpeaking, the figurative fenfe of a word is derived
from its proper fenfe, which holds remarkably at
prefent. Beauty in its original fignification is confined

---

* Kempfer's hiftory of Japan, b. 5. ch. 2.

fined to objects of fight; but, as many other objects, intellectual as well as moral, raife emotions refembling that of beauty, the refemblance of the effects prompts us to extend the term *beauty* to thefe objects. This equally accounts for the terms *grandeur* and *fublimity* taken in a figurative fenfe. Every emotion, from whatever caufe proceeding, that refembles an emotion of grandeur or elevation, is called by the fame name : thus generofity is faid to be an *elevated* emotion, as well as great courage; and that firmnefs of foul which is fuperior to misfortunes, obtains the peculiar name of *magnanimity*. On the other hand, every emotion that contracts the mind, and fixeth it upon things trivial or of no importance, is termed *low*, by its refemblance to an emotion produced by a little or low object of fight : thus an appetite for trifling amufements is called *a low tafte*. The fame terms are applied to characters and actions : we talk familiarly of an *elevated* genius, of a *great* man, and equally fo of *littlenefs* of mind : fome actions are *great* and *elevated*, and others are *little* and *groveling*. Sentiments, and even expreffions, are characterifed in the fame manner: an expreffion or fentiment that raifes the mind is denominated *great* or *elevated ;* and hence the SUBLIME* in poetry. In fuch figurative terms, we lofe the diftinction between *great* and

elevated

---

* Longinus gives a defcription of the fublime that is not amifs, though far from being juft in every circumftance, " That the mind is elevated by it, and fo fenfibly affected, as to fwell in tranfport and inward pride, as if what is only heard or read, were its own invention." But he adheres not to this defcription ; in his 6th chapter, he juftly obferves, that many paffions have nothing of the grand, fuch as grief, fear, pity, which deprefs the mind inftead of raifing it ; and yet in chap. 8. he mentions Sappho's ode upon love as fublime : beautiful it is undoubtedly, but it cannot be fublime, becaufe it really depreffes the mind inftead of raifing it.   His tranflator Boileaux is not more fuccefsful in his inftances : in his 10th reflection, he cites a paffage from Demofthenes and another from Herodotus as fublime, which have not the leaft tincture of that quality.

elevated in their proper fenfe ; for the refemblance is not fo entire as to preferve thefe terms diftinct in their figurative application. We carry this figure ftill farther. Elevation in its proper fenfe, imports fuperiority of place ; and lownefs, inferiority of place : and hence a man of *fuperior* talents, of *fuperior* rank, of *inferior* parts, of *inferior* tafte, and fuch like. The veneration we have for our anceftors, and for the ancients in general, being fimilar to the emotion produced by an elevated object of fight, juftifies the figurative expreffion, of the ancients being *raifed* above us, or poffeffing a *fuperior* place. And we may remark in paffing, that as words are intimately connected with ideas, many, by this form of expreffion, are led to conceive their anceftors as really above them in place, and their pofterity below them :

A grandam's name is litttle lefs in love,
Than is the doting title of a mother :
They are as children but one ftep below.
Richard III. *act* 4. *fc.* 5.

The notes of the gamut, proceeding regularly from the blunter or groffer founds to the more acute and piercing, produce in the hearer a feeling fomewhat fimilar to what is produced by mounting upward ; and this gives occafion to the figurative expreffions, *a high note, a low note.*

Such is the refemblance in feeling between real and figurative grandeur, that among the nations on the eaft coaft of Afric, who are directed purely by nature, the officers of ftate are, with refpect to rank, diftinguifhed by the length of the batoon each carries in his hand : and in Japan, princes and great lords fhew their rank by the length and fize of their
fedan-poles.

fedan-poles.* Again, it is a rule in painting, that figures of a fmall fize are proper for grotefque pieces ; but that an hiftorical fubject, grand and important, requires figures as great as the life. The refemblance of thefe feelings is in reality fo ftrong, that elevation, in a figurative fenfe, is obferved to have the fame effect, even externally, with real elevation :

K. Henry. This day is call'd the feaft of Crifpian.
He that outlives this day, and comes fafe home,
Will ftand a-tiptoe when this day is nam'd,
And roufe him at the name of Crifpian.
Henry V. *act* 4. *fc.* 8.

The refemblance in feeling between real and figurative grandeur, is humoroufly illuftrated by Addifon in criticifing upon Englifh tragedy : " The ordinary method of making an hero, is to clap a huge plume of feathers upon his head, which rifes fo high, that there is often a greater length from his chin to the top of his head, than to the fole of his foot. One would believe, that we thought a great man and a tall man the fame thing. As thefe fuperfluous ornaments upon the head make a great man, a princefs generally receives her grandeur from thofe additional incumbrances that fall into her tail : I mean the broad fweeping train, that follows her in all her motions ; and finds conftant employment for a boy, who ftands behind her to open and fpread it to advantage.†" The Scythians, impreffed with the fame of Alexander, were aftonifhed when they found him a little man.

A gradual progrefs from fmall to great is no lefs remarkable in figurative, than in real grandeur or elevation,

---

* Kempfer's hiftory of Japan.

† Spectator, No. 42.

elevation. Every one muſt have obſerved the delightful effect of a number of thoughts or ſentiments, artfully diſpoſed like an aſcending ſeries, and
making impreſſions deeper and deeper : ſuch diſpoſition of members in a period is termed a *climax*.

Within certain limits, grandeur and ſublimity produce their ſtrongeſt effects, which leſſen by exceſs as
well as by defect. This is remarkable in grandeur
and ſublimity taken in their proper ſenſe : the grand-
eſt emotion that can be raiſed by a viſible object, is
where the object can be taken in at one view ; if ſo
immenſe as not to be comprehended but in parts, it
tends rather to diſtract than ſatisfy the mind :* in
like manner, the ſtrongeſt emotion produced by elevation, is where the object is ſeen diſtinctly; a greater
elevation leſſens in appearance the object, till it vaniſhes out of ſight with its pleaſant emotion. The
ſame is equally remarkable in figurative grandeur and
elevation, which ſhall be handled together, becauſe,
as obſerved above, they are ſcarce diſtinguiſhable.
Sentiments may be ſo ſtrained, as to become obſcure,
or to exceed the capacity of the human mind: againſt
ſuch licence of imagination, every good writer will
be upon his guard. And therefore it is of greater
importance to obſerve, that even the true ſublime
may be carried beyond that pitch which produces
the higheſt entertainment : we are undoubtedly ſuf-
ceptible of a greater elevation, than can be inſpired
by human actions, the moſt heroic and magnani-
mous ; witneſs what we feel from Milton's deſcription

---

* It is juſtly obſerved by Addiſon, that perhaps a man would have
been more aſtoniſhed with the majeſtic air that appeared in one of Lyſip-
pus' ſtatues of Alexander, though no bigger than the life, than he might
have been with Mount Athos, had it been cut into the figure of the
hero, according to the propoſal of Phidias, with a river in one hand, and
a city in the other. *Spectator*, No. 415.

tion of fuperior beings : yet every man muft be fenfible of a more conftant and fweet elevation, when
the hiftory of his own fpecies is the fubject ; he enjoys an elevation equal to that of the greateft hero,
of an Alexander or a Cæfar, of a Brutus or an Epaminondas ; he accompanies thefe heroes in their fub-
limeft fentiments and moft hazardous exploits, with
a magnanimity equal to theirs ; and finds it no ftretch,
to preferve the fame tone of mind, for hours together, without finking. The cafe is not the fame in
defcribing the actions or qualities of fuperior beings:
the reader's imagination cannot keep pace with that of
the poet ; the mind, unable to fupport itfelf in a
ftrained elevation, falls as from a height ; and the
fall is immoderate, like the elevation : where that
effect is not felt, it muft be prevented by fome obfcurity in the conception, which frequently attends
the defcription of unknown objects. Hence the St.
Francifes, St. Dominics, and other tutelary faints,
among the Roman Catholics. A mind unable to
raife itfelf to the Supreme Being felf-exiftent and
eternal, or to fupport itfelf in a ftrained elevation,
finds itfelf more at eafe in ufing the interceffion of
fome faint whofe piety and penances while on earth
are fuppofed to have made him a favourite in heaven.

A ftrained elevation is attended with another in-
convenience, that the author is apt to fall fuddenly
as well as the reader ; becaufe it is not a little difficult, to defcend fweetly and eafily from fuch elevation, to the ordinary tone of the fubject. The
following paffage is a good illuftration of that obfervation :

Sæpe etiam immenfum cœlo venit agmen aquarum,
Et fœdam glomerant tempeftatem imbribus atris
Conlectæ ex alto nubes. Ruit arduus æther,
Et pluvia ingenti fata læta boumque labores
                                              Diluit.

Diluit. Inplentur foffæ, et cava flumina crefcunt
Cum fonitu, fervetque fretis fpirantibus æquor.
Ipfe Pater, media nimborum in noĉte, corufcâ
Fulmina molitur dextra. Quo maxima motu
Tera tremit : fugere feræ ! et mortalia corda
Per gentes humilis ftravit pavor. Ille flagranti
Aut Atho, aut Rhodopen, aut alta Ceraunia telo
Dejicit : *ingeminant auftri, et denfiffimus imber.*

Virg. Georg. l. I.

In the defcription of a ftorm, to figure Jupiter throwing down huge mountains with his thunder-bolts, is
hyperbollically fublime, if I may ufe the expreffion :
the tone of mind produced by that image is fo diftant from the tone produced by a thick fhower of
rain, that the fudden tranfition muft be unpleafant.

Objeĉts of fight that are not remarkably great nor
high, fcarce raife any emotion of grandeur or of fublimity : and the fame holds in other objeĉts ; for we
often find the mind roufed and animated, without being carried to that height. This difference may be
difcerned in many forts of mufic, as well as in fome
mufical inftruments : a kettle drum roufes, and a
hautboy is animating ; but neither of them infpires
an emotion of fublimity : revenge animates the mind
in a confiderable degree ; but I think it never produceth an emotion that can be termed *grand* or *fublime ;* and I fhall have occafion afterward to obferve,
that no difagreeable paffion ever has that effeĉt. I
am willing to put this to the teft, by placing before
my reader a moft fpirited piĉture of revenge : it is a
fpeech of Antony wailing over the body of Cæfar :

Wo to the hand that fhed this coftly blood !
Over thy wounds now do I prophefy,
(Which, like dumb mouths, do ope their ruby lips
To beg the voice and utterance of my tongue,)
A curfe fhall light upon the kind of men ;

Domeftic

Domeſtic fury, and fierce civil ſtrife,
Shall cumber all the parts of Italy ;
Blood and deſtruction ſhall be ſo in uſe,
And dreadful objects ſo familiar,
That mothers ſhall but ſmile when they behold
Their infants quarter'd by the hand of war.
All pity chok'd with cuſtom of fell deeds,
And Cæſar's ſpirit, ranging for revenge,
With *Atè* by his ſide come hot from hell,
Shall in theſe confines, with a monarch's voice,
Cry, *Havock !* and let ſlip the dogs of war.

Julius Cæſar, act 3. ſc. 4.

No deſire is more univerſal than to be exalted and honoured ; and upon that account chiefly are we ambitious of power, riches, titles, fame, which would ſuddenly loſe their reliſh, did they not raiſe us above others, and command ſubmiſſion and deference ;* and it may be thought that our attachment to things grand and lofty proceeds from their connection with our favourite paſſion. This connection has undoubtedly an effect ; but that the preference given to things grand and lofty muſt have a deeper root in human nature, will appear from conſidering, that many beſtow their time upon low and trifling amuſements, without having the leaſt tincture of this favourite paſſion : yet theſe very perſons talk the ſame language with the reſt of mankind, and prefer the more elevated pleaſures : they acknowledge a more refined taſte, and are aſhamed of their own as low and groveling. This ſentiment, conſtant and univerſal, muſt be the work of nature ; and it plainly indicates an original

* Honeſtum per ſe eſſe expetendum indicant pueri, in quibus, ut in ſpeculis, natura cernitur. Quanta ſtudia decertantum ſunt ! Quanta ipſa certamina ! Ut illi efferuntur lætitia, cum vicerunt ! Ut pudet victos ! Ut ſe accuſari nolunt ! Ut cupiunt laudari ! Quos illi labores non perſerunt, ut æqualium principes ſint ! *Cicero de finibus.*

original attachment in human nature to every object that elevates the mind : fome men may have a greater relifh for an object not of the higheft rank; but they are confcious of the preference given by mankind in general to things grand and fublime ; and they are fenfible that their peculiar tafte ought to yield to the general tafte.

What is faid above fuggefts a capital rule for reaching the fublime in fuch works of art as are fufceptible of it ; and that is, to prefent thofe parts or circumftances only which make the greateft figure, keeping out of view every thing low or trivial ; for the mind, elevated by an important object, cannot, without reluctance, be forced down to beftow any fhare of its attention upon trifles. Such judicious felection of capital circumftances, is by an eminent critic ftyled *grandeur of manner.** In none of the fine arts is there fo great a fcope for that rule as in poetry ; which, by that means, enjoys a remarkable power of beftowing upon objects and events an air of grandeur : when we are fpectators, every minute object prefents itfelf in its order ; but, in defcribing at fecond hand, thefe are laid afide, and the capital objects are brought clofe together. A judicious tafte in thus felecting the moft interefting incidents, to give them an united force, accounts for a fact that may appear furprifing ; which is, that we are more moved by a fpirited narrative at fecond hand, than by being fpectators of the event itfelf, in all its circumftances.

Longinus exemplifies the foregoing rule by a comparifon of two paffages.† The firft, from Ariftæus, is thus tranflated :

Ye

---

* Spectator, No. 415.

† Chap. 8. of the Sublime.

Ye pow'rs, what madnefs! how on fhips fo frail
(Tremendous thought !) can thoughtlefs mortals fail ?
For ftormy feas they quit the pleafing plain,   .
Plant woods in waves, and dwell amidft the main.
Far o'er the deep (a tracklefs path) they go,
And wander oceans in purfuit of wo.
No eafe their hearts, no reft their eyes can find,
On heaven their looks, and on the waves their mind,
Sunk are their fpirits, while their arms they rear,
And gods are wearied with their fruitlefs prayer.

The other, from Homer, I fhall give in Pope's tranflation :

Burft as a wave that from the cloud impends,
And fwell'd with tempefts on the fhip defcends,
White are the decks with foam : the winds aloud
Howl o'er the mafts, and fing through every fhroud.
Pale, trembling, tir'd, the failors freeze with fears,
And inftant death on every wave appears.

In the latter paffage, the moft ftriking circumftances
are felected to fill the mind with terror and aftonifhment. The former is a collection of minute and
low circumftances which fcatter the thought, and
make no impreffion : it is at the fame time full of
verbal antithefes and low conceit, extremely im- .
proper in a fcene of diftrefs. But this laft obfervation belongs to another head.

The following defcription of a battle is remarkably fublime, by collecting together, in the feweft
words, thofe circumftances which make the greateft
figure.

Like Autumn's dark ftorms pouring from two echoing
hills, toward each other approached the heroes : as two
dark ftreams from high rocks meet and roar on the plain,
loud, rough, and dark in battle, meet Lochlin and Inisfail.
                                                        Chief   .
        N 2

Chief mixes his ftrokes with chief, and man with man :
fteel founds on fteel, and helmets are cleft on high ; blood
burfts and fmokes around : ftrings murmur on the polifh'd
yew : darts rufh along the fky : fpears fall like fparks of
flame that gild the ftormy face of night.

As the noife of the troubled ocean when roll the waves
on high, as the laft peal of thundering heaven, fuch is the
noife of battle.   Though Cormac's hundred bards were
there, feeble were the voice of a hundred bards to fend the
deaths to future times ; for many were the deaths of the
heroes, and wide poured the blood of the valiant.

Fingal.

The following paffage in the 4th book of the Iliad
is a defcription of a battle wonderfully ardent.
" When now gathered on either fide, the hofts
plunged together in fight ; fhield is harfhly laid
to fhield ; fpears crafh on the brazen corflets ; boffy
buckler with buckler meets ;   loud tumult rages over
all ; groans are mixed with boafts of men ; the flain
and flayer join in noife ; the earth is floating round
with blood.   As when two rufhing ftreams from
two mountains come roaring down, and throw together their rapid waters below, they roar along the
gulphy vale.   The ftartled fhepherd hears the found,
as he ftalks o'er the diftant hills ; fo, as they mixed
in fight, from both armies clamour with loud terror
arofe."   But fuch general defcriptions are not frequent in Homer.   Even his fingle combats are rare.
The fifth book is the longeft account of a battle that
is in the Iliad ; and yet contains nothing but a long
catalogue of chiefs killing chiefs, not in fingle combat neither, but at a diftance, with an arrow or jave-
lin ; and thefe chiefs named for the firft time and the
laft.   The fame fcene is continued through a great
part of the fixth book.   There is at the fame time a
minute defcription of every wound, which for accuracy may do honour to an anatomift, but in an epic

poem

poem is tirefome and fatiguing. There is no relief from horrid languor, but the beautiful Greek language, and melody of Homer's verfification.

In the twenty-firft book of the Odyfiey, there is a paffage which deviates widely from the rule above laid down : it concerns that part of the hiftory of Penelope and her fuitors, in which fhe is made to declare in favour of him who fhould prove the moft dextrous in fhooting with the bow of Ulyfies :

.. Now gently winding up the fair afcent,
By many an eafy ftep, the matron went :
Then o'er the pavement glides with grace divine,
(With polifh'd oak the level pavements fhine ;)
The folding gates a dazzling light difplay'd,
With pomp of various architrave o'erlay'd.
The bolt, obedient to the filken ftring,
Forfakes the ftaple as fhe pulls the ring ;
The wards refpondent to the key turn'd round ;
The bars fall back ; the flying valves refound.
Loud as a bull makes hill and valley ring ;
So roard the lock when it releas'd the fpring.
She moves majeftic through the wealthy room
Where treafur'd garments caft a rich perfume ;
There from the column where aloft it hung,
Reach'd in its fplendid cafe, the bow unftrung.

Virgil fometimes errs againft this rule : in the following paffages minute circumftances are brought into full view ; and, what is ftill worfe, they are defcribed with all the pomp of poetical diction ; *Æneid*, *L.* 1. *l.* 214. *to* 219. *L.* 6. *l.* 176. *to* 182. *L.* 6. *l.* 212. *to* 231. and the laft, which defcribes a funeral, is the lefs excufable, as the man whofe funeral it is makes no figure in the poem.

The

N 3

The fpeech of Clytemneftra, defcending from her chariot in the Iphigenia of Euripidies,* is ftuffed with a number of common and trivial circumftances. But of all writers, Lucan, as to this article, is the moft injudicious : the fea-fight between the Romans and Mafillians,† is defcribed fo much in detail, without exhibiting any grand or total view, that the reader is fatigued with endlefs circumftances, without ever feeling any degree of elevation.; and yet there are fome fine incidents, thofe for example of the two brothers, and of the old man and his fon, which, taken feparately, would affect us greatly. But Lucan, once engaged in a defcription, knows no end. See other paffages of the fame kind, *L.* 4. *l.* 292. *to* 337. *L.* 4. *l.* 750. *to* 765. The epifode of the for- cerefs Erictho, end of book 6. is intolerably minute and prolix.

To thefe I venture to oppofe a paffage from an old hiftorical ballad :

> Go, little page, tell Hardiknute
>   That lives on hill fo high,‡
> To draw his fword, the dread of faes,
>   And hafte to follow me.
>
> The little page flew fwift as dart
>   Flung by his mafter's arm.
> "Come down, come down, Lord Hardiknute,
> "And rid your king from harm."

This rule alfo is applicable to other fine arts. In paint- ing it is eftablifhed, that the principal figure muft be put

---

* Beginning of act 3.

† Lib. 3. beginning at line 567.

‡ *High*, in the old Scotch language, is pronounced *hee*.

put in the ftrongeft light; that the beauty of attitude confifts in placing the nobler parts moft in view, and in fuppreffing the fmaller parts as much as poffible; that the folds of the drapery muft be few and large; that forefhortenings are bad, becaufe they make the parts appear little; and that the mufcles ought to be kept as entire as poffible, without being divided into fmall fections. Every one at prefent fubfcribes to that rule as applied to gardening, in oppofition to parterres fplit into a thoufand fmall parts in the ftiffeft regularity of figure. The moft eminent architects have governed themfelves by the fame rule in all their works.

Another rule chiefly regards the fublime, though it is applicable to every fort of literary performance intended for amufement; and that is, to avoid as much as poffible abftract and general terms. Such terms, fimilar to mathematical figns, are contrived to exprefs our thoughts in a concife manner; but images, which are the life of poetry, cannot be raifed in any perfection but by introducing particular objects. General terms that comprehend a number of individuals, muft be excepted from that rule: our kindred, our clan, our country, and words of the like import, though they fcarce raife any image, have however a wonderful power over our paffions: the greatnefs of the complex object overbalances the obfcurity of the image.

Grandeur, being an extreme vivid emotion, is not readily produced in perfection but by reiterated impreffions. The effect of a fingle impreffion can be but momentary; and if one feel fuddenly fomewhat like a fwelling or exaltation of mind, the emotion vanifheth as foon as felt. Single thoughts or fentiments, I know, are often cited as examples of the fublime; but their effect is far inferior to that of a

grand

grand fubject difplayed in its capital parts. I fhall give a few examples, that the reader may judge for himfelf. In the famous action of Thermopylæ, where Leonidas the Spartan king, with his chofen band, fighting for their country, were cut off to the laft man, a faying is reported of Dieneces, one of the band, which, exprefting cheerful and undifturbed bravery, is well entitled to the firft place in examples of that kind. Refpecting the number of their enemies, it was obferved, that the arrows fhot by fuch a multitude would intercept the light of the fun. So much the better, fays he, for we fhall then fight in the fhade.*

Somerfet. Ah! Warwick, Warwick, wert thou as
  we are,
We might recover all our lofs again.
The Queen from France hath brought a puiffant power,
Ev'n now we heard the news. Ah! couldft thou fly !
Warwick. Why, then I would not fly.
    Third part, Henry VI. *act 5. fc. 3.*

Such a fentiment from a man expiring of his wounds, is truly heroic, and muft elevate the mind to the greateft height that can be done by a fingle expreffion : it will not fuffer in a comparifon with the famous fentiment *Qu'il mourut* of Corneille : the latter is a fentiment of indignation merely, the former of firm and cheerful courage.

To cite in oppofition many a fublime paffage, enriched with the fineft images, and dreffed in the moft nervous expreffions, would fcarce be fair : I fhall produce but one inftance from Shakefpear, which fets a few objects before the eye, without much pomp of language : it operates its effect by reprefenting thefe
         objects

* Herodotus, book 7.

objects in a climax, raifing the mind higher and
higher till it feel the emotion of grandeur in perfection:

> •The cloud-capt towr's, the gorgeous palaces,
> The folemn temples, the great globe itfelf,
> Yea all which it inherit, fhall diffolve, &c.

The cloud-capt tower's produce an elevating emotion,
heightened by the *gorgeous palaces ;* and the mind is
carried ftill higher and higher by the images that
follow. Succeflive images, making thus deeper and
deeper impreflions, muft elevate more than any fingle
image can do.

As, on the one hand, no means directly applied
have more influence to raife the mind than grandeur
and fublimity ; fo, on the other, no means indirectly
applied have more influence to fink and deprefs it :
for in a ftate of elevation, the artful introduction of
an humbling object, makes the fall great in proportion to the elevation. Of this obfervation Shakefpear gives a beautiful example, in the paflage laft
quoted:

> The cloud-capt tow'rs, the gorgeous palaces,
> The folemn temples, the great globe itfelf,
> Yea all which it inherit, fhall diflolve,
> And, like the bafelefs fabric of a vifion,
> Leave not a wreck behind.——
>
> *Tempeft, act* 4. *fc.* 4.

The elevation of the mind in the former part of this
beautiful paffage, makes the fall great in proportion,
when the moft humbling of all images is introduced,
that of an utter diffolution of the earth and its inhabitants. The mind, when warmed, is more fufceptible of impreflions than in a cool ftate ; and a
depreffing

deprefling or melancholy object liftened to, makes the ftrongeft impreffion when it reaches the mind in its higheft ftate of elevation or cheerfulnefs.

But a humbling image is not always neceffary to produce that effect : a remark is made above, that, in defcribing fuperior beings, the reader's imagination, unable to fupport itfelf in a ftrained elevation, falls often as from a height, and finks even below its ordinary tone. The following inftance comes luckily in view; for a better cannot be given : "God faid, Let there be light, and there was light." Longinus quotes this paffage from Mofes as a fhining example of the fublime; and it is fcarce poffible, in fewer words, to convey fo clear an image of the infinite power of the Deity : but then it belongs to the prefent fubject to remark, that the emotion of fublimity raifed by this image is but momentary ; and that the mind, unable to fupport itfelf in an elevation fo much above nature, immediately finks down into humility and veneration for a being fo far exalted above groveling mortals. Every one is acquainted with a difpute, about that paffage between two French critics,* the one pofitively affirming it to be fublime, the other as pofitively denying. What I have remarked fhows that both of them have reached the truth, but neither of them the whole truth : the primary effect of the paffage is undoubtedly an emotion of grandeur ; which fo far juftifies Boileau : but then every one muft be fenfible, that the emotion is merely a flafh, which, vanifhing inftantaneoufly, gives way to humility and veneration. That indirect effect of fublimity juftifies Huet, who, being a man of true piety, and probably not much carried by imagination, felt the humbling paffion more fenfibly than his antagonift did. And, laying

---

* Boileau and Huet.

laying afide difference of character, Huets opinion may, I think, be defended as the more folid; becaufe in fuch images, the depreffing emotions are the more fenfibly felt, and have the longer endurance.

The ftraining an elevated fubject beyond due bounds, is a vice not fo frequent as to require the correction of criticifm. But falfe fublime is a rock that writers of more fire than judgment commonly fplit on; and therefore a collection of examples may be of ufe as a beacon to future adventurers. One fpecies of falfe fublime, known by the name of *bombaft*, is common among writers of a mean genius: it is a ferious endeavour, by ftrained defcription, to raife a low or familiar fubject above its rank; which, inftead of being fublime, becomes ridiculous. I am extremely fenfible how prone the mind is, in fome animating paffions, to magnify its objects beyond natural bounds: but fuch hyperbolical defcription has its limits; and, when carried beyond the impulfe of the propenfity, it degenerates into burlefque. Take the following examples.

> *Sejanus.*————————Great and high
> The world knows only two, that's Rome and I.
> My roof receives me not; 'tis air I tread,
> And at each ftep I feel my advanc'd head
> Knock out a ftar in heav'n.
>
> *Sejanus, Ben Johnfon, act 5.*

A writer who has no natural elevation of mind, deviates readily into bombaft: he ftrains above his natural powers; and the violent effort carries him beyond the bounds of propriety. Boileau expreffes this happily:

L'autre à peur de ramper, il fe perd dans la nue.*

The

* L'art poet. chant. 1. l. 68.

The fame author, Ben Johnſon, abounds in the bombaſt :

———————————————The mother,
Th' expulſed Apicata, finds them there ;
Whom when ſhe ſaw lie ſpread on the degrees,
After a world of fury on herſelf,
Tearing her hair, defacing of her face,
Beating her breaſts and womb, kneeling amaz'd,
Crying to heav'n, then to them ; at laſt
Her drowned voice got up above her woes :
And with ſuch black and bitter execrations,
(As might affright the gods, and force the ſun
Run backward to the eaſt ; nay, make the old
Deformed chaos riſe again t'" o'erwhelm
'Them, us, and all the world,) ſhe fills the air,
Upbraids the heavens with their partial dooms,
Defies their tyrannous powers, and demands
What ſhe and thoſe poor innocents have tranſgreſs'd,
That they muſt ſuffer ſuch a ſhare in vengeance.
                                    Sejanus, act 5. *ſc. laſt.*

———————————————Lentulus, the man,
If all our fire were out, would fetch down new
Out of the hand of Jove ; and rivet him
To Caucaſus, ſhould he but frown ; and let
His own gaunt eagle fly at him to tire.
                                    Catiline, act 3.

Can theſe, or ſuch, be any aid to us ?
Look they as they were built to ſhake the world,
Or be a moment to our enterpriſe ?
A thouſand, ſuch as they are, could not make
One atom of our ſouls.   They ſhould be men
Worth heaven's fear, that looking up but thus,
Would make Jove ſtand upon his guard, and draw
Himſelf within his thunder ; which, amaz'd,
He ſhould diſcharge in vain, and they unhurt.
Or, if they were, like Capaneus at Thebes,
They ſhould hang dead upon the higheſt ſpires
And aſk the ſecond bolt to be thrown down.
                                    Why

Why Lentulus talk you fo long ? This time
Had been enough t'have fcatter'd all the ftars,
T''have quench'd the fun and moon, and made the world
Defpair of day, or any light but ours.

Catiline, act 4.

This is the language of a madman :

Guildford. Give way, and let the gufhing torrent come,
Behold the tears we bring to fwell the deluge,
Till the flood rife upon the guilty world
And make the ruin common.

Lady Jane Gray, act 4. near the end.

I am forry to obferve that the following bombaft
ftuff dropt from the pen of Dryden.

To fee this fleet upon the ocean move,
Angels drew wide the curtains of the fkies ;
And heaven, as if there wanted lights above,
For tapers made two glaring comets rife.

Another fpecies of falfe fublime is ftill more faulty
than bombaft ; and that is, to force elevation by introducing imaginary beings without preferving any
propriety in their actions ; as if it were lawful to afcribe every extravagance and inconfiftence to beings
of the poet's creation. No writer's are more licentious in that article than Johnfon and Dryden :

Methinks I fee Death and the furies waiting
What we will do, and all the heaven at leifure
For the great fpectacle. Draw then your fwords :
And if our deftiny envy our virtue
The honour of the day, yet let us care
To fell ourfelves at fuch a price, as may
Undo the world to buy us, and make Fate,
While fhe tempts ours, to fear her own eftate.

Catiline, act 5.

----The

———————————The furies ftood on hill
Circling the place, and trembled to fee men
Do more than they ; whilft Piety left the field,
Griev'd for that fide, that in fo bad a caufe
They knew not what a crime their valour was.
The fun ftood ftill, and was, behind the cloud
The battle made, feen fweating to drive up
His frighted horfe, whom ftill the noife drove backward.

Ibid. act 5.

Ofmyn. While we indulge our common happinefs,
He is forgot by whom we all poffefs,
The brave Almanzor, to whofe arms we owe
All that we did, and all that we fhall do ;
Who like a tempeft that outrides the wind,
Made a juft battle ere the bodies join'd.
   Abdalla. His victories we fcarce could keep in view,
Or polifh 'em fo faft as he rough drew.
   Abdemelech. Fate after him below with pain did move,
And victory could fcarce keep pace above.
Death did at length fo many flain forget,
And loft the tale, and took 'em by the great.

Conqueft of Grenada, act 2. *at beginning.*

The gods of Rome fight for ye ; loud Fame calls ye,
Pitch'd on the toplefs Apenine, and blows
To all the under world, all nations
The feas, and unfrequented defarts, where the fnow dwells,
Wakens the ruin'd monuments, and there,
Where nothing but eternal death and fleep is,
Informs again the dead bones.

Beaumont and Fletcher, Bonduca, act 3. *fc.* 3.

   An actor on the ftage may be guilty of bombaft
as well as an author in his clofet ; a certain manner
of acting, which is grand when fupported by dignity
in the fentiment and force in the expreffion, is ridiculous where the fentiment is mean, and the expreffion flat.

This

This chapter fhall be clofed with fome obfervations. When the fublime is carried to its due height,
and circumfcribed within proper bounds, it enchants
the mind, and raifes the moft delightful of all emotions : the reader engroffed by a fublime object, feels
himfelf raifed as it were to a higher rank. Confidering that effect, it is not wonderful that the hiftory
of conquerors and heroes, fhould be univerfally the
favourite entertainment. And this fairly accounts
for what I once erroneoufly fufpected to be a wrong
bias originally in human nature ; which is, that the
groffeft acts of oppreffion and injuftice fcarce blem-
ifh the character of a great conqueror: we, never-
thelefs, warmly efpoufe his intereft, accompany him
in his exploits, and are anxious for his fuccefs : the
fplendour and enthufiafm of the hero transfufed into
the readers, elevate their minds far above the rules
of juftice, and render them in a great meafure infenfible of the wrongs that are committed :

> For in thofe days might only fhall be admir'd,
> And valour and heroic virtue call'd ;
> To overcome in battle, and fubdue
> Nations, and bring home fpoils with infinite
> Manflaughter, fhall be held the higheft pitch
> Of human glory, and for glory done
> Of triumph, to be ftyl'd great conquerors,
> Patrons of mankind, gods, and fons of gods ;
> Deftroyers rightlier call'd, and plagues of men.
> Thus fame fhall be achiev'd, renown on earth,
> And what moft merits fame in filence hid.
> .   *Milton, b.* 11.

The irregular influence of grandeur reaches alfo
to other matters : however good, honeft, or ufeful, a
man may be, he is not fo much refpected as is one
of a more elevated character, though of lefs integri-
ty ;

ty ;' nor do the misfortunes of the former affect us fo much as thofe of the latter. And I add, becaufe it cannot be difguifed, that the remorfe which attends breach of engagement, is in a great meafure propor- tioned to the figure that the injured perfon makes : the vows and proteftations of lovers are an illuftrious example ; for thefe commonly are little regarded when made to women of inferior rank.

CHAP.

CHAP. V.

Motion and Force.

THAT motion is agreeable to the eye without relation to purpofe or defign, may appear from the amufement it gives to infants : juvenile exercifes are relifhed chiefly on that account.

If a body in motion be agreeable, one will be apt to conclude that at reft it muft be difagreeable : but we learn from experience, that this would be a rafh conclufion. Reft is one of thofe circumftances that are neither agreeable nor difagreeable, being viewed with perfect indifferency. And happy is it for mankind to have the matter fo ordered : if reft were agreeable, it would difincline us to motion, by which all things are performed : if it were difagreeable, it would be a fource of perpetual uneafinefs ; for the bulk of the things we fee appear to be at reft. A fimilar inftance of defigning wifdom I have had occafion to explain, in oppofing grandeur to littlenefs, and elevation to lownefs of place.* Even in the fimpleft matters, the finger of God is confpicuous : the happy adjuftment of the internal nature of man to his external circumftances, difplayed in the inftances here given, is indeed admirable.

Motion is agreeable in all its varieties of quicknefs and flownefs ; but motion long continued admits fome exceptions. That degree of continued motion which correfponds to the natural courfe of our perceptions,

* See Chap. ▲.

O

ceptions, is the moſt agreeable. The quickeſt motion
is for an inſtant delightful ; but ſoon appears to be
too rapid : it becomes painful by forcibly accelerating
the courſe of our perceptions. Slow continued motion becomes diſagreeable from an oppoſite cauſe,
that it retards the natural courſe of our perceptions.*
There are other varieties in motion, beſide quickneſs and ſlowneſs, that make it more or leſs agreeable:
regular motion is preferred before what is irregular ;
witneſs the motion of the planets in orbits nearly circular : the motion of the comets in orbits leſs regular,
is leſs agreeable.

Motion uniformly accelerated, reſembling an aſcending ſeries of numbers, is more agreeable than
when uniformly retarded : motion upward is agreeable, by tendency to elevation. What then ſhall we
ſay of downward motion regularly accelerated by the
force of gravity, compared with upward motion regularly retarded by the ſame force ? Which of theſe is
the moſt agreeable ? This queſtion is not eaſily ſolved.

Motion in a ſtraight line is agreeable : but we prefer undulating motion, as of waves, of a flame, of a
ſhip under ſail ; ſuch motion is more free, and alſo
more natural. Hence the beauty of a ſerpentine river.

The eaſy and ſliding motion of a fluid, from the
lubricity of its parts, is agreeable upon that account :
but the agreeableneſs chiefly depends on the following circumſtance, that the motion is perceived, not
as of one body, but as of an endleſs number moving
together with order and regularity. Poets ſtruck
with that beauty, draw more images from fluids in
motion than from ſolids.

Force is of two kinds ; one quieſcent, and one exerted in motion. The former, dead weight for example, muſt be laid aſide ; for a body at reſt is not,

by

---

* This will be explained more fully afterward, ch. 9.

by that circumſtance, either agreeable or diſagreeable. Moving force only is my province ; and, though
it is not ſeparable from motion, yet by the power of
abſtraction, either of them may be conſidered independent of the other. Both of them are agreeable,
becauſe both of them include activity. It is agreeable to ſee a thing move : to ſee it moved, as when it
is dragged or puſhed along, is neither agreeable nor
diſagreeable, more than when at reſt. It is agreeable to ſee a thing exert force ; but it makes not the
thing either agreeable or diſagreeable to ſee force exerted upon it.

Though motion and force are each of them agreeable, the impreſſions they make are different. This
difference, clearly felt, is not eaſily deſcribed. All
we can ſay is, that the emotion raiſed by a moving
body, reſembling its cauſe, is felt as if the mind were
carried along : the emotion raiſed by force exerted, reſembling alſo its cauſe, is felt as if force were exerted within the mind.

To illuſtrate that difference, I give the following
examples. It has been explained why ſmoke aſcending in a calm day, ſuppoſe from a cottage in a wood,
is an agreeable object ;* ſo remarkably agreeable,
that landſcape painters introduce it upon all occaſions. The aſcent being natural, and without effort,
is pleaſant in a calm ſtate of mind : it reſembles a
gently-flowing river, but is more agreeable, becauſe
aſcent is more to our taſte than deſcent. A fire-work
or a *jet d'eau* rouſes the mind more ; becauſe the
beauty of force viſibly exerted, is ſuperadded to that
of upward motion. To a man reclining indolently
upon a bank of flowers, aſcending ſmoke in a ſtill
morning is charming ; but a fire-work or a *jet d'eau*
rouſes him from that ſupine poſture, and puts him in
motion.

A *jet*

O 2   * Chap. 1.

A *jet d'eau* makes an impreffion diftinguifhable from that of a water fall. Downward motion being natural and without effort, tends rather to quiet the mind than to roufe it : upward motion, on the contrary, overcoming the refiftance of gravity, makes an impreffion of a great effort, and thereby roufes and enlivens the mind.

The public games of the Greeks and Romans, which gave fo much entertainment to the fpectators, confifted chiefly in exerting force, wreftling, leaping, throwing great ftones, and fuch-like trials of ftrength. When great force is exerted, the effort felt internally is animating. The effort may be fuch, as in fome meafure to overpower the mind : thus the explofion of gun-powder, the violence of a torrent, the weight of a mountain, and the crufh of an earthquake, create aftonifhment rather than pleafure.

No quality nor circumftance contributes more to grandeur than force, efpecially where exerted by fenfible beings. I cannot make the obfervation more evident than by the following quotations.

———————Him the Almighty power
Hurl'd headlong flaming from th' ethereal fky,
With hideous ruin and combuftion, down
To bottomlefs perdition, there to dwell
In adamantine chains and penal fire,
Who durft defy th' Omnipotent to arms.
Paradife Loft, book 1.

————————Now ftorming fury rofe,
And clamour fuch as heard in heaven till now
Was never ; arms on armour clafhing bray'd
Horrible difcord, and the madding wheels
Of brazen chariots rag'd ; dire was the noife
Of conflict ; over head the difmal hifs
Of fiery darts in flaming vollies flew,
And flying vaulted either hoft with fire.
So under fiery cope together rufh'd
Both battles main, with ruinous affault

And

And inextinguifhable rage ; all heaven ·
Refounded ; and had earth been then, all earth
Had to her center fhook.

Ibid. book 6.

They ended parle, and both addrefs'd for fight
Unfpeakable ; for who, though with the tongue
Of angels, can relate, or to what things
Liken on earth confpicuous, that may lift
Human imagination to fuch height
Of god-like pow'r ? for likeft gods they feem'd,
Stood they or mov'd, in ftature, motion, arms,
Fit to decide the empire of great Heav'n.
Now wav'd their fiery fwords, and in the air
Made horrid circles : two broad funs their fhields
Blaz'd oppofite, while expectation ftood
In horror : from each hand with fpeed retir'd,
Where erft was thickeft fight, th' angelic throng,
And left large field, unfafe within the wind
Of fuch commotion ; fuch as, to fet forth
Great things by fmall, if Nature's concord broke,
Among the conftellations war were fprung,
Two planets, rufhing from afpect malign
Of fierceft oppofition, in mid fky
Should combat, and their jarring fpheres confound.

Ibid. book 6.

We fhall next confider the effect of motion and force in conjunction. In contemplating the planetary fyftem, what ftrikes us the moft, is the fpherical figures of the planets, and their regular motions ; the conception we have of their activity and enormous bulk being more obfcure : the beauty accordingly of that fyftem, raifes a more lively emotion than its grandeur. But if we could comprehend the whole fyftem at one view, the activity and irrefiftible force of thefe immenfe bodies would fill us with amazement : nature cannot furnifh another fcene fo grand.

Motion

Motion and force, agreeable in themfelves, are alfo agreeable by their utility when employed as means
to accomplifh fome beneficial end. Hence the fuperior beauty of fome machines, where force and
motion concur to perform the work of numberlefs
hands. Hence the beautiful motions, firm and regular, of a horfe trained for war : every fingle ftep is
the fitteft that can be, for obtaining the purpofed
end. But the grace of motion is vifible chiefly in
man, not only for the reafons mentioned, but becaufe every gefture is fignificant. The power however of agreeable motion is not a common talent :
every limb of the human body has an agreeable and
difagreeable motion ; fome motions being extremely
graceful, others plain and vulgar ; fome expreffing
dignity, others meannefs. But the pleafure here,
arifing, not fingly from the beauty of motion, but
from indicating character and fentiment, belongs to
different chapters.*

I fhould conclude with the final caufe of the relifh
we have for motion and force, were it not fo evident
as to require no explanation. We are placed here
in fuch circumftances as to make induftry effential to
our well-being ; for without induftry the plaineft
neceffaries of life are not obtained. When our fituation, therefore, in this world requires activity and a
conftant exertion of motion and force, Providence
indulgently provides for our welfare by making thefe
agreeable to us : it would be a grofs imperfection in
our nature, to make any thing difagreeable that we
depend on for exiftence : and even indifference
would flacken greatly that degree of activity which is
indifpenfable.

CHAP.

* Chap. 11. and 15.

Novelty, and the unexpected appearance of objects.

O F all the circumſtances that raiſe emotions, not excepting beauty, nor even greatneſs,
novelty hath the moſt powerful influence. A new object produceth inſtantaneouſly an emotion termed *wonder*, which totally occupies the mind, and for a time excludes all other objects. Converſation among the
vulgar never is more intereſting than when it turns
upon ſtrange objects and extraordinary events. Men
tear themſelves from their native country in ſearch
of things rare and new ; and novelty converts
into a pleaſure, the fatigues and even perils of travelling. To what cauſe ſhall we aſcribe theſe ſingular
appearances ? To curioſity undoubtedly, a principle
implanted in human nature for a purpoſe extremely
beneficial, that of acquiring knowledge ; and the
emotion of wonder, raiſed by new and ſtrange objects, inflames our curioſity to know more of them.
This emotion is different from *admiration :* novelty
wherever found, whether in a quality or action, is the
cauſe of wonder ; admiration is directed to the perſon who performs any thing wonderful.

During infancy, every new object is probably the
occaſion of wonder, in ſome degree ; becauſe, during infancy, every object at firſt ſight is ſtrange as
well as new : but as objects are rendered familiar by
cuſtom, we ceaſe by degrees to wonder at new appearances, if they have any reſemblance to what we
are acquainted with ; for a thing muſt be ſingular as

well

well as new, to raife our wonder. To fave multiplying words, I would be underftood to comprehend
both circumftances when I hereafter talk of novelty.

In an ordinary train of perceptions where one
thing introduces another, not a fingle object makes
its appearance unexpectedly:* the mind thus prepared for the reception of its objects, admits them
one after another without perturbation. But when
a thing breaks in unexpectedly, and without the
preparation of any connection, it raifes an emotion,
known by the name of *furprife*. That emotion may
be produced by the moft familiar object, as when
one unexpectedly meets a friend who was reported
to be dead ; or a man in high life lately a beggar.
On the other hand, a new object, however ftrange,
will not produce the emotion, if the fpectator be prepared for the fight : an elephant in India will not
furprife a traveller who goes to fee one ; and yet its
novelty will raife his wonder : an Indian in Britain
would be much furprifed to ftumble upon an elephant feeding at large in the open fields : but the
creature itfelf, to which he was accuftomed, would
not raife his wonder.

Surprife thus in feveral refpects differs from wonder : unexpectednefs is the caufe of the former emotion ; novelty is the caufe of the latter. Nor differ
they lefs in their nature and circumftances, as will
be explained by and by. With relation to one circumftance they perfectly agree ; which is, the fhortnefs of their duration : the inftantaneous production
of thefe emotions in perfection, may contribute to
that effect, in conformity to a general law, That
things foon decay which foon come to perfection :
the violence of the emotions may alfo contribute ;
for

* See Chap. 1.

for an ardent emotion, which is not fufceptible of increafe, cannot have a long courfe. But their fhort
duration is occafioned chiefly by that of their caufes :
we are foon reconciled to an object, however unexpected ; and novelty foon degenerates into familiarity.

Whether thefe emotions be pleafant or painful, is
not a clear point. It may appear ftrange, that our
own feelings and their capital qualities, fhould afford any matter for a doubt : but when we are engroffed by any emotion, there is no place for fpeculation ; and when fufficiently calm for fpeculation,
it is not eafy to recal the emotion with accuracy.
New objects are fometimes terrible, fometimes delightful : The terror which a tyger infpires is greateft at firft, and wears off gradually by familiarity :
on the other hand, even women will acknowledge
that it is novelty which pleafes the moft in a new
fafhion. It would be rafh however to conclude, that
wonder is in itfelf neither pleafant nor painful, but that
it affumes either quality according to circumftances.
An object it is true, that hath a threatening appearance, adds to our terror by its novelty : but from
that experiment it doth not follow, that novelty is in
itfelf difagreeable ; for it is perfectly confiftent, that
we be delighted with an object in one view, and terrified with it in another : a river in flood fwelling
over its banks, is a grand and delightful object ; and
yet it may produce no fmall degree of fear when we
attempt to crofs it : courage and magnanimity are
agreeable ; and yet, when we view thefe qualities
in an enemy, they ferve to increafe our terror. In
the fame manner, novelty may produce two effects
clearly diftinguifhable from each other : it may, directly and in itfelf, be agreeable ; and it may have an
oppofite effect indirectly, which is, to infpire terror ;

for

for when a new object appears in any degree dangerous, our ignorance of its powers and qualities, affords ample fcope for the imagination to drefs it in
the moft frightful colours.*   The firft fight of a lion,
for example, may at the fame inftant produce two
oppofite feelings, the pleafant emotion of wonder,
and the painful paffion of terror : the novelty of the
object produces the former directly, and contributes
to the latter indirectly.   Thus, when the fubject is
analyfed, we find; that the power which novelty hath
indirectly to inflame terror, is perfectly confiftent
with its being in every circumftance agreeable.   The
matter may be put in the cleareft light, by adding
the following circumftances.   If a lion be firft feen
from a place of fafety, the fpectacle is altogether agreeable without the leaft mixture of terror.   If, again, the
firft fight puts us within reach of that dangerous animal,
our terror may be fo great as quite to exclude any
fenfe of novelty.   But this fact proves not that wonder is painful : it proves only, that wonder may be
excluded by a more powerful paffion.   Every man
may be made certain from his own experience, that
wonder raifed by a new object which is inoffenfive, is
always pleafant ; and with refpect to offenfive objects, it appears from the foregoing deduction, that
the fame muft hold as long as the fpectator can attend to the novelty.

Whether furprife be in itfelf pleafant or painful,
is a queftion no lefs intricate than the former.   It is
certain that furprife inflames our joy, when unexpectedly we meet with an old friend, and our terror when
we ftumble upon any thing noxious.   To clear that
queftion, the firft thing to be remarked is, that in
                                                   fome

* Effays on the Principles of Morality and Natural Religion, part 2.
eff. 6.

fome inftances an unexpected object overpowers the
mind, fo as to produce a momentary ftupefaction :
where the object is dangerous, or appears fo, the fudden alarm it gives, without preparation, is apt totally to unhinge the mind, and for a moment to fufpend all its faculties, even thought itfelf ;* in which
ftate a man is quite helplefs ; and if he move at all,
is as like to run upon the danger as from it. Surprife carried to fuch a height, cannot be either pleafant or painful ; becaufe the mind, during fuch momentary ftupefaction, is in a good meafure, if not
totally, infenfible.

If we then inquire for the character of this emotion, it muft be where the unexpected object or event
produceth lefs violent effects. And while the mind
remains fenfible of pleafure and pain, is it not natural
to fuppofe, that furprife, like wonder, fhould have an
invariable character ? I am inclined however to think,
that furprife has no invariable character, but affumes that of the object which raifes it. Wonder
being an emotion invariably raifed by novelty, and
being diftinguifhable from all other emotions, ought
naturally to poffefs one conftant character. The unexpected appearance of an object, feems not equally
entitled to produce an emotion diftinguifhable from
that which is produced by the object in its ordinary
appearance : the effect it ought naturally to have, is
only to fwell that emotion, by making it more pleafant or more painful than it commonly is. And that
conjecture is confirmed by experience, as well as by
language, which is built upon experience : when a
man meets a friend unexpectedly, he is faid to be
agreeably furprifed ; and when he meets an enemy
unexpectedly, he is faid to be difagreeably furprifed.

It

* Hence the Latin names for furprife, *torpor, animi, ftupor.*

It appears, then, that the fole effect of furprife is to
fwell the emotion raifed by the object. And that effect can be clearly explained : a tide of connected
perceptions glide gently into the mind, and produce
no perturbation ; but an object breaking in unexpectedly, founds an alarm, roufes the mind out of its
calm ftate, and directs its whole attention to the object, which, if agreeable becomes doubly fo. Several circumftances concur to produce that effect :
on the one hand, the agitation of the mind, and its
keen attention, prepare it in the moft effectual manner for receiving a deep impreffion : on the other
hand, the object, by its fudden and unforefeen appearance, makes an impreffion, not gradually as expected objects do, but as at one ftroke with its whole
force. The circumftances are precifely fimilar where
the object is in itfelf difagreeable.*

The

* What the Marefchal Saxe terms *le cœur humain* is no other than
fear occafioned by furprife. It is owing to that caufe that an ambufh is
generally fo deftructive : intelligence of it beforehand renders it harm-
lefs. The Marefchal gives from Cæfar's Commentaries two examples of
what he calls *le cœur humain*. At the fiege of Amiens by the Gauls,
Cæfar came up with his army, which did not exceed 7000 men, and began to intrench himfelf in fuch hurry, that the barbarians, judging him
to be afraid, attacked his intrenchments with great fpirit. During the
time they were filling up the ditch, he iffued out with his cohorts ; and,
by attacking them unexpectedly, ftruck a panic that made them fly
with precipitation, not a fingle man offering to make a ftand. At the
fiege of Alefia, the Gauls, infinitely fuperior in number, attacked the
Roman lines of circumvallation, in order to raife the fiege. Cæfar ordered a body of his men to march out filently, and to attack them on the
one flank, while he with another body did the fame on the other
flank. The furprife of being attacked when they expected a de-
fence only, put the Gauls into diforder, and gave an eafy victory to
Cæfar.
    A third may be added, no lefs memorable. In the year 846, an ob-
ftinate battle was fought between Xamire King of Leon, and Abdoul-
rahman the Moorifh King of Spain. After a very long conflict, the
night only prevented the Arabians from obtaining a complete victory.
The King of Leon, taking advantage of the darknefs, retreated to a
neighbouring hill, leaving the Arabians mafters of the field of battle.
                                                                 Next

The pleafure of novelty is eafily diftinguifhed from that of variety: to produce the latter, a plurality of objects is neceffary; the former arifes from a circum- ftance found in a fingle object. Again, where ob- jects, whether coexiftent or in fucceffion, are fuffi- ciently diverfified, the pleafure of variety is com- plete, though every fingle object of the train be fa- miliar: but the pleafure of novelty, directly oppofite to familiarity, requires no diverfification.

There are different degrees of novelty, and its ef- fects are in proportion. The loweft degree is found in objects furveyed a fecond time after a long inter- val; and that in this cafe an object takes on fome ap- pearance of novelty, is certain from experience: a large building of many parts varioufly adorned, or an extenfive field embellifhed with trees, lakes, temples, ftatues, and other ornaments, will appear new oft- ener than once: the memory of an object fo com- plex is foon loft, of its parts at leaft, or of their ar- rangement. But experience teaches, that even with- out any decay of remembrance, abfence alone will give an air of novelty to a once familiar object; which is not furprifing, becaufe familiarity wears off gradually by abfence: thus a perfon with whom we have been intimate, returning after a long interval, appears like a new acquaintance: and diftance of place contributes to this appearance, no lefs than diftance of time: a friend, for example, after a fhort abfence in a remote country, has the fame air of

Novelty

Next morning, perceiving that he could not maintain his place for want of provifions, nor be able to draw off his men in the face of a victorious army, he ranged his men in order of battle, and, without lofing a mo- ment, marched to attack the enemy, refolving to conquer or die. The Arabians, aftonifhed to be attacked by thofe who were conquered the night before, loft all heart: fear fucceeded to aftonifhment, the panic was univerfal, and they all turned their backs almoft without drawing a fword.

novelty as if he had returned after a longer interval
from a place near home : the mind forms a connection between him and the remote country, and beſtows upon him the ſingularity of the objects he has
ſeen. For the ſame reaſon, when two things equally
new and ſingular are preſented, the ſpectator balances
between them ; but when told that one of them is
the product of a diſtant quarter of the world, he no
longer heſitates, but clings to it as the more ſingular.
Hence the preference given to foreign luxuries, and
to foreign curioſities, which appear rare in proportion to their original diſtance.

The next degree of novelty, mounting upward, is
found in objects of which we have ſome information
at ſecond hand ; for deſcription, though it contribute to familiarity, cannot altogether remove the appearance of novelty when the object itſelf is preſented : the firſt ſight of a lion occaſions ſome wonder,
after a thorough acquaintance with the correcteſt
pictures and ſtatues of that animal.

A new object that bears ſome diſtant reſemblance
to a known ſpecies, is an inſtance of a third degree
of novelty : a ſtrong reſemblance among individuals
of the ſame ſpecies, prevents almoſt entirely the effect of novelty, unleſs diſtance of place or ſome other
circumſtance concur ; but where the reſemblance is
faint, ſome degree of wonder is felt, and the emotion
riſes in proportion to the faintneſs of the reſemblance.

The higheſt degree of wonder ariſeth from unknown objects that have no analogy to any ſpecies
we are acquainted with. Shakeſpear in a ſimile introduces that ſpecies of novelty :

As glorious to the ſight
As is a winged meſſenger from heaven
                                        Unto

Unto the white up-turning wond'ring eye
Of mortals, that fall back to gaze on him
When he beſtrides the lazy-pacing clouds,
And ſails upon the boſom of the air.
Romeo and Juliet.

One example of that ſpecies of novelty deſerves peculiar attention ; and that is, when an object altogether new is ſeen by one perſon only, and but once. Theſe circumſtances heighten remarkably the emotion : the ſingularity of the ſpectator concurs with the ſingularity of the object, to inflame wonder to its higheſt pitch.

In explaining the effects of novelty, the place a being occupies in the ſcale of exiſtence, is a circumſtance that muſt not be omitted. Novelty in the individuals of a low claſs is perceived with indifference, or with a very ſlight emotion : thus a pebble, however ſingular in its appearance, ſcarce moves our wonder. The emotion riſes with the rank of the object ; and, other circumſtances being equal, is ſtrongeſt in the higheſt order of exiſtence : a ſtrange infect affects us more than a ſtrange vegetable : and a ſtrange quadruped more than a ſtrange infect.

However natural novelty may be, it is a matter of experience, that thoſe who reliſh it the moſt are careful to conceal its influence. Love of novelty, it is true, prevails in children, in idlers, and in men of ſhallowunderſtanding : and yet, after all, why ſhould one be aſhamed of indulging a natural propenſity ? A diſtinction will afford a ſatisfactory anſwer. No man is aſhamed of curioſity when it is indulged in order to acquire knowledge. But to prefer any thing merely becauſe it is new, ſhows a mean taſte, which one ought to be aſhamed of : vanity is commonly at the bottom, which leads thofe who are deficient in tafte to prefer things odd, rare, or fingular, in order to diftinguifh themfelves from others. And in fact, that appetite, as above mentioned, reigns chiefly among perfons of a mean tafte, who are ignorant of refined and elegant pleafures.

One final caufe of wonder, hinted above, is, that this emotion is intended to ftimulate our curiofity. Another, fomewhat different, is, to prepare the mind for receiving deep impreffions of new objects. An acquaintance with the various things that may affect us and with their properties, is effential to our wellbeing : nor will a flight or fuperficial acquaintance be fufficient; they ought to be fo deeply engraved on the mind, as to be ready for ufe upon every occafion. Now, in order to make a deep impreffion, it is wifely contrived, that things fhould be introduced to our acquaintance with a certain pomp and folemnity productive of a vivid emotion. When the impreffion is once fairly made, the emotion of novelty, being no longer neceffary, vanifheth almoft inftantaneoufly ; never to return, unlefs where the impreffion happens to be obliterated by length of time or other means ; in which cafe, the fecond introduction hath nearly the fame folemnity with the firft.

Defigning wifdom is no where more legible than in this part of the human frame. If new objects did not affect us in a very peculiar manner, their impreffions would be fo flight as fcarce to be of any ufe in life : on the other hand, did objects continue to affect us as deeply as at firft, the mind would be totally engroffed with them, and have no room left either for action or reflection.

The final caufe of furprife is ftill more evident than of novelty. Self-love makes us vigilantly attentive to felf-prefervation ; but felf-love, which operates by

means

means of reafon and reflection, and impels not the
mind to any particular object or from it, is a principle too cool for a fudden emergency : an object
breaking in unexpectedly, affords no time for deliberation ; and, in that cafe, the agitation of furprife
comes in feafonably to roufe felf-love into action :
furprife gives the alarm ; and if there be any appearance of danger, our whole force is inftantly fummon-
ed up to fhun or to prevent it.

C H A P.

C H A P. VII.

Rifible Objects.

SUCH is the nature of man, that his powers and faculties are foon blunted by exercife. The
returns of fleep, fufpending all activity, are not alone
fufficient to preferve him in vigor : during his walking hours, amufement by intervals is requifite to un-
bend his mind from ferious occupation. To that
end, nature hath kindly made a provifion of many
objects, which may be diftinguifhed by the epithet of
rifible, becaufe they raife in us a peculiar emotion expreffed externally by *laughter :* that emotion is pleafant ; and being alfo mirthful, it moft fuccefsfully
unbends the mind, and recruits the fpirits. Imagination contributes a part by multiplying fuch objects
without end.

    Ludicrous is a general term, fignifying, as may ap-
pear from its derivation, what is playfome, fportive,
or jocular. *Ludicrous*, therefore, feems the genus,
of which *rifible* is a fpecies, limited as above to what
makes us laugh.

    However eafy it may be, concerning any particu-
lar object, to fay whether it be rifible or not, it
feems difficult, if at all practicable, to eftablifh any
general character, by which objects of that kind may
be diftinguifhed from others. Nor is that a fingular
cafe ; for, upon a review, we find the fame difficulty in moft of the articles already handled. There
is nothing more eafy, viewing a particular object,
than to pronounce that it is beautiful or ugly, grand

or

or little : but were we to attempt general rules for ranging objects under different claffes, according to thefe qualities, we fhould be much gravelled. A feparate caufe increafes the difficulty of diftinguifhing rifible objects by a general character : all men are not equally affected by rifible objects ; nor the fame man at all times ; for in high fpirits a thing will make him laugh outright, which fcarce provokes a fmile in a grave mood. Rifible objects, however, are circumfcribed within certain limits ; which I fhall fuggeft, without pretending to accuracy. And, in the firft place, I obferve, that no object is rifible but what appears flight, little, or trivial ; for we laugh at nothing that is of importance to our own intereft, or to that of others. A real diftrefs raifes pity, and therefore cannot be rifible ; but a flight or imaginary diftrefs, which moves not pity, is rifible. The adventure of the fulling-mills in Don Quixote, is extremely rifible ; fo is the fcene where Sancho, in a dark night, tumbling into a pit, and attaching himfelf to the fide by hand and foot, hangs there in terrible difmay till the morning, when he difcovers himfelf to be within a foot of the bottom. A nofe remarkably long or fhort, is rifible : but to want it altogether, far from provoking laughter, raifes horror in the fpectator. Secondly, With refpect to works both of nature and of art, none of them are rifible but what are out of rule, fome remarkable defect or excefs ; a very long vifage, for example, or a very fhort one. Hence nothing juft, proper, decent, beautiful, proportioned, or grand, is rifible.

Even from this flight fketch it will readily be conjectured, that the emotion raifed by a rifible object is of a nature fo fingular, as fcarce to find place while the mind is occupied with any other paffion or emo-

tion :

tion : and the conjecture is verified by experience ;
for we fcarce ever find that emotion blended with any
other.   One emotion I muft except ; and that is,
contempt raifed by certain improprieties : every improper act infpires us with fome degree of contempt
for the author ; and if an improper act be at the
fame time rifible to provoke laughter, of which
blunders and abfurdities are noted inftances, the two
emotions of contempt and of laughter unite intimately
in the mind, and produce externally what is termed
a laugh of derifion or *of fcorn*.   Hence objects that caufe
laughter may be diftinguifhed into two kinds : they
are either *rifible* or *ridiculous*.   A rifible object is
mirthful only : a ridiculous object is both mirthful and
contemptible. The firft raifes an emotion of laughter that
is altogether pleafant: the pleafant emotion of laughter
raifed by the other, is blended with the painful emotion of contempt ; and the mixed emotion is termed
the emotion of ridicule.   The pain a ridiculous object
gives me is refented and punifhed by a laugh of derifion.   A rifible object, on the other hand, gives me
no pain : it is altogether pleafant by a certain fort of
titillation, which is exprefled externally by mirthful
laughter.   Ridicule will be more fully explained afterward : the prefent chapter is appropriated to the
other emotion.

Rifible objects are fo common, and fo well underftood, that it is unneceffary to confume paper or time
upon them.   Take the few following examples.

Falftaff. I do remember him at Clement's inn, like a
man made after fupper of a cheefe-paring.   When he was
naked, he was for all the world like a forked radifh, with
a head fantaftically carved upon it with a knife.

Second Part, Henry IV. act. 3. fc. 5.

The foregoing is of difproportion.   The following
examples are of flight or imaginary misfortunes.

Falftaff.

Falftaff. Go fetch me a quart of fack ; put a toaft in't. Have I liv'd to be carried in a bafket, like a barrow of butcher's offal, and to be thrown into the Thames ! Well, if I be ferved fuch another trick, I'll have my brains ta'en out and butter'd, and give them to a dog for a new year's gift. The rogues flighted me into the river with as little remorfe as they would have drown'd a bitch's blind puppies, fifteen i'th'litter ; and you may know by my fize, that I have a kind of alacrity in finking : if the bottom were as deep as hell, I fhould down. I had been drown'd, but that the fhore was fhelvy and fhallow ; a death that I abhor ; for the water fwells a man : and what a thing fhould I have been when I had been fwell'd ? I fhould have been a mountain of mummy.

Merry Wives of Windfor, act 3. *fc.* 15.

Falftaff. Nay, you fhall hear, Mafter Brook, what I have fuffer'd to bring this woman to evil for your good. Being thus cramm'd in the bafket, a couple of Ford's knaves, his hinds, were call'd forth by their miftrefs, to carry me in the name of foul cloaths to Datchet-lane. They took me on their fhoulders, met the jealous knave their mafter in the door, who afk'd them once or twice what they had in their bafket. I quak'd for fear, left the lunatick knaves would have fearch'd it ; but Fate, ordaining he fhould be a cuckold, held his hand. Well, on went he for a fearch, and away went I for foul cloaths. But mark the fequel, Mafter Brook. I fuffer'd the pangs of three egregious deaths ; firft, an intolerable fright, to be detected by a jealous rotten bell-weather ; next, to be com-pafs'd like a good bilbo, in the circumference of a peck, hilt to point, heel to head ; and then to be ftopt in, like a ftrong diftillation, with ftinking cloaths that fretted in their own greafe. Think of that, a man of my kidney ; think of that, that am as fubject to heat as butter ; a man of continual diffo-lution and thaw ; it was a miracle to 'fcape fuffocation. And in the height of this bath, when I was more than half ftew'd in greafe, like a Dutch difh, to be thrown into the Thames, and cool'd glowing hot, in that furge, like a horfe fhoe ; think of that ; hiffing hot ; think of that, Mafter Brook.

Merry Wives of Windfor, act 3. *fc.* 17.

P 3　　　　　　　　　　CHAP.

CHAP. VIII.

Reſemblance and Diſſimilitude.

HAVING diſcuſſed thoſe qualities and circumſtances of ſingle objects that ſeem peculiarly connected with criticiſm, we proceed, according to the method propoſed in the chapter of beauty, to the relations of objects, beginning with the relations of reſemblance and diſſimilitude.

The connection that man hath with the beings around him, requires ſome acquaintance with their nature, their powers, and their qualities, for regulating his conduct. For acquiring a branch of knowledge ſo eſſential to our well-being, motives alone of reaſon and intereſt are not ſufficient : nature hath providently ſuperadded curioſity, a vigorous propenſity, which never is at reſt. This propenſity attaches us to every new object ;* and incites us to compare objects, in order to diſcover their differences and reſemblances.

Reſemblance among objects of the ſame kind, and diſſimilitude among objects of different kinds, are too obvious and familiar to gratify our curioſity in any degree : its gratification lies in diſcovering differences among things where reſemblance prevails, and reſemblances where difference prevails. Thus a difference in individuals of the ſame kind of plants or animals is deemed a diſcovery ; while the many particulars in which they agree are neglected : and in different kinds, any reſemblance is greedily remarked,
without

---

* See chap. 6.

without attending to the many particulars in which they differ.

A comparifon, however, may be too far ftretched. When differences or refemblances are carried beyond certain bounds, they appear flight and trivial ; and for that reafon will not be relifhed by a man of tafte : yet fuch propenfity is there to gratify paffion, curiofity in particular, that even among good writers we find many comparifons too flight to afford fatisfaction. Hence the frequent inftances among logicians of diftinctions without any folid difference : and hence the frequent inftances among poets and orators, of fimilies without any juft refemblance. With regard to the latter, I fhall confine myfelf to one inftance, which will probably amufe the reader, being a quotation, not from a poet nor orator, but from a grave author, writing an inftitute of law. " Our ftudent fhall obferve, that the knowledge of the law is like a deep well, out of which each man draweth according to the ftrength of his underftanding. He that reacheth deepeft, feeth the amiable and admirable fecrets of the law, wherein I affure you the fages of the law in former times have had the deepeft reach. And, as the bucket in the depth is eafily drawn to the uppermoft part of the water, (for *nullum elementum in fuo proprio loco eft grave*) but take it from the water, it cannot be drawn up but with a great difficulty ; fo, albeit beginnings of this ftudy feem difficult, yet, when the profeffor of the law can dive into the depth, it is delightful, eafy, and without any heavy burden, fo long as he keep himfelf in his own proper element.*" Shakefpear, with uncommon humour, ridicules fuch difpofition to fimile-making,

by

* Coke upon Lyttleton, p. 71.

P 4

by putting in the mouth of a weak man a refemblance much of a piece with that now mentioned.

Fluellen. I think it is in Macedon, where Alexander is porn : I tell you, Captain, if you look in the maps of the orld, I warrant that you fall find, in the comparifons between Macedon and Monmouth, that the fituations, look you, is both alike. There is a river in Macedon, there is alfo moreover a river in Monmouth : it is called *Wye* at Monmouth, but it is out of my prains what is the name of the other river ; but it is all one, 'tis as like as my fingers to my fingers, and there is falmons in both. If you mark Alexander's life well, Harry of Monmouth's life is come after it indifferent well ; for there is figures in all things. Alexander, God knows, and you know, in his rages, and his furies, and his wraths, and his cholers, and his moods, and his difpleafures, and his indignations ; and alfo being a little, intoxicates in his prains, did, in his ales and his angers, look you, kill his peft friend Clytus.

Gower. Our King is not like him in that ; he never kill'd any of his friends.

Fluellen. It is not well done, mark you now, to take the tales out of my mouth, ere it is made and finifhed. I fpeak but in figures, and comparifons of it : As Alexander kill'd his friend Clytus, being in his ales and his cups ; fo alfo Harry Monmouth, being in his right wits and his good judgments, turn'd away the fat knight with the great belly doublet ; he was full of jefts, and gypes, and knaveries, and mocks : I have forgot his name.

Gower. Sir John Falftaff.

Fluellen. That is he : I tell you there is good men porn at Monmouth.

K. Henry V, *act* 4. *fc.* 13.

Inftruction, no doubt, is the chief end of comparifon ; but that it is not the only end will be evident from confidering, that a comparifon may be employed with fuccefs to put a fubject in a ftrong point of view. A lively idea is formed of a man's courage,

by

by likening it to that of a lion ; and eloquence is exalted in our imagination, by comparing it to a river
overflowing its banks, and involving all in its impetuous courſe.   The ſame effect is produced by contraſt : a man in proſperity becomes more ſenſible of
his happineſs by oppoſing his condition to that of a
perſon in want of bread.   Thus, compariſon is ſubſervient to poetry as well as to philoſophy : and,
with reſpect to both, the foregoing obſervation holds
equally, that reſemblance among objects of the ſame
kind, and diffimilitude among objects of different
kinds, have no effect : ſuch a compariſon neither tends
to gratify our curioſity, nor to ſet the objects compared in a ſtronger light : two apartments in a palace, ſimilar in ſhape, ſize, and furniture, make ſeparately as good a figure as when compared ; and the
ſame obſervation is applicable to two ſimilar compartments in a garden : on the other hand, oppoſe a
regular building to a fall of water, or a good picture to a towering hill, or even a little dog to a large
horſe, and the contraſt will produce no effect.   But
a reſemblance between objects of different kinds, and
a difference between objects of the ſame kind, have
remarkably an enlivening effect.   The poets, ſuch of
them as have a juſt taſte, draw all their ſimilies from
things that in the main differ widely from the principal ſubject ; and they never attempt a contraſt but
where the things have a common genus and a reſemblance in the capital circumſtances : place together a
large and a ſmall ſized animal of the ſame ſpecies,
the one will ·appear greater, the other leſs, than
when viewed ſeparately : when we oppoſe beauty to
deformity, each makes a greater figure by the compariſon.   We compare the dreſs of different nations
with curioſity, but without ſurpriſe ; becauſe they
have no ſuch reſemblance in the capital parts as to
                                                      pleaſe

pleafe us by contrafting the fmaller parts. But a new
cut of a fleeve or of a pocket enchants by its novelty, and in oppofition to the former fafhion raifes fome
degree of furprife.

That refemblance and diffimilitude have an enlivening effect upon objects of fight, is made fufficiently
evident: and that they have the fame effect upon objects
of the other fenfes, is alfo certain. Nor is that law
confined to the external fenfes ; for characters contrafted make a greater figure by the oppofition : Iago,
in the tragedy of *Othello*, fays,

> He hath a daily beauty in his life
> That makes me ugly.

The character of a fop, and of a rough warrior,
are no were more fuccefsfully contrafted than in
Shakefpear :

> *Hotfpur.* My liege, I did deny no prifoners :
> But I remember, when the fight was done,
> When I was dry with rage, and extreme toil,
> Breathlefs and faint, leaning upon my fword ;
> Came there a certain Lord, neat, trimly drefs'd,
> Frefh as a bridegroom ; and his chin, new-reap'd,
> Shew'd like a ftubble-land at harveft home.
> He was perfumed like a milliner ;
> And 'twixt his finger and his thumb he held
> A pouncet-box, which ever and anon
> He gave his nofe ;—and ftill he fmil'd and talk'd ;
> And as the foldiers bear dead bodies by,
> He call'd them untaught knaves, unmannerly,
> To bring a flovenly unhandfome corfe !
> Betwixt the wind and his nobility.
> With many holiday and lady terms
> He queftion'd me : among the reft, demanded
> My pris'ners, in your Majefty's behalf.
> I then all fmarting with my wounds ; being gall'd
> To be fo pefter'd with a popinjay,

Out

Out of my grief, and my impatience,.
Anfwer'd, negleſtingly, I know not what :
He ſhould, or ſhould not ; for he made me mad,
To fee him ſhine ſo briſk, and ſmell ſo ſweet,
And talk ſo like a waiting gentlewoman,
Of guns, and drums, and wounds ; (God ſave the mark !)
And telling me, the ſov'reigneſt thing on earth
Was parmacity, for an inward bruiſe ;
And that it was great pity, ſo it was,
This villainous faltpetre ſhould be digg'd
Out of the bowels of the harmleſs earth,
Which many a good, tall fellow had deſtroy'd
So cowardly : and but for theſe vile guns
He would himſelf have been a ſoldier.————

Firſt part, Henry IV. *aſt* 1. *ſc.* 4.

Paffions and emotions are alſo inflamed by comparifon. A man of high rank humbles the by-ſtanders,
even to annihilate them in their own opinion : Cæſar,
beholding the ſtatue of Alexander, was greatly mor-
tified, that now at the age of thirty-two when Alexander died, he had not performed one memorable
aſtion.

Our opinions alſo are much influenced by comparifon. A man whoſe opulence exceeds the ordinary
ſtandard, is reputed richer than he is in reality ; and
wiſdom or weakneſs, if at all remarkable in an individual, is generally carried beyond the truth.

The opinion a man forms of his preſent diſtreſs is
heightened by contraſting it with his former happineſs :

Could 1 forget
What I have been, I might the better bear
What I am deſtin'd to.   I'm not the firſt
That have been wretched : but to think how much
I have been happier.

Southern's Innocent Adultery, aſt 2.

The

The diflrefs of a long journey makes even an indifferent inn agreeable : and in travelling, when the
road is good, and the horfeman well covered, a bad
day may be agreeable by making him fenfible how
fnug he is.

The fame effeâ is equally remarkable, when a man
oppofes his condition to that of others. A fhip toffed
about in a florm, makes the fpeâator refleâ upon
his own eafe and fecurity, and puts thefe in the
ftrongeft light :

> Suave, mari magno turbantibus æquora ventis,
> E terra magnum alterius fpeâare laborem ;
> Non quia vexari quemquam eft jucunda voluptas,
> Sed quibus ipfe malis careas, quia cernere fuave eft.
> *Lucret. l. 2. principio.*

A man in grief cannot bear mirth : it gives him a
more lively notion of his unhappinefs, and of courfe
makes him more unhappy. Satan contemplating
the beauties of the terreftrial paradife, has the following exclamation :

> With what delight could I have walk'd thee round,
> If I could joy in ought, fweet interchange
> Of hill and valley, rivers, woods, and plains,
> Now land, now fea, and fhores with foreft crown'd,
> Rocks, dens, and caves ! but I in none of thefe
> Find place or refuge ; and the more I fee
> Pleafures about me, fo much more I feel
> Torment within me, as from the hateful fiege
> Of contraries : all good to me becomes
> Bane, and in heav'n much worfe would be my ftate.
> *Paradife Loft, book 9. l. 114.*

> *Gaunt.* All places that the eye of heaven vifits,
> Are to a wife man ports and happy havens.
> Teach thy neceffity to reafon thus :
> There is no virtue like neceffity.

Think

Think not the King did banifh thee ;
But thou the King. Wo doth the heavier fit,
Where it perceives it is but faintly borne.
Go fay, I fent thee forth to purchafe honour :
And not, the King exil'd thee.   Or fuppofe,
Devouring peftilence hangs in our air,
And thou art flying to a frefher clime,
Look what thy foul holds dear, imagine it
To lie that way thou go'ft, not whence thou com'ft.
Suppofe the finging birds muficians ;
The grafs whereon thou tread'ft, the prefence-floor ;
The flow'rs, fair ladies ; and thy fteps, no more
Than a delightful meafure or a dance.
For gnarling Sorrow hath lefs power to bite
The man that mocks at it, and fets it light.

Bolingbroke. Oh, who can hold a fire in his hand,
By thinking on the frofty Caucafus ?
Or cloy the hungry edge of Appetite,
By bare imagination of a feaft ?
Or wallow naked in December fnow,
By thinking on fantaftic fummer's heat ?
Oh, no ! the apprehenfion of the good
Gives but the greater feeling to the worfe.
                King Richard II. *act* 1. *fc.* 6.

The appearance of danger gives fometimes pleafure, fometimes pain.   A timorous perfon upon the
battlements of a high tower, is feized with fear, which
even the confcioufnefs of fecurity cannot diffipate.
But upon one of a firm head, this fituation has a
contrary effect : the appearance of danger heightens,
by oppofition, the confcioufnefs of fecurity, and confequently, the fatisfaction that arifes from fecurity :
here the feeling refembles that above mentioned, occafioned by a fhip labouring in a ftorm.

The effect of magnifying or leffening objects by
means of comparifon, is fo familiar, that no philof-
                                        opher

opher has thought of fearching for a caufe.* The obfcurity of the fubjeft may poffibly have contributed to their filence ; but luckily, we difcover the caufe to be a principle unfolded above, which is, the influence of paffion over our opinions†. We have had occafion to fee many illuftrious effects of that fingular power of paffion ; and that the magnifying or diminifhing objects by means of comparifon, proceeds from the fame caufe, will evidently appear, by reflecting in what manner a fpectator is affected, when a very large animal is for the firft time placed befide a very fmall one of the fame fpecies. The firft thing that ftrikes the mind, is the difference between the two animals, which is fo great as to occafion furprife; and this, like other emotions, magnifying its objects, makes us conceive the difference to be the greateft that can be : we fee, or feem to fee, the one animal extremely little, and the other extremely large. The emotion of furprife arifing from any unufual refemblance, ferves equally to explain, why at firfl view we are apt to think fuch refemblance more entire than it is in reality. And it muft not efcape obfervation, that the circumftances of more and lefs, which are the proper fubjects of comparifon, raife a perception fo indiftinct and vague as to facilitate the effect defcribed : we have no mental ftandard of great and little, nor of the feveral degrees of any attribute ; and the mind thus unreftrained, is naturally difpofed to indulge its furprife to the utmoft extent.

In

---

* Practical writers upon the fine arts will attempt any thing, being blind both to the difficulty and danger. De Piles, accounting why contraft is agreeable, fays, '' That it is a fort of war, which puts the oppofite parties in motion.'' Thus, to account for an effect of which there is no doubt, any caufe, however foolifh, is made welcome.

† Chap. 2. part 5.

In exploring the operations of the mind, fome of which are extremely nice and flippery, it is neceffary to proceed with the utmoft caution : and after all, feldom it happens that fpeculations of that kind af‐ ford any fatisfaction. Luckily, in the prefent cafe, our fpeculations are fupported by facts and folid ar‐ gument. Firft, a fmall object of one fpecies oppof‐ ed to a great object of another, produces not, in any degree, that deception which is fo remarkable when both objects are of the fame fpecies. The greateft difparity between objects of different kinds, is fo common as to be obferved with perfect indifference ; but fuch difparity between objects of the fame kind, being uncommon, never fails to produce furprife : and may we not fairly conclude, that furprife, in the latter cafe, is what occafions the deception, when we find no deception in the former ? In the next place, if furprife be the fole caufe of the deception, it fol‐ lows neceffarily, that the deception will vanifh as foon as the objects compared become familiar. This holds fo unerringly, as to leave no reafonable doubt that furprife is the prime mover : our furprife is great the firft time a fmall lap-dog is feen with a large maftiff ; but when two fuch animals are constantly together, there is no furprife, and it makes no dif‐ ference whether they be viewed feparately or in com‐ pany : we fet no bounds to the riches of a man who has recently made his fortune, the furprifing difpropor‐ tion between his prefent and his paft fituation being carried to an extreme; but with regard to a family that for many generations hath enjoyed great wealth, the fame falfe reckoning is not made : it is equally re‐ markable, that a trite fimile has no effect ; a lover compared to a moth fcorching itfelf at the flame of a

candle,

candle, originally a fprightly fimile, has by frequent ufe loft all force ; love cannot now be compared to fire, without fome degree of difguft : it has been juftly objected againft Homer, that the lion is too often introduced into his fimilies ; all the variety he is able to throw into them, not being fufficient to keep alive the reader's furprife.

To explain the influence of comparifon upon the mind, I have chofen the fimpleft cafe, to wit, the firft fight of two animals of the fame kind, differing in fize only ; but to complete the theory, other circum- ftances muft be taken in. And the next fuppofition I make, is where both animals, feparately familiar to the fpectator, are brought together for the firft time. In that cafe, the effect of magnifying and diminifh- ing, is found remarkably greater than in that firft mentioned ; and the reafon will appear upon analyf- ing the operation : the firft feeling we have is of fur- prife at the uncommon difference of two creatures of the fame fpecies ; we are next fenfible, that the one appears lefs, the other larger than they did for- merly; and that new circumftance, increafing our fur- prife, makes us imagine a ftill greater oppofition be- tween the animals than if we had formed no notion of them beforehand.

I fhall confine myfelf to one other fuppofition ; That the fpectator was acquainted beforehand with one of the animals only, the lap-dog for example. This new circumftance will vary the effect : for in- ftead of widening the natural difference, by enlarg- ing in appearance the one animal, and diminifhing the other in proportion, the whole apparent alteration will reft upon the lap-dog : the furprife to find it lefs than it appeared formerly, directs to it our whole at- tention, and makes us conceive it to be a moft dimin- utive creature : the maftiff in the mean time is quite
overlooked

overlooked. I am able to illuftrate this effect by a familiar example. Take a piece of paper, or of linen tolerably white, and compare it with a pure white of the fame kind : the judgment we formed of the firft object is inftantly varied ; and the furprife occafioned by finding it lefs white than was thought, produceth a hafty conviction that it is much lefs white than it is in reality : withdrawing now the pure white, and putting in its place a deep black, the furprife occafioned by that new circumftance carries us to the other extreme, and makes us conceive the object firft mentioned to be a pure white : and thus experience compels us to acknowledge, that our emotions have an influence even upon our eye-fight. This experiment leads to a general obfervation. That whatever is found more ftrange or beautiful than was expected, is judged to be more ftrange or beautiful than it is in reality. Hence a common artifice to depreciate beforehand what we wifh to make a figure in the opinion of others.

The comparifons employed by poets and orators, are of the kind laft mentioned ; for it is always a known object that is to be magnified or leffened. The former is effected by likening it to fome grand object, or by contrafting it with one of an oppofite character. To effectuate the latter, the method muft be reverfed : the object muft be contrafted with fomething fuperior to it, or likened to fomething inferior. The whole effect is produced upon the principal object, which by that means is elevated above its rank, or depreffed below it.

In accounting for the effect that any unufual refemblance or diffimilitude hath upon the mind, no caufe has been mentioned but furprife ; and to prevent confufion, it was proper to difcufs that caufe firft.

firſt. But ſurpriſe is not the only cauſe of the ef-
fe& deſcribed : another concurs, which operates perhaps not leſs powerfully, namely, a principle in human nature that lies ſtill in obſcurity, not having
been unfolded by any writer, though its effe&s are
extenſive ; and as it is not diſtinguiſhed by a proper
name, the reader muſt be ſatisfied with the following deſcription. Every man who ſtudies himſelf or
others, muſt be ſenſible of a tendency or propenſity
in the mind, to complete every work that is begun,
and to carry things to their full perfeɑtion. There
is little opportunity to diſplay that propenſity upon
natural operations, which are ſeldom left imperfe&;
but in the operations of art, it hath great ſcope : it
impels us to perſevere in our own work, and to wiſh
for the completion of what another is doing : we
feel a ſenſible pleaſure when the work is brought to
perfe&ion ; and our pain is no leſs ſenſible when we
are diſappointed. Hence our uneaſineſs, when an
intereſting ſtory is broke off in the middle, when a
piece of muſic ends without a cloſe, or when a building or garden is left unfiniſhed. The ſame propenſity operates in making colle&ions, ſuch as the
whole works good and bad of any author. A certain perſon attempted to colle& prints of all the capital paintings, and ſucceeded except as to a few.
La Bruyere remarks, that an anxious ſearch was
made for theſe ; not for their value, but to complete
the ſet.*

The

---

* The examples above given, are of things that can be carried to an
end or concluſion. But the ſame uneaſineſs is perceptible with reſpe&
to things that admit not any concluſion; witneſs a ſeries that has no end,
commonly called *an infinite ſeries*. The mind moving along ſuch a ſeries, begins ſoon to feel an uneaſineſs, which becomes more and more
ſenſible, in continuing its progreſs without hope of an end.
An unbounded proſpe& doth not long continue agreeable : we ſoon
feel

The final caufe of the propenfity is an additional proof of its exiftence : human , works are of no fignificancy till they be completed ; and reafon is not always a fufficient counterbalance to indolence : fome principle over and above is neceffary, to excite our induftry, and to prevent our ftopping fhort in the middle of the courfe. We need not lofe time to defcribe the co-operation of the foregoing propenfity with furprife, in producing the effect that follows any unufual refemblance or diffimilitude. Surprife firft operates, and carries

feel a flight uneafinefs, which increafes with the time we beftow upon the profpect. An avenue without a terminating object, is one inftance of an unbounded profpect ; and we might hope to find the caufe of its difagreeablenefs, if it refembled an infinite feries. The eye indeed promifes no refemblance ; for the fharpeft eye commands but a certain length of fpace, and there it is bounded, however obfcurely. But the mind perceives things as they exift ; and the line is carried on in idea without end ; in which refpect an unbounded profpect is fimilar to an infinite feries. In fact, the uneafinefs of an unbounded profpect, differs very little in its feeling from that of an infinite feries ; and therefore we may reafonably prefume, that both proceed from the fame caufe. We next confider a profpect unbounded every way, as, for example, a great plain or the ocean, viewed from an eminence. We feel here an uneafinefs occafioned by the want of an end or termination, precifely as in the other cafes. A profpect unbounded every way, is indeed fo far fingular, as at firft to be more pleafant than a profpect that is unbounded in one direction only, and afterward to be more painful. But thefe circumftances are eafily explained, without wounding the general theory : the pleafure we feel at firft, is a vivid emotion of grandeur, arifing from the immenfe extent of the object : and to increafe the pain we feel afterward for the want of a termination, there concurs a pain of a different kind, occafioned by ftretching the eye to comprehend fo wide a profpect ; a pain that gradually increafes with the repeated efforts we make to grafp the whole. It is the fame principle, if I miflake not, which operates imperceptibly with refpect to quantity and number. Another's property indented into my field, gives me uneafinefs ; and I am eager to make the purchafe, not for profit, but in order to fquare my field. Xerxes and his army, in their paffage to Greece, were fumptuoufly entertained by Pythius the Lydian : Xerxes recompenfed him with 7000 Darics, which he wanted to complete the fum of four millions.

carries our opinion of the refemblance or diffimilitude beyond truth. The propenfity we have been defcribing carries us ftill farther; for it forces upon the mind a conviction, that the refemblance or diffimilitude is complete. We need no better illuftration, than the refemblance that is fancied in fome pebbles to a tree or an infect; which refemblance, however faint in reality, is conceived to be wonderfully perfect. The tendency to complete a refemblance acting jointly with furprife, carries the mind fometimes fo far, as even to prefume upon future events. In the Greek tragedy entitled *Phineides*, thofe unhappy women, feeing the place where it was intended they fhould be flain, cried out with anguifh, " They now faw their cruel deftiny had condemned them to die in that place, being the fame where they had been expofed in their infancy.*"

The propenfity to advance every thing to its perfection, not only co-operates with furprife to deceive the mind, but of itfelf is able to produce that effect. Of this [we fee many inftances where there is no place for furprife; and the firft I fhall give is of refemblance. *Unumquodque eodem modo diffolvitur quo colligatum eft*, is a maxim in the Roman law that has no foundation in truth; for tying and loofing, building and demolifhing, are acts oppofite to each other, and are performed by oppofite means: but when thefe acts are connected by their relation to the fame fubject, their connection leads us to imagine a fort of refemblance between them, which by the foregoing propenfity is conceived to be as complete as poffible. The next inftance fhall be of contraft. Addifon obferves,

---

* Ariftotle, poet. cap. 17.

obferves,* "That the paleft features look the moft agreeable in white ; that a face which is overfluflhed appears to advantage in the deepeft fcarlet ; and that a dark complexion is not a little alleviated by a black hood." The foregoing propenfity ferves to account for thefe appearances ; to make which evident, one of the cafes fhall fuffice. A complexion, however dark, never approaches to black : when thefe colours appear together, their oppofition ftrikes us ; and the propenfity we have to complete the oppofition makes the darknefs of complexion vanifh out of fight.

The operation of this propenfity, even where there is no ground for furprife, is not confined to opinion or conviction : fo powerful it is, as to make us fometimes proceed to action, in order to complete a refemblance or diffimilitude. If this appear obfcure, it will be made clear by the following inftances. Upon what principle is the *lex talionis* founded, other than to make the punifhment refemble the mifchief ? Reafon dictates, that there ought to be a conformity or refemblance between a crime and its punifhment; and the foregoing propenfity impels us to make the refemblance as complete as poffible. Titus Livius, under the influence of that propenfity, accounts for a certain punifhment by a refemblance between it and the crime, too fubtile for common apprehenfion. Treating of Mettus Fuffetius, the Alban general, who, for treachery to the Romans his allies, was fentenced to be torn to pieces by horfes, he puts the following fpeech in the mouth of Tullus Hoftilius, who decreed the punifhment. "Mette Fuffeti, inquit, fi ipfe difcere poffes fidem ac fœdera, fervare, vivo tibi ca difciplina a me adhibita effet. Nunc, quoniam tuun infanabile

* Spectator, No. 265.

infanabile ingenium eft, at tu tuo fupplicio doce hu-
manum genus, ea fanƈta credere, quae a te violata
funt. Ut igitur paulo ante animum inter Fidenatem
Romanamque rem ancipitem geffifti, ita jam corpus
paffim diftrahendum dabis.*" By the fame influence, the fentence is often executed upon the very
fpot where the crime was committed. In the *Eleƈtra*
of Sophocles, Egiftheus is dragged from the theatre
into an inner room of the fuppofed palace, to fuffer
death where he murdered Agamemnon. Shakefpear,
whofe knowledge of nature is no lefs profound than
extenfive, has not overlooked this propenfity :

Othello. Get me fome poifon, Iago, this night ; I'll
not expoftulate with her, left her body and her beauty un-
provide my mind again ; this night, Iago.
Iago. Do it not with poifon ; ftrangle her in bed, even
in the bed fhe hath contaminated.
Othello. Good, good : The juftice of it pleafes ; very
good.

Othello, aƈt 4. fc. 5.

Warwick. From off the gates of York fetch down the
          head,
Your father's head, which Clifford placed there.
Inftead whereof let his fupply the room.
Meafure for meafure muft he anfwered.

Third Part of Henry VI. aƈt 2. fc. 9.

Perfons in their laft moments are generally feized
with an anxiety to be buried with their relations. In
the *Amynta* of Taffo, the lover, hearing that his miftrefs was torn to pieces by a wolf, expreffes a defire
to die the fame death.†

Upon the fubjeƈt in general I have two remarks to
add. The firft concerns refemblance, which, when
                                                        too

---

* Lib. 1. feƈt. 28,   † Aƈt 4. fc. 2.

too entire, hath no effect, however different in kind
the things compared may be. The remark is applicable to works of art only ; for natural objects of
different kinds have fcarce ever an entire refemblance. To give an example in a work of art, marble is a fort of matter very different from what com-
pofes an animal ; and marble cut into a human figure produces great pleafure by the refemblance : but,
if a marble ftatue be coloured like a picture, the refemblance is fo entire, as at a diftance to make the
ftatue appear a perfon : we difcover the miftake
when we approach ; and no other emotion is raifed,
but furprife occafioned by the deception : The figure ftill appears a real perfon, rather than an imitation ; and we muft ufe reflection to correct the miftake. This cannot happen in a picture ; for the refemblance can never be fo entire as to difguife the
imitation.

The other remark relates to contraft. Emotions
make the greateft figure when contrafted in fucceffion ; but the fucceffion ought neither to be rapid,
nor immoderately flow : if too flow, the effect of
contraft becomes faint by the diftance of the emotions ; and if rapid, no fingle emotion has room to
expand itfelf to its full fize, but is ftifled, as it were,
in the birth, by a fucceeding emotion. The funeral
oration of the Bifhop of Meaux upon the Duchefs of
Orleans is a perfect hodge-podge of cheerful and melancholy reprefentations following each other in the
qiuckeft fucceffion : oppofite emotions are beft felt
in fucceffion ; but each emotion feparately fhould be
raifed to its due pitch, before another be introduced.

What is above laid down, will enable us to determine a very important queftion concerning emotions
raifed by the fine arts, namely, Whether ought fim-

ilar

ilar emotions to succeed each other or dissimilar ? The emotions raised by the fine arts are for the most part too nearly related to make a figure by resemblance; and for that reason their succession ought to be regulated as much as possible by contrast. This holds confessedly in epic and dramatic compositions; and the best writers, led perhaps by taste more than by reasoning, have generally aimed at that beauty. It holds equally in music; in the same cantata, all the variety of emotions that are within the power of music may not only be indulged, but, to make the greatest figure, ought to be contrasted. In gardening, there is an additional reason for the rule: the emotions raised by that art are at best so faint, that every artifice should be employed to give them their utmost vigor: a field may be laid out in grand, sweet, gay, neat, wild, melancholy scenes; and when these are viewed in succession, grandeur ought to be contrasted with neatness, regularity with wildness, and gaiety with melancholy, so as that each emotion may succeed its opposite: nay it is an improvement to intermix in the succession rude uncultivated spots as well as unbounded views, which in themselves are disagreeable, but in succession heighten the feeling of the agreeable objects; and we have nature for our guide, which in her most beautiful landscapes often intermixes rugged rocks, dirty marshes, and barren stony heaths. The greatest masters of music have the same view in their compositions: the second part of an Italian song seldom conveys any sentiment; and, by its harshness, seems purposely contrived to give a greater relish for the interesting parts of the composition.

A small garden comprehended under a single view, affords little opportunity for that embellishment. Dissimilar emotions require different tones of mind;

and therefore in conjunction can never be pleafant :*
gaiety and fweetnefs may be combined, or wildnefs
and gloominefs ; but a compofition of gaiety and
gloominefs is diftafteful.	The rude uncultivated
compartment of furze and broom in Richmond
garden hath a good effect in the fucceffion of objects ;
but a fpot of that nature would be infufferable in the
midft of a polifhed parterre or flower-plot. A garden,
therefore, if not of great extent, admits not diffimilar
emotions ; and in ornamenting a fmall garden, the
the fafeft courfe is to confine it to a fingle expreffion.
For the fame reafon, a landfcape ought alfo to be
confined to a fingle expreffion ; and accordingly it is
a rule in painting, That if the fubject be gay, every
figure ought to contribute to that emotion.

It follows from the foregoing train of reafoning,
that a garden near a great city ought to have an air
of folitude.	The folitarinefs again of a wafte coun-
try ought to be contrafted in forming a garden ; no
temples, no obfcure walks : but *jets d'eau*, cafcades,
objects active, gay and fplendid.	Nay, fuch a gar-
den fhould in fome meafure avoid imitating nature,
by taking on an extraordinary appearance of regularity and art, to fhow the bufy hand of man, which
in a wafte country has a fine effect by contraft.

It may be gathered from what is faid above,† that
wit and ridicule make not an agreeable mixture with
grandeur.	Diffimilar emotions have a fine effect in
a flow fucceffion ; but in a rapid fucceffion, which
appproaches to coexiftence, they will not be relifhed :
in the midft of a laboured and elevated defcription of
a battle, Virgil introduces a ludicrous image, which
is certainly out of its place :

Obvius

---

* See chap. 2, part 4.	† Chap. 2. part 4.

Obvíus ambuſtum torrem Chorinæus ab ara
Corripit, et venienti Ebuſo plagamque ferenti
Occupat os flammis : illi ingens barba reluxit,
Nidoremque ambuſta dedit.

Æn. xii. 298.

The following image is no leſs ludicrous, nor leſs improperly placed.

Mentre fan queſti i bellici ſtromenti
Perche debbiano toſto in uſo porſe,
Il gran nemico de l'humane genti
Contra i Chriſtiani i lividi occhi torſe :
E lor veggendo à le bell' opre intenti,
Ambo le labra per furor ſi morſe :
E qual tauro ferito, il ſuo dolore
Verſo mugghiando e ſofpirando fuore.

Gerufal. cant. 4. *ſt.* 1.

It would, however, be too auſtere to baniſh altogether ludicrous images from an epic poem. This poem doth not always ſoar above the clouds : it admits great variety ; and upon occaſion can defcend even to the ground without finking. In its more familiar tones, a ludicrous ſcene may be introduced without impropriety. This is done by Virgil* in a foot-race ; the circumſtances of which, not excepting the ludicrous part, are copied from Homer.†
After a fit of merriment, we are, it is true, the leſs difpofed to the ferious and fublime : but then, a ludicrous ſcene, by unbending the mind from fevere application to more intereſting ſubjeƈts, may prevent fatigue, and preferve our reliſh entire.

* Æn. lib. 5.   † Iliad, book 23. l. 879.

CHAP.

CHAP. IX.

Uniformity and Variety.

IN attempting to explain uniformity and variety, in order to fhow how we are affected by thefe circumftances, a doubt occurs, what method ought to be followed. In adhering clofe to the fubject, I forefee difficulties ; and yet by indulging fuch a circuit as may be neceffary for a fatisfactory view, I probably fhall incur the cenfure of wandering.— Yet the dread of cenfure ought not to prevail over what is proper : befide that the intended circuit will lead to fome collateral matters, that are not only curious, but of confiderable importance in the fcience of human nature.

The neceffary fucceffion of perceptions may be examined in two different views ; one with refpect to order and connection, and one with refpect to uniformity and variety. In the firft view it is handled above :* and I now proceed to the fecond. The world we inhabit is replete with things no lefs remarkable for their variety than for their number : thefe, unfolded by the wonderful mechanifm of external fenfe, furnifh the mind with many perceptions; which, joined with ideas of memory, of imagination, and of reflection, form a complete train that has not a gap or interval. This train of perceptions and ideas depends very little on will. The mind, as has been obferved,† is fo conftituted, " That it can by

no

* Chap. 1.

† Locke, book 2. chap. 14.

no effort break off the fucceffion of its ideas, nor keep its attention long fixed upon the fame object ;" we can arreft a perception in its courfe ; we can fhorten its natural duration, to make room for another ; we can vary the fucceffion, by change of place or of amufement ; and we can in fome meaf-ure prevent variety, by frequently recalling the fame object after fhort intervals : but ftill there muft be a fucceffion and a change from one perception to another. By artificial means, the fucceffion may be retarded or accelerated, may be rendered more various or more uniform, but in one fhape or another is unavoidable.

The train, even when left to its ordinary courfe, is not always uniform in its motion; there are natural caufes that accelerate or retard it confiderably. The firft I fhall mention, is a peculiar conftitution of mind. One man is diftinguifhed from another, by no circumftance more remarkably, than his train of perceptions : to a cold languid temper belongs a flow courfe of perceptions, which occafions dulnefs of ap-prehenfion and fluggifhnefs in action : to a warm tem-per, on the contrary, belongs a quick courfe of per-ceptions, which occafions quicknefs of apprehenfion and activity in bufinefs. The Afiatic nations, the Chinefe efpecially, are obferved to be more cool and deliberate than the Europeans : may not the reafon be, that heat enervates by exhaufting the fpirits ? and that a certain degree of cold, as in the middle regions of Europe, bracing the fibres, roufeth the mind, and produceth a brifk circulation of thought, accompanied with vigor in action ? In youth is ob-fervable a quicker fucceffion of perceptions than in old age : and hence, in youth, a remarkable avid-ity for variety of amufements, which in riper years give place to more uniform and more fedate occupa-tion.

tion. This qualifies men of middle age for bufinefs; where activity is required, but with a greater propor. tion of uniformity than variety. In old age, a flow and languid fucceffion makes variety unneceffary; and for that reafon, the aged in all their motions, are gen- erally governed by an habitual uniformity. Whatever be the caufe, we may venture to pronounce, that heat in the imagination and temper, is always connected with a brifk flow of perceptions.

The natural rate of fucceffion, depends alfo, in fome degree, upon the particular perceptions that compofe the train. An agreeable object, taking a ftrong hold of the mind, occafions a flower fuccef- fion than when the objects are indifferent : grandeur and novelty fix the attention for a confiderable time, excluding all other ideas : and the mind thus occu- pied is fenfible of no vacuity. Some emotions, by hurrying the mind from object to object, accelerate the fucceffion. Where the train is compofed of con- nected perceptions or ideas, the fucceffion is quick ; for if it is fo ordered by nature, that the mind goes eafily and fweetly along connected objects;* On the other hand, the fucceffion muft be flow, where the train is compofed of unconnected perceptions or ideas, which find not ready accefs to the mind ; and that an unconnected object is not admitted without a ftruggle, appears from the unfettled ftate of the mind for fome moments after fuch an object is prefented, wavering between it and the former train : during that fhort period, one or other of the former objects will intrude, perhaps oftener than once, till the at- tention be fixt entirely upon the new object. The fame obfervations are applicable to ideas fuggefted by language ; the mind can bear a quick fucceffion of

related

related ideas ; but an unrelated idea, for which the mind is not prepared, takes time to make an impreſſion ; and therefore a train compoſed of ſuch ideas, ought to proceed with a ſlow pace. Hence an epic poem, a play, or any ſtory connected in all its parts, may be peruſed in a ſhorter time, than a book of maxims or apothegms, of which a quick ſucceſſion creates both confuſion and fatigue.

Such latitude·hath nature indulged in the rate of ſucceſſion : what latitude it indulges with reſpect to uniformity, we proceed to examine. The uniformity or variety of a train, ſo far as compoſed of perceptions, depends on the particular objects that ſurround the percipient at the time. The preſent occupation muſt alſo have an influence ; for one is ſometimes engaged in a multiplicity of affairs, ſometimes altogether vacant. A natural train of ideas of memory is more circumſcribed, each object being, by ſome connection, linked to what precedes and to what follows it : theſe connections, which are many, and of different kinds, afford ſcope for a ſufficient degree of variety ; and at the ſame time prevent that degree which is unpleaſant by exceſs. Temper and conſtitution alſo have an influence here, as well as upon the rate of ſucceſſion : a man of a calm and ſedate temper, admits not willingly any idea but what is regularly introduced by a proper connection : one of a roving diſpoſition embraces with avidity every new idea, however ſlender its relation be to thoſe that preceded it. Neither muſt we overlook the nature of the perceptions that compoſe the train ; for their influence is no leſs with reſpect to uniformity and variety, than with reſpect to the rate of ſucceſſion. The mind engroſſed by any paſſion, love or hatred, hope or fear, broods over its object, and can bear no interruption ; and in ſuch a ſtate, the train of percep-

tions

tions muft not only be flow, but extremely uniform. Anger newly inflamed eagerly grafps its object, and leaves not a cranny in the mind for another thought but of revenge.   In the character of Hotfpur, that ftate of mind is reprefented to the life ; a picture remarkable for likenefs as well as for high colouring.

> *Worcefter.*   Peace, Coufin, fay no more.
> And now I will unclafp a fecret book,
> And to your quick-conceiving difcontents
> I'll read you matter deep and dangerous ;
> As full of peril and and advent'rous fpirit
> As to o'erwalk a current roaring loud,
> On the unftedfaft footing of a fpear.
>   *Hotfpur.* If he fall in, good night. Or fink or fwim,
> Send danger from the eaft into the weft,
> So honour crofs it from the north to fouth ;
> And let them grapple. Oh ! the blood more ftirs
> To roufe a lion than to ftart a hare.
>   *Worcefter.*   Thofe fame Noble Scots,
> That are your prifoners————
>   *Hotfpur.*   I'll keep them all ;
> By Heav'n, he fhall not have a Scot of them :
> No ; if a Scot would fave his foul, he fhall not ;
> I'll keep them, by this hand.
>   *Worcefter.*   You ftart away,
> And lend no ear unto my purpofes :
> Thofe prif'ners you fhall keep.
>   *Hotfpur.*   I will, that's flat :
> He faid he would not ranfom Mortimer ;
> Forbade my tongue to fpeak of Mortimer :
> But I will find him when he lies afleep,
> And in his ear I'll holla *Mortimer !*
> Nay, I will have a ftarling taught to fpeak
> Nothing but *Mortimer*, and give it him,
> To keep his anger ftill in motion.
>   *Worcefter.*   Hear you, coufin, a word.
>   *Hotfpur.*   All ftudies here I folemnly defy,
> Save how to gall and pinch this Bolingbroke :
> And that fame fword-and-buckler Prince of Wales,
>   (But

(But that I think his father loves him not,
And would be glad he met with fome mifchance,)
I'd have him poifon'd with a pot of ale.
Worcefter. Farewell, my kinfman, I will talk to you
When you are better temper'd to attend.
Firſt part, Henry IV. *act* 1. *fc.* 4.

Having viewed a train of perceptions as directed
by nature, and the variations it is fufceptible of from
different neceffary caufes, we proceed to examine
how far it is fubjected to will ; for that this faculty
hath fome influence, is obferved above. And firſt,
the rate of fucceffion may be retarded by infifting upon one object, and propelled by difmiffing another
before its time. But fuch voluntary mutations in the
natural courfe of fucceffion, have limits that cannot
be extended by the moſt painful efforts : which will
appear from confidering, that the mind circumfcribed in its capacity, cannot, at the fame inftant, admit many perceptions ; and when replete, that it
hath not place for new perceptions, till others are removed ; confequently, that a voluntary change of
perceptions cannot be inftantaneous, as the time it
requires fets bounds to the velocity of fucceffion. On
the other hand, the power we have to arreft a flying
perception is equally limited : and the reafon is, that
the longer we detain any perception, the more difficulty we find in the operation ; till, the difficulty becoming infurmountable, we are forced to quit our
hold, and to permit the train to take its ufual courfe.

The power we have over this train as to uniformity and variety, is in fome cafes very great, in others
very little. A train compofed of perceptions of external objects, depends entirely on the place we occupy, and admits not more nor lefs variety but by
change of place. A train compofed of ideas of
memory, is ftill lefs under our power ; becaufe we
cannot

cannot at will call up any idea that is not connected with the train.* But a train of ideas fuggefted by reading, may be varied at will, provided we have books at hand. The power that nature hath given us over our train of perceptions may be greatly ftrengthened by proper difcipline, and by an early application to bufinefs ; witnefs fome mathematicians, who go far beyond common nature in flownefs and uniformity ; and ftill more perfons devoted to religious exercifes, who pafs whole days in contemplation, and impofe upon themfelves long and fevere penances. With refpect to celerity and variety, it is not eafily conceived what length a habit of activity in affairs will carry fome men. Let a ftranger, or let any perfon to whom the fight is not familiar, attend the chancellor of Great Britain through the labours but of one day, during a feffion of parliament : how great will be his aftonifhment ! what multiplicity of lawbufinefs, what deep thinking, and what elaborate application to matters of government ! The train of perceptions muft in that great man be accelerated far beyond the ordinary courfe of nature ; yet no confufion or hurry ; but in every article the greateft order and accuracy. Such is the force of habit. How happy is man, to have the command of a principle of action that can elevate him fo far above the ordinary condition of humanity !†

We are now ripe for confidering a train of perceptions, with refpect to pleafure and pain : and to that fpeculation peculiar attention muft be given, becaufe it ferves to explain the effects that uniformity and

---

* See chap. I.

† This chapter was compofed in the year 1752.

and variety have upon the mind. A man, when his perceptions flow in their natural courfe, feels himfelf free, light, and eafy, efpecially after any forcible acceleration or retardation. On the other hand, the accelerating or retarding the natural courfe, excites a pain, which, though fcarcely felt in fmall removes, becomes confiderable toward the extremes. Averfion to fix on a fingle object for a long time, or to take in a multiplicity of objects in a fhort time, is remarkable in children ; and equally fo in men unaccuftomed to bufinefs : a man languifhes when the fucceffion is very flow ; and, if he grow not impatient, is apt to fall afleep : during a rapid fucceffion, he hath a feeling as if his head were turning round ; he is fatigued, and his pain refembles that of wearinefs after bodily labour.

But a moderate courfe will not fatisfy the mind, unlefs the perceptions be alfo diverfified : number without variety is not fufficient to conftitute an agreeable train. In comparing a few objects, uniformity is pleafant ; but the frequent reiteration of uniform objects becomes unpleafant : one tires of a fcene that is not diverfified ; and foon feels a fort of unnatural reftraint when confined within a narrow range, whether occafioned by a retarded fucceffion or by too great uniformity. An excefs in variety is, on the other hand, fatiguing : which is felt even in a train of related perceptions ; much more of unrelated perceptions, which gain not admittance without effort : the effort, it is true, is fcarce perceptible in a fingle inftance ; but by frequent reiteration it becomes exceedingly painful. Whatever be the caufe, the fact is certain, that a man never finds himfelf more at eafe, than when his perceptions fucceed each other with a certain degree, not only of velocity, but alfo of variety. The pleafure that arifes from a train

of

of connected ideas, is remarkable in a reverie; efpecially where the imagination interpofeth, and is active in coining new ideas, which is done with wonderful facility : one muft be fenfible, that the ferenity and eafe of the mind in that ftate, makes a great part of the enjoyment. The cafe is different where external objects enter into the train ; for thefe, making their appearance without order, and without connection fave that of contiguity, form a train of perceptions that may be extremely uniform or extremely diverfified ; which, for oppofite reafons, are both of them painful.

To alter, by an act of will, that degree of variety which nature requires, is not lefs painful, than to alter that degree of velocity which it requires. Contemplation, when the mind is long attached to one fubject, becomes painful by reftraining the free range of perception : curiofity, and the profpect of ufeful difcoveries, may fortify one to bear that pain : but it is deeply felt by the bulk of mankind, and produceth in them averfion to all abftract fciences. In any profeflion or calling, a train of operation that is fimple and reiterated without intermiffion, makes the operator languifh, and lofe vigor : he complains neither of too great labour, nor of too little action ; but regrets the want of variety, and the being obliged to do the fame thing over and over : where the operation is fufficiently varied, the mind retains its vigor, and is pleafed with its condition. Actions again create uneafinefs when exceflive in number or variety, though in every other refpect pleafant : thus a throng of bufinefs in law, in phyfic, or in traffic, diftreffes and diftracts the mind, unlefs where a habit of application is acquired by long and conftant exercife : the exceffive variety is the diftreffing circumftance ; and the mind fuffers grievoufly by being kept conftantly upon the ftretch. With

R 2

With relation to involuntary caufes difturbing that degree of variety which nature requires, a flight pain affecting one part of the body without variation, becomes, by its conftancy and long duration, almoft infupportable : the patient, fenfible that the pain is not increafed in degree, complains of its conftancy more than of its feverity, of its engroffing his whole thoughts, and admitting no other object. A fhifting pain is more tolerable, becaufe change of place contributes to variety : and an intermitting pain, fuffering other objects to intervene, ftill more fo. Again, any fingle colour or found often returning becomes unpleafant ; as may be obferved in viewing a train of fimilar apartments in a great houfe painted with the fame colour, and in hearing the prolonged tollings of a bell. Colour and found varied within certain limits, though without any order, are pleafant ; witnefs the various colours of plants and flowers in a field, and the various notes of birds in a thicket : increafe the number or variety, and the feeling becomes unpleafant ; thus a great variety of colours, crowded upon a fmall canvas or in quick fucceffion, create an uneafy feeling, which is prevented by putting the colours at a greater diftance from each other either of place or of time. A number of voices in a crowded affembly, a number of animals collected in a market, produce an unpleafant feeling ; though a few of them together, or all of them in a moderate fucceffion, would be pleafant. And becaufe of the fame excefs in variety, a number of pains felt in different parts of the body, at the fame inftant or in a rapid fucceffion, are an exquifite torture.

The pleafure or pain refulting from a train of perceptions in different circumftances, are a beautiful contrivance of nature for valuable purpofes. But being fenfible, that the mind, inflamed with fpecula-

tions

tions fo highly interefting, is beyond meafure difpofed
to conviction; I fhall be watchful to admit no argument nor remark, but what appears folidly founded :
and with that caution I proceed to unfold thefe purpofes. It is occafionally obferved above, that perfons
of a phlegmatic temperament, having a fluggifh train
of perceptions are indifpofed to action ; and that activity conftantly accompanies a brifk flow of perceptions. To afcertain that fact, a man need not go
abroad for experiments : reflecting on things paffing
in his own mind, he will find, that a brifk circulation
of thought conftantly prompts him to action; and
that he is averfe to action when his perceptions languifh in their courfe. But as man by nature is formed for action, and muft be active in order to be ·
happy, nature hath kindly provided againft indolence,
by annexing pleafure to a moderate courfe of perceptions, and by making any remarkable retardation
painful. A flow courfe of perceptions is attended
with another bad effect : man, in a few capital cafes,
is governed by propenfity or inftinct ; but in matters
that admit deliberation and choice, reafon is affigned
him for a guide : now as reafoning requires often a
great compafs of ideas, their fucceffion ought to be
fo quick as readily to furnifh every motive that may
be neceffary for mature deliberation ; in a languid fucceffion, motives will often occur after action is commenced when it is too late to retreat.

Nature hath guarded man, her favourite, againft
a fucceffion too rapid, no lefs carefully than againft
one too flow : both are equally painful, though the
pain is not the fame in both. Many are the good effects of that contrivance. In the firft place, as the
exertion of bodily faculties is by certain painful fenfations confined within proper limits, Nature is equally provident with refpect to the nobler faculties of
the

the mind : the pain of an accelerated courfe of perceptions, is Nature's admonition to relax our pace, and to admit a more gentle exertion of thought. Another valuable purpofe is difcovered upon reflecting in what manner objects are imprinted on the mind : to give the memory firm hold of an external object, time is required, even where attention is the greateft; and a moderate degree of attention, which is the common cafe, muft be continued ftill longer, to produce the fame effect: a rapid fucceffion, accordingly, muft prevent objects from making an impreffion fo deep as to be of real fervice in life; and Nature, for the fake of memory, has, by a painful feeling, guarded againft a rapid fucceffion. But a ftill more valuable purpofe is anfwered by the contrivance; as, on the one hand, a fluggifh courfe of perceptions indifpofeth to action; fo, on the other, a courfe too rapid impels to rafh and precipitant action: prudent conduct is the child of deliberation and clear conception, for which there is no place in a rapid courfe of thought. Nature therefore, taking meafures for prudent conduct, has guarded us effectually from precipitancy of thought, by making it painful.

Nature not only provides againft a fucceffion too flow or too quick, but makes the middle courfe extremely pleafant. Nor is that courfe confined within narrow bounds : every man can naturally, without pain, accelerate or retard in fome degree the rate of his perceptions. And he can do it in a ftill greater degree by the force of habit: a habit of contemplation annihilates the pain of a retarded courfe of perceptions; and a bufy life, after long practice, makes acceleration pleafant.

Concerning the final caufe of our tafte for variety, it will be confidered, that human affairs, complex by

variety

variety as well as number, require the diſtributing our attention and activity in meaſure and proportion. Nature therefore, to ſecure a juſt diſtribution correſponding to the variety of human affairs, has made too great uniformity or too great variety in the courſe of perceptions, equally unpleaſant : and indeed, were we addicted to either extreme, our internal conſtitution would be ill ſuited to our external circumſtances. At the ſame time, where great uniformity of operation is required, as in ſeveral manufactures, or great variety, as in law or phyſic, Nature, attentive to all our wants, hath alſo provided for theſe caſes, by implanting in the breaſt of every perſon, an efficacious principle that leads to habit : an obſtinate perſeverance in the ſame occupation, relieves from the pain of exceſſive uniformity ; and the like perſeverance in a quick circulation of different occupations, relieves from the pain of exceſſive variety. And thus we come to take delight in ſeveral occupations, that by nature, without habit, are not a little diſguſtful.

A middle rate alſo in the train of perceptions between uniformity and variety, is no leſs pleaſant than between quickneſs and ſlowneſs. The mind of man, ſo framed, is wonderfully adapted to the courſe of human affairs, which are continually changing, but not without connection : it is equally adapted to the acquiſition of knowledge, which reſults chiefly from diſcovering reſemblances among different objects, and differences among reſembling objects : ſuch occupation, even abſtracting from the knowledge we acquire, is in itſelf delightful, by preſerving a middle rate between too great uniformity and too great variety.

We are now arrived at the chief purpoſe of the preſent chapter ; which is to conſider uniformity and variety with relation to the fine arts, in order to diſcover if we can, when it is that the one ought to

prevail,

prevail, and when the other. And the knowledge we have obtained, will even at firſt view ſuggeſt a general obſervation, That in every work of art, it muſt be agreeable, to find that degree of variety which correſponds to the natural courſe of our perceptions ; and that an exceſs in variety or in uniformity muſt be diſagreeable, by varying that natural courſe. For that reaſon, works of art admit more or leſs variety according to the nature of the ſubjeƈt : in a piƈture of an intereſting event that ſtrongly attaches the ſpectator to a ſingle objeƈt, the mind reliſheth not a multiplicity of figures nor of ornaments : a piƈture repreſenting a gay ſubjeƈt, admits great variety of figures and ornaments ; becauſe theſe are agreeable to the mind in a cheerful tone. The ſame obſervation is applicable to poetry·and to muſic.

It muſt at the ſame time be remarked, that one can bear a greater variety of natural objeƈts, than of objeƈts in a piƈture ; and a greater variety in a piƈture than in a deſcription. A real objeƈt preſented to view, makes an impreſſion more readily than when repreſented in colours, and much more readily than when repreſented in words. Hence it is, that the profuſe variety of objeƈts in ſome natural landſcapes, neither breed confuſion nor fatigue : and for the ſame reaſon, there is place for greater variety of ornament in a piƈture than in·a poem. A piƈture, however, like a building, ought to be ſo ſimple as to be comprehended in one view. Whether every one of Le Brun's piƈtures of Alexander's hiſtory will ſtand this teſt, is ſubmitted to judges.

From theſe general obſervations, I proceed to particulars. In works expoſed continually to public view, variety ought to be ſtudied. It is a rule accordingly in ſculpture, to contraſt the different limbs of a ſtatue, in order to give it all the variety poſſible. Though
the

the cone, in a fingle view, be more beautiful than the pyramid ; yet a pyramidal fteeple, becaufe of its variety, is juftly preferred. For the fame reafon, the oval is preferred before the circle ; and painters, in copying buildings or any regular work, give an air of variety, by reprefenting the fubject in an angular view : we are pleafed with the variety, without lofing fight of the regularity. In a landfcape reprefenting animals, thofe efpecially of the fame kind, contraft ought to prevail : to draw one fleeping, another awake ; one fitting, another in motion ; one moving toward the fpectator, another from him, is the life of fuch a performance.

In every fort of writing intended for amufement, variety is neceffary in proportion to the length of the work. Want of variety is fenfibly felt in Davila's hiftory of the civil wars of France : the events are indeed important and various ; but the reader languifhes by a tirefome monotony of character, every perfon engaged being figured a confummate politician, governed by intereft only. It is hard to fay, whether Ovid difgufts more by too great variety, or too great uniformity : his ftories are all of the fame kind, concluding invariably with the transformation of one being into another ; and fo far he is tirefome by excefs in uniformity : he is not lefs fatiguing by excefs in variety, hurrying his reader inceffantly from ftory to ftory. Ariofto is ftill more fatiguing than Ovid, by exceeding the juft bounds of variety : not fatisfied, like Ovid, with a fucceffion in his ftories, he diftracts the reader, by jumbling together a multitude of them without any connection. Nor is the Orlando Furiofo lefs tirefome by its uniformity than the Metamorphofes, though in a different manner : after a ftory is brought to a crifis, the reader, intent on the cataftrophe, is fuddenly fnatched away to a new ftory, which makes no impreffion fo long as the mind is occupied with the former. This tantalizing method, from which the author never once fwerves during the courfe of a long work, befide its uniformity, hath another bad effect : it prevents that fympathy, which is raifed by an interefting event when the reader meets with no interruption.

The emotions produced by our perceptions in a train, have been little confidered, and lefs underftood; the fubject therefore required an elaborate difcuffion. It may furprife fome readers to find variety treated as only contributing to make a train of perceptions pleafant, when it is commonly held to be a neceffary ingredient in beauty of whatever kind ; according to the definition, " That beauty confifts in uniformity amid variety." But, after the fubject is explained and illuftrated as above, I prefume it will be evident, that this definition, however applicable to one or other fpecies, is far from being juft with refpect to beauty in general : variety contributes no fhare to the beauty of a moral action, nor of a mathematical theorem : and numberlefs are the beautiful objects of fight that have little or no variety in them ; a globe, the moft uniform of all figures, is of all the moft beautiful ; and a fquare, though more beautiful than a trapezium, hath lefs variety in its conftituent parts. The foregoing definition, which at beft is but obfcurely expreffed, is only applicable to a number of objects in a group or in fucceffion, among which indeed a due mixture of uniformity and variety is always agreeable; provided the particular object, feparately confidered, be in any degree beautiful, for uniformity amid variety among ugly objects, affords no pleafure. This circumftance is totally omitted in the definition ; and indeed to have mentioned it, would at the firft glance have fhown the definition to be imperfect : for to define beauty as arifing from beautiful objects blended

together

together in a due proportion of uniformity and variety, would be too grofs to pafs current : as nothing can be more grofs, than to employ in a definition the very term that is to be explained.

APPENDIX to CHAP. IX.

Concerning the Works of Nature, chiefly with refpect to Uniformity and Variety.

In things of Nature's workmanfhip, whether we regard their internal or external ftructure, beauty and defign are equally confpicuous. We fhall begin with the outfide of nature, as what firft prefents itfelf.

The figure of an organic body is generally regular. The trunk of a tree, its branches, and their ramifications, are nearly round, and form a feries regularly decreafing from the trunk to the fmalleft fibre : uniformity is no where more remarkable than in the leaves, which, in the fame fpecies, have all the fame colour, fize, and fhape : the feeds and fruits are all regular figures, approaching for the moft part to the globular form. Hence a plant, efpecially of the larger kind, with its trunk, branches, foliage, and fruit, is a charming object.

In an animal, the trunk, which is much larger than the other parts, occupies a chief place : its fhape, like that of the ftem of plants, is nearly round : a figure which of all is the moft agreeable : its two fides are precifely fimilar : feveral of the under parts go off in pairs ; and the two individuals of each pair are accurately uniform : the fingle parts are placed in the middle : the limbs, bearing a certain proportion to

the

the trunk, ferve to fupport it, and to give it a proper
elevation : upon one extremity are difpofed the neck
and head, in the direction of the trunk : the head
being the chief part, poffeffes with great propriety the
chief place. Hence, the beauty of the whole figure,
is the refult of many equal and proportional parts
orderly difpofed ; and the fmalleft variation in number, equality, proportion, or order, never fails to
produce a perception of deformity.

Nature in no particular feems more profufe of
ornament, than in the beautiful colouring of her
works. The flowers of plants, the furs of beafts,
and the feathers of birds, vie with each other in the
beauty of their colours, which in luftre as well as in
harmony are beyond the power of imitation. Of
all natural appearances, the colouring of the human
face is the moft exquifite : it is the ftrongeft inftance
of the ineffable art of nature, in adapting and propor-
tioning its colours to the magnitude, figure and pofition, of the parts. In a word, colour feems to live
in nature only, and to languifh under the fineft
touches of art.

When we examine the internal ftructure of a plant
or animal, a wonderful fubtility of mechanifm is difplayed. Man, in his mechanical operations, is confined to the furface of bodies ; but the operations of
nature are exerted through the whole fubftance, fo .
as to reach even the elementary parts. Thus the body
of an animal, and of a plant, are compofed of certain great veffels ; thefe of fmaller; and thefe again
of ftill fmaller, without end, as far as we can difcover.
This power of diffufing mechanifm through the
moft intimate parts, is peculiar to nature, and diftinguifhes her operations, moft remarkably, from
every work of art. Such texture, continued from
the groffer parts to the moft minute, preferves all
                                                      along

along the ſtricteſt regularity: the fibres of plants
are a bundle of cylindric canals, lying in the ſame
direction, and parallel or nearly parallel to each
other : in ſome inſtances, a moſt accurate arrangement of parts is diſcovered, as in onions, formed of
concentric coats, one within another, to the very centre.   An animal body is ſtill more admirable, in the
diſpoſition of its internal parts, and in their order
and ſymmetry : there is not a bone, a muſcle, a
blood veſſel, a nerve, that hath not one correſponding
to it on the oppoſite ſide ; and the ſame order is carried through the moſt minute parts ; the lungs are
compoſed of two parts, which are diſpoſed upon the
ſides of the thorax ; and the kidneys, in a lower ſituation, have a poſition no leſs orderly : as to the parts
that are ſingle, the heart is advantageouſly ſituated
near the middle : the liver, ſtomach, and ſpleen, are
diſpoſed in the upper region of the abdomen, about
the ſame height : the bladder is placed in the middle of the body, as well as the inteſtinal canal, which
fills the whole cavity with its convolutions.

The mechanical power of nature, not confined to
ſmall bodies, reacheth equally thoſe of the greateſt
ſize ; witneſs the bodies that compoſe the ſolar ſyſtem, which, however large, are weighed, meaſured,
and ſubjected to certain laws, with the utmoſt accuracy. Their places round the ſun, with their diſtances,
are determined by a preciſe rule, correſponding
to their quantity of matter. The ſuperior dignity of
the central body, in reſpect to its bulk and lucid appearance, is ſuited to the place it occupies. The
globular figure of theſe bodies, is not only in itſelf
beautiful, but is above all others fitted for regular
motion. Each planet revolves about its own axis in
a given time ; and each moves round the ſun, in an
orbit nearly circular, and in a time proportioned to.

its diftance. Their velocities, directed by an eftablifhed law, are perpetually changing by regular accele-
rations and retardations.   In fine, the great variety of
regular appearances, joined with the beauty of the
fyftem itfelf, cannot fail to produce the higheft delight in every one who is fenfible of defign, power,
or beauty.

Nature hath a wonderful power of connecting fyftems with each other, and of propagating that connection through all her works.   Thus the conftituent parts of a plant, the roots, the ftem, the branches,
the leaves, the fruit, are really different fyftems, united by a mutual dependence on each other : in an
animal, the lymphatic and lacteal ducts, the blood-
veffels and nerves, the mufcles and glands, the bones
and cartilages, the membranes and bowels, with the
other organs, form diftinct fyftems, which are united
into one whole.   There are, at the fame time, other
connections lefs intimate : every plant is joined to
the earth by its roots ; it requires rain and dews to
furnifh it with juices ; and it requires heat to preferve thefe juices in fluidity and motion : every animal,
by its gravity, is connected with the earth, with the
element in which it breathes, and with the fun, by
deriving from it cherifhing and enlivening heat : the
earth furnifheth aliment to plants, thefe to animals,
and thefe again to other animals, in a long train of
dependence : that the earth is part of a greater fyftem, comprehending many bodies mutually attracting
each other, and gravitating all toward one common
centre, is now thoroughly explored.   Such a regular and uniform feries of connections, propagated
through fo great a number of beings, and through
fuch wide fpaces is wonderful : and our wonder muft
increafe when we obferve thefe connections propa-

gated

gated from the minuteft atoms to bodies of the moft enormous fize, and fo widely diffufed as that we can neither perceive their beginning nor their end. That thefe connections are not confined within our own planetary fyftem, is certain : they are diffuffed over fpaces ftill more remote, where new bodies and fyftems rife without end. All fpace is filled with the works of God, which are conducted by one plan, to anfwer unerringly one great end.

But the moft wonderful connection of all, though not the moft confpicuous, is that of our interual frame with the works of nature : man is obvioully fitted for contemplating thefe works, becaufe in this contemplation he has great delight. The works of nature are remarkable in their uniformity no lefs than in their variety : and the mind of man is fitted to receive pleafure equally from both. Uniformity and variety are interwoven in the works of nature with furprifing art : variety, however great, is never without fome degree of uniformity ; nor the greateft uniformity without fome degree of variety : there is great variety in the fame plant, by the different appearances of its ftem, branches, leaves, bloffoms, fruit, fize, and colour ; and yet, when we trace that variety through different plants, efpecially of the fame kind, there is difcovered a furprifing uniformity : again, where nature feems to have intended the moft exact uniformity, as among individuals of the fame kind, there ftill appears a diverfity, which ferves readily to diftinguifh one individual from another. It is indeed admirable, that the human vifage, in which uniformity is fo prevalent, fhould yet be fo marked, as to leave no room, among millions, for miftaking one perfon for another : thefe marks, though clearly perceived, are generally fo delicate, that words cannot be found to defcribe them. A correfpondence fo

perfect

perfect between the human mind and the works of nature, is extremely remarkable. The oppofition between variety and uniformity is fo great, that one
would not readily imagine they could both be relifhed
by the fame palate ; at leaft not in the fame object, nor at the fame time : it is however true, that
the pleafures they afford, being happily adjufted
to each other, and readily mixing in intimate
union, are frequently produced by the fame individual object. Nay, further, in the objects that
touch us the moft, uniformity and variety are conftantly combined ; witnefs natural objects, whero
this combination is always found in perfection.
Hence it is, that natural objects readily form themfelves into groups, and are agreeable in whatever
manner combined : a wood with its trees, fhrubs and
herbs, is agreeable : the mufic of birds, the lowing
of cattle, and the murmuring of a brook, are in conjunction delightful ; though they ftrike the ear without modulation or harmony. In fhort, nothing can
be more happily accommodated to the inward conftitution of man, than that mixture of uniformity with
variety, which the eye difcovers in natural objects ;
and, accordingly, the mind is never more highly
gratified than in contemplating a natural landfcape.

CHAP.

CHAP. X.

Congruity and Propriety.

MAN is fuperior to the brute, not more by his rational faculties, than by his fenfes. With re-fpect to external fenfes, brutes probably yield not to men; and they may alfo have fome obfcure percep-tion of beauty : but the more delicate fenfes of reg-ularity, order, uniformity, and congruity, being connected with morality and religion, are referved to dignify the chief of the terreftrial creation. Upon that account, no difcipline is more fuitable to man, nor more *congruous* to the dignity of his nature, than that which refines his tafte, and leads him to diftin-guifh, in every fubject, what is regular, what is or-derly, what is fuitable, and what is fit and proper.*

It is clear from the very conception of the terms *congruity* and *propriety*, that they are not applicable to any fingle object : they imply a plurality, and ob-vioufly fignify a particular *relation* between different objects. Thus we fay currently, that a decent garb is fuitable or *proper* for a judge, modeft behaviour for a young woman, and a lofty ftyle for an epic poem : and,

---

* Nec vero illa parva vis naturæ eft rationifque, quod unum hoc ani-mal fentit quid fit ordo, quid fir quod deceat in factis dictifque, qui mo-dus. Itaque eorum ipforum, quæ afpectu fentiuntur, nullum aliud ani-mal, pulchritudinem, venuftatem, convenientiam partium fentit. Quam fimilitudinem natu·a ratioque ab oculis ad animum transferens, multo etiam magis pulchritudinem, conftantiam, ordinem, in conciliis factifque· confervandum putat, cavetque ne quid indecore effeminateve faciat ; tum in omnibus et opinionibus et factis ne quid libidinofe aut faciat aut cogi-tet. Quibus ex rebus conflatur et efficitur id, quod quærimus, honef-tum. *Cicero de Officiis, l.* 1.

and, on the other hand, that it is unsuitable or *in-congruous* to see a little woman sunk in an overgrown farthingale, a coat richly embroidered covering coarse and dirty linen, a mean subject in an elevated style, an elevated subject in a mean style, a first minister darning his wife's stocking, or a reverend prelate in lawn sleeves dancing a hornpipe.

The perception we have of this relation, which seems peculiar to man, cannot proceed from any other cause, but from a *sense* of congruity or propriety ; for, supposing us destitute of that sense, the terms would be to us unintelligible.*

It is matter of experience, that congruity or propriety, wherever perceived, is agreeable ; and that incongruity or impropriety, wherever perceived, is disagreeable. The only difficulty is, to ascertain what are the particular objects that in conjunction suggest these relations ; for there are many objects that do not : the sea, for example, viewed in conjunction with a picture, or a man viewed in conjunction with a mountain, suggest not either congruity or incongruity. It seems natural to infer, what will be found true by induction, that we never perceive con-

gruity

---

* From many things that pass current in the world without being generally condemned, one at first view would imagine, that the sense of congruity or propriety hath scarce any foundation in nature ; and that it is rather an artificial refinement of those who affect to distinguish themselves from others. The fulsome panegyrics bestowed upon the great and opulent, in epistles dedicatory and other such compositions, would incline us to think so. Did there prevail in the world, it will be said, or did nature suggest, a taste of what is suitable, decent, or proper, would any good writer deal in such compositions, or any man of sense receive them without disgust ? Can it be supposed that Lewis XIV. of France was endued by nature with any sense of propriety, when, in a dramatic performance purposely composed for his entertainment, he suffered himself, publicly and in his presence, to be styled the greatest king ever the earth produced ? These, it is true, are strong facts; but luckily they do not prove the sense of propriety to be artificial : they only prove, that the sense of propriety is at times overpowered by pride and vanity ; which is no singular case, for that sometimes is the fate even of the sense of justice.

gruity nor incongruity but among things that are connected by fome relation ; fuch as a man and his actions, a principal and its acceffories, a fubject and its
ornaments. We are indeed fo framed by nature, as,
among things fo connected, to require a certain fuitablenefs or correfpondence, termed *congruity* or *propriety ;* and to be difpleafed when we find the oppofite relation of *incongruity* or *impropriety.**

If things connected be the fubject of congruity, it
is reafonable beforehand to expect a degree of congruity proportioned to the degree of the connection.
And, upon examination we find our expectation to be
well founded : where the relation is intimate, as between a caufe and its effect, a whole and its parts,
we require the ftricteft congruity ; but where the relation is flight, or accidental, as among things jum-
bled together, we require little or no congruity : the
ftricteft propriety is required in behaviour and manner of living ; becaufe a man is connected with thefe
by the relation of caufe and effect : the relation between an edifice and the ground it ftands upon is of
the moft intimate kind, and therefore the fituation of
a great houfe ought to be lofty : its relation to neighbouring

---

* In the chapter of beautv, qualities are diftinguifhed into primary and
fecondary : and to clear fome obfcuritv that may appear in the text, it is
proper to be obferved, that the fame diftinction is applicable to relations.
Refemblance, equality, uniformity, proximity, are relations that depend
not on us, but exift equally whether perceived or not ; and upon that account may juftly be termed *primary* relations. But there are other relations, that only appear fuch to us, and that have not any external exiftence like primary relations ; which is the cafe of congruity, incongruitv,
propriety, impropriety : thefe may be properly termed *fecondary* relations. Thus it appears from what is faid in the text, that the fecondary
relations mentioned arife from objects connected by fome primarv relation. Property is an example of a fecondary relation, as it exifts no
where but in the mind. I purchafe a field or a horfe : the covenant
makes the primary relation; and the fecondary relation built on it is
property.

bouring hills, rivers, plains, being that of propinquity
only, demands but a fmall fhare of congruity : among
members of the fame club, the congruity ought to be
confiderable, as well as among things placed for fhow
in the fame niche : among paffengers in a ftage-coach
we require very little congruity; and lefs ftill at a
public fpeɕacle.

Congruity is fo nearly allied to beauty, as commonly to be held a fpecies of it ; and yet they differ
fo effentially, as never to coincide : beauty, like
colour, is placed upon a fingle fubjeɕ : congruity
upon a plurality : further, a thing beautiful in itfelf,
may, with relation to other things, produce the
ftrongeft fenfe of incongruity.

Congruity and propriety are commonly reckoned
fynonimous terms ; and hitherto in opening the fubjeɕ they have been ufed indifferently ; but they are
diftinguifhable ; and the precife meaning of each muft
be afcertained. Congruity is the genus, of which
propriety is a fpecies ; for we call nothing *propriety*,
but that congruity or fuitablenefs, which ought to
fubfift between fenfible beings and their thoughts,
words, and aɕions.

In order to give a full view of thefe fecondary relations, I fhall trace them through fome of the moft
confiderable primary relations. The relation of a
part to the whole, being extremely intimate, demands
the utmoft degree of congruity : even the flighteft
deviation is difguftful ; witnefs the *Lutrin*, a burlefque poem, which is clofed with a ferious and warm
panegyric on Lamoignon, one of the King's judges :

      —————Amphora cœpit
  Inftitui ; currente rota, cur urceus exit ?

Examples of congruity and incongruity are furnifhed in plenty by the relation between a fubjeɕ and
                            its

its ornaments.   A literary performance intended
merely for amufement is fufceptible of much ornament, as well as a mufic-room or a playhoufe ; for in
gaiety the mind hath a peculiar relifh for fhow and
decoration.   The moft gorgeous apparel, however
improper in tragedy, is not unfuitable to opera-ac-
tors : the truth is, an opera, in its prefent form, is
a mighty fine thing ; but, as it deviates from nature
in its capital circumftances, we look not for nature
nor propriety in thofe which are acceffory.   On the
other hand, a ferious and important fubject admits
not much ornament ;* nor a fubject that of itfelf is
extremely beautiful : and a fubject that fills the mind
with its loftinefs and grandeur, appears beft in a drefs
altogether plain.

To a perfon of a mean appearance, gorgeous apparel is unfuitable ; which, befide the incongruity,
fhows by contraft the meannefs of appearance in the
ftrongeft light.   Sweetnefs of look and manner requires fimplicity of drefs joined with the greateft elegance.   A ftately and majeftic air requires fumptu-
ous apparel, which ought not to be gaudy, nor
crowded with little ornaments.   A woman of confummate beauty can bear to be highly adorned, and
yet fhows beft in a plain drefs,

————————For lovelinefs
Needs not the foreign aid of ornament,
But is, when unadorn'd, adorn'd the moft.
                              Thompfon's Autumn, 208.

                                        Congruity

* Contrary to this rule, the introduction to the third volume of the
Characteriftics. is a continued chain of metaphors : thefe in fuch profu-
fion are too florid for the fubject ; and have befide the bad effect of removing our attention from the principal fubject, to fix it upon fplendid
trifles.

Congruity regulates not only the quantity of ornament, but alfo the kind. The decorations of a
dancing-room ought all of them to be gay. No picture is proper for a church but what has religion for
its fubject. Every ornament upon a fhield fhould relate to war ; and Virgil, with great judgment, confines the carvings upon the fhield of Æneas to the
military hiftory of the Romans : that beauty is overlooked by Homer : for the bulk of the fculpture upon the fhield of Achilles is of the arts of peace in general, and of joy and feftivity in particular : the author of Telemachus betrays the fame inattention, in
defcribing the fhield of that young hero.

In judging of propriety with regard to ornaments,
we muft attend, not only to the nature of the fubject
that is to be adorned, but alfo to the circumftances
in which it is placed : the ornaments that are proper
for a ball will appear not altogether fo decent at public worfhip : and the fame perfon ought to drefs differently for a marriage-feaft and for a funeral.

Nothing is more intimately related to a man than
his fentiments, words, and actions ; and therefore
we require here the ftricteft conformity. When we
find what we thus require, we have a lively fenfe of
propriety : when we find the contrary, our fenfe of
impropriety is no lefs lively. Hence the univerfal
diftafte of affectation, which confifts in making a fhew
of greater delicacy and refinement, than is fuited
either to the character or circumftances of the perfon. Nothing in epic or dramatic compofitions is
more difguftful than impropriety of manners. In
Corneille's tragedy of *Cinna*, Æmilia, a favourite of
Auguftus, receives daily marks of his affection, and is
loaded with benefits : yet all the while is laying plots
to affaffinate her benefactor, directed by no other motive

tive but to avenge her father's death :* revenge
againſt a benefactor, founded ſolely upon filial piety,
cannot be directed by any principle but that of juſtice, and therefore never can ſuggeſt unlawful means;
yet the crime here attempted, a treacherous murder,
is what even a miſcreant will ſcarce attempt againſt
his bittereſt enemy.   What is ſaid might be thought
ſufficient to explain the relations of congruity and
propriety.   And yet the ſubject is not exhauſted : on
the contrary, the proſpect enlarges upon us, when
we take under view the effects theſe relations produce in the mind.   Congruity and propriety, wherever perceived, appear agreeable; and every agreeable object produceth in the mind a pleaſant emotion :
incongruity and impropriety, on the other hand, are
diſagreeable : and of courſe produce painful emotions.   Theſe emotions, whether pleaſant or painful,
ſometimes vaniſh without any conſequence ; but more
frequently occaſion other emotions, to which I proceed.

When any ſlight incongruity is perceived in an accidental combination of perſons or things, as of paſſengers in a ſtage-coach, or of individuals dining at
an ordinary ; the painful emotion of incongruity, after a momentary exiſtence, vaniſheth without producing any effect.   But this is not the caſe of propriety and impropriety : voluntary acts, whether
words or deeds, are imputed to the author ; when
proper, we reward him with our eſteem ; when
improper, we puniſh him with our contempt.   Let us
ſuppoſe, for example, a generous action ſuited to the
character of the author, which raiſes in him and every ſpectator the pleaſant emotion of propriety : this
emotion generates in the author both ſelf-eſteem and
joy ; the former when he conſiders his relation to
the

* See act 1. ſc. 2.

the action, and the latter when he confiders the good
opinion that others will entertain of him : the fame
emotion of propriety produceth in the fpectators efteem for the author of the action : and when they
think of themfelves, it alfo produceth by contraft an
emotion of humility. To difcover the effects of an
unfuitable action, we muft invert each of thefe circumftances : the painful emotion of impropriety generates in the author of the action both humility and
fhame ; the former when he confiders his relation to
the action, and the latter when he confiders what
others will think of him : the fame emotion of impropriety produceth in the fpectators contempt for
the author of the action : and it alfo produceth, by
contraft when they think of themfelves, an emotion
of felf-efteem. Here then are many different emotions, derived from the fame action confidered in different views by different perfons ; a machine provided with many fprings, and not a little complicated.
Propriety of action, it would feem, is a favourite of
nature, or of the author of nature, when fuch care
and folicitude is beftowed on it. It is not left to our
own choice ; but, like juftice, is required at our
hands ; and, like juftice, is enforced by natural rewards and punifhments : a man cannot, with impu-
nity, do any thing unbecoming or improper ; he
fuffers the chaftifement of contempt inflicted by others, and of fhame inflicted by himfelf. An appara-
tus fo complicated, and fo fingular, ought to roufe
our attention : for nature doth nothing in vain ; and
we may conclude with certainty, that this curious
branch of the human conftitution is intended for
fome valuable purpofe. To the difcovery of that
purpofe or final caufe I fhall with ardour apply my
thoughts, after difcourfing a little more at large upon
the punifhment, as it may now be called, that nature

hath

hath provided for indecent and unbecoming behaviour. This, at any rate, is neceffary, in order to
give a full view of the fubject : and who knows
whether it may not, over and above, open fome
tract that will lead us to the final caufe we are in
queft of ?

A grofs impropriety is punifhed with contempt and
indignation, which are vented againft the offender
by external expreffions ; nor is even the flighteft impropriety fuffered to pafs without fome degree of
contempt. But there are improprieties of the flighter
kind, that provoke laughter ; of which we have examples without end in the blunders and abfurdities of
our own fpecies : fuch improprieties receive a different punifhment, as will appear by what follows. The
emotions of contempt and of laughter occafioned by
an impropriety of that kind, uniting intimately in the
mind of the fpectator, are expreffed externally by a
peculiar fort of laugh, termed *a laugh of derifion or
fcorn.* An impropriety that thus moves not only
contempt but laughter, is diftinguifhed by the epithet of *ridiculous ;* and a laugh of derifion or fcorn is
the punifhment provided for it by nature. Nor
ought it to efcape obfervation, that we are fo fond of
inflicting that punifhment, as fometimes to exert it
even againft creatures of an inferior fpecies : witnefs
a turkeycock fwelling with pride, and ftrutting with
difplayed feathers, which in a gay mood is apt to
provoke a laugh of derifion.

We muft not expect, that thefe different improprieties are feparated by diftinct boundaries : for of improprieties, from the flighteft to the moft grofs, from
the moft rifible to the moft ferious, there are degrees without end. Hence it is, that in viewing fome
                                                    unbecoming

* See chap. 7.

unbecoming actions, too rifible for anger, and too ferious for derifion, the fpectator feels a fort of mixt
emotion, partaking both of derifion and of anger :
which accounts for an expreffion, common with refpect to the impropriety of fome actions. That we
know not whether to laugh or be angry.

It cannot fail to be obferved, that in the cafe of a
rifible impropriety, which is always flight, the contempt we have for the offender is extremely faint,
though derifion, its gratification, is extremely pleafant. This difproportion between a paffion and its
gratification, may feem not conformable to the analogy of nature. In looking about for a folution, I reflect upon what is laid down above, that an improper
action, not only moves our contempt for the author,
but alfo, by means of contraft, fwells the good opinion we have of ourfelves. This contributes, more
than any other particular, to the pleafure we have in
ridiculing follies and abfurdities : and accordingly, it
is well known, that thofe who have the greateft fhare
of vanity ; are the moft prone to laugh at others.
Vanity, which is a vivid paffion, pleafant in itfelf,
and not lefs fo in its gratification, would fingly be
fufficient to account for the pleafure of ridicule, without borrowing any aid from contempt. Hence appears the reafon of a noted obfervation, That we
are the moft difpofed to ridicule the blunders and
abfurdities of others, when we are in high fpirits ;
for in high fpirits, felf-conceit difplays itfelf with
more than ordinary vigour.

Having with wary fteps traced an intricate road,
not without danger of wandering ; what remains to
complete our journey, is to account for the final caufe
of congruity and propriety, which make fo great a
figure in the human conftitution. One final caufe,
regarding congruity, is pretty obvious, that the fenfe
of

of congruity, as one principle of the fine arts, contributes in a remarkable degree to our entertainment ;
which is the final caufe affigned above for our fenfe of
proportion,* and need not be enlarged upon here.
Congruity, indeed, with refpect to quantity, coincides
with proportion : when the parts of a building are
nicely adjufted to each other, it may be faid indifferently, that it is agreeable, by the congruity of its
parts, or by the proportion of its parts. But propriety, which regards voluntary agents only, can never be
the fame with proportion : a very long nofe is dif-
proportioned, but cannot be termed *improper*. In
fome inftances, it is true, impropriety coincides with
difproportion in the fame fubject, but never in the
fame refpect. I give for an example a very little man
buckled to a long toledo : confidering the man and
the fword with refpect to fize, we perceive a difproportion : confidering the fword as the choice of the
man, we perceive an impropriety.

The fenfe of impropriety with refpect to miftakes,
blunders, and abfurdities, is evidently calculated for
the good of mankind. In the fpectators it is productive of mirth and laughter, excellent recreation in an
interval from bufinefs. But this is a trifle compared
to what follows. It is painful to be the fubject of
ridicule ; and to punifh with ridicule the man who is
guilty of an abfurdity, tends to put him more on his
guard in time coming. It is well ordered, that even
the moft innocent blunder is not committed with im-
punity : becaufe, were errors licenfed where they do
no hurt, inattention would grow into habit, and be
the occafion of much hurt.

The final caufe of propriety, as to moral duties, is of all
the moft illuftrious. To have a juft notion of it, the
moral

---

* See chap. 3.

moral duties that refpect others muft be diftinguifhed from thofe that refpect ourfelves. Fidelity, gratitude, and abftinence from injury, are examples of the firft fort; temperance, modefty, firmnefs of mind, are examples of the other : the former are made duties by the fenfe of juftice ; the latter, by the fenfe of propriety. Here is a final caufe of the fenfe of propriety that will roufe our attention. It is undoubtedly the intereft of every man to fuit his behaviour to the dignity of his nature, and to the ftation alloted him by Providence ; for fuch rational conduct contributes in every refpect to happinefs, by preferving health, by procuring plenty, by gaining the efteem of others, and, which of all is the greateft blefling, by gaining a juftly founded felf-efteem. But in a matter fo effential to our well-being, even felf-intereft is not relied on : the powerful authority of duty is fuperadded to the motive of intereft. The God of nature, in all things effential to our happinefs, hath obferved one uniform method : to keep us fteady in our conduct, he hath fortified us with natural laws and principles, preventive of many aberrations, which would daily happen were we totally furrendered to fo fallible a guide as is human reafon. Propriety cannot rightly be confidered in another light, than as the natural law that regulates our conduct with refpect to ourfelves ; as juftice is the natural law that regulates our conduct with refpect to others. I call propriety a law, no lefs than juftice ; becaufe both are equally rules of conduct that *ought* to be obeyed : propriety includes that obligation ; for to fay an action is proper, is in other words to fay, that it *ought* to be performed ; and to fay it is improper, is in other words to fay, that it *ought* to be forborne. It is that very character of *ought* and *fhould* which makes juftice a law to us ; and the fame character is applicable to propriety,

priety, though perhaps more faintly than to juſtice : but the difference is in degree only, not in kind ; and we ought, without heſitation or reluctance, to ſubmit equally to the government of both.

But I have more to urge upon that head. To the ſenſe of propriety as well as of juſtice, are annexed the ſanctions of rewards and puniſhments ; which evidently prove the one to be a law as well as the other. The ſatisfaction a man hath in doing his duty, joined to the eſteem and good-will of others, is the reward that belongs to both equally. The puniſhments alſo, though not the ſame, are nearly allied ; and differ in degree more than in quality. Diſobedience to the law of juſtice is puniſhed with remorſe ; diſobedience to the law of propriety, with ſhame, which is remorſe in a lower degree. Every tranſgreſſion of the law of juſtice raiſes indignation in the beholder ; and ſo doth every flagrant tranſgreſſion of the law of propriety. Slighter improprieties receive a milder puniſhment : they are always rebuked with ſome degree of contempt, and frequently with deriſion. In general, it is true, that the rewards and puniſhments annexed to the ſenſe of propriety are ſlighter in degree than thoſe annexed to the ſenſe of juſtice : which is wiſely ordered, becauſe duty to others is ſtill more eſſential to ſociety than duty to ourſelves : ſociety, indeed, could not ſubſiſt a moment, were individuals not protected from the headſtrong and turbulent paſſions of their neighbours.

The final cauſe now unfolded of the ſenſe of propriety, muſt, to every diſcerning eye, appear delightful : and yet this is but a partial view ; for that ſenſe reaches another illuſtrious end, which is, in conjunction with the ſenſe of juſtice, to enforce the performance of ſocial duties. In fact, the ſanctions viſibly contrived to compel a man to be juſt to himſelf,

are

are equally ferviceable to compel him to be juft to
others ; which will be evident from a fingle reflection,   That an action, by being unjuft, ceafes not to
be improper: an action never appears more eminently improper, than when it is unjuft : it is obvioufly becoming, and fuitable to human nature, that
each man do his duty to others ; and, accordingly,
every tranfgreffion of duty to others, is at the fame
time a tranfgreffion of duty to one's felf.   This is a
plain truth without exaggeration ; and it opens a new
and enchanting view in the moral landfcape, the
profpect being greatly enriched by the multiplication
of agreeable objects.   It appears now, that nothing
is overlooked, nothing left undone, that can poffibly
contribute to the enforcing focial duty ; for to all
the fanctions that belong to it fingly, are fuperadded
the fanctions of felf-duty.   A familiar example fhall
fuffice for illuftration.   An act of ingratitude, confidered in itfelf, is to the author difagreeable, as well
as to every fpectator : confidered by the author with
relation to himfelf, it raifes felf-contempt : confidered by him with relation to the world, it makes him
afhamed : confidered by others, it raifes their contempt and indignation againft the author.   Thefe
feelings are all of them occafioned by the impropriety
of the action.   When the action is confidered as unjuft, it occafions another fet of feelings : in the author it produces remorfe, and a dread of merited
punifhment ; and in others, the benefactor chiefly,
indignation and hatred directed to the ungrateful
perfon.   Thus fhame and remorfe united in the ungrateful perfon, and indignation united with hatred
in the hearts of others, are the punifhments provided
by nature for injuftice.   Stupid and infenfible muft
he be, who, in a contrivance fo exquifite, perceives
not the benevolent hand of our Creator.

CHAP.

Dignity and Grace.

THE terms *dignity* and *meanness* are applied to man in point of character, fentiment, and behaviour : we fay, for example, of one man, that he hath natural dignity in his air and manner ; of another, that he makes a mean figure : we perceive dignity in every action and fentiment of fome perfons ; meannefs and vulgarity in the actions and fentiments of others. With refpect to the fine arts, fome performances are faid to be manly, and fuitable to the dignity of human nature ; others are termed low, mean, trivial. Such expreffions are common, though they have not always a precife meaning. With refpect to the art of criticifm, it muft be a real acquifition to afcertain what thefe terms truly import ; which poffibly may enable us to rank every performance in the fine arts according to its dignity.

Inquiring firft to what fubjects the terms *dignity* and *meanness* are appropriated, we foon difcover, that they are not applicable to any thing inanimate : the moft magnificent palace that ever was built, may be lofty, may be grand, but it has no relation to dignity: the moft diminutive fhrub may be little, but it is not mean. Thefe terms muft belong to fenfitive beings, probably to man only ; which will be evident when we advance in the inquiry.

Human actions appear in many different lights : in themfelves they appear grand or little ; with refpect to the author, they appear proper or improper; with refpect to thofe affected by them, juft or unjuft :
and

and I now add, that they are alfo diftinguifhed by dignity and meannefs. If any one incline to think, that, with refpect to human actions, dignity coincides with grandeur, and meannefs with littlenefs, the difference will be evident upon reflecting, that an action may be grand without being virtuous, and little without being faulty ; but that we never attribute dignity to any action but what is virtuous, nor meannefs to any but what is faulty. Every action of dignity creates refpect and efteem for the author ; and a mean action draws upon him contempt. A man is admired for a grand action, but frequently is neither loved nor efteemed for it : neither is a man always contemned for a low or little action. The action of Cæfar paffing the Rubicon was grand ; but there was no dignity in it, confidering that his purpofe was to enflave his country : Cæfar, in a march, taking opportunity of a rivulet to quench his thirft, did a low action, but the action was not mean.

As it appears to me, dignity and meannefs are founded on a natural principle not hitherto mentioned. Man is endowed with a SENSE of the worth and excellence of his nature : he deems it more perfect than that of the other beings around him ; and he perceives, that the perfection of his nature confifts in virtue, particularly in virtues of the higheft rank. To exprefs that fenfe, the term _dignity_ is appropriated. Further, to behave with dignity, and to refrain from all mean actions, is felt to be, not a virtue only, but a duty : it is a duty every man owes to himfelf. By acting in that manner, he attracts love and efteem : by acting meanly, or below himfelf, he is difapproved and contemned.

According to the defcription here given of dignity and meannefs, they appear to be a fpecies of propriety and impropriety. Many actions may be proper or improper, to which dignity or meannefs cannot be

applied :

applied : to eat when one is hungry, is proper, but there is no dignity in that action ; revenge fairly taken, if againſt law, is improper, but not mean. But every actionof dignity is alſo proper, and every mean action is alſo improper.

This ſenſe of the dignity of human nature, reaches even our pleaſures and amuſements: if they enlarge the mind by raiſing grand or elevated emotions, or if they humanize the mind by exerciſing our ſympathy, they are approved as ſuited to the dignity of our nature : if they contract the mind by fixing it on trivial objects, they are contemned as not ſuited to the dignity of our nature. Hence, in general, every occupation, whether of uſe or amuſement, that correſponds to the dignity of man, is termed *manly ;* and every occupation below his nature, is termed *childiſh.*

To thoſe who ſtudy human nature, there is a point which has always appeared intricate : How comes it that generoſity and courage are more eſteemed, and beſtow more dignity, than good-nature, or even juſtice ; though the latter contribute more than the former to private as well as to public happineſs ? This queſtion, bluntly propoſed, might puzzle a cunning philoſopher : but, by means of the following obſervations, will eaſily be ſolved. Human virtues, like other objects, obtain a rank in our eſtimation, not from their utility, which is a ſubject of reflection, but from the direct impreſſion they make on us. Juſtice and good-nature are a ſort of negative virtues, that ſcarce make any impreſſion but when they are trangreſſed : courage and generoſity, on the contrary, producing elevated emotions, enliven greatly the ſenſe of a man's dignity, both in himſelf and in others ; and for that reaſon, courage and generoſity are in higher regard than the other virtues mentioned :

ed : we defcribe them as grand and elevated, as of greater dignity, and more praife-worthy.

This leads us to examine more direftly emotions and paffions with refpeft to the prefent fubjeft ; and it will not be difficult to form a fcale of them, beginning with the meaneft, and afccnding gradually to thofe of the higheft rank and dignity. Pleafure felt as at the organ of fenfe, named *corporeal plcafure*, is perceived to be low ; and when indulged to excefs, is perceived alfo to be mean : for that reafon, perfons of any delicacy diffemble the pleafure they take in eating and drinking. The pleafures of the eye and ear, having no organic feeling,* and being free from any fenfe of meannefs, are indulged without any fhame : they even rife to a certain degree of dignity when their objefts are grand or elevated. The fame is the cafe of the fympathetic paffions : a virtuous perfon behaving with fortitude and dignity under cruel misfortunes, makes a capital figure ; and the fympathifing fpeftator feels in himfelf the fame dignity. Sympathetic diftrefs at the fame time never is mean : on the contrary, it is agreeable to the nature of a focial being, and has general approbation. The rank that love poffeffes in the fcale, depends in a great meafure on its objeft : it poffeffes a low place when founded on external propcrties merely ; and is mean when beftowed on a perfon of inferior rank without any extraordinary qualification : but when founded on the more elevated internal properties, it affumes a confiderable degree of dignity. The fame is the cafe of friendfhip. When gratitude is warm, it animates the mind ; but it fcarce rifes to dignity. Joy beftows dignity when it proceeds from an elevated caufe.

If I can depend upon induftion, dignity is not a property of any difagreeable paffion : one is flight, another

---

* See the Introduftion.

another fevere; one depreffes the mind, another animates it ; but there is no elevation, far lefs dignity,
in any of them. Revenge, in particular, though it
inflame and fwell the mind, is not accompanied with
dignity, nor even with elevation : it is not, however,
felt as mean or groveling, unlefs when it takes indirect meafures for gratification. Shame and remorfe,
though they fink the fpirits, are not mean. Pride, a
difagreeable paffion, beftows no dignity in the eye of
a fpectator. Vanity always appears mean ; and extremely fo where founded, as commonly happens, on
trivial qualifications.

I proceed to the pleafures of the underftanding,
which poffefs a high rank in point of dignity. Of
this every one will be fenfible, when he confiders the
important truths that have been laid open by fcience ;
fuch as general theorems, and the general laws that
govern the material and moral worlds. The pleafures of the underftanding are fuited to man as a rational and contemplative being ; and they tend not a
little to ennoble his nature ; even to the Deity he
ftretcheth his contemplations, which, in the difcovery
of infinite power, wifdom, and benevolence, afford
delight of the moft exalted kind. Hence it appears,
that the fine arts ftudied as a rational fcience, afford
entertainment of great dignity ; fuperior far to what
they afford as a fubject of tafte merely.

But contemplation, however in itfelf valuable, is
chiefly refpected as fubfervient to action ; for man is
intended to be more an active than a contemplative
being. He accordingly fhows more dignity in action
than in contemplation : generofity, magnanimity,
heroifm, raife his character to the higheft pitch : thefe
beft exprefs the dignity of his nature, and advance
him nearer to divinity than any other of his attributes.

By

T 2

By every production that shows art and contrivance, our curiofity is excited upon two points; firſt,
how it was made ; and next, to what end. Of the
two, the latter is the more important inquiry, becaufe
the means are ever fubordinate to the end ; and, in
fact, our curiofity is always more inflamed by the
final than by the *efficient* caufe. This preference is
no where more vifible, than in contemplating the
works of nature : if in the efficient caufe wifdom and
power be difplayed, wifdom is no lefs confpicuous in
the final caufe ; and from it only can we infer benevolence, which of all the divine attributes is to man
the moſt important.

Having endeavoured to affign the efficient caufe of
dignity and meannefs, by unfolding the principle on
which they are founded, we proceed to explain the
final caufe of the dignity or meannefs beſtowed upon
the feveral particulars above mentioned, beginning
with corporeal pleafures. Thefe, as far as ufeful, are,
like juſtice, fenced with fufficient fanctions to prevent
their being neglected : hunger and thirſt are painful
fenfations ; and we are incited to animal love by a
vigorous propenfity : were coporeal pleafures dignified over and above with a place in a high clafs, they
would infallibly difturb the balance of the mind, by
outweighing the focial affections. This is a fatisfactory final caufe for refufing to thefe pleafures any degree of dignity ; and the final caufe is no lefs evident
of their meannefs, when they are indulged to excefs.
The more refined pleafures of external fenfe, con-
veyed by the eye and the ear from natural objects and
from the fine arts, deferve a high place in our eſteem,
becaufe of their fingular and extenfive utility : in
fome cafes they rife to a confiderable dignity ; and the
very loweſt pleafures of the kind are never eſteemed
mean or groveling. The pleafure arifing from wit,

humour,

humour, ridicule, or from what is fimply ludicrous, is ufeful, by relaxing the mind after the fatigue of more manly occupation : but the mind, when it furrenders itfelf to pleafure of that kind, lofes its vigour, and finks gradually into floth.* The place this pleafure occupies in point of dignity, is adjufted to thefe views : to make it ufeful as a relaxation, it is not branded with meannefs ; to prevent its ufurpation, it is removed from that place but a fingle degree : no man values himfelf for that pleafure, even during gratification ; and if it have engroffed more of his time than is requifite for relaxation, he looks back with fome degree of fhame.

In point of dignity, the focial emotions rife above the felfifh, and much above thofe of the eye and ear : man is by his nature a focial being ; and to qualify him for fociety, it is wifely contrived, that he fhould value himfelf more for being focial than felfifh.†

The excellency of man is chiefly difcernible in the great improvements he is fufceptible of in fociety : thefe, by perfeverance, may be carried on progreffively above any affignable limits ; and, even abftracting from revelation, there is great probability, that the progrefs begun here will be completed in fome future ftate. Now, as all valuable improvements proceed from the exercife of our rational faculties, the author of our nature, in order to excite us

to

---

* Neque enim ita generati à natura fumus, ut ad ludum et jocum facti efle videamur, fed ad feveritatem potius et ad quaedam ftudia graviora atque majora. Ludo autem et joco, uti illis quidem licet, fed ficut fomno et quietibus cacteris, tum cum gravibus feriifque rebus fatisfecerimus. *Cicero de offic. lib.* 1.

† For the fame reafon, the felfifh emotions that are founded upon a focial principle, rife higher in our efteem than thofe that are founded upon a felfifh principle. As to which fee above, p. 46. note.

T 3

to a due ufe of thefe faculties, hath affigned a high rank to the pleafures of the underftanding : their utility, with refpect to this life as well as a future, entitles them to that rank.

But as action is the aim of all our improvements, virtuous actions juftly poffefs the higheft of all the ranks. Thefe, we find, are by nature diftributed into different claffes, and the firft in point of dignity affigned to actions that appear not the firft in point of ufe : generofity for example, in the fenfe of mankind is more refpected than juftice, though the latter is undoubtedly more effential to fociety ; and magnanimity, heroifm, undaunted courage, rife ftill higher in our efteem. One would readily think, that the moral virtues fhould be efteemed according to their importance. Nature has here deviated from her ordinary path, and great wifdom is fhown in the deviation : the efficient caufe is explained above, and the final caufe is explained in the Effays of morality and natural religion.*

We proceed to analyfe *grace*, which being in a good meafure an uncultivated field, requires more than ordinary labour :

Graceful is an attribute : *grace* and *gracefulnefs* exprefs that attribute in the form of a noun.

That this attribute is agreeable, no one doubts.

As grace is difplayed externally, it muft be an object of one or other of our five fenfes. That it is an object of fight, every perfon of tafte can bear witnefs ; and that it is confined to that fenfe, appears from induction ; for it is not an object of fmell, nor of tafte, nor of touch. Is it an object of hearing ? Some mufic indeed is termed graceful ; but that expreffion is metaphorical, as when we fay of other mufic that it is beautiful : the latter metaphor, at the fame time is

more

more fweet and eafy ; which fhows how little applicable to mufic or to found the former is, when taken
in its proper fenfe.

That it is. an attribute of man, is beyond difpute.
But of what other beings is it alfo an attribute ? We
perceive at firft fight that nothing inanimate is
entitled to that epithet. What animal then, befide
man, is entitled ? Surely, not an elephant, nor even
a lion. A horfe may have a delicate fhape with a
lofty mein, and all his motions may be exquifite ;
but he is never faid to be graceful. Beauty and
grandeur are common to man with fome other beings : but dignity is not applied to any being inferior to man ; and upon the ftricteft examination, the
fame appears to hold in grace.

Confining then grace to man, the next inquiry is,
whether, like beauty, it makes a conftant appearance,
or in fome circumftances only. Does a perfon difplay this attribute at reft as well as in motion, afleep
as when awake ? It is undoubtedly connected with
motion ; for when the moft graceful perfon is at reft,
neither moving nor fpeaking, we lofe fight of that
quality as much as of colour in the dark. Grace
then is an agreeable attribute, infeparable from motion as oppofed to reft, and as comprehending fpeech,
looks, geftures, and loco-motion.

As fome motions are homely, the oppofite to
graceful, the next inquiry is, with what motions is
this attribute connected ? No man appears graceful
in a mafk ; and, therefore, laying afide the expreffions of the countenance, the other motions may be
genteel, may be elegant, but of themfelves never are
graceful. A motion adjufted in the moft perfect
manner to anfwer its end, is elegant; but ftill fomewhat
more

T 4

more is required to complete our idea of grace, or gracefulnefs.

What this unknown *more* may be, is the nice point. One thing is clear from what is faid, that this *more* muft arife from the expreffion of the countenance : and from what expreffions fo naturally as from thofe which indicate mental qualities, fuch as fweetnefs, benevolence, elevation, dignity? This promifes to be a fair analyfis ; becaufe of all objects mental qualties affect us the moft ; and the impreffion made by graceful appearance upon every fpecta- tor of tafte, is too deep for any caufe purely corporeal.

The next ftep is, to examine what are the men- tal qualities, that, in conjunction with elegance of motion, produce a graceful appearance. Sweetnefs, cheerfulnefs, affability, are not feparately fufficient, nor even in conjunction. As it appears to me, dignity alone with elegant motion may produce a graceful ap- pearance; but ftill more graceful, with the aid of other qualities, thofe efpecially that are the moft exalted.

But this is not all. The moft exalted virtues may be the lot of a perfon whofe countenance has little ex- preffion : fuch a perfon cannot be graceful. There- fore, to produce this appearance, we muft add another circumftance, namely, an expreffive countenance, difplaying to every fpectator of tafte, with life and energy, every thing that paffes in the mind.

Collecting thefe circumftances together, grace may be defined, that agreeable appearance which arifes from elegance of motion, and from a countenance expreffive of dignity. Expreffions of other mental qualities are not effential to that appearance, but they heighten it greatly.

Of all external objects, a graceful perfon is the moft agreeable.

Dancing

Dancing affords great opportunity for diſplaying grace, and haranguing ſtill more.

I conclude with the following reflection, That in vain will a perſon attempt to be graceful, who is de- ficient in amiable qualities. A man, it is true, may form an idea of qualities he is deſtitute of ; and, by means of that idea, may endeavour to expreſs theſe qualities by looks and geſtures : but ſuch ſtudied ex- preſſion will be too faint and obſcure to be graceful.

C H A P.

Ridicule.

To define ridicule has puzzled and vex-
ed every critic. The definition given by Ariftotle is
obfcure and imperfect.* Cicero handles it at great
length† but without giving any fatisfaction : he
wanders in the dark, and miffes the diftinction between rifible and ridiculous. Quintilian is fenfible
of the diftinction‡ but has not attempted to explain
it. Luckily this fubject lies no longer in obfcurity : a
rifible object produceth an emotion of laughter merely :∥ a ridiculous object is improper as well as rifible ; and produceth a mixt emotion, which is vented by a laugh of derifion or fcorn.∥∥

Having therefore happily unravelled the knotty
part, I proceed to other particulars.

Burlefque, though a great engine of ridicule, is
not confined to that fubject ; for it is clearly diftinguifhable into burlefque that excites laughter merely,
and burlefque that provokes derifion or ridicule. A
grave fubject in which there is no impropriety, may
be brought down by a certain colouring fo as to be
rifible ; which is the cafe of *Virgil Traveftie ;*∥∥∥ and
alfo

---

* Poet. cap. 5.   † L. 2. De Oratore.

‡ Idcoque anceps ejus rei ratio eft, quod a derifu non procul abeft rifus
lib. 6. *cap.* 3. § 1.

∥ See chap. 7.   [∥ See chap. 10.   ∥∥ Scarron.

alfo the cafe of the *Secchia Rapita* :* the authors
laugh firft, in order to make their readers laugh.
The *Lutrin* is a burlefque poem of the other fort,
laying hold of a low and trifling incident, to expofe
the luxury, indolence, and contentious fpirit of a fet
of monks. Boileau, the author, gives a ridiculous
air to the fubject, by drefling it in the heroic ftyle,
and affecting to confider it as of the utmoft dignity
and importance. In a compofition of this kind, no
image profeffedly ludicrous ought to find quarter,
becaufe fuch images deftroy the contraft ; and, accordingly, the author fhows always the grave face,
and never once betrays a fmile.

Though the burlefque that aims at ridicule, produces its effect by elevating the ftyle far above the fubject, yet it has limits beyond which the elevation ought
not to be carried : the poet, confulting the imagination
of his readers, ought to confine himfelf to fuch images as are lively, and readily apprehended : a ftrained elevation, foaring above an ordinary reach of fancy makes not a pleafant impreffion : the reader, fatigued with being always upon the ftretch, is foon
difgufted ; and if he perfevere, becomes thoughtlefs
and indifferent. Further, a fiction gives no pleafure
unlefs it be painted in colours fo lively as to produce
fome perception of reality ; which never can be done
effectually where the images are formed with labour
or difficulty. For thefe reafons, I cannot avoid condemning the *Batrachomuomachia*, faid to be the compofition of Homer : It is beyond the power of imagination to form a clear and lively image of frogs and
mice, acting with the dignity of the higheft of our
fpecies ; nor can we form a conception of the reality
of fuch an action, in any manner fo diftinct as to intereft our affections even in the flighteft degree.

The

* Taffoni.

The *Rape of the Lock* is of a character clearly diſtinguiſhable from thoſe now mentioned : it is not properly a burleſque performance, but what may rather be termed *an heroi-comical poem :* it treats a gay and familiar ſubject with pleaſantry, and with a moderate degree of dignity : the author puts not on a maſk like Boileau, nor profeſſes to make us laugh like Taſſoni. The *Rape of the Lock* is a genteel ſpecies of writing, leſs ſtrained than thoſe mentioned ; and is pleaſant or ludicrous without having ridicule for its chief aim : giving way however to ridicule where it ariſes naturally from a particular character, ſuch as that of Sir Plume. Addiſon's *Spectator* upon the exerciſe of the fan* is extremely gay and ludicrous, reſembling in its ſubject the *Rape of the Lock.*

Humour belongs to the preſent chapter, becauſe it is connected with ridicule. Congreve defines humour to be " a ſingular and unavoidable manner of doing or ſaying any thing, peculiar and natural to one man only, by which his ſpeech and actions are diſtinguiſhed from thoſe of other men." Were this definition juſt, a majeſtic and commanding air, which is a ſingular property, is humour ; as alſo a natural flow of correct and commanding eloquence, which is no leſs ſingular. Nothing juſt or proper is denominated humour ; nor any ſingularity of character, words, or actions, that is valued or reſpected. When we attend to the character of an humouriſt, we find that it ariſes from circumſtances both riſible and improper, and therefore that it leſſens the man in our eſteem, and makes him in ſome meaſure ridiculous.

Humour in writing is very different from humour in character. When an author infiſts upon ludicrous ſubject with a profeſſed purpoſe to make his

readers

readers laugh, he may be ſtyled a *ludicrous writer ;* but is ſcarce entitled to be ſtyled *a writer of humour.* This quality belongs to an author, who, affecting to be grave and ſerious, paints his objects in ſuch colours as to provoke mirth and laughter. A writer that is really an humouriſt in character, does this without deſign : if not, he muſt affect the character in order to ſucceed. Swift and Fontaine were humouriſts in character, and their writings are full of humour. Addiſon was not an humouriſt in character ; and yet in his proſe writings a moſt delicate and refined humour prevails. Arbuthnot exceeds them all in drollery and humourous painting ; which ſhows a great genius, becauſe, if I am not miſinformed, he had nothing of that peculiarity in his character.

There remains to ſhow by examples the manner of treating ſubjects, ſo as to give them a ridiculous appearance.

Il ne dit jamais, je vous donne, mais, je vous prete le bon jour.

Moliere.

Orleans. I know him to be valiant.
Conſtable. I was told that by one that knows him better than you.
Orleans. What's he ?
Conſtable. Marry, he told me ſo himſelf ; and he ſaid, he car'd not who knew it.

Henry V. *Shakeſpear.*

He never broke any man's head but his own, and that was againſt a poſt when he was drunk.

Ibid.

Millament. Sententious Mirabell ! pr'ythee don't look with that violent and inflexible wiſe face, like Solomon at the dividing of the child in an old tapeſtry hanging.

Way of the World.

A true

. A true critic in the perufal of a book, is like a dog at a feaſt, whoſe thoughts and ſtomach are wholly ſet upon what the gueſts fling away, and confequently is apt to ſnarl moſt when there are the feweſt bones.

Tale of a Tub.

In the following inſtances, the ridicule ariſes from abſurd conceptions in the perſons introduced.

Mafcarille. Te ſouvient-il, vicomte de cette demi-lune, que nous emportâmes ſur les ennemis au ſiege d'arras ?
Jodelet. Que veux tu dire avec ta demi-lune ? c'étoit bien une lune tout entiere.

Moliere les Precieuſes Ridicules, ſc. II.

Slender. I came yonder at Eaton to Marry Mrs. Anne Page ; and ſhe's a great lubberly boy.
Page. Upon my life then you took the wrong.
Slender. What need you tell me that ? I think ſo when I took a boy for a girl ; if I had been marry'd to him, for all he was in woman's apparel, I would not have had him.

Merry Wives of Windſor.

Valentine. Your bleſſing, Sir.
Sir Sampſon. You've had it already, Sir ; I think I ſent it you to day in a bill for four thouſand pound ; a great deal of money, Brother Foreſight.
Foreſight. Ay indeed, Sir Sampſon, a great deal of money for a young man ; I wonder what he can do with it.

Love for Love, act 2. *ſc.* 7.

Millament. I nauſeate walking ; 'tis a country-diverſion ; I loathe the country, and every thing that relates to it.
Sir Wilful. Indeed ! hah ! look ye, look ye, you do ? nay, 'tis like you may——here are choice of paſtimes here in town, as plays and the like ; that muſt be confeſs'd indeed.
Millament. Ah l'etourdie ! I hate the town too.
Sir Wilful. Dear heart, that's much——hah ! that you ſhould hate 'em both ! hah ! 'tis like you may ; there are ſome can't reliſh the town, and others can't away with the country——'tis like you may be one of theſe, Couſine.

Way of the World, act 4. *ſc.* 4.
Lord Froth.

Lord Froth. I affure you, Sir Paul, I laugh at nobody's jefts but my own, or a lady's : I affure, you, Sir Paul.

Brifk. How ? how, my Lord ? what, affront my wit! Let me perifh, do I never fay any thing worthy to be laugh'd at ?

Lord Froth. O foy, don't mifapprehend me, I don't fay fo, for I often fmile at your conceptions. But there is nothing more unbecoming a man of quality than to laugh ; 'tis fuch a vulgar expreffion of the paffion ! every body can laugh. Then efpecially to laugh at the jeft of an inferior perfon, or when any body elfe of the fame quality does not laugh with one ; ridiculous ! To be pleas'd with what pleafes the crow'd ! Now, when I laugh I always laugh alone.

Double Dealer, act 1. fc. 4.

So fharp-fighted is pride in blemifhes, and fo willing to be gratified, that it takes up with the very flighteft improprieties ; fuch as a blunder by a foreigner in fpeaking our language, efpecially if the blunder can bear a fenfe that reflects on the fpeaker.

Quickly. The young man is an honeft man.

Caius. What fhall de honeft man do in my clofet ? dere is no honeft man dat fhall come in my clofet.

Merry Wives of Windfor.

Love-fpeeches are finely ridiculed in the following paffage.

Quoth he, My faith as adamantine,
As chains of deftiny, I'll maintain ;
True as Apollo ever fpoke,
Or oracle from heart of oak ;
And if you'll give my flame but vent,
Now in clofe hugger mugger pent,
And fhine upon me but benignly,
With that one, and that other pigfneye,
The fun and day fhall fooner part,
Than love, or you, fhake off my heart ;

The

  The fun that fhall no more difpenfe
His own but your bright influence :
I'll carve your name on barks of trees,
With true love-knots, and flourifhes ;
That fhall infufe eternal fpring,
And everlafting flourifhing :
Drink ev'ry letter on't in ftum,
And make it brifk champaign become.
Where-e'er you tread, your foot fhall fet
The primrofe and the violet ;
All fpices, perfumes, and fweet powders,
Shall borrow from your breath their odours !
Nature her charter fhall renew,
And take all lives of things from you ;
The world depend upon your eye,
And when you frown upon it, die.
Only our loves fhall ftill furvive,
New worlds and natures to outlive ;
And, like to herald's moons, remain
All crefcents, without change or wane.

Hudibras, part 2. *canto* 1.

Irony turns things into ridicule in a peculiar
manner ; it confifts in laughing at a man under difguife of appearing to praife or fpeak well of him.
Swift affords us many illuftrious examples of that
fpecies of ridicule. Take the following.

By thefe methods, in a few weeks, there ftarts up many
a writer, capable of managing the profoundeft and moft
univerfal fubjects. For what though his head be empty,
provided his common-place book be full ! And if you will
bate him but the circumftances of method, and ftyle, and
grammar, and invention ; allow him but the common priv-
ileges of tranfcribing from others, and digreffing from himfelf, as often as he fhall fee occafion ; he will defire no more
ingredients towards fitting up a treatife that fhall make a
very comely figure on a bookfeller's fhelf, there to be preferved neat and clean, for a long eternity, adorned with the
heraldry of its title, fairly infcribed on a label ; never to
be thumbed or greafed by ftudents, nor bound to everlafting
                                                        chains

chains of darknefs in a library ; but when the fulnefs of
time is come, fhall happily undergo the trial of purgatory,
in order to afcend the fky.*

I cannot but congratulate our age on this peculiar fe-
licity, that though we have indeed made great progrefs in
all other branches of luxury, we are not yet debauch'd with
any *high relifh* in poetry, but are in this one tafte lefs *nice*
than our anceftors.

If the Reverend clergy fhewed more concern than others,
I charitably impute it to their great charge of fouls ; and
what confirmed me in this opinion was, that the degrees of
apprehenfion and terror could be diftinguifhed to be greater
or lefs, according to their ranks and degrees in the church.†

A parody muft be diftinguifhed from every fpecies of ridicule : it enlivens a gay fubject by imitating fome important incident that is ferious ; it is ludicrous, and may be rifible ; but ridicule is not a
neceffary ingredient. Take the following examples,
the firft of which refers to an expreffion of Mofes.

> The fkilful nymph reviews her force with care :
> Let fpades be trumps ! fhe faid, and trumps they were.
> *Rape of the Lock, Canto* iii. 45.

The next is in imitation of Achilles's oath in Homer : ʻ

> But by this lock, this facred lock, I fwear,
> (Which never more fhall join its parted hair,
> Which never more its honours fhall renew,
> Clip'd from the lovely head where late it grew,)
> That while my noftrils draw the vital air,
> This hand, which won it, fhall for ever wear.
>   He

* Tale of a Tub, fect. 7.

† A true and faithful narrative of what paffed in London during the
general confternation of all ranks and degrees of mankind.

He fpoke, and fpeaking, in proud triumph fpread
The long-contended honours of her head.
                              Ibid. canto iv. 133.

The following imitates the hiftory of Agamemnon's
fceptre in Homer.

Now meet thy fate, incens'd Belinda cry'd,
And drew a deadly bodkin from her fide,
(The fame, his ancient perfonage to deck,
Her great-great-grandfire wore about his neck,
In three feal-rings ; which after, melted down,
Form'd a vaft buckle for his widow's gown :
Her infant grandame's whiftle next it grew,
The bells fhe jingled, and the whiftle blew ;
Then in a bodkin grac'd her mother's hairs,
Which long fhe wore, and now Belinda wears.)
                              Ibid. canto 5. 87.

Though ridicule, as obferved above, is no neceffary
ingredient in a parody, yet there is no oppofition between them : ridicule may be fuccefsfully employed
in a parody : and a parody may be employed to promote ridicule ; witnefs the following example, with
refpect to the latter, in which the goddefs of Dull-
nefs is addreffed upon the fubject of modern education :

Thou gav'ft that ripenefs, which fo foon began,
And ceas'd fo foon, he ne'er was boy nor man ;
Through fchool and college, thy kind cloud o'ercaft,
Safe and unfeen the young Æneas paft ;*
Thence burfting glorious, all at once let down,
Stunn'd with his giddy larum half the town.
                              Dunciad, b. iv. 287.

The interpofition of the gods, in the manner of
Homer and Virgil, ought to be confined to ludicrous
                              fubjects,

* Æu. l. 1. *At Venus obfcuro,* &c.

fubjects, which are much enlivened by fuch interpofition handled in the form of a parody ; witnefs the
cave of Spleen, *Rape of the Lock*, canto 4. the goddefs of Difcord, *Lutrin*, canto 1. and the goddefs of
Indolence, *canto* 2.

Thofe who have a talent for ridicule, which is feldom united with a tafte for delicate and refined beauties, are quick-fighted in improprieties ; and thefe
they eagerly grafp, in order to gratify their favourite propenfity. Perfons galled are provoked to
maintain that ridicule is improper for grave fubjects.
Subjects really grave are by no means fit for ridicule :
but then it is urged againft them, that when it is
called in queftion whether a certain fubject be really
grave, ridicule is the only means of determining the
controverfy. Hence a celebrated queftion, Whether
ridicule be or be not a teft of truth ? I give this queftion a place here, becaufe it tends to illuftrate the
nature of ridicule.

The queftion ftated in accurate terms is, Whether
the fenfe of ridicule be the proper teft for diftinguifhing ridiculous objects, from what are not fo. Taking it for granted, that ridicule is not a fubject of reafoning, but of fenfe or tafte,* I proceed thus. No perfon
doubts but that our fenfe of beauty is the true teft of what
is beautiful ; and our fenfe of grandeur, of what is great
or fublime. Is it more doubtful whether our fenfe of
ridicule be the true teft of what is ridiculous ? It is not
only the true teft, but indeed the only teft ; for this
fubject comes not, more than beauty or grandeur, under the province of reafon. If any fubject, by the influence of fafhion or cuftom, have acquired a degree
of veneration to which naturally it is not entitled,
what

---

* See chap. 10. compared with chap. 7.

what are the proper means for wiping off the artificial colouring, and diſplaying the ſubjeſt in its true light ? A man of true taſte ſees the ſubjeſt without diſguiſe : but if he heſitate, let him apply the teſt of ridicule, which ſeparates it from its artificial conneſtions, and expoſes it naked with all its native improprieties.

But it is urged, that the graveſt and moſt ſerious matters may be ſet in a ridiculous light. Hardly ſo ; for where an objeſt is neither riſible nor improper, it lies not open in any quarter to an attack from ridicule. But ſuppoſing the faſt, I foreſee not any harmful conſequence. By the ſame ſort of reaſoning, a talent for wit ought to be condemned, becauſe it may be employed to burleſque a great or lofty ſubjeſt. Such irregular uſe made of a talent for wit or ridicule, cannot long impoſe upon mankind : it cannot ſtand the teſt of correſt and delicate taſte ; and truth will at laſt prevail even with the vulgar. To condemn a talent for ridicule becauſe it may be perverted to wrong purpoſes, is not a little ridiculous : could one forbear to ſmile, if a talent for reaſoning were condemned becauſe it alſo may be perverted ? and yet the concluſion in the latter caſe, would be not leſs juſt than in the former : perhaps more juſt ; for no talent is more frequently perverted than that of reaſon.

We had beſt leave nature to her own operations : the moſt valuable talents may be abuſed, and ſo may that of ridicule : let us bring it under proper culture if we can, without endeavouring to pluck it up by the root. Were we deſtitute of this teſt of truth, I know not what might be the conſequences : I ſee not what rule would be left us to prevent ſplendid trifles paſſing for matters of importance, ſhow and form for ſubſtance, and ſuperſtition or enthuſiaſm for pure religion.

CHAP.

Wit.

WIT is a quality of certain thoughts and expreffions : the term is never applied to an action nor to a paffion, and as little to an external object. However difficult it may be, in many inftances, to diftinguifh a witty thought or expreffion from one that is not fo, yet, in general, it may be laid down, that the term *wit* is appropriated to fuch thoughts and expreffions as are ludicrous, and alfo occafion fome degree of furprife by their fingularity. Wit, alfo, in a figurative fenfe, expreffes a talent for inventing ludicrous thoughts or expreffions : we fay commonly, *a witty man*, or *a man of wit*.

Wit in its proper fenfe, as explained above, is diftinguifhable into two kinds ; wit in the thought, and wit in the words or expreffion. Again, wit in the thought is of two kinds ; ludicrous images, and ludicrous combinations of things that have little or no natural relation.

Ludicrous images that occafion furprife by their fingularity, as having little or no foundation in nature, are fabricated by the imagination : and the imagination is well qualified for the office ; being of all our faculties the moft active, and the leaft under reftraint. Take the following example.

Shylock. You knew (none fo well, none fo well as you) of my daughter's flight.
Salino. That's certain ; I for my part knew the tailor that made the wings fhe flew withal.
Merchant of Venice, act 3. *fc.* 1.

The

U 3

The image here is undoubtedly witty. It is ludicrous : and it muſt occaſion ſurprife ; for having no
natural foundation, it is altogether unexpected.

The other branch of wit in the thought, is that
only which is taken notice of by Addifon, following
Locke, who defines it " to lie in the aſſemblage of
ideas ; and putting thofe together, with quicknefs
and variety, wherein can be found any refemblance
or congruity, thereby to make up pleafant pictures
and agreeable viſions in the fancy.*" It may be defined more concifely, and perhaps more accurately,
" A junction of things by diſtant and fanciful relations, which furprife becaufe they are unexpected.†"
The following is a proper example.

> We grant although he had much wit,
> He was very ſhie of uſing it,
> As being loth to wear it out ;
> . And therefore bore it not about,
> Unleſs on holidays, or fo,
> As men their beſt apparel do.
>
> *Hudibras, canto* i.

Wit is of all the moſt elegant recreation : the image enters the mind with gaiety, and gives a ſudden
fiaſh, which is extremely pleafant. Wit thereby gently
elevates without ſtraining, raifes mirth without diſſo-
lutenefs, and relaxes while it entertains.

Wit in the expreſſion, commonly called *a play of
words*, being a baſtard fort of wit, is referved for the
laſt place. I proceed to examples of wit in the
thought ; and firſt of ludicrous images.

Falſtaff, ſpeaking of his taking Sir John Colevile
of the Dale.

> Here he is, and here I yield him ; and I befeech your
> Grace, let it be book'd with the reſt of this day's deeds ;
> or, by the Lord, I will have it in a particular ballad elfe,
> with

with mine own picture on the top of it, Colevile kissing my
foot : to the which courfe if I be enforc'd,· if you do not all
fhew like gilt twopences to me ; and I, in the clear fky of
fame, o'erfhine you as much as the full moon doth the
cinders of the element, which fhew like pins' heads to her ;
believe not the word of the noble. Therefore let me have
right, and let defert mount.

Second part, Henry IV. *act* 4. *fc.* 6.

I knew, when feven juftices could not take up a quar-
rel, but when the parties were met themfelves, one of them
thought but of an *if ;* as, if you faid fo, then I faid fo ;
and they fhook hands, and fwore brothers ; Your *if* is the
only peacemaker ; much virtue is in *if.*

Shakefpear.

For there is not through all nature, another fo callous,
and infenfible a member, as the world's pofteriors, whether
you apply to it the toe or the birch.

Preface to the tale of a Tub.

The war hath introduced abundance of polyfyllables,
which will never be able to live many more campaigns.
Speculations, operations, preliminaries, ambaffadors, pali-
fadoes, communication, circumvallation, battalions, as
numerous as they are, if they attack us too frequently in
our coffee-houfes, we fhall certainly put them to flight, and
cut off the rear.

Tatler, No. 230.

Speaking of Difcord.

She never went abroad, but fhe brought home fuch a
bundle of monftrous lies, as would have amazed any mortal, but fuch as knew her ; of a whale that had fwallowed
a fleet of fhips ; of the lions being let out of the tower to
deftroy the Proteftant religion ; of the Pope's being feen in
a brandy-fhop at Wapping, &c.

Hiftory of John Bull, part 1. *ch.* 16.

The

U 4

The other branch of wit in the thought, namely, ludicrous combinations and oppofitions, may be traced through various ramifications. And, firft, fanciful caufes affigned that have no natural rela-tion to the effects produced :

Lancafter.   Fare you well, Falftaff; I, in my condition, Shall better fpeak of you than you deferve.   [*Exit.*

Falftaff.   I would you had but the wit ; 'twere better than your dukedom.   Good faith, this fame young fober-blooded boy doth not love me ; nor a man cannot make him laugh ; but that's no marvel, he drinks no wine.   There's never any of thefe demure boys come to any proof ; for thin drink doth fo overcool their blood, and making many fifh-meals, that they fall into a kind of male green-ficknefs; and then, when they marry, they get wenches.   They are generally fools and cowards ; which fome of us fhould be too, but for inflammation.   A good fherris-fack hath a two-fold operation in it : it afcends me into the brain ; dries me there all the foolifh, dull, and crudy vapours which environ it, makes it apprehenfive, quick, forgetive, full of nimble, fiery, and delectable fhapes ; which deliver'd o'er to the voice, the tongue, which is the birth, becomes excellent wit.   The fecond property of your excellent fherris is, the warming of the blood ; which before cold and fettled, left the liver white and pale ; which is the badge of pufillanimity and cowardice : but the fherris warms it, and makes it courfe from the inwards to the parts extreme ; it illuminateth the face, which, as a beacon, gives warning to all the reft of this little kingdom, man, to arm ; and then the vital commoners and inland petty fpirits mufter me all to their captain, the heart, who, great, and puff'd up with this retinue, doth any deed of courage : and thus valour comes of fherris.   So that fkill in the weapon is nothing without fack, for that fets it a-work ; and learning a mere hoard of gold kept by a devil, till fack commences it, and fets it in act and ufe.   Hereof comes it, that Prince Harry is valiant ; for the cold blood he did naturally inherit of his father, he hath, like lean, fteril, and bare land, manured, hufbanded, and till'd with excellent endeavour of drinking good and good ftore of fertile fherris, that he is become very hot and valiant.   If I had a
                                            thoufand

thoufand fons, the firft human principle I would teach
them, fhould be to forfwear thin potations, and to addict
themfelves to fack.

Second part of Henry IV. *act* 4. *fc.* 7.

The trenchant blade, toledo trufty,
For want of fighting was grown rufty,
And ate into itfelf, for lack
Of fome body to hew and hack.
The peaceful fcabbard where it dwelt,
The rancor of its edge had felt ;
For of the lower end two handful,
It had devoured, 'twas fo manful ;
And fo much fcorn'd to lurk in cafe,
As if it durft not fhew its face.

Hudibras, canto 1.

Speaking of phyficians,

Le bon de cette profeffion eft, qu'il y a parmi les morts
une honnêteté, une difcrétion la plus grande du monde ;
jamais on n'en voit fe plaindre du médicin qui l'a tué.

Le medicin malgré lui.

Admirez les bontez, admirez les tendreffes,
De ces vieux efclaves du fort.
Ils ne font jamais las d'aquérir des richeffes,
Pour ceux qui fouhaitent leur mort.

Belinda. Lard, he has fo peftered me with flames and
ftuff—I think I fhant endure the fight of a fire this twelve-
month.

Old Backelor, act 2. *fc.* 4.

To account for effects by fuch fantaftical caufes,
being highly ludicrous, is quite improper in any ferious compofition. Therefore the following paffage
from Cowley, in his poem on the death of Sir Henry Wooton, is in a bad tafte,

He

He did the utmoſt bounds of knowledge find,
He found them not ſo large as was his mind.
But, like the brave pellæan youth, did moan,
Becauſe that Art had no more worlds than one.
And when he ſaw that he through all had paſt,
He dy'd, left he ſhould idle grow at laſt.

Fanciful reaſoning :

Falſtaff. Imbowell'd !——if thou imbowel me to-day,
I'll give you leave to powder me, and eat me to-morrow!
'Sblood, 'twas time to counterfeit, or that hot termagant
Scot had paid me ſcot and lot too. Counterfeit! I lie, I
am no counterfeit ; to die is to be a counterfeit ; for he is
but the counterfeit of a man, who hath not the life of a
man ; but to counterfeit dying, when a man thereby liveth,
is to be no counterfeit, but the true and perfect image of
life, indeed.
Firſt part, Henry IV. *act* 1. *ſc.* 10.

Clwn. And the more pity that great folk ſhould have
countenance in this world to drown or hang themſelves,
more than their even Chriſtian.
Hamlet, act 5. *ſc.* 1.

Pedro. Will you have me, Lady ?
Beatrice. No, my Lord, unleſs I might have another for
working days. Your Grace is too coſtly to wear every
day.
Much ado about nothing, act, 2. *ſc.* 5.

Jeſſica. I ſhall be ſaved by my huſband ; he hath made
me a Chriſtian.
Launcelot. Truly the more to blame he ; we were Chriſtians enough before e'en as many as could well live by one
another : this making of Chriſtians will raiſe the price of
hogs ; if we grow all to be pork-eaters, we ſhall not have
a raſher on the coals for money.
Merchant of Venice, act 3. *ſc.* 6.

In

In weftern clime there is a town,
To thofe that dwell therein well known ;
Therefore there needs no more be faid here,
We unto them refer our reader :
For brevity is very good
When w'are, or are not underftood.
                    Hudibras, canto 1.

But Hudibras gave him a twitch,
As quick as lightning, in the breech,
Juft in the place where honour's lodg'd,
As wife philofophers have judg'd ;
Becaufe a kick in that part, more
Hurts honour, than deep wounds before.
                    Ibid. canto 3.

Ludicrous·junction of fmall things with great, as of equal importance :

This day black omens threat the brighteft fair,
That e'er deferv'd a watchful fpirit's care ,
Some dire difafter or by force or flight ;
But what, or where, the fates have wrapt in night :
Whether the nymph fhall break Diana's law ;
Or fome frail china jar receive a flaw ;
Or ftain her honour, or her new brocade ;
Forget her pray'rs or mifs a mafquerade ;
Or lofe her heart, or necklace, at a ball ;
Or whether heaven has doom'd that fhock muft fall.
                    Rape of the Lock, canto ii. 101.

One fpeaks the glory of the Britifh Queen,
And one defcribes a charming Indian fcreen.
                    Ibid. canto iii. 13.

Then flafh'd the living lightning from her eyes,
And fcreams of horror rend th' affrighted fkies.
Not louder fhrieks to pitying heav'n are caft,
When hufbands, or when lapdogs, breathe their laft ;
Or when rich china veffels fall'n from high,
In glittering duft and painted fragments lie !
                    Ibid. canto iii. 155.

Not

Not youthful kings in battle feiz'd alive,
Not fcornful virgins who their charms furvive,
Not ardent lovers robb'd of all their blifs,
Not ancient ladies when refus'd a kifs,
Not tyrants fierce that unrepenting die,
Not Cynthia when her manteau's pinn'd awry,
E'er felt fuch rage, refentment, and defpair,
As thou fad virgin for thy ravifh'd hair.

Ibid. canto iv. 3.

Joining things that in appearance are oppofite.
As for example, where Sir Roger de Coverley, in
the Spectator, fpeaking of his widow,

That he would have given her a coal-pit to have kept her
in clean linen ; and that her finger fhould have fparkled
with one hundred of his richeft acres.

Premifes that promife much and perform nothing.
Cicero upon that article fays,

Sed fcitis effe notiffimum ridiculi genus, cum aliud ex-
pectamus, aliud dicitur : hic nobifmetipfis nofter error
rifum movet.*

Beatrice.————With a good leg and a good foot, uncle, and money enough in his purfe, fuch a man would win
any woman in the world if he could get her good-will.

Much ado about nothing, act 2. *fc.* 1.

Beatrice. I have a good eye, uncle, I can fee a church
by day-light.   *Ibid.*

Le medicin que l'on m'indique
Sait le Latin, le Grec, l'Hebreu,
Les belles lettres, la phyfique,
La chimie et la botanique.
Chacun lui donne fon aveu :
Il auroit auffi ma pratique ;
Mais je veux vivre encore un peu.

* De oratore, l. 2. cap. 63.

Again,

Again,

> Vingt fois le jour le bon Grégoire
> A foin de fermer fon armoire.
> De quoi penfez vous qu'il a peur ?
> Belle demande ! Qu'un voleur
> Trouvante une facile proie,
> Ne lui ravilfe tout fon bien.
> Non ; Grégoire a peur qu'on ne voie
> Que dans fon armoire il n'a rien.

Again,

> L'athfmatique Damon a cru que l'air des champs
> Repareroit en lui le ravage des ans,
>   Il s'eft fuit, a grands fraix, tranfporter en Bretagne.
> Or voiez ce qu'a fait l'air natal qu'il a pris !
>   Damon feroit mort à Paris :
>   Damon eft mort à la campagne.

Having difcuffed wit in the thought, we proceed to what is verbal only, commonly called *a play of words*. This fort of wit depends, for the moft part, upon choofing a word that hath different fignifications : by that artifice hocus-pocus tricks are played in language, and thoughts plain and fimple take on a very different appearance. Play is neceffary for man, in order to refrefh him after labour ; and accordingly man loves play, even fo much as to relifh a play of words : and it is happy for us, that words can be employed not only for ufeful purpofes, but alfo for our amufement. This amufement, though humble and low, unbends the mind ; and is relifhed by fome at all times, and by all at fome times.

It is remarkable, that this low fpecies of wit, has among all nations been a favourite entertainment, in a certain ftage of their progrefs toward refinement of tafte and manners, and has gradually gone into difrepute.

difrepute. As foon as a language is formed into a fyftem, and the meaning of words is afcertained with tolerable accuracy, opportunity is afforded for expreffions that, by the double meaning of fome words, give a familiar thought the appearance of being new ; and the penetration of the reader or hearer is gratified in detecting the true fenfe difguifed under the double meaning. That this fort of wit was in England deemed a reputable amufement, during the reigns of Elifabeth and James I. is vouched by the works of Shakefpear, and even by the writings of grave divines. But it cannot have any long endurance; for as language ripens, and the meaning of words is more and more afcertained, words held to be fynonymous diminifh daily; and when thofe that remain have been more than once employed, the pleafure vanifheth with the novelty.

I proceed to examples, which, as in the former cafe, fhall be diftributed into different claffes.

A feeming refemblance from the double meaning of a word :

> Beneath this ftone my wife doth lie ;
> She's now at reft and fo am I.

A feeming contraft from the fame caufe, termed, *a verbal antithefis*, which hath no defpicable effect in ludicrous fubjects :

> Whilft Iris his cofmetic wafh would try
> To make her bloom revive, and lovers die,
> Some afk for charms and others philters chufe,
> To gain Corinna, and their quartans lofe.
>   *Difpenfary, canto* 2.

> And how frail nymphs, oft by abortion, aim
> To lofe a fubftance, to preferve a name.
>   *Ibid. canto* 3.
>   While

While nymphs take treats, or affignations give.
Rape of the Lock.

Other feeming connections from the fame caufe:

Will you employ your conqu'ring fword,
To break a fiddle, and your word?
Hudibras, canto 2.

To whom the knight with comely grace
Put off his hat to put his cafe.
Ibid. part 3. *canto* 3.

Here Britain's ftatefmen oft the fall foredoom
Of foreign tyrants, and of nymphs at home;
Here thou, great Anna! whom three realms obey,
Doft fometimes counfel take—and fometimes tea.
Rape of the Lock, canto 3. *l.* 5.

O'er their quietus where fat judges dofe,
And lull their cough and confcience to repofe
Difpenfary, canto 1.

Speaking of Prince Eugene:

This general is a great taker of fnuff as well as of towns.
Pope, Key to the Lock.

Exul mentifque domufque.
Metamorphofes, l. ix. 409.

A feeming oppofition from the fame caufe:

Hic quiefcit qui nunquam quievit.

Again,

Quel âge a cette Iris, dont on fait tant de bruit?
Me demandoit Cliton n'aguere.
Il faut, dis-je, vous fatisfaire,
Elle a vingt ans le jeur, et cinquante ans la nuit.

Again,

Again,

> So like the chances are of love and war,
> That they alone in this diftinguifh'd are ;
> In love the victors from the vanquifh'd fly,
> They fly that wound, and they purfue that die.
>
> *Waller.*

> What new found witchcraft was in thee,
> With thine own cold to kindle me ?
> Strange art ; like him that fhould devife
> To make a burning glafs of ice.
>
> *Cowley.*

Wit of this kind is unfuitable in a ferious poem ; witnefs the following line in Pope's Elegy to the memory of an unfortunate lady :

> Cold is that breaft which warm'd the world before.

This fort of writing is finely burlefqued by Swift :

> Her hands the fofteft ever felt,
> Though cold would burn, though dry would melt.
>
> *Strephon and Chloe.*

Taking a word in a different fenfe from what is meant, comes under wit, becaufe it occafions fome flight degree of furprife :

> *Beatrice.* I may fit in a corner and cry *Heigh ho !* for a hufband.
> *Pedro.* Lady Beatrice, I will get you one.
> *Beatrice.* I would rather have one of your father's getting. Hath your grace ne'er a brother like you ? Your father got excellent hufbands, if a maid could come by them.
>
> *Much ado about nothing; act 2. fc. 5.*

> *Falftaff.* My honeft lads, I will tell you what I am about.
>
> *Piftol.*

Piſtol. Two yards and more.

Falſtaff. No quips now, Piſtol : indeed I am in the waſte two yards about : but I am now about no waſte ; I am about thrift.

Merry Wives of Windſor, act 1. *ſc.* 7.

Lo. Sands.————By your leave ſweet ladies,
If I chance to talk a little wild, forgive me :
I had it from my father.
Anne Bullen. Was he mad, Sir !
Sands. O, very mad, exceeding mad, in love too ;
But he would bite none————

K. Henry VIII.

An aſſertion that bears a double meaning, one right, one wrong, but ſo introduced as to direct us to the wrong meaning, is a ſpecies of baſtard wit, which is diſtinguiſhed from all others by the name *pun.* For example,

Paris.————Sweet Helen, I muſt woo you,
To help unarm our Hector : his ſtubborn buckles,
With theſe your white enchanting fingers touch'd,
Shall more obey, than to the edge of ſteel,
Or force of Greekiſh ſinews ; you ſhall do more
Than all the iſland Kings, diſarm great Hector.

Troilus and Creſſida, act 3. *ſc.* 2.

The pun is in the cloſe. The word *diſarm* has a double meaning : it ſignifies to take off a man's armour, and alſo to ſubdue him in fight. We are directed to the latter ſenſe by the context ; but, with regard to Helen, the word holds only true in the former ſenſe. I go on with other examples :

Eſſe nihil dicis quicquid petis, improbe Cinna :
Si nil, Cinna, petis, nil tibi, Cinna, nego.

Martial, l. 3. *epigr.* 61.
Jocondus

Jocondus geminum impofuit tibi, Sequana, pontem ;
Hunc tu jure potes dicere pontificem.

Sanzaarius.

N. B. *Jecondus was a monk.*

Chief Juftice. Well ! the truth is, Sir Joh● you live in
great infamy.

Falftaff. He that buckles him in my belt cannot live in
lefs.

Chief Juftice. Your means are very flender, and your
wafte is great.

Falftaff. I would it were otherwife : I would my means
were greater and my wafte flenderer.

Second Part, Henry IV. act 1. fc. 5.

Celia. I pray you bear with me I can go no further.

Clown.. For my part, I had rather bear with you than
bear you : yet I fhould bear no crofs if I did bear you ;
for I think you have no money in your purfe.

As you like it, act 2. fc. 4.

He that impofes an oath makes it,
Not he that for convenience takes it ;
Then how can any man be faid
To break an oath he never made ?

Hudibras, part 2. canto 2.

The feventh fatire of the firft book of Horace is purpofely contrived to introduce at the clofe a moft execrable pun. Talking of fome infamous wretch whofe
name was *Rex Rupilius,*

Perfius exclamat, Per magnos, Brute, deos te
Oro, qui reges confueris tollere, cur non ,
Hunc regem jugulas ? Operum hoc, mihi crede, tuo-
rum eft.

Though playing with words is a mark of a mind
at eafe, and difpofed to any fort of amufement, we

muft

muſt not thence conclude that playing with words is always ludicrous. Words are ſo intimately con-nected with thought, that if the ſubject be really grave, it will not appear ludicrous even in that fan-taſtic dreſs. I am, however, far from recommending it in any ſerious performance : on the contrary, the diſcordance between the thought and expreſſion muſt be diſagreeable ; witneſs the following ſpecimen.

He hath abandoned his phyſicians, Madam, under whoſe practiſes he hath perſecuted time with hope : and finds no other advantage in the proceſs, but only the loſing of hope by time.

All's well that ends well, act 1. ſc. 1.

K. Henry. O my poor kingdom ſick with civil blows !
When that my care could not with-hold thy riots,
What wilt thou do when riot is thy care ?

Second part, K. Henry IV.

If any one ſhall obſerve, that there is a third ſpe-cies of wit, different from thoſe mentioned, conſiſt-ing in ſounds merely, I am willing to give it place. And indeed it muſt be admitted, that many of Hu-dibras's double rhymes come under the definition of wit given in the beginning of this chapter : they are ludicrous and their ſingularity occaſions ſome de-gree of ſurprize. Swift is no leſs ſucceſsful than Butler in this ſort of wit ; witneſs the following in-ſtances : *Goddeſs—Boadice. Pliny—Nicolini. Iſca-riots—Chariots. Mitre—Nitre. Dragon—Suffragan.*

A repartee may happen to be witty : but it cannot be conſidered as a ſpecies of wit ; becauſe there are many repartees extremely ſmart and yet extremely ſe-rious. I give the following example. A certain petu-lant Greek, objecting to Anacharſis that he was a Scythian : True, ſays Anacharſis, my country diſ-graces me, but you diſgrace your country. This fine turn gives ſurprize ; but it is far from being ludicrous.

C H A P.

W 2

Cuſtom and Habit.

VIEWING man as under the influence
of novelty, would one ſuſpeᴄt that cuſtom alſo ſhould
influence him?. and yet our nature is equally ſuſceptible
of each ; not only in different objeᴄts, but frequently
in the ſame. When an objeᴄt is new, it is enchanting : familiarity renders it indifferent ; and cuſtom,
after a longer familiarity, makes it again diſagreeable. Human nature diverſified with many and various ſprings of aᴄtion, is wonderfully, and, indulging
the expreſſion, intricately conſtruᴄted.

Cuſtom hath ſuch influence upon many of our
feelings, by warping and varying them, that we muſt
attend to its operations if we would be acquainted
with human nature. This ſubjeᴄt, in itſelf obſcure,
has been much negleᴄted ; and a complete analyſis
of it would be no eaſy taſk. I pretend only to touch
it curſorily ; hoping, however, that what is here
laid down, will diſpoſe diligent inquirers to attempt
further diſcoveries.

Cuſtom reſpeᴄts the aᴄtion, *habit* the agent. By
cuſtom we mean a frequent reiteration of the ſame aᴄt ;
and by *habit*, the effeᴄt that cuſtom has on the agent.
This effeᴄt may be either aᴄtive, witneſs the dexterity
produced by cuſtom in performing certain exerciſes ;
or paſſive, as when a thing makes an impreſſion on
us different from what it did originally. The latter
only as relative to the ſenſitive part of our nature,
comes under the preſent undertaking.

This ſubjeᴄt is intricate : ſome pleaſures are fortified by cuſtom ; and yet cuſtom begets familiarity,
and

and confequently indifference :* in many inftances, fatiety and difguft are the confequences of reiteration : again, though cuftom blunts the edge of diftrefs and of pain, yet the want of any thing to which we have been long accuftomed, is a fort of torture. A clue to guide us through all the intricacies of this labyrinth, would be an acceptable prefent.

Whatever be the caufe, it is certain that we are much influenced by cuftom : it hath an effect upon our pleafures, upon our actions, and even upon our thoughts and fentiments. Habit makes no figure during the vivacity of youth : in middle age it gains ground ; and in old age governs without control. In that period of life, generally fpeaking, we eat at a certain hour, take exercife at a certain hour, go to reft at a certain hour, all by the direction of habit : nay, a particular feat, table, bed, comes to be effential ; and a habit in any of thefe cannot be controlled without uneafinefs.

Any flight or moderate pleafure frequently reiterated for a long time, forms a peculiar connection between us and the thing that caufes the pleafure. This connection termed *habit*, has the effect to awaken our defire or appetite for that thing when it returns not as ufual. During the courfe of enjoyment, the pleafure rifes infenfibly higher and higher till a habit be eftablifhed ; at which time the pleafure is at its height. It continues not however ftationary : the fame cuftomary•reiteration which carried it to its height, brings it down again by infenfible degrees .

t veas

---

* If all the year were playing holidays,
To fport would be as t dious as to work :
But when they feldom come, they wifh'd for come,
And nothing pleafeth but rare accidents.

Firft part, Henry IV. act 1. f. 1.

W 3

even lower than it was at firſt : but of that circum-ſtance afterward. What at preſent we have in view, is to prove by experiments, that thoſe things which at firſt are but moderately agreeable, are the apteſt to become habitual. Spirituous liquors, at firſt ſcarce agreeable, readily produce an habitual appe-tite : and cuſtom prevails ſo far, as even to make us fond of things originally diſagreeable, ſuch as coffee, aſſa-foetida, and tobacco ; which is pleaſantly illuſ-trated by Congreve :

Fainall. For a paſſionate lover, methinks you are a man ſomewhat too diſcerning in the failings of your miſtreſs.
Mirabell. And for a diſcerning man, ſomewhat too paſſionate a lover ; for I like her with all her faults ; nay like her for her faults. Her follies are ſo natural, or ſo artful, that they become her ; and thoſe affeĉtations which in another woman would be odious, ſerve but to make her more agreeable. I'll tell thee, Fainall, ſhe once us'd me with that inſolence, that in revenge I took her to pieces, lifted her, and ſeparated her failings ; I ſtudy'd 'em, and got 'em by rote. The catalogue was ſo large, that I was not without hopes, one day or other, to hate her heartily : to which end I ſo us'd myſelf to think of 'em, that at length, contrary to my deſign and expeĉtation, they gave me every hour leſs and leſs diſturbance ; till in a few days, it became habitual to me to remember 'em without being diſpleaſed. They are now grown as familiar to me as my own frailties ; and in all probabiiity, in a little time longer, I ſhall like 'em as well.

The way of the world, aĉt 1. ſc. 3.

A walk upon the quarter-deck, though intolerably confined, becomes however ſo agreeable by cuſtom, that a ſailor in his walk on ſhore, confines himſelf commonly within the ſame bounds. I knew a man who had relinquiſhed the ſea for a country-life : in the corner of his garden he reared an artificial mount with a level ſummit, reſembling moſt accurately a

quarter-

quarter-deck, not only in ſhape but in ſize; and here he generally walked. In Minorca Governor Kane made an excellent road the whole length of the iſland; and yet the inhabitants adhere to the old road, though not only longer but extremely bad.* Play or gaming, at firſt barely amuſing by the occupation it affords, becomes in time extremely agreeable; and is frequently proſecuted with avidity, as if it were the chief buſineſs of life. The ſame obſervation is applicable to the pleaſures of the internal ſenſes, thoſe of knowledge and virtue in particular: children have ſcarce any ſenſe of theſe pleaſures; and men very little who are in the ſtate of nature without culture: our taſte for virtue and knowledge improves ſlowly; but is capable of growing ſtronger than any other appetite in human nature.

To introduce an active habit, frequency of acts is not ſufficient without length of time: the quickeſt ſucceſſion of acts in a ſhort time, is not ſufficient; nor a ſlow ſucceſſion in the longeſt time. The effect muſt be produced by a moderate ſoft action, and a long ſeries of eaſy touches, removed from each other by ſhort intervals. Nor are theſe ſufficient without regularity in the time, place, and other circumſtances of the action: the more uniform any operation is, the ſooner it becomes habitual. And this holds equally in a paſſive habit; variety in any remarkable degree, prevents the effect; thus any particular food will ſcarce ever become habitual, where the manner of dreſſing is varied. The circumſtances then

---

* Cuſtom is a ſecond nature. Formerly, the merchants of Briſtol had no place for meeting but the ſtreet, open to every variety of weather. An exchange was erected for them with convenient piazzas. But ſo riveted were they to their accuſtomed place, that in order to diſlodge them, the magiſtrates were forced to break up the pavement, and to render the place a heap of rough ſtones.

then requiſite to augment a moderate pleaſure, and at the long run to form a habit, are weak uniform acts, reiterated during a long courſe of time without any conſiderable interruption : every agreeable cauſe that operates in this manner, will grow habitual.

Affection and *averſion*, as diſtinguiſhed from paſſion on the one hand, and on the other from original diſpoſition, are in reality habits refpecting particular objects, acquired in the manner above ſet forth. The pleaſure of ſocial intercourſe with any perſon, muſt originally be faint, and frequently reiterated, in order to eſtabliſh the habit of affection. Affection thus generated, whether it be friendſhip or love, ſeldom ſwells into any tumultuous or vigorous paſſion ; but is however the ſtrongeſt cement that can bind together two individuals of the human ſpecies. In like manner, a ſlight degree of difguſt often reiterated with regularity, grows into the habit of averſion, which commonly ſubſiſts for life.

Objects of taſte that are delicious, far from tending to become habitual, are apt by indulgence to produce ſatiety and difguſt : no man contracts a habit of ſugar, honey, or ſweet-meats, as he doth of tobacco :

> Dulcia non ferimus ; fucco renovamur amaro.
> > *Ovid. art. amand. l.* 3.

> Inſipido è quel dolce, che condito
> Non è di qualche amaro, e toſto ſatia.
> > *Aminta di Taſſo.*

> Theſe violent delights have violent ends,
> And in their triumph die. The ſweeteſt honey
> Is loathſome in its own delicioufnefs,
> And in the taſte confounds the appetite ;
> > Therefore

Therefore love mod'rately, long love doth ſo ;
Too ſwift arrives as tardy as too flow.
Romeo and Juliet, act 2. ſc. 6.

The ſame obſervation holds with reſpect to all objects that being extremely agreeable raiſe violent paſſions : ſuch paſſions are incompatible with a habit of any ſort ; and in particular they never produce affection nor averſion : a man who at firſt ſight falls violently in love, has a ſtrong deſire of enjoyment, but no affection for the woman :* a man who is ſurpriſed with an unexpected favour burns for an opportunity to exert his gratitude, without having any affection for his benefactor :

---

* Violent love without affection is finely exemplified in the following ſtory. When Conſtantinople was taken by the Turks, Irene, a young Greek of an illuſtrious family, fell into the hands of Mahomet II, who was at that time in the prime of youth and glory. His ſavage heart being ſubdued by her charms, he ſhut himſelf up with her, denying acceſs even to his miniſters. Love obtained ſuch aſcendant as to make him frequently abandon the army, and fly to his Irene. War relaxed, for victory was no longer the monarch's favourite paſſion. The ſoldiers, accuſtomed to booty, began to murmur : and the infection ſpread even among the commanders. The Baſha Muſtapha, conſulting the fidelity he owed his maſter, was the firſt who durſt acquaint him of the diſcourſes held publicly to the prejudice of his glory.

The Sultan, after a gloomy ſilence, formed his reſolution. He ordered Muſtapha to aſſemble the troops next morning ; and then with precipitation retired to Irene's apartment. Never before did that princeſs appear ſo charming ; never before did the prince beſtow ſo many warm careſſes. To give a new luſtre to her beauty, he exhorted her women next morning, to beſtow their utmoſt art and care on her dreſs. He took her by the hand, led her into the middle of the army, and pulling off her vail, demanded of the Baſhas with a fierce look, whether they had ever beheld ſuch a beauty ? After an awful pauſe. Mahomet with one hand laying hold of the young Greek by her beautiful locks, and with the other pulling out his ſcimitar, ſevered the head from the body at one ſtroke. Then turning to his grandees, with eyes wild and furious, " This ſword," ſaid he, " when it is my will, knows to cut the bands of love." However ſtrange it may appear, we learn from experience, that deſire of enjoyment may conſiſt with the moſt brutal averſion, directed both to the ſame woman. Of this we have a noted example in the firſt book of Sully's Memoirs ; to which I chooſe to refer the reader, for it is too groſs to be tranſcribed.

benefactor : neither does defire of vengeance for an atrocious injury, involve averfion.

It is perhaps not eafy to fay why moderate pleafures gather ftrength by cuftom : but two caufes concur to prevent that effect in the more intenfe pleafures. Thefe by an original law in our nature, increafe quickly to their full growth, and decay with no lefs precipitation ;* and cuftom is too flow in its operation to overcome that law. The other caufe is no lefs powerful : exquifite pleafure is extremely fatiguing ; occafioning, as a naturalift would fay, great expenfe of animal fpirits ;† and of fuch the mind cannot bear fo frequent gratification, as to fuperinduce a habit : if the thing that raifes the pleafure return before the mind have recovered its tone and relifh, difguft enfues inftead of pleafure.

A habit never fails to admonifh us of the wonted time of gratification, by raifing a pain for want of the object, and a defire to have it. The pain of want is always firft felt : the defire naturally follows ; and upon prefenting the object both vanifh inftantaneoufly. Thus a man accuftomed to tobacco, feels, at the end of the ufual interval, a confufed pain of want ; which at firft points at nothing in particular, though it foon fettles upon its accuftomed object ; and the fame may be obferved in perfons addicted to drinking, who are often in an uneafy reftlefs ftate before they think of the bottle. In pleafures indulged regularly, and at equal intervals, the appetite, remarkably obfequious to cuftom, returns regularly with the ufual time of gratification ; not fooner, even though the object be prefented. This pain of want

arifing

---

* See chap. 2. part 3.

† Lady Eafy, upon her hufband's reformation, expreffes to her friend the following fentiment : "Be fatisfied ; Sir Charles has made me happy, even to a pain of joy."

ariſing from habit, ſeems directly oppoſite to that of fatiety ; and it muſt appear ſingular, that frequency of gratification ſhould produce effects ſo oppoſite, as are the pains of exceſs and of want.

The appetites that reſpect the preſervation and propagation of our ſpecies, are attended with a pain of want ſimilar to that occaſioned by habit : hunger and thirſt are uneaſy ſenſations of want, which always precede the deſire of eating or drinking ; and a pain for want of carnal enjoyment precedes the deſire of an object. The pain being thus felt independent of an object, cannot be cured but by gratification. Very different is an ordinary paſſion, in which deſire precedes the pain of want : ſuch a paſſion cannot exiſt but while the object is in view ; and therefore, by removing the object out of thought, it vaniſheth, with its deſire, and pain of want.*

The natural appetites above mentioned differ from habit in the following particular : they have an undetermined direction toward all objects of gratification in general ; whereas an habitual appetite is directed to a particular object : the attachment we have by habit to a particular woman, differs widely from the natural paſſion which comprehends the whole ſex ; and the habitual reliſh for a particular diſh is far from being the ſame with a vague appetite for food. That difference notwithſtanding, it is ſtill remarkable, that nature hath enforced the gratification of certain natural appetites eſſential to the ſpecies, by a pain of the ſame ſort with that which habit produceth.

The pain of habit is leſs under our power than any other pain that ariſes from want of gratification : hunger and thirſt are more eaſily endured, eſpecially

at

* See chap. 2. part 3.

at firſt, than an unuſual intermiſſion of any habitual
pleaſure: perſons are often heard declaring, they
would forego ſleep or food, rather than tobacco.
We muſt not, however, conclude, that the gratification of an habitual appetite affords the ſame delight
with the gratification of one that is natural : far from
it ; the pain of want only is greater.

The flow and reiterated acts that produce a habit,
ſtrengthen the mind to enjoy the habitual pleaſure
in greater quantity and more frequency than originally ; and by that means a habit of intemperate gratification is often formed : after unbounded acts of
intemperance, the habitual reliſh is ſoon reſtored, and
the pain for want of enjoyment returns with freſh
vigour.

The cauſes of the preſent emotions hitherto in
view, are either an individual, ſuch as a companion,
a certain dwelling-place, a certain amuſement ; or a
particular ſpecies, ſuch as coffee, mutton, or any
other food. But habit is not confined to ſuch. A
conſtant train of trifling diverſions, may form ſuch a
habit in the mind, that it cannot be eaſy a moment
without amuſement : a variety in the objects prevents
a habit as to any one in particular ; but as the train
is uniform with reſpect to amuſement, the habit is
formed accordingly ; and that ſort of habit may be
denominated *a generic habit*, in oppoſition to the former, which is *a ſpecific habit*. A habit of a town-life,
of country ſports, of ſolitude, of reading, or of buſineſs, where ſufficiently varied, are inſtances of generic habits. Every ſpecific habit hath a mixture of
the generic ; for the habit of any one ſort of food
makes the taſte agreeable, and we are fond of that
taſte wherever found. Thus a man deprived of an
habitual object, takes up with what moſt reſembles it ;
deprived of tobacco, any bitter herb will do, rather
than

than want: a habit of punch, makes wine a good
reſource : accuſtomed to the ſweet ſociety and com-
forts of matrimony, the man, unhappily deprived of
his beloved object, inclines the ſooner to a ſecond.
In general, when we are deprived of an habitual object, we are fond of its qualities in any other object.

The reaſons are aſſigned above, why the cauſes of
intenſe pleaſure become not readily habitual : but
now we diſcover, that theſe reaſons conclude only
againſt ſpecific habits.   In the caſe of a weak pleaſure, a habit is formed by frequency and uniformity
of reiteration, which, in the caſe of an intenſe pleaſure, produceth ſatiety and diſguſt.   But it is remarkable, that ſatiety and diſguſt have no effect, except as
to that thing ſingly which occaſions them : a ſurfeit
of honey produceth not a loathing of ſugar ; and
intemperance with one woman produceth no diſreliſh
of the ſame pleaſure with others.   Hence it is eaſy
to account for a generic habit in any intenſe pleaſure.:
the delight we had in the gratification of the appetite inflames the imagination, and makes us with avid-
ity, ſearch for the ſame gratification in whatever
other ſubject it can be found.   And thus uniform frequency in gratifying the ſame paſſion upon different
objects, produceth at length a generic habit.   In this
manner one acquires an habitual delight, in high
and poignant ſauces, rich dreſs, fine equipages, crowds
of company, and in whatever is commonly termed *pleaſure*.   There concurs, at the ſame time, to introduce this
habit, a peculiarity obſerved above, that reiteration of
acts enlarges the capacity of the mind, to admit a
more plentiful gratification than originally, with regard to frequency as well as quantity.

Hence it appears, that though a ſpecific habit,
cannot be formed but upon a moderate pleaſure, a
generic habit may be formed upon any ſort of pleaſ-

ure, moderate or immoderate, that hath variety of objects. The only difference is that a weak pleaſure runs naturally into a ſpecific habit ; whereas an intenſe pleaſure is altogether averſe to ſuch a habit. In a word, it is only in ſingular caſes that a moderate pleaſure produces a generic habit ; but an intenſe pleaſure cannot produce any other habit.

The appetites that reſpect the preſervation and propagation of the ſpecies are formed into habit in a peculiar manner : the time as well as meaſure of their gratification are much under the power of cuſtom ; which, by introducing a change upon the body, occaſions a proportional change in the appetites. Thus, if the body be gradually formed to a certain quantity of food at ſtated times, the appetite is regulated accordingly ; and the appetite is again changed, when a different habit of body is introduced by a different practice. Here it would ſeem, that the change is not made upon the mind, which is commonly the caſe in paſſive habits, but upon the body

When rich food is brought down by ingredients of a plainer taſte, the compoſition is ſuſceptible of a a ſpecifiic habit. Thus the ſweet taſte of ſugar, rendered leſs poignant in a mixture may, in courſe of time, produce a ſpecific habit for ſuch mixture. As moderate pleaſures, by becoming more intenſe, tend to generic habits ; ſo intenſe pleaſures, by becoming more moderate, tend to ſpecific habits.

The beauty of the human figure, by a ſpecial recommendation of nature, appears to us ſupreme, amid the great variety of beauteous forms beſtowed upon animals. The various degrees in which individuals enjoy that property, render it an object ſometimes of a moderate, ſometimes of an intenſe paſſion. The moderate paſſion, admitting frequent reiteration without

out diminution, and occupying the mind without ex-
hauſting it, turns gradually ſtronger till it becomes
a habit.   Nay, inſtances are not wanting, of a face,
at firſt diſagreeable, afterward rendered indifferent
by familiarity, and at length agreeable by cuſtom.
On the other hand, conſummate beauty, at the very
firſt glance, fills the mind ſo as to admit no increaſe.
Enjoyment leſſens the pleaſure ;* and if often repeated ends commonly in ſatiety and difguſt.   The
impreſſions made by conſummate beauty, in a gradual fucceſſion from lively to faint, conſtitute a feries
oppoſite to that of faint impreſſions, waxing gradually more lively, till they produce a ſpecific habit.
But the mind, when accuſtomed to beauty, contracts
a reliſh for it in general, though often repelled from
particular objects by the pain of ſatiety : and thus a
generic habit is formed, of which inconſtancy in
love is the neceſſary conſequence ; for a generic habit, comprehending every beautiful object, is an invincible obſtruction to a ſpecific habit, which is confined to one.

But a matter which is of great importance to the
youth of both ſexes deſerves more than a curſory
view.   Though the pleaſant emotion of beauty differs widely from the corporeal appetite, yet when
both are directed to the ſame object, they produce a
very ſtrong complex paſſion :† enjoyment in that
caſe muſt be exquiſite ; and therefore more apt to
produce ſatiety, than in any other caſe whatever.
This is a never-failing effect, where conſummate
beauty in the one party, meets with a warm imagination
and great ſenſibility in the other.   What I am here
explaining, is true without exaggeration ; and they
muſt be inſenſible upon whom it makes no impreſ-
fion : it deſerves well to be pondered by the young
and

---

* See chap, 2. part 3.   * See chap. 2. part 4.

and the amorous, who, in forming the matrimonial
ſociety, are too often blindly impelled by the animal
pleaſure merely, inflamed by beauty. It may indeed
happen, after the pleaſure is gone, and go it muſt
with a ſwift pace, that a new connection is formed upon more dignified and more laſting principles : but this is a dangerous experiment ; for,
even ſuppoſing good ſenſe, good temper, and internal merit of every ſort, yet a new connection
upon ſuch qualifications is rarely formed : it commonly, or rather always happens, that ſuch qualifications, the only ſolid foundation of an indiſſoluble
connection, are rendered altogether inviſible by ſatiety of enjoyment creating diſguſt.

One effect of cuſtom, different from any that have
been explained, muſt not be omitted, becauſe it
makes a great figure in human nature : Though cuſtom augments moderate pleaſures, and leſſens thoſe
that are intenſe, it has a different effect with reſpect
to pain ; for it blunts the edge of every ſort of pain
and diſtreſs, faint or acute. Uninterrupted miſery,
therefore, is attended with one good effect : if its
torments be inceſſant, cuſtom hardens us to bear
them.

The changes made in forming habits, are curious.
Moderate pleaſures are augmented gradually by reiteration, till they become habitual ; and then are at
their height : but they are not long ſtationary ; for
from that point they gradually decay, till they vaniſh
altogether. The pain occaſioned by want of gratification, runs a different courſe : it increaſes uniformly ;
and at laſt becomes extreme, when the pleaſure of
gratification is reduced to nothing :

————————————It ſo falls out,
That what we have we prize not to the worth,
While we enjoy it ; but being lack'd and loſt,

Why

Why then we rack the value : then we find
The virtue that poſſeſſion would not ſhew us
Whilſt it was ours.
Much ado about nothing, *act* 4. *ſc.* 2.

The effect of cuſtom with relation to a ſpecific
habit, is diſplayed through all its varieties in the uſe
of tobacco. The taſte of that plant is at firſt extremely unpleaſant ; our diſguſt leſſens gradually, till
it vaniſh altogether ; at which period the taſte is
neither agreeable nor diſagreeable : continuing the
uſe of the plant, we begin to reliſh it ; and our reliſh improves by uſe, till it arrive at perfection : from
that period it gradually decays, while the habit is in
a ſtate of increment, and conſequently the pain
of want. The reſult is, that when the habit has
acquired its greateſt vigour, the reliſh is gone ; and
accordingly we often ſmoke and take ſnuff habitually,
without ſo much as being conſcious of the operation.
We muſt except gratification after the pain of want ;
the pleaſure of which gratification is the greateſt when
the habit is the moſt vigorous : it is of the ſame kind
with the pleaſure one feels upon being delivered from
the rack, the cauſe of which is explained above.*
This pleaſure, however, is but occaſionally the
effect of habit ; and however exquiſite, is avoided as
much as poſſible becauſe of the pain that precedes it.

With regard to the pain of want, I can diſcover no
difference between a generic and a ſpecific habit. But
theſe habits differ widely with reſpect to the poſitive
pleaſure : I have had occaſion to obſerve, that the
pleaſure of a ſpecific habit decays gradually till it turn
imperceptible : the pleaſure of a generic habit, on
the contrary, being ſupported by variety of gratification, ſuffers little or no decay after it comes to its
height.

* Chap. 2. part 1. ſect. 3.

height. However it may be with other generic hab‑
its, the obſervation, I am certain, holds with reſpect
to the pleaſures of virtue and of knowledge : the
pleaſure of doing good has an unbounded ſcope, and
may be ſo variouſly gratified that it can never decay :
ſcience is equally unbounded ; our appetite for knowl‑
edge having an ample range of gratification, where
diſcoveries are recommended by novelty, by variety,
by utility, or by all of them.

In this intricate inquiry, I have endeavoured, but
without ſucceſs, to diſcover by what particular means
it is that cuſtom hath influence upon us : and now
nothing ſeems left, but to hold our nature to be ſo
framed as to be ſuſceptible of ſuch influence. And
ſuppoſing it purpoſely ſo framed, it will not be diffi‑
cult to find out ſeveral important final cauſes. That
the power of cuſtom is a happy contrivance for our
good, cannot have eſcaped any one who reflects, that
buſineſs is our province, and pleaſure our relaxation
only. Now ſatiety is neceſſary to check exquiſite
pleaſures, which otherwiſe would engroſs the mind,
and unqualify us for buſineſs. On the other hand, as
buſineſs is ſometimes painful, and is never pleaſant
beyond moderation, the habitual increaſe of mode‑
rate pleaſure, and the converſion of pain into pleaſ‑
ure, are admirably contrived for diſappointing the
malice of Fortune, and for reconciling us to what‑
ever courſe of life may be our lot :

How uſe doth breed a habit in a man !
This ſhadowy deſart, unfrequented woods,
I better brook than flouriſhing peopled towns.
Here I can ſit alone, unſeen of any,
And to the nightingale's complaining notes
Tune my diſtreſſes, and record my woes.
　　　　　Two Gentlemen of Verona, act 5. ſc. 4.

　　　　　　　　　　　　　　　　As

As the foregoing diſtinction between intenſe and moderate holds in pleaſure only, every degree of pain being ſoftened by time, cuſtom is a catholicon for pain and diſtreſs of every ſort ; and of that regulation the final cauſe requires no illuſtration.

Another final cauſe of cuſtom will be highly reliſhed by every perſon of humanity, and yet has in a great meaſure been overlooked ; which is, that cuſtom hath a greater influence than any other known cauſe, to put the rich and the poor upon a level : weak pleaſures, the ſhare of the latter, become fortunately ſtronger by cuſtom ; while voluptuous pleaſures, the ſhare of the former, are continually loſing ground by ſatiety. Men of fortune, who poſſeſs palaces, ſumptuous gardens, rich fields, enjoy them leſs than paſſengers do. The goods of Fortune are not unequally diſtributed : the opulent poſſeſs what others enjoy.

And indeed, if it be the effect of habit, to produce the pain of want in a high degree while there is little pleaſure in enjoyment, a voluptuous life is of all the leaſt to be envied. Thoſe who are habituated to high feeding, eaſy vehicles, rich furniture, a crowd of valets, much deference and flattery, enjoy but a ſmall ſhare of happineſs, while they are expoſed to manifold diſtreſſes. To ſuch a man, enſlaved by eaſe and luxury, even the petty inconveniencies in travelling, of a rough road, bad weather, or homely fare, are ſerious evils : he loſes his tone of mind, turns peeviſh, and would wreak his reſentment even upon the common accidents of life. Better far to uſe the goods of Fortune with moderation : a man who by temperance and activity hath acquired a hardy conſtitution, is, on the one hand, guarded againſt external accidents ; and, on the other, is provided with great variety of enjoyment ever at command.

I ſhall

I fhall clofe this chapter with an article more delicate than abftrufe, namely, what authority cuftom
ought to have over our tafte in the fine arts. One particular is certain, that we cheerfully abandon to the
authority of cuftom things that nature hath left indifferent. It is cuftom not nature that hath eftablifhed a difference between the right hand and the
left, fo as to make it awkward and difagreeable to
ufe the left where the right is commonly ufed. The
various colours, though they affeⅽt us differently, are
all of them agreeable in their purity : but cuftom has
regulated that matter in another manner ; a black
fkin upon a human being, is to us difagreeable ; and
a white fkin probably no lefs fo to a negro. Thus
things, originally indifferent, become agreeable or
difagreeable, by the force of cuftom. Nor will this
be furprifing after the difcovery made above, that the
original agreeablenefs or difagreeablenefs of an ob-
jeⅽt, is, by the influence of cuftom, often converted
into the oppofite quality.

Proceeding to matters of tafte, where there is naturally a preference of one thing before another ; it
is certain, in the firft place, that our faint and more
delicate feelings are readily fufceptible of a bias from
cuftom ; and therefore that it is no proof of a defective tafte to find thefe in fome meafure influenced by
cuftom : drefs and the modes of external behaviour
are regulated by cuftom in every country : the deep
red or vermilion with which the ladies in France
cover their cheeks, appears tò them beautiful in fpite
of nature ; and ftrangers cannot altogether be juftified in condemning that praⅽtice, confidering the
lawful authority of cuftom, or of the *fafhion*, as it is
called : It is told of the people who inhabit the fkirts
of the Alps facing the north, that the fwelling they
have univerfally in the neck is to them agreeable.
So

So far has cuſtom power to change the nature of things, and to make an object originally diſagreeable take on an oppoſite appearance.

But, as to every particular that can be denominated proper or improper, right or wrong, cuſtom has little authority, and ought to have none. The principle of duty takes naturally place of every other ; and it argues a ſhameful weakneſs or degeneracy of mind, to find it in any caſe ſo far ſubdued as to ſubmit to cuſtom.

Theſe few hints may enable us to judge in ſome meaſure of foreign manners, whether exhibited by foreign writers or our own. A compariſon between the ancients and the moderns was ſome time ago a favourite ſubject : thoſe who declared for ancient manners thought it ſufficient that theſe manners were ſupported by cuſtom : their antagoniſts, on the other hand, refuſing ſubmiſſion to cuſtom as a ſtandard of taſte, condemned ancient manners as in ſeveral inſtances irrational. In that controverſy, an appeal being made to different principles, without the ſlighteſt attempt to eſtabliſh a common ſtandard, the diſpute could have no end. The hints above given tend to eſtabliſh a ſtandard for judging how far the authority of cuſtom ought to be held lawful ; and, for the ſake of illuſtration, we ſhall apply that ſtandard in a few inſtances.

Human ſacrifices, the moſt diſmal effect of blind and groveling ſuperſtition, wore gradually out of uſe by the prevalence of reaſon and humanity. In the days of Sophocles and Euripides, traces of that practice were ſtill recent ; and the Athenians, through the prevalence of cuſtom, could without diſguſt ſuffer human ſacrifices to be repreſented in their theatre, of which the *Iphigenia* of Euripides is a proof.

But

X 3

But a human ſacrifice, being altogether inconſiſtent with modern manners as producing horror inſtead of pity, cannot with any propriety be introduced upon a modern ſtage. I muſt therefore condemn the *Iphi-genia* of Racine, which, inſtead of the tender and ſympathetic paſſions, ſubſtitutes diſguſt and horror. Another objeƈtion occurs againſt every fable that de-viates ſo remarkably from improved notions and ſen-timents ; which is, that if it ſhould even command our belief by the authority of hiſtory, it appears too fiƈtitious and unnatural to produce a perception of reality :* a human ſacrifice is ſo unnatural, and to us ſo improbable, that few will be affeƈted with the repre-ſentation of it more than with a fairy tale. The ob-jeƈtion firſt mentioned ſtrikes alſo againſt the *Phedra* of that author : the Queen's paſſion for her ſtepſon, tranſgreſſing the bounds of nature, creates averſion and horror rather than compaſſion. The author in his preface obſerves, that the Queen's paſſion, how-ever unnatural, was the effeƈt of deſtiny and the wrath of the gods ; and he puts the ſame excuſe in her own mouth. But what is the wrath of a heathen God to us Chriſtians ? we acknowledge no deſtiny in paſſion : and if love be unnatural, it never can be rel-iſhed. A ſuppoſition like what our author lays hold of, may poſſibly cover ſlight improprieties ; but it will never engage our ſympathy for what appears to us frantic or extravagant.

Neither can I reliſh the cataſtrophe of that tragedy. A man of taſte may peruſe, without diſguſt, a Grecian performance deſcribing a ſea-monſter ſent by Neptune to deſtroy Hippolytus : he conſiders, that ſuch a ſtory might agree with the religious creed of Greece, and may be pleaſed with the ſtory, as what probably had a ſtrong effeƈt upon a Grecian audience.

But

---

* See chap. 2. part 1. ſeƈt. 7.

But he cannot have the ſame indulgence for ſuch a repreſentation upon a modern ſtage ; becauſe no ſtory that carries a violent air of fiction can ever moves us in any conſiderable degree.

In the *Coephores* of Eſchylus,* Oreſtes is made to ſay, that he was commanded by Apollo to avenge his father's murder ; and yet if he obeyed, that he was to be delivered to the furies, or be ſtruck with ſome horrid malady : the tragedy accordingly con-cludes with a chorus, deploring the fate of Oreſtes, obliged to take vengeance againſt a mother, and in-volved thereby in a crime againſt his will. It is im-poſſible for any modern to bend his mind to opinions ſo irrational and abſurd, which muſt diſguſt him in peruſing even a Grecian ſtory. Again, among the Greeks, groſsly ſuperſtitious, it was a common opin-ion that the report of a man's death was a preſage of his death ; and Oreſtes, in the firſt act of *Electra*, ſpreading a report· of his own death in order to blind his mother and her adulterer, is even in that caſe af-fected with the preſage. Such imbecility can never find grace with a modern audience : it may indeed produce ſome compaſſion for a people afflicted with abſurd terrors, ſimilar to what is felt in peruſing a deſcription of the Hottentots ; but ſuch manners will not intereſt our affections, nor attach us to the per-ſonages repreſented.

* Act 2.

C H A P.

C H A P. XV.

External Signs of Emotions and Paſſions.

SO intimately connected are the ſoul and body, that every agitation in the former produceth a viſible effect upon the latter. There is, at the ſame time, a wonderful uniformity in that operation ; each claſs of emotions and paſſions being invariably attended with an external appearance peculiar to itſelf.* Theſe external appearances or ſigns may not improperly be conſidered as a natural language, expreſſing to all beholders emotions and paſſions as they ariſe in the heart. Hope, fear, joy, grief, are diſplayed externally : the character of a man can be read in his face ; and beauty, which makes ſo deep an impreſſion, is known to reſult, not ſo much from regular features and a fine complexion, as from good nature, good ſenſe, ſprightlineſs, ſweetneſs, or other mental quality, expreſſed upon the countenance. Though perfect ſkill in that language be rare, yet what is generally known is ſufficient for the ordinary purpoſes of life. But by what means we come to underſtand the language, is a point of ſome intricacy : it cannot be by ſight merely ; for, upon the moſt attentive inſpection of the human face, all that can be diſcerned, are figure, colour, and motion, which, ſingly or combined, never can repreſent a paſſion, nor a ſentiment : the external ſign is indeed viſible ; but to underſtand its meaning, we muſt be able to connect it with the paſſion that cauſes it, an operation far beyond

yond

---

* Omnis enim motus animi, ſuum quemdam a natura habet vultum et ſonum et geſtum. *Cicero, l. 3. De Oratore.*

yond the reach of eye-fight. Where then is the in-
ftruffor to be found that can unveil this fecret con-
nefction? If we apply to experience, it is yielded, that
from long and diligent obfervation, we may gather,
in fome meafure, in what manner thofe we are acquainted with exprefs their paffions externally : but
with refpeff to ftrangers, we are left in the dark ;
and yet we are not puzzled about the meaning of
thefe external expreffions in a ftranger, more than in
a bofom companion. Further, had we no other
means but experience for underftanding the external
figns of paffion, we could not expeff any degree of
fkill in the bulk of individuals : yet matters are fo
much better ordered, that the external expreffions of
paffion form a language underftood by all, by the
young as well as the old, by the ignorant as well as the
learned : I talk of the plain and legible charaffers of
that language : for undoubtedly we are much indebted to experience in deciphering the dark and more
delicate expreffions. Where then fhall we apply for
a folution of this intricate problem, which feems to
penetrate deep into human nature ? In my mind it
will be convenient to fufpend the inquiry, till we are
better acquainted with the nature of external figns,
and with their operations. Thefe articles, therefore,
fhall be premifed.

The external figns of paffion are of two kinds,
voluntary and involuntary. The voluntary figns are
alfo of two kinds : fome are arbitrary, fome natural.
Words are obvioufly voluntary figns : and they are
alfo arbitrary ; excepting a few fimple founds expreffive of certain internal emotions, which founds being
the fame in all languages, muft be the work of nature ; thus the unpremeditated tones of admiration
are the fame in all men ; as alfo of compaffion, refentment, and defpair. Dramatic writers ought to be
well

well acquainted with this natural language of paſſion : the chief talent of ſuch a writer is a ready command of the expreſſions that nature dictates to every perſon, when any vivid emotion ſtruggles for utterance ; and the chief talent of a fine reader is a ready command of tones ſuited to theſe expreſſions.

The other kind of voluntary ſigns comprehends certain attitudes or geſtures that naturally accompany certain emotions with a ſurpriſing uniformity ; exceſſive joy is expreſſed by leaping, dancing, or ſome elevation of the body : exceſſive grief, by ſinking or depreſſing it : and proſtration and kneeling have been employed by all nations, and in all ages, to ſignify profound veneration. Another circumſtance, ſtill more than uniformity, demonſtrates theſe geſtures to be natural, viz. their remarkable conformity or reſemblance to the paſſions that produce them.* Joy, which is a cheerful elevation of mind, is expreſſed by an elevation of body : pride, magnanimity, courage, and the whole tribe of elevating paſſions, are expreſſed by external geſtures that are the ſame as to the circumſtance of elevation, however diſtinguiſhable in other reſpects ; and hence an erect poſture is a ſign or expreſſion of dignity :

> Two of far nobler ſhape, erect and tall,
> Godlike erect, with native honour clad,
> In naked majeſty, ſeem'd lords of all,
> *Paradiſe Loſt, book* 4.

Grief, on the other hand, as well as reſpect, which depreſs the mind, cannot, for that reaſon, be expreſſed more ſignificantly than by a ſimilar depreſſion of the body ; and hence, *to be caſt down*, is a common phraſe, ſignifying to be grieved or diſpirited.†

One

---

* See chap. 9. part 6.

† Inſtead of a complimental ſpeech in addreſſing a ſuperior the Chineſe deliver the compliment in writing, the ſmallneſs of the letters being proportioned

One would not imagine who has not given peculiar attention, that the body should be susceptible of
such variety of attitude and motion, as readily to
accompany every different emotion with a corres-
ponding expression. Humility, for example, is ex-
pressed naturally by hanging the head ; arrogance,
by its elevation ; and languor or despondence by reclining it to one side. The expressions of the hands
are manifold : by different attitudes and motions,
they express desire, hope, fear ; they assist us in
promising, in inviting, in keeping one at a distance ;
they are made instruments of threatening, of suppli-
cation, of praise, and of horror ; they are employed
in approving, in refusing, in questioning ; in showing
our joy, our sorrow, our doubts, our regret, our admiration. These expressions, so obedient to passion, are extremely difficult to be imitated in a calm state : the ancients, sensible of the advantage as well as difficulty of
having these expressions at command, bestowed much
time and care in collecting them from observation, and
in digesting them into practical art, which was taught
in their schools as an important branch of education.
Certain sounds are by nature allotted to each passion
for expressing it externally. The actor who has these
sounds at command to captivate the ear, is mighty :
if he have also proper gestures at command to captivate the eye, he is irresistible.

The foregoing signs, though in a strict sense voluntary, cannot however be restrained but with the
utmost difficulty when prompted by passion. We
scarce need a stronger proof than the gestures of a
keen

proportioned to the degree of respect ; and the highest compliment is, to
make the letters so small as not to be legible. Here is a clear evidence
of a mental connection between respect and littleness : a man humbles
himself before his superior ; and endeavours to contract himself and his
hand-writing within the smallest bounds.

keen player at bowls : obferve only how he writhes his body, in order to reftore a ftray bowl to the right track. It is one article of good breeding, to fupprefs, as much as poffible, thefe external figns of paffion, that we may not in company appear too warm, or too interefted. The fame obfervation holds in fpeech : a paffion, it is true, when in extreme, is filent ;* but when lefs violent it muft be vented in words, which have a peculiar force not to be equalled in a fedate compofition. The eafe and fecurity we have in a confident, may encourage us to talk cf ourfelves and of our feelings : but the caufe is more general; for it operates when we are alone as well as in company. Paffion is the caufe ; for in many inftances it is no flight gratification, to vent a paffion externally by words as well as by geftures. Some paffions, when at a certain height, impel us fo ftrongly to vent them in words, that we fpeak with an audible voice even when there is none to liften. It is that circumftance in paffion which juftifies foliloquies ; and it is that circumftance which proves them to be natural.† The mind fometimes favours this impulfe of paffion, by beftowing a temporary fenfibility upon any objeét at hand, in order

to

* See chap. 17.

† Though a foliloquy in the perturbation of paffion is undoubtedly natural, and indeed not unfrequent in real life ; yet Congreve, who himfelf has penned feveral good foliloquies, yields, with more candour than knowledge, that they are unnatural ; and he only pretends to juftify them from neceffity. This he does in his dedication of the *Double Dealer*, in the following words : " When a man in a foliloquy reafons with himfelf, and *pro's* and *con's*, and weighs all his defigns ; we ought not to imagine, that this man either talks to us, or to himfelf : he is only thinking, and thinking (frequently) fuch matter as it were inexcufable folly in him to fpeak. But becaufe we are concealed fpeétators of the plot in agitation, and the poet finds it neceffary to let us know the whole myftery of his contrivance, he is willing to inform us of this perfon's thoughts ; and to that end is forced to make ufe of the expedient of fpeech, no other better way being yet invented for the communication of thought."

to make it a confident. Thus in the *Winter's Tale,*＊ Antigonus addreſſes himſelf to an infant whom he was ordered to expoſe ;

> Come, poot babe,
> I have heard, but not believ'd, the ſpirits of the dead,
> May walk again ;˙if ſuch things be, thy mother
> Appear'd to me laſt night ; for ne'er was dream
> So like a waking.

The involuntary figns, which are all of them natural, are either peculiar to one paſſion, or common to many. Every vivid paſſion hath an external expreſſion peculiar to itſelf ; not excepting pleaſant paſſions ; witneſs admiration and mirth. The pleaſant emotions that are leſs vivid have one common expreſſion ; from which we may gather the ſtrength of the emotion, but ſcarce the kind : we perceive a cheerful or contented look ; and we can make no more of it. Painful paſſions, being all of them violent, are diſtinguiſhable from each other by their external expreſſions : thus fear, ſhame, anger, anxiety, dejection, deſpair, have each of them peculiar expreſſions ; which are apprehended without the leaſt confuſion : ſome painful paſſions produce violent effects upon the body, trembling, for example, ſtarting, and ſwooning ; but theſe effects, depending in a good meaſure upon ſingularity of conſtitution, are not uniform in all men.

The involuntary figns, ſuch of them as are diſplayed upon the countenance, arc of two kinds : ſome. are temporary, making their appearance with the. emotions that produce them, and vaniſhing with theſe emotions ; others, being formed gradually by ſome violent paſſion often recurring, become permanent

nent figns of that paffion, and ferve to denote the difpofition or temper. The face of an infant indicates no particular difpofition, becaufe it cannot be marked with any character, to which time is neceffary : even the temporary figns are extremely awkward, being the firft rude effays of Nature to difcover internal feelings ; thus the fhrieking of a new born infant, without tears or fobbings, is plainly an attempt to weep ; and fome of thefe temporary figns, as fmiling and frowning, cannot be obferved for fome months after birth. Permanent figns, formed in youth while the body is foft and flexible, are preferved entire by the firmnefs and folidity that the body acquires, and are never obliterated even by a change of temper. Such figns are not produced after the fibres become rigid : fome violent cafes excepted, fuch as reiterated fits of the gout or ftone through a courfe of time : but thefe figns are not fo obftinate as what are produced in youth ; for when the caufe is removed, they gradually wear away, and at laft vanifh.

The natural figns of emotions, voluntary and involuntary, being nearly the fame in all men, form an univerfal language, which no diftance of place, no difference of tribe, no diverfity of tongue, can darken or render doubtful : even education, though of mighty influence, hath not power to vary nor fophifticate, far lefs to deftroy, their fignification. This is a wife appointment of Providence : for if thefe figns were, like words, arbitrary and variable, the thoughts and volitions of ftrangers would be entirely hid from us : which would prove a great, or rather invincible, obftruction to the formation of focieties : but as matters are ordered, the external appearances of joy, grief, anger, fear, fhame, and of the other paffions, forming an univerfal language, open a direct

rect avenue to the heart. As the arbitrary figns vary
in every country, there could be no communication
of thoughts among different nations, were it not for
the natural figns, in which all agree : and as the dif-
covering paffions inftantly at their birth, is effential
to our well being, and often neceffary for felf-prefervation, the author of our nature, attentive to our
wants, hath provided a paffage to the heart, which
never can be obftructed while eye-fight remains.

In an inquiry concerning the external figns of
paffion, actions muft not be overlooked : for though
fingly they afford no clear light, they are, upon the
whole, the beft interpreters of the heart.* By obferving a man's conduct for a courfe of time, we
difcover unerringly the various paffions that move
him to action, what he loves, and what he hates. In
our younger years, every fingle action is a mark, not
at all ambiguous, of the temper ; for in childhood
there is little or no difguife : the fubject becomes
more intricate in advanced age ; but even there,
diffimulation is feldom carried on for any length of
time. And thus the conduct of life is the moft perfect expreffion of the internal difpofition. It merits
not indeed the title of an univerfal language ; becaufe it is not thoroughly underftood but by thofe of
a penetrating genius or extenfive obfervation : it is a
language

---

* The actions here chiefly in view, are what a paffion fuggefts in order
to its gratification. Befide thefe, actions are occafionally exerted to give
fome vent to a paffion, without any view to an ultimate gratification.
Such occafional action is characteriftical of the paffion in a high degree ;
and for that reafon, when happily invented, has a wonderfully good
effect :

> *Hamlet.* Oh moft pernicious woman !
> Oh villain, villain, fmiling damned villain !
> My tables—meet it is I fet it down,
> That one may fmile, and fmile, and be a villain ;
> At leaft I'm fure it may be fo in Denmark. [*Writing.*
> So, uncle, there you are.
>
> *Hamlet, act* i. *fc.* 8.

language, however, which every one can decipher in fome meafure; and which, joined with the other external figns, affords fufficient means for the direction of our conduct with regard to others: if we commit any miftake when fuch light is afforded, it never can be the effect of unavoidable ignorance, but of rafhnefs or inadvertence.

Reflecting on the various expreffions of our emotions, we recognife the anxious care of Nature, to difcover men to each other. Strong emotions, as above hinted, beget an impatience to exprefs them externally by fpeech and other voluntary figns, which cannot be fuppreffed without a painful effort: thus a fudden fit of paffion, is a common excufe for indecent behaviour or opprobrious language. As to involuntary figns, thefe are altogether unavoidable: no volition nor effort can prevent the fhaking of the limbs nor a pale vifage, in a fit of terror: the blood flies to the face upon a fudden emotion of fhame, in fpite of all oppofition:

> Vergogna, che'n altrui ftampo natura,
> Non fi puo' rinegar : che fe tu' tenti
> Di cacciarla dal cor, fugge nel volto.
> *Paftor Fido, act* 2. *fc.* 5.

Emotions indeed, properly fo called, which are quiefcent, produce no remarkable figns externally. Nor is it neceffary that the more deliberate paffions fhould, becaufe the operation of fuch paffions is neither fudden nor violent: thefe, however, remain not altogether in obfcurity; for being more frequent than violent paffion, the bulk of our actions are directed by them. Actions therefore difplay, with fufficient evidence, the more deliberate paffions; and complete the admirable fyftem of external figns, by which we become fkilful in human nature.

What

What comes next in order is, to examine the effects produced upon a spectator by external signs, of paffion. None of these signs are beheld with indifference; they are productive of various emotions, tending all of them to ends wise and good. This curious subject makes a capital branch of human nature: it is peculiarly useful to writers who deal in the pathetic; and to history painters it is indispensable.

It is mentioned above, that each paffion, or class of paffions, hath its peculiar signs; and, with respect to the present subject, it must be added, that these invariably make certain impressions on a spectator: the external signs of joy, for example, produce a cheerful emotion; the external signs of grief produce pity; and the external signs of rage produce a sort of terror even in those who are not aimed at.

Secondly, It is natural to think, that pleasant paffions should express themselves externally by signs that to a spectator appear agreeable, and painful paffions by signs that to him appear disagreeable. This conjecture, which Nature suggests, is confirmed by experience. Pride possibly may be thought an exception, the external signs of which are disagreeable, though it be commonly reckoned a pleasant paffion: but pride is not an exception, being in reality a mixed paffion, partly pleasant, partly painful; for when a proud man confines his thoughts to himself, and to his own dignity or importance, the paffion is pleasant, and its external signs agreeable; but as pride chiefly confists in undervaluing or contemning others, it is so far painful, and its external signs disagreeable.

Thirdly, It is laid down above, that an agreeable object produceth always a pleasant emotion, and a disagreeable object one that is painful.* According to

* See chap. 2. part 7.

to this law, the external figns of a pleafant paffion, being agreeable, muft produce in the fpectator a pleaf-ant emotion : and the external figns of a painful paffion, being difagreeable, muft produce in him a painful emotion.

Fourthly, in the prefent chapter it is obferved, that pleafant paffions are, for the moft part, expreff-ed externally in one uniform manner ; but that all the painful paffions are diftinguifhable from each other by their external expreffions. The emotions accordingly raifed in a fpectator by external figns of pleafant paffions, have little variety : thefe emotions are pleafant or cheerful, and we have not words to reach a more particular defcription. But the exter-nal figns of painful paffions produce in the fpectator emotions of different kinds : the emotions, for ex-ample, raifed by external figns of grief, of remorfe, of anger, of envy, of malice, are clearly diftinguifh-able from each other.

Fifthly, External figns of painful paffions are fome of them *attractive* fome *repulfive*. Of every painful paffion that is alfo difagreeable,* the external figns are repulfive, repelling the fpectator from the object : and the paffion raifed by fuch external figns may be alfo confidered as repulfive. Painful paffions that are agreeable produce an oppofite effect : their ex-ternal figns are attractive, drawing the fpectator to them, and producing in him benevolence to the per-fon upon whom thefe figns appear ; witnefs diftrefs painted on the countenance, which inftantaneoufly infpires the fpectator with pity, and impels him to af-ford relief. And the paffion raifed by fuch external figns may alfo be confidered as attractive. The caufe

of

---

* See paffions explained as agreeable or difagreeable, chap. 2. part 2.

of this difference among the painful paſſions raiſed by their external ſigns may be readily gathered from what is laid down, chap. 2. part 7.

It is now time to look back to the queſtion propoſed in the beginning, How we come to underſtand external ſigns, ſo as to refer each ſign to its proper paſſion ? We have ſeen that this branch of knowledge cannot be derived orignally from ſight, nor from experience. Is it then implanted in us by nature ? The following conſiderations will incline us to anſwer the queſtion in the affirmative. In the firſt place, the external ſigns of paſſion muſt be natural ; for they are invariably the ſame in every country, and among the different tribes of men : pride, for example, is always expreſſed by an erect poſture, reverence by proſtration, and ſorrow by a dejected look. Secondly, we are not even indebted to experience for the knowledge that theſe expreſſions are natural and univerſal : for we are ſo framed as to have an innate conviction of the fact : let a man change his habitation to the other ſide of the globe, he will, from the accuſtomed ſigns, infer the paſſion of fear among his new neighbours, with as little heſitation as he did at home. But why, after all, involve ourſelves in preliminary obſervations, when the doubt may be directly ſolved as follows ? That, if the meaning of external ſigns be not derived to us from ſight, nor from experience, there is no remaining ſource whence it can be derived but from nature.

We may then venture to pronounce, with ſome degree of aſſurance, that man is provided by nature with a ſenſe or faculty that lays open to him every paſſion by means of its external expreſſions. And we cannot entertain any reaſonable doubt of this, when

Y 2

when we reflect, that the meaning of external figns
is not hid even from infants : an infant is remarkably
affected with the paffions of its nurfe expreffed in
her countenance ; a fmile cheers it, a frown makes
it afraid : but fear cannot be without apprehending
danger ; and what danger can the infant apprehend,
unlefs it be fenfible that its nurfe is angry ? We muft
therefore admit, that a child can read anger in its
nurfe's face : of which it muft be fenfible intuitively,
for it has no other mean of knowledge.   I do not affirm, that thefe particulars are clearly apprehended
by the child ; for to produce clear and diftinct perceptions, reflection and experience are requifite : but
that even an infant, when afraid, muft have fome
notion of its being in danger is evident.

That we fhould be confcious intuitively of a paffion
from its external expreffions, is conformable to the
analogy of nature : the knowledge of that language
is of too great importance to be left upon experience ;
becaufe a foundation fo uncertain and precarious,
would prove a great obftacle to the formation of focieties.   Wifely therefore is it ordered, and agreeably to the fyftem of Providence, that we fhould have
nature for our inftructor.

Manifold and admirable are the purpofes to which
the external figns of paffion are made fubfervient by
the author of our nature : thofe occafionally mentioned above, make but a part.   Several final caufes
remain to be unfolded ; and to that tafk I proceed
with alacrity.   In the firft place, the figns of internal agitation difplayed externally to every fpectator,
tend to fix the fignification of many words.   The only
effectual means to afcertain the meaning of any doubtful word, is an appeal to the thing it reprefents :
and hence the ambiguity of words expreffive of things
that are not objects of external fenfe ; for in that
                                                        cafe

caſe an appeal is denied. Paſſion, ſtrictly ſpeaking, is not an object of external ſenſe : but its external ſigns are ; and by means of theſe ſigns, paſſions may be appealed to with tolerable accuracy : thus the words that denote our paſſions, next to thoſe that de-note external objects, have the moſt diſtinct meaning. Words ſignifying internal action and the more deli-cate feelings, are leſs diſtinct. This defect with re-gard to internal action, is what chiefly occaſions the intricacy of logic : the terms of that ſcience are far from being ſufficiently aſcertained, even after much care and labour beſtowed by an eminent writer ;* to whom, however, the world is greatly indebted, for removing a mountain of rubbiſh, and moulding the ſubject into a rational and correct form. The ſame defect is remarkable in criticiſm, which has for its object the more delicate feelings ; the terms that denote theſe feelings being not more diſtinct than thoſe of logic. To reduce the ſcience of criticiſm, to any regular form, has never once been attempted : however rich the ore may be, no critical chemiſt has been found, to analyſe its conſtituent parts, and to diſtinguiſh each by its own name,

In the ſecond place, Society among individuals is greatly promoted by that univerſal language. Looks and geſtures give direct acceſs to the heart, and lead us to ſelect, with tolerable accuracy, the perſons who are worthy of our confidence. It is ſurpriſing how quickly, and for the moſt part how correctly, we judge of character from external appearance.

Thirdly, After ſocial intercourſe is commenced, theſe external ſigns, which diffuſe through a whole aſſembly the feelings of each individual, contribute

* Locke,

Y 3

ute above all other means to improve the social affections. Language, no doubt, is the moft comprehenfive vehicle for communicating emotions : but in expedition, as well as in power of conviction, it falls fhort of the figns under confideration ; the involuntary figns efpecially, which are incapable of deceit. Where the countenance, the tones, the gef-tures, the actions, join with the words in communicating emotions, thefe united have a force irrefifti-ble : thus all the pleafant emotions of the human heart, with all the focial and virtuous affections, are, by means of thefe external figns, not only perceived, but felt. By this admirable contrivance, converfa-tion becomes that lively and animating amufement, without which life would at beft be infipid : one joy-ful countenance fpreads cheerfulnefs inftantaneoufly through a multitude of fpectators.

Fourthly, Diffocial paffions, being hurtful by prompting violence and mifchief, are noted by the moft confpicuous external figns, in order to put us upon our guard : thus anger and revenge, efpecially when fudden, difplay themfelves on the countenance in legible characters.* The external figns again of every paffion that threatens danger raife in us the paffion of fear : which frequently operating without reafon

* Rough and blunt manners are allied to anger by an internal feeling, as well as by external expreffions refembling in a faint degree thofe of anger : therefore fuch manners are eafily heightened into anger ; and favages for that reafon are prone to anger. Thus rough and blunt manners are unhappy in two refpects : firft, they are readily converted into anger ; and next the change being imperceptible becaufe of the fimili-tude of their external figns, the perfon againft whom the anger is directed is not put upon his guard. It is for thefe reafons a great object in fociety, to correct fuch manners, and to bring on a habit of fweetnefs and calmnefs. This temper has two oppofite good effects. Firft, it is not eafily pro-voked to wrath. Next, the interval being great between it and real an-ger, a perfon of that temper who receives an affront, has many changes to go through before his anger be inflamed : thefe changes have each of them their external fign ; and the offending party is put upon his guard, to retire, or to endeavour a reconciliation,

ŗeaſon or reflection, moves us by a ſudden impulſe to avoid the impending danger.*

In the fifth place, Theſe external ſigns are remarkably ſubſervient to morality. A painful paſſion, being accompanied with diſagreeable external ſigns, muſt produce in every ſpectator a painful emotion.: but then, if the paſſion be ſocial, the emotion it produces is attractive, and connects the ſpectator with the perſon who ſuffers. Diſſocial paſſions only are productive of repulſive emotions, involving the ſpectator's averſion, and frequently his indignation. This beautiful contrivance makes us cling to the virtuous, and abhor the wicked.

Sixthly, Of all the external ſigns of paſſion, thoſe of affliction or diſtreſs are the moſt illuſtrious with reſpect to a final cauſe. They are illuſtrious by the ſingularity of their contrivance, and alſo by inſpiring ſympathy, a paſſion to which human ſociety is indebted for its greateſt bleſſing, that of providing relief for the diſtreſſed. A ſubject ſo intereſting deſerves a leiſurely and attentive examination. The conformity of the nature of man to his external circumſtances is in every particular wonderful : his nature makes him prone to ſociety ; and ſociety is neceſſary to his well-being, becauſe in a ſolitary ſtate he is a helpleſs being, deſtitute of ſupport, and in his manifold diſtreſſes deſtitute of relief : but mutual ſupport, the ſhining attribute of ſociety, iſ of too great moment to be left dependent upon cool reaſon ; it is ordered more wiſely, and with greater conformity to the analogy of nature that it ſhould be enforced even inſtinctively by the paſſion of ſympathy. Here ſympathy makes a capital figure, and contributes, more than any

other

* See chap. 2. part 1. ſect. 6.

other means, to make life eafy and comfortable.
But, however effential the fympathy of others may be-
to our well-being, one beforehand would not readily conceive how it could be raifed by external figns
of diftrefs : for confidering the analogy of nature, if
thefe figns be agreeable, they muft give birth to a
pleafant emotion leading every beholder to be pleafed
with human woes : if difagreeable, as they undoubtedly are; ought they not naturally to repel the fpectator from them, in order to be relieved from pain ?
Such would be the reafoning beforehand ; and fuch
would be the effect were man purely a felfifh being.
But the benevolence of our nature gives a very different direction to the painful paffion of fympathy, and
to the defire involved in it : inftead of avoiding diftrefs, we fly to it in order to afford relief : and our
fympathy cannot be otherwife gratified but by giving
all the fuccour in our power.* Thus external figns
of diftrefs, though difagreeable, are attractive ; and
the fympathy they infpire is a powerful caufe, impelling us to afford relief even to a ftranger as if he were
our friend or relation.†

The

* See chap. 2. part 7.

† It is a noted obfervation, that the deepeft tragedies are the moft
crowded ; which in a flight view will be thought an unaccountable bias
in human nature. Love of novelty, defire of occupation, beauty of action, make us fond of theatrical reprefentations ; and, when once engaged we muft follow the ftory to the conclufion, whatever diftrefs it may
create. But we generally become wife by experience ; and when we
forefee what pain we fhall fuffer during the courfe of the reprefentation,
is it not furprifing that perfons of reflection do not avoid fuch fpectacles
altogether ? And yet one who has fcarce recovered from the diftrefs of a
deep tragedy, refolves coolly and deliberately to go to the very next,
without the flighteft obftruction from felf-love. The whole myftery is
explained by a fingle obfervation, That fympathy, though painful, is attractive, and attaches us to an object in diftrefs, the oppofition of felf-
love notwithftanding, which fhould prompt us to fly from it. And by
this curious mechanifm it is, that perfons of any degree of fenfibility are
attracted by affliction ftill more than by joy.

The effects produced in all beholders by external figns of paffion, tend fo vifibly to advance the focial ftate, that I muft indulge my heart with a more narrow infpection of this admirable branch of the human conftitution. Thefe external figns, being all of them refolvable into colour, figure, and motion, fhould not naturally make any deep impreffion on a fpectator ; and fuppofing them qualified for making deep impreffions, we have feen above, that the effects they produce are not fuch as might be expected. We cannot therefore account otherwife for the operation of thefe external figns, but by afcribing it to the original conftitution of human nature: to improve the focial ftate, by making us inftinctively rejoice with the glad of heart, weep with the mourner, and fhun thofe who threaten danger, is a contrivance no lefs. illuftrious for its wifdom than for its benevolence. With refpect to the external figns of diftrefs in particular, to judge of the excellency of their contrivance, we need only reflect upon feveral other means feemingly more natural, that would not have anfwered the end purpofed. What if the external figns of joy were difagreeable, and the external figns of diftrefs agreeable? This is no whimfical fuppofition, becaufe there appears not any neceffary connection between thefe figns and the emotions produced by them in a fpectator. Admitting then the fuppofition, the queftion is, How would our fympathy operate ? There is no occafion to deliberate for an anfwer : fympathy would be deftructive, and not beneficial : for, fuppofing the external figns of joy difagreeable, the happinefs of others would be our averfion ; and fuppofing the external figns of grief agreeable, the diftreffes of others would be our entertainment. I make a fecond fuppofition, That the external figns of diftrefs were indifferent to us, and productive

neither

neither of pleafure nor of pain. This would annihil-ate the ftrongeft branch of fympathy, that which is raifed by means of fight : and it is evident, that re-flective fympathy, felt by thofe only who have great fenfibility, would not have any extenfive effect. I fhall draw nearer to truth in a third fuppofition, That the external figns of diftrefs being difagreeable, were productive of a painful repulfive emotion. Sympa-thy upon that fuppofition would not be annihilated : but it would be rendered ufelefs ; for it would be gratified by flying from or avoiding the object, in-ftead of clinging to it and affording relief : the con-dition of man would in reality be worfe than if fym-pathy were totally eradicated ; becaufe fympathy would only ferve to plague thofe who feel it, without producing any good to the afflicted.

　　Loath to quit fo interefting a fubject, I add a re-flection, with which I fhall conclude. The external figns of paffion are a ftrong indication, that man, by his very conftitution, is framed to be open and fin-cere. A child in all things obedient to the impulfes of nature, hides none of its emotions : the favage and clown, who have no guide but pure nature, expofe their hearts to view, by giving way to all the natural figns. And even when men learn to diffemble their fentiments, and when behaviour degenerates into art, there ftill remain checks, that keep diffimulation within bounds, and prevent a great part of its mif-chievous effects : the total fuppreffion of the volun-tary figns during any vivid paffion, begets the utmoft uneafinefs, which cannot be endured for any confid-erable time : this operation becomes indeed lefs pain-ful by habit; but, luckily, the involuntary figns cannot, by any effort, be fuppreffed, nor even dif-fembled. An abfolute hypocrify, by which the character

character is concealed, and a fictitious one affumed, is made impracticable ; and nature has thereby prevented much harm to fociety.   We may pronounce, therefore, that Nature, herfelf fincere and candid, intends that mankind fhould preferve the fame character, by cultivating fimplicity and truth, and banifhing every fort of diffimulation that tends to mifchief.

C H A P.

Sentiments.

EVERY thought prompted by paſſion, is termed *a ſentiment.** To have a general notion of the different paſſions, will not alone enable an artiſt to make a juſt repreſentation of any paſſion : he ought, over and above, to know the various appearances of the ſame paſſion in different perſons. Paſſions re-ceive a tincture from every peculiarity of character ; and for that reaſon it rarely happens, that a paſſion, in the different circumſtances of feeling, of ſentiment, and of expreſſion, is preciſely the ſame in any two perſons. Hence the following rule concerning dra-matic and epic compoſitions, That a paſſion be adjuſt-ed to the character, the ſentiments to the paſſion, and the language to the ſentiments. If nature be not faithfully copied in each of theſe, a defect in ex-ecution is perceived : there may appear ſome reſem-blance ; but the picture, upon the whole, will be in-ſipid, through want of grace and delicacy. A paint-er, in order to repreſent the various attitudes of the body, ought to be intimately acquainted with muſ-cular motion : no leſs intimately acquainted with emotions and characters ought a writer to be, in or-der to repreſent the various attitudes of the mind. A general notion of the paſſions, in their groſſer differ-ences of ſtrong and weak, elevated and humble, ſe-vere and gay, is far from being ſufficient : pictures formed ſo ſuperficially have little reſemblance, and no expreſſion ; yet it will appear by and by, that in

many

* See Appendix, § 30.

many inflances our artifts are deficient even in that fuperficial knowledge.

In handling the prefent fubject, it would be end-lefs to trace even the ordinary paffions through their nice and minute differences. Mine fhall be an humbler tafk ; which is, to felect from the beft writers inflances of faulty fentiments, after paving the way by fome general obfervations.

To talk in the language of mufic, each paffion hath a certain tone, to which every fentiment proceeding from it ought to be tuned with the greateft accuracy : which is no eafy work, efpecially where fuch harmony ought to be fupported during the courfe of a long theatrical reprefentation. In order to reach fuch delicacy of execution, it is neceffary that a writer affume the precife character and paffion of the perfonage reprefented ; which requires an uncommon genius. But it is the only difficulty ; for the writer, who, annihilating himfelf, can thus become another perfon, need be in no pain about the fentiments that belong to the affumed character : thefe will flow without the leaft ftudy, or even preconception ; and will frequently be as delightfully new to himfelf as to his reader. But if a lively picture even of a fingle emotion require an effort of genius, how much greater the effort to compofe a paffionate dialogue with as many different tones of paffion as there are fpeakers ? With what ductility of feeling muft that writer be endowed, who approaches perfection in fuch a work ; when it is neceffary to affume different and even oppofite characters and paffions, in the quickeft fucceffion ? Yet this work, difficult as it is, yields to that of compofing a dialogue in genteel comedy, exhibiting characters without paffion. The reafon is, that the different tones of character are more delicate and lefs in fight, than thofe of paffion ;

and,

and, accordingly, many writers, who have no genius for drawing characters, make a shift to reprefent tolerably well, an ordinary paffion in its fimple movements. But of all works of this kind, what is truly the moft difficult, is a characteriftical dialogue upon any philofophical fubject : to interweave characters with reafoning, by fuiting to the character of each fpeaker, a peculiarity not only of thought, but of expreffion, requires the perfection of genius, tafte, and judgment.

How nice dialogue-writing is, will be evident, even without reafoning, from the miferable compofitions of that kind found without number in all languages. The art of mimicking any fingularity in gefture or in voice, is a rare talent, though directed by fight and hearing, the acuteft and moft lively of our external fenfes : how much more rare muft the talent be, of imitating characters and internal emotions, tracing all their different tints, and reprefenting them in a lively manner by natural fentiments properly expreffed ? The truth is, fuch execution is too delicate for an ordinary genius ; and for that reafon, the bulk of writers, inftead of expreffing a paffion as one does who feels it, content themfelves with defcribing it in the language of a fpectator. To awake paffion by an internal effort merely, without any external caufe, requires great fenfibility : and yet that operation is neceffary, no lefs to the writer than to the actor ; becaufe none but thofe who actually feel a paffion, can reprefent it to the life. The writer's part is the more complicated : he muft add compofition to paffion ; and muft, in the quickeft fucceffion, adopt every different character. But a very humble flight of imagination, may ferve to convert a writer into a fpectator ; fo as to figure, in fome obfcure manner, an action as paffing in his fight and hearing. In that figured fituation being led naturally to write like a

fpectator,

ſpectator, he entertains his readers with his own reflections, with cool deſcription, and florid declamation ; inſtead of making them eye-witneſſes, as it
were, to a real event, and. to every movement of
genuine paſſion.* Thus moſt of our plays appear to
be caſt in the ſame mould ; perſonages without
character, the mere outlines of paſſion, a tireſome
monotony, and a pompous declamatory ſtyle.†

This deſcriptive manner of repreſenting paſſion, is
a very cold entertainment : our ſympathy is not raiſed by deſcription ; we muſt firſt be lulled into a
dream of reality, and every thing muſt appear as
paſſing in our ſight .‡ Unhappy is the player of genius who acts a capital part in what may be termed a
deſcriptive tragedy ; after aſſuming the very paſſion
that is to be repreſented, how is he cramped in action, when he muſt utter, not the ſentiments of the
paſſion he feels, but a cold deſcription in the language of a byſtander ? It is that imperfection, I am
perſuaded, in the bulk of our plays, which confines
our ſtage almoſt entirely to Shakeſpear, notwithſtanding his many irregularities. In our late Engliſh
tragedies,

---

* In the *Æneid,* the hero is made to deſcribe himſelf in the following
words : *Sum pius Æneas, fama ſuper æthera notus.* Virgil could never
have been guilty of an impropriety ſo groſs, had he aſſumed the perſonage
of his hero, inſtead of uttering the ſentiments of a ſpectator. Nor would
Xenophon have made the following ſpeech for Cyrus the younger, to
his Grecian auxiliaries, whom he was leading againſt his brother Artax-
erxes : " I have choſen you, O Greeks ! my auxiliaries, not to enlarge
my army, for I have *Barbarians* without number ; but becauſe you ſurpaſs all the *Barbarians* in valour and military diſcipline." This ſentiment is Xenophon's ; for ſurely Cyrus did not reckon his countrymen
Barbarians.

† Chez Racine tout eſt ſentiment ; il a ſu faire parler *chacun pour ſoi,*
et c'eſt en cela qu'il eſt vraiment unique parmi les auteurs dramatiques
de ſa nation.
Rouſſeau.

‡ See chap. 2. part 1. ſect. 7.

tragedies, we fometimes find fentiments tolerably well adapted to a plain paffion : but we muft not, in any of them, expeĉt a fentiment expreffive of charaĉter ; and, upon that very account, our late performances of the dramatic kind are for the moft part intolerably infipid.

Looking back upon what is faid, I am in fome apprehenfion of not being perfeĉtly underftood ; for it is not eafy to avoid obfcurity in handling a matter fo complicated : but I promife to fet it in the cleareft light, by adding example to precept. The firft examples fhall be of fentiments that appear the legitimate offspring of paffion ; to which fhall be oppofed what are defcriptive only, and illegitimate : and in making this comparifon, I borrow my inftances from Shakefpear and Corneille, who for genius in dramatic compofition ftand uppermoft in the rolls of fame.

Shakefpear fhall furnifh the firft example, being of fentiments diĉtated by a violent and perturbed paffion :

> *Lear.*——————————Filial ingratitude!
> Is it not, as if this mouth, fhould tear this hand
> For lifting food to't ?—But I'll punifh home ;
> No, I will weep no more.——In fuch a night,
> To fhut me out !——Pour on, I will endure.
> In fuch a night as this ! O Regan, Gonerill,
> Your old kind father, whofe frank heart gave all—
> O ! that way madnefs lies ; let me fhun that ;
> No more of that.——————
>   *Kent.* Good, my Lord, enter here.
>   *Lear.* Pr'ythee, go in thyfelf, feek thine own eafe,
> This tempeft will not give me leave to ponder
> On things would hurt me more :—but I'll go in ;
> In, boy, go firft. You houfelefs poverty——
> Nay, get thee in ; I'll pray, and then I'll fleep—
> Poor naked wretches, wherefoe'er you are,
> That bide the pelting of this pitilefs ftorm !
> How fhall your houfelefs heads, and unfed fides,

Your

Your loop'd and window'd raggednefs defend you
From feafons fuch as thefe ?——O I have ta'en
Too little care of this ! take phyfic, Pomp ;'
Expofe thyfelf to feel what wretches feel,
That thou may'ft fhake the fuperflux to them,
And fhow the heavens more juft.

King Lear, act 3. *fc.* 5.

I give another example of the fame kind, exprefling
fentiments arifing from remorfe and defpair :

Othello. Lo ! I have a weapon :
A better never did itfelf fuftain
Upon a foldier's thigh. I've feen the day,
That with this little arm, and this good fword,
I've made my way through more impediments
Than twenty times your ftop. But, oh vain boaft !
Who can controul his fate ? 'tis not fo now.
Be not afraid, though you do fee me weapon'd ;
Here is my journey's end, here is my butt,
The very fea-mark of my outmoft fail.
Do you go back difmay'd ? 'tis a loft fear.
Man but a rufh againft Othello's breaft,
And he retires. Where fhould Othello go ?
Now—how doft thou look now ? Oh ill-ftarr'd wench !
Pale as thy fmock ! when we fhall meet at compt,
This look of thine will hurl my foul from heav'n
And fiends will fnatch at it. Cold, cold, my girl ;
Ev'n like thy chaftity. O curfed flave !
Whip me, ye devils,
From the poffeffion of this heav'nly fight ;
Blow me about in winds, roaft me in fulphur,
Wafh me in fteep-down gulphs of liquid fire——
Oh, Defdemona ! Defdemona ! dead ! dead ! oh ! oh !

Othello, act 5. *fc.* 9.

The fentiments here difplayed flow fo naturally from
the paffions reprefented, that we cannot conceive any
imitation more perfect.

With

With regard to the French author, truth obliges me to acknowledge, that he defcribes in the ftyle of a fpectator, inftead of expreffing paffion like one who feels it ; which naturally betrays him into a tirefome monotony, and a pompous declamatory ftyle.* It is fcarce neceffary to give examples, for

he

---

* This criticifm reaches the French dramatic writers in general, with very few exceptions : their tragedies, excepting thofe of Racine, are moftly, if not totally, defcriptive. Corneille led the way ; and later writers, imitating his manner, have accuftomed the French ear to a ftyle, formal, pompous, declamatory, which fuits not with any paffion. Hence, to burlefque a French tragedy, is not more difficult than to burlefque a ftiff folemn fop. The facility of the operation has in Paris introduced a fingular amufement, which is, to burlefque the more fuccefsful tragedies in a fort of farce called a *parody*. La Motte, who himfelf appears to have been forely galled by fome of thefe productions, acknowledges, that no more is neceffary to give them currency but barely to vary the *dramatis perfonæ*, and inftead of kings and heroes, queens and princeffes, to fubftitute tinkers and taylors, milkmaids and feamftreffes. The declamatory ftyle, fo different from the genuine expreffion of paffion, paffes in fome meafure unobferved, when great perfonages are the fpeakers ; but in the mouths of the vulgar, the impropriety with regard to the fpeaker as well as to the paffion reprefented, is fo remarkable as to become ridiculous. A tragedy, where every paffion is made to fpeak in its natural tone, is not liable to be thus burlefqued : the fame paffion is by all men exprefs'd nearly in the fame manner ; and, therefore, the genuine expreffions of a paffion cannot be ridiculous in the mouth of any man who is fufceptible of the paffion.

It is a well known fact, that to an Englifh ear, the French actors appear to pronounce with too great rapidity : a complaint much infifted on by Cibber in particular, who had frequently heard the famous Baron upon the French ftage. This may in fome meafure be attributed to our want of facility in the French tongue ; as foreigners generally imagine that every language is pronounced too quick by natives. But that it is not the fole caufe, will be probable from a fact directly oppofite, that the French are not a little difgufted with the langu'dnefs, as they term it, of the Englifh pronunciation. May not this difference of tafte be derived from what is obferved above ? The pronunciation of the genuine language of a paffion is neceffarily directed by the nature of the paffion, particularly by the flownefs or celerity of its progrefs : plaintive paffions, which are the moft frequent in tragedy, having a flow motion, dictate a flow pronunciation : in declamation, on the contrary, the fpeaker warms gradually ; and, as he warms, he naturally accelerates his pronunciation. But, as the French have formed their tone of pronunciation upon Corneille's declamatory tragedies, and the Englifh upon the more natural language of Shakefpear, it is not furprifing that cuftom fhould produce fuch difference of tafte in the two nations.

he never varies from that tone. I ſhall, however, take two paſſages at a venture, in order to be confronted with thoſe tranſcribed above. In the tragedy of *Cinna*, Æmilia, after the conſpiracy ‚was diſcovered, having nothing in view but racks and death to herſelf and her lover, receives a pardon from Auguſtus, attended with the brighteſt circumſtances of magnanimity and tenderneſs. This is a lucky ſituation for repreſenting the paſſions of ſurpriſe and gratitude in their different ſtages, which ſeem naturally to be what follow. Theſe paſſions, raiſed at once to the utmoſt pitch, and being at firſt too big for utterance, muſt, for ſome moments be expreſſed by violent geſtures only : as ſoon as there is vent for words, the firſt expreſſions are broken and interrupted : at laſt we ought to expect a tide of intermingled ſentiments, occaſioned by the fluctuation of the mind between the two paſſions. Æmilia is made to behave in a very different manner : with extreme coolneſs ſhe deſcribes her own ſituation, as if ſhe were merely a ſpectator, or rather the poet takes the taſk off her hands :

Et je me rens, Seigneur, à ces hautes bontés :
Je recouvre la vûe auprès de leurs clartés.
Je connois mon forfait qui me ſembloit juſtice ;
Et ce que n'avoit pû la terreur du ſupplice,
Je ſens naitre en mon ame un repentir puiſſant,
Et mon cœur en ſecret me dit, qu'il y conſent.
Le ciel a réſolu votre grandeur ſuprême ;
Et pour preuve, Seigneur, je n'en veux que moi-même.
J'oſe avec vanité me donner cet éclat,
Puiſqu'il change mon cœur, qu'il veut changer l'état,
Ma haine vamourir, que j'ai crue immortelle ;
Elle eſt morte, et ce cœur devient ſujet fidele ;
Et prenant déſormais cette haine en horreur,
L'ardeur de vous ſervir ſuccede à ſa fureur.

Act 5. *ſc.* 3.
In

In the tragedy of *Sertorius*, the Queen, furprifed with the news that her lover was affaffinated, inftead of venting any paffion, degenerates into a cool fpectator, and undertakes to inftruĉt the by-ftanders how a queen ought to behave on fuch an occafion :

> *Viriate.* Il m'en fait voir enfemble, et l'auteur, et la caufe. -
> Par cet affaffinat c'eft de moi qu'on difpofe,
> C'eft mon trône, c'eft moi qu'on pretend conquerir ;
> Et c'eft mon jufte choix qui feul l'a fait perir.
> Madame, après fa perte, et parmi ces alarmes,
> N'attendez point de moi de foupirs, ni de larmes ;
> Ce font amufemens que dédaigne aifement
> Le prompt et noble orgueil d'un vif reffentiment.
> Qui pleure, l'affoiblit ; qui foupire, l'exhale :
> Il faut plus de fierté dans une ame royale ;
> Et ma douleur foumife aux foins de le venger, &c.
> > *Aĉt* 5. *fc.* 3.

So much in general upon the genuine fentiments of paffion. I proceed to particular obfervations. And, firft, paffions feldom continue uniform any confiderable time : they generally fluĉtuate, fwelling and fubfiding by turns, often in a quick fucceffion ;[*] and the fentiments cannot be juft unlefs they correfpond to fuch fluĉtuation. Accordingly, a climax never fhows better than in expreffing a fwelling paffion : the following paffages may fuffice for an illuftration.

> *Oroonoko.*———Can you raife the dead ?
> Purfue and overtake the wings of time ?
> And bring about again, the hours, the days,
> The years, that made me happy ?
> > *Oroonoko, aĉt* 2. *fc.* 2.

> *Almeria.*———How haft thou charm'd
> The wildnefs of the waves and rocks to this ?
> > That

[*] See chap. 2. part 3.

That thus relenting they have giv'n thee back
· To earth, to light and life, to love and me ?
>> *Mourning Bride, act 1. fc. 7.*

I would not be the villain that thou think'ft
For the whole fpace that's in the tyrant's grafp,
And the rich earth to boot.
>> *Macbeth act 4. fc. 4.*

The following paffage expreffes finely the progrefs
of conviction.

Let me not ftir, nor breathe, left I diffolve
That tender, lovely form, of painted air,
So like Almeria. Ha ! it finks, it falls ;
I'll catch it ere it goes, and grafp her fhade.
'Tis life ! 'tis warm ! 'tis fhe ! 'tis fhe herfelf !
It is Almeria, 'tis, it is my wife !
>> *Mourning Bride, act 2. fc. 6.*

In the progrefs of thought our refolutions become
more vigorous as well as our paffions :

If ever I do yield or give confent,
By any action, word, or thought, to wed
Another Lord ; may then juft heav'n fhow'r down, &c.
>> *Mourning Bride, act 1. fc. 1.*

And this leads to a fecond obfervation, That the
different ftages of a paffion, and its different direc-
tions, from birth to extinction, muft be carefully
reprefented in their order : becaufe other wife the
fentiments, by being mifplaced, will appear forced
and unnatural. Refentment, for example, when
provoked by an atrocious injury, difcharges itfelf
firft upon the author : fentiments therefore of revenge come always firft, and muft in fome meafure
be exhaufted before the perfon injured think of
>> grieving

grieving for himfelf. In the *Cid* of Corneille, Don Diegue having been affronted in a cruel manner, ex- preffes fcarce any fentiment of revenge, but is totally occupied in contemplating the low fituation to which he is reduced by the affront :

O rage ! ô defefpoir ! ô vieilleffe ennemie !
N'ai je donc tant vecu que pour cette infamie ?
Et ne fuis-je blanchi dans les travaux guerriers,
Que pour voir en un jour fletrir tant de lauriers ?
Mon bras, 'qu'avec refpeĉt toute l'Efpagne admire,
Mon bras, qui tant de fois a fauvé cet empire,
Tant de fois affermi le trône de fon Roi,
Trahit donc ma querelle, et ne fait rien pour moi !
O cruel fouvenir de ma gloire paffée !
Oeuvre de tant de jours en un jour effacée !
Nouvelle dignité fatale à mon bonheur !
Precipice elevé d'où tombe mon honneut !
Faut il de votre éclat voir triompher le Comte,
Et mourir fans vengeance, ou vivre dans la honte ?
Comte, foi; de mon Prince à prefent goyerneur,
Ce haut rang n'admet point un homme fans honneur ;
Et ton jaloux orgueil par cet affront infigne,
Malgré le choix du Roi, m'en à fû rendre indigne.
Et toi, de mes exploits glorieux inftrument,
Mais d'un corps tout de glace inutile ornement,
Fer jadis tant à craindre, et qui dans cette offenfe,
M'as fervi de parade, et non pas de defenfe,
Va, quitte deformais le dernier des humains,
Paffe pour me venger en de meilleures mains,

　　　　　　　　Le Cid, aĉt 1. *fc.* 7.

Thefe fentiments are certainly not the firft that are fuggefted by the paffion of refentment. As the firft movements of refentment are always direĉted to its objeĉt, the very fame is the cafe of grief. Yet with relation to the fudden and fevere diftemper that feiz- ed Alexander bathing in the river Cydnus, Quintus Curtius defcribes the firft emotions of the army as di- reĉted to themfelves, lamenting that they were left

　　　　　　　　　　　　　　　　　　without .

without a leader, far from home, and had fcarce any hopes of returning in fafety : their King's diftrefs, which muft naturally have been their firft concern, occupies them but in the fecond place, according to that author.   In the *Aminta* of Taffo, Sylvia, upon a report of her lover's death, which fhe believed certain, inftead of bemoaning the lofs of her beloved, turns her thoughts upon herfelf, and wonders her heart does not break :

> Ohime, ben fon di faffo,
> Poi che quefta novella non m'uccide.
>
> *Act 4. fc. 2.*

In the tragedy of *Jane Shore*, Alicia, in the full purpofe of deftroying her rival, has the the following reflection :

> Oh Jealoufy ! thou bane of pleafing friendfhip,
> Thou worft invader of our tender bofoms ;
> How does thy rancour poifon all our foftnefs,
> And turn our gentle natures into bitternefs ?
> See where fhe comes ! once my hearts deareft bleffing,
> Now my chang'd eyes are blafted with her beauty,
> Loathe that known face, and ficken to behold her.
>
> *Act 3. fc. 1.*

Thefe are the reflections of a cool fpectator.   A paffion while it has the afcendant, and is freely indulged, fuggefts not to the perfon who feels it any fentiment to its own prejudice : reflections like the foregoing occur not readily till the paffion has fpent its vigour.

A perfon fometimes is agitated at once by different paffions ; and the mind, in that cafe, vibrating like a pendulum, vents itfelf in fentiments that partake of the fame vibration.   This I give as a third obfervation ;

Queen.

Z 4

Queen. 'Would I had never trod this Englifh earth,
Or felt the flatteries that grow upon it !
Ye've angels faces, but Heaven knows your hearts.
What fhall become of me now ! wretched lady !
I am the moft unhappy woman living.
Alas ! poor wenches, where are now your fortunes ?

(To her women.

Shipwreck'd upon a kingdom, where no pity,
No friends, no hope ! no kindred weep for me !
Almoft no grave allow'd me.

Henry, VIII. *act* 3. *fc.* 1.

Othello. Oh devil, devil !
If that the earth could teem with woman's tears,
Each drop fhe falls would prove a crocodile.
Out of my fight !
Defdemona. I will not ftay t'offend you. *(going.*
Lodovico. Truly, an obedient lady :
I do befeech your Lordfhip call her back.
Oth. Miftrefs——
Def. My Lord.
Oth. What would you with her, Sir ?
Lod. Who, I, my Lord ?
Oth. Ay ; you did wifh that I would make her turn :
Sir, fhe can turn and turn, and yet go on ;
And turn again. And fhe can weep, Sir, weep :
And fhe's obedient : as you fay, obedient ;
Very obedient—proceed you in your tears—
Concerning this, Sir,—oh well painted paffion !—
I am commanded home, get you away,
I'll fend for you anon—Sir, I obey the mandate,
And will return to Venice.——Hence, avaunt !

[Exit Defdemona.
Othello, act 4. *fc.* 6.

Æmilia. Oh ! my good Lord, I would fpeak a word
with you.
Othello. Yes, 'tis Æmilia—By and by—She's dead.
'Tis like fhe come's to fpeak of Caffio's death ;
The noife was high—Ha ! no more moving ?
Still as the grave. Shall fhe come in ? were't good ?
I think fhe ftirs again—No—What's the beft ?
If fhe come in, fhe'll fure fpeak to my wife ;

My

My wife ! my wife ! What wife! I have no wife ;
Oh infupportable ! O heavy hour !

　　　　　　　　Othello, act 5. *fc.* 7.

A fourth obfervation is, That nature, which gave
us paffions, and made them extremely beneficial when
moderate, intended undoubtedly that they fhould be
fubjected to the government of reafon and confcience.*
It is therefore againft the order of nature, that paffion in any cafe fhould take the lead in contradiction
to reafon and confcience : fuch a ftate of mind is a
fort of anarchy, which every one is afhamed of, and
endeavours to hide or diffemble. Even love, however laudable, is attended with a confcious fhame
when it becomes immoderate : it is covered from the
world, and difclofed only to the beloved object :

Et que l'amour fouvent de remors combattu
Paroiffe une foibleffe, et non une vertu.
　　　　　　Boileau, L'art poet. chant. 3. *l.* 101.

O, they love leaft that let men know their love.
　　　　　　Two gentlemen of Verona, act 1. *fc.* 3.

Hence a capital rule in the reprefentation of immoderate paffions, that they ought to be hid or diffem-
bled as much as poffible. And this holds in an
efpecial manner with refpect to criminal paffions :
one never counfels the commiffion of a crime in plain
terms : guilt muft not appear in its native colours,
even in thought : the propofal muft be made by
hints, and by reprefenting the action in fome favourable light. Of the propriety of fentiment upon
fuch an occafion, Shakefpear, in the *Tempeft*,
has given us a beautiful example, in a fpeech by the
　　　　　　　　　　　　　　　　　　ufurping

* See chap. 2. part 7.

ufurping Duke of Milan, advifing Sebaftian to murder his brother the King of Naples :

> *Antonio.*————————What might,
> Worthy Sebaftian,—O, what might—no more.
> And yet methinks, I fee it in thy face,
> What thou fhouldft be : th' occafion fpeaks thee, and
> My ftrong imagination fees a crown   ·
> Dropping upon thy head.
>
> *Act* 2. *fc.* 1.

There never was drawn a more complete picture of
this kind, than that of King John foliciting Hubert
to murder the young Prince Arthur :

> *K. John.* Come hither, Hubert. O my gentle Hubert,
> We owe thee much ; within this wall of flefh
> There is a foul counts thee her creditor,
> And with advantage means to pay thy love.
> And, my good friend, thy voluntary oath
> Lives in this bofom, dearly cherifhed.
> Give me thy hand, I had a thing to fay————
> But I will fit it with fome better time.
> By heav'n, Hubert, I'm almoft afham'd
> To fay what good refpect I have of thee.
> *Hubert.* I am much bounden to your Majefty.
> *King John.* Good friend, thou haft no caufe to fay fo
>   yet————
> But thou fhalt have—and creep time ne'er fo flow,
> Yet it fhall come for me to do thee good.
> I had a thing to fay——but let it go ;
> The fun is in the heav'n ; and the proud day,
> Attended with the pleafures of the world,
> Is all too wanton, and too full of gawds,
> To give me audience. If the midnight-bell
> Did with his iron-tongue and brazen mouth
> Sound one into the drowfy race of night ;
> If this fame were a church-yard where we ftand,
> And thou poffeffed with a thoufand wrongs ;
> Or if that furly fpirit Melancholy
> Had bak'd thy blood, and made it heavy-thick,
>
> Which

Which elſe runs tickling up and down the veine,
Making that idiot Laughter keep men's eyes,
And ſtrain their cheeks to idle merriment,
(A paſſion hateful to my purpoſes ;)
Or if that thou couldſt ſee me without eyes,
Hear me without thine ears, and make reply
Without a tongue, uſing conceit alone,
Without eyes, ears, and harmful ſound of words ;
Then, in deſpite of broad-ey'd watchful day,
I would into thy boſom pour my thoughts.
But ah, I will not—Yet I love thee well ;
And, by my troth, I think thou lov'ſt me well.
     Hubert. So well, that what you bid me undertake,
Though that my death were adjunct to my act,
By Heav'n, I'd do't.
     K. John. Do not I know thou wouldſt ?
Good Hubert, Hubert, Hubert, throw thine eye
On yon young boy.   I'll tell thee what, my friend ;
He is a very ſerpent in my way.
And, whereſoe'er this foot of mine doth tread,
He lies before me.   Doſt thou underſtand me ?
Thou art his keeper.   *King John, act 3. ſc. 5.*

As things are beſt illuſtrated by their contraries, I
proceed to faulty ſentiments, diſdaining to be indebted for examples to any but the moſt approved authors.   The firſt claſs ſhall conſiſt of ſentiments that
accord not with the paſſion ; or, in other words, ſentiments that the paſſion does not naturally ſuggeſt.
In the ſecond claſs, ſhall be ranged ſentiments that
may belong to an ordinary paſſion, but unſuitable to
it as tinctured by a ſingular character.   Thoughts
that properly are not ſentiments, but rather deſcrip-
tions, make a third.   Sentiments that belong to the
paſſion repreſented, but are faulty as being introduced too early or too late, make a fourth.   Vicious
ſentiments expoſed in their native dreſs, inſtead of
being concealed or diſguiſed, make a fifth.   And in
the laſt claſs, ſhall be collected ſentiments ſuited to
no character nor paſſion, and therefore unnatural.
                                                      The

The firſt claſs contains faulty ſentiments of various kinds, which I ſhall endeavour to diſtinguiſh from each other ; beginning with ſentiments that are faulty by being above the tone of the paſſion :

> *Othello.* ———————— O my ſoul's joy !
> If after every tempeſt come ſuch calms,
> May the winds blow till they have waken'd death !
> And let the labouring bark climb hills of ſeas
> Olympus high, and duck again as low
> As hell's from heaven !
> > *Othello, act* 2. *ſc.* 6.

This ſentiment may be ſuggeſted by violent and inflamed paſſion, but is not ſuited to the calm ſatiſfaction that one feels upon eſcaping danger.

> *Philaſter.* Place me ſome god, upon a pyramid
> Higher than hills of earth, and lend a voice
> Loud as your thunder to me, that from thence
> I may diſcourſe to all the under-world
> The worth that dwells in him.
> > *Philaſter of Beaumont and Fletcher, act* 4.

Second. Sentiments below the tone of the paſſion. Ptolemy, by putting Pompey to death, having incurred the diſpleaſure of Cæſar was in the utmoſt dread of being dethroned : in that agitating ſituation, Corneille makes him utter a ſpeech full of cool reflection, that is in no degree expreſſive of the paſſion.

> Ah ! ſi je t'avois crû, je n'aurois pas de maitre,
> Je ſerois dans le trône où le Ciel m'a fait naître ;
> Mais c'eſt une imprudence aſſez commune aux rois,
> D'écouter trop d'avis, et ſe tromper aux choix.
> Le Deſtin les aveugle au bord du précipice,
> Où ſi quelque lumiere en leur ame ſe gliſſe,

Cette

Cette fauffe clarté dont il les eblouit,
Le plonge dans une gouffre, et puis s'evanouit.
La morte de Pompée, act 4. fc. 1.

In *Les Freres ennemies* of Racine, the fecond act is opened with a love fcene : Hemon talks to his miftrefs of the torments of abfence, of the luftre of her eyes, that he ought to die no where but at her feet, and that one moment of abfence is a thoufand years. Antigone on her part acts the coquette ; pretends fhe muft be gone to wait on her mother and brother, and cannot ftay to liften to his courtfhip. This is odious French gallantry, below the dignity of the paffion of love : it would fcarce be excufable in painting modern French manners ; and is infufferable where the ancients are brought upon the ftage. The manners painted in the *Alexandre* of the fame author are not more juft : French gallantry prevails there throughout.

Third. Sentiments that agree not with the tone of the paffion ; as where a pleafant fentiment is grafted upon a painful paffion, or the contrary. In the following inftances the fentiments are too gay for a ferious paffion :

No happier tafk thefe faded eyes purfue ;
To read and weep is all they now can do.
Eloifa to Abelard, l. 47.

Again,
Heav'n firft taught letters for fome wretch's aid,
Some banifh'd lover, or fome captive maid ;
They live, they fpeak, they breathe what love infpires,
Warm from the foul, and faithful to its fires ;
The virgin's wifh without her fears impart,
Excufe the blufh, and pour out all the heart ;
Speed the foft intercourfe from foul to foul,
And waft a figh from Indus to the pole.
Eloifa to Abelard, l. 51.

Thefe

Thefe thoughts are pretty : they fuit Pope, but not
Eloifa.

Satan, enraged by a threatening of the angel Gabriel,
anfwer thus :

> Then when I am thy captive talk of chains,
> Proud limitary cherub ; but ere then
> Far heavier load thyfelf expect to feel
> From my prevailing arm, though Heaven's King
> Ride on thy wings, and thou with thy compeers,
> Us'd to the yoke, draw'ft his triumphant wheels
> In progrefs through the road of heav'n *ftar-pav'd.*
> > *Paradife loft, book* 4.

The concluding epithet forms a grand and delightful
image, which cannot be the genuine offspring of
rage.

Fourth. Sentiments too artificial for a ferious
paffion. I give for the firft example a fpeech of
Piercy expiring :

> O, Harry, thou haft robb'd me of my growth :
> I better brook the lofs of brittle life,
> Than thofe proud titles thou haft won of me ;
> They wound my thoughts, worfe than thy fword my
> > flefh.
> But thought's the flave of life, and life time's fool ;
> And time, that takes furvey of all the world,
> Muft have a ftop.
> > *Firft part, Henry IV. act* 5. *fc.* 9.

Livy inferts the following paffage in a plaintive oration of the Locrenfes, accufing Pleminius the Roman legate of oppreffion.

In hoc legato veftro, nec hominis quicquam eft, Patres
Confcripti, præter figuram et fpeciem ; neque Ro-
mani

mani civis, præter habitum veſtitumque, et ſonum linguæ
Latinæ. Peſtis et bellua immanis, quales fretum, quon-
dam, quo ab Sicilia dividimur, ad perniciem navigantium
circumſediſſe, fabulæ ferunt.*

The ſentiments of the *Mourning Bride* are for the
moſt part no leſs delicate than juſt copies of nature :
in the following exception the picture is beautiful,
but too artful to be ſuggeſted by ſevere grief.

> *Almeria.* O no ! Time gives increaſe to my afflictions.
> The circling hours, that gather all the woes
> Which are diffus'd through the revolving year,
> Come heavy laden with th' oppreſſive weight
> To me ; with me, ſucceſſively they leave
> The ſighs, the tears, the groans, the reſtleſs cares,
> And all the damps of grief, that did retard their flight :
> They ſhake their downy wings, and ſcatter all
> The dire collected dews on my poor head ;
> Then fly with joy and ſwiftneſs from me.
>
> 　　　　　　　　*Act* 1. *ſc.* 1.

In the ſame play, Almeria ſeeing a dead body, which
ſhe took to be Alphonſo's, expreſſes ſentiments
ſtrained and artificial, which nature ſuggeſts not to
any perſon upon ſuch an occaſion :

> Had they, or hearts, or eyes, that did this deed ?
> Could eyes endure to guide ſuch cruel hands ?
> Are not my eyes guilty alike with theirs,
> That thus can gaze, and yet not turn to ſtone ?
> —I do not weep ! The ſprings of tears are dry'd ?
> And of a ſudden I am calm, as if
> All things were well ; and yet my huſband's murder'd !
> Yes, yes, I know to mourn : I'll ſluice this heart,
> The ſource of wo, and let the torrent looſe.
>
> 　　　　　　　　*Act* 5. *ſc.* 11.
> 　　　　　　　　　　*Lady*

* Titus Livius, l. 29. § 17.

Lady Trueman. How could you be fo cruel to defer giving me that joy which you knew I muſt receive from your
prefence ? You have robb'd my life of fome hours of happinefs that ought to have been in it.

                           Drummer, act 5.

Pope's Elegy to the memory of an unfortunate lady,
expreſſes delicately the moſt tender concern and forrow that one can feel for the deplorable fate of a perfon of worth. Such a poem, deeply ferious and pathetic, rejects with difdain all fiction. Upon that account, the following paſſage deferves no quarter ; for
it is not the language of the heart, but of the imagination, indulging its flights at cafe ; and by that
means is eminently difcordant with the fubject. It
would be a ſtill more fevere cenfure, if it ſhould be
afcribed to imitation, copying indifcreetly what has
been faid by others :

> What though no weeping loves thy aſhes grace,
> Nor poliſh'd marble emulate thy face ?
> What though no facred earth allow thee room,
> Nor hallow'd dirge be mutter'd o'er thy tomb ?
> Yet ſhall thy grave with rifing flowr's be dreſt,
> And the green turf lie lightly on thy breaſt :
> There ſhall the morn her earlieſt tears beſtow,
> There the firſt rofes of the year ſhall blow ;
> While angels with their filver wings o'erſhade
> The ground, now facred by thy reliques made.

Fifth. Fanciful or finical fentiments. Sentiments
that degenerate into point or conceit, however they
may amufe in an idle hour, can never be the offspring
of any ferious or important paſſion. In the *Jerufa-
lem* of Taſſo, Tancred, after a fingle combat, fpent
with fatigue and lofs of blood, falls into a fwoon ;
in which fituation, underſtood to be dead, he is dif-
                                 cover'd

covered by Erminia, who was in love with him to dif-
traction. A more happy fituation cannot be imagined, to raife grief in an inftant to its height; and
yet, in venting her forrow, fhe defcends moft abominably into antithefis and conceit, even of the loweft kind :

> E in lui versò d'inefficabil vena
> Lacrime, e voce, di fofpiri mifta.
> In che mifero punto hor qui me mena
> Fortuna ? a che veduta amara e trifta ?
> Dopo gran tempo i' ti ritrovo à pena
> Tancredi, e ti riveggio, e non fon vifta,
> Vifta non fon da te, benche prefente
> E trovando ti perdo eternamente.
>
> > *Canto* 19. *ft.* 105.

Armida's lamentation refpecting her lover Rinaldo,*
is in the fame vicious tafte.

> ● *Queen.* Give me no help in lamentation,
> I am not barren to bring forth complaints :
> All fprings reduce their currents to mine eyes
> That I being govern'd by the wat'ry moon,
> May fend forth plenteous tears to drown the world,
> Ah, for my hufband, for my dear Lord Edward.
> > *King Richard,* III. *act* 2. *fc.* 2.

> *Jane Shore.* Let me be branded for the public fcorn,
> Turn'd forth, and driven to wander like a vagabond,
> Be friendlefs and forfaken, feek my bread
> Upon the barren wild, and defolate wafte,
> *Feed on my fighs, and drink my falling tears ;*
> Ere I confent to teach my lips injuftice,
> Or wrong the Orphan who has none to fave him.
> > *Jane Shore,* act 4.

> Give me your drops, ye foft-defcending rains,
> Give me your ftreams, ye never-ceafing fprings,
> > That

* Canto 20. ftan. 124. 125. & 126.

That my fad eyes may ftill fupply my duty,
And feed an everlafting flood of forrow.
Jane Shore, aft 5.

Jane Shore utters her laft breath in a witty conceit.

Then all is well, and I fhall fleep in peace—
'Tis very dark, and I have loft you now—
Was there not fomething I would have bequeath'd you?
But I have nothing left me to beftow,
Nothing but one fad figh. Oh mercy, Heav'n! [*Dies.*
Aft 5.

Guilford to Lady Jane Gray, when both were con-
• demned to die :

Thou ftand'ft unmov'd ;
Calm temper fits upon thy beauteous brow ;
Thy eyes that flow'd fo faft for Edward's lofs,
Gaze unconcern'd upon the ruin round thee,
As if thou hadft refolv'd to brave thy fate,
And triumph in the midft of defolation.
Ha! fee, it fwells, the liquid cryftal rifes,
It ftarts in fpite of thee—but I will catch it,
Nor let the earth be wet with dew fo rich.
Lady Jane Gray, aft 4. *near the end.*

The concluding fentiment is altogether finical, unfuitable to the importance of the occafion, and even
to the dignity of the paffion of love.

Corneille in his *Examen of the Cid,** anfwering an
objection, That his fentiments are fometimes too
much refined for perfons in deep diftrefs, obferves, that
if poets did not indulge fentiments more ingenious or
refined than are prompted by paffion, their performances would often be low, and extreme grief would
never fuggeft but exclamations merely. This is in
plain language to affert, that forced thoughts are
more agreeable than thofe that are natural, and
ought to be preferred.

The

* Page 316.

The fecond clafs is of fentiments that may belong to an ordinary paffion, but are not perfectly concordant with it, as tinctured by a fingular character.

In. the laft act of that excellent comedy, *The Carelefs Hufband*, Lady Eafy, upon Sir Charles' reformation, is made to exprefs more violent and turbulent fentiments of joy, than are confiftent with the mildnefs of her character :

Lady Eafy. O the foft treafure ! O the dear reward of long defiring love.—Thus ! thus to have you mine, is fomething more than happinefs ; 'tis double life, and madnefs of abounding joy.

If the fentiments of a paffion ought to be fuited to a peculiar character, it is ftill more neceffary that actions be fuited to the character. In the 5th act of the *Drummer*, Addifon makes his gardner act even below the character of an ignorant credulous ruftic : he gives him the behaviour of a gaping idiot.

The following inftances are defcriptions rather than fentiments, which compofe a third clafs.

Of this defcriptive manner of painting the paffions, there is in the *Hyppolitus* of Euripides, act 5, an illuftrious inftance, namely, the fpeech of Thefeus, upon hearing of his fon's difmal exit. In Racine's tragedy of *Efther*, the Queen hearing of the decree iffued againft her people, inftead of expreffing fentiments fuitable to the occafion, turns her attention upon herfelf, and defcribes with accuracy her own fituation :

Jufte Ciel ! tout mon fang dans mes veines fe glace.

Act 1. *fc.* 3.

Again,

Aman.

Aman. C'en eſt fait. Mon orgueil eſt forcé de plier.
L'inexorable Aman eſt reduit à prier.

> *Eſther, act* 3. *ſc.* 5.

Athalie. Quel prodige nouveau me trouble et m'embar-
raſſe ?
La douceur de ſa voix, ſon enfance, ſa grace,
Font inſenſiblement à mon inimitié
Succeder—Je ſerois ſenſible à la pitié ?

> *Athalie,* act 2. *ſc.* 7.

Titus. O de ma paſſion fureur deſeſperée !

> *Brutus of Voltaire,* act 3. *ſc.* 6.

What other are the foregoing inſtances but deſcribing the paſſion another feels ?

A man ſtabbed to the heart in a combat with his
enemy expreſſes himſelf thus :

> So, now I am at reſt :————
> I feel death riſing higher ſtill, and higher,
> Within my boſom ; every breath I fetch
> Shuts up my life within a ſhorter compaſs :
> And like the vaniſhing ſound of bells, grows leſs
> And leſs each pulſe, 'till it be loſt in air.
>
> > *Dryden.*

Captain Flaſh, in a farce compoſed by Garrick, endeavours to hide his fear by ſaying, "What a damn'd
paſſion I am in."

An example is given above of remorſe and deſpair
expreſſed by genuine and natural ſentiments. In the
fourth book of *Paradiſe Loſt*, Satan is made to expreſs his remorſe and deſpair in ſentiments, which,
though beautiful, are not altogether natural : they are
rather the ſentiments of a ſpectator, than of a perſon
who actually is tormented with theſe paſſions.

The fourth claſs is of ſentiments introduced too
early or too late.

> Some

Some examples mentioned above belong to this
clafs.   Add the following from *Venice Preferv'd*, act
5, at the clofe of the fcene between Belvidera and her
father Priuli.   The account given by Belvidera of
the danger fhe was in, and of her hufband's threatening to murder her, ought naturally to have alarmed her relenting father, and to have made him exprefs the moft perturbed fentiments.   Inftead of
which he diffolves into tendernefs and love for his
daughter, as if he had already delivered her from
danger, and as if there were a perfect tranquillity :

Canft thou forgive me all my follies paft ?
I'll henceforth be indeed a father ; never,
Never more thus expofe but cherifh thee,
Dear as the vital warmth that feeds my life,
Dear as thofe eyes that weep in fondnefs o'er thee:
Peace to thy heart.

Immoral fentiments expofed in their native colours, inftead of being concealed or difguifed, compofe the fifth clafs.

The Lady Macbeth, projecting the death of the
King, has the following foliloquy :

————————The raven himfelf's not hoarfe
That croaks the fatal entrance of Duncan
Under my battlements.   Come all you fpirits
That tend on mortal thoughts, unfex me here,
And fill me from the crown to the toe, top-full
Of direct cruelty ; make thick my blood,
Stop up th' accefs and paffage to remorfe,
That no compunctious vifitings of nature
Shake my fell purpofe.   *Macbeth*, act 1. fc. 7.

This fpeech is not natural.   A treacherous murder
was never perpetrated even by the moft hardened
mifcreant, without compunction : and that the lady here muft have been in horrible agitation, ap-

A a 3   pears

pears from her invoking the infernal fpirits to fill her
with cruelty, and to ftop up all avenues to remorfe.
But in that ftate of mind, it is a never-failing arti‐
fice of felf-deceit, to draw the thickeft veil over the
wicked action, and to extenuate it by all the circum‐
ftances that imagination can fuggeft : and if the
crime cannot bear difguife, the next attempt is to
thruft it out of mind altogether, and to rufh on
to action without thought. This laft was the huf‐
band's method :

Strange things I have in head, that will to hand ;
Which muft be acted ere they muft be fcann'd.

Act 3. *fc.* 5.

The lady follows neither of thefe courfes, but in a
deliberate manner endeavours to fortify her heart in
the commiffion of an execrable crime, without even
attempting to colour it. This I think is not natural,
I hope there is no fuch wretch to be found as is here
reprefented. In the *Pompey* of Corneille,* Photine
counfels a wicked action in the plaineft terms with‐
out difguife :

Seigneur, n'attirez point le tonnerre en ces lieux,
Rangez vous du parti des deftins et des dieux,
Et fans les accufer d'injuftice, ou d'outrage ;
Puis qu'ils font les heureux, adorez leur ouvrage ;
Quels que foient leurs decrets, déclarez-vous pour eux,
Et pour leur obéir, perdez le mal hereux.
Prefs de touts parts des coléres celeftes,
Il en vient deffus vous faire fondre les reftes ;
Et fa tête qu' à peine il a pû dérober,
Tout prête dechoir, cherche avec qui tomber.
Sa retraite chez vous en effet n'eft qu'un crime ;
Elle marque fa haine, et non pas fon eftime ;
Il ne vient que vous perdre en venant prendre port,
Et vous pouvez douter s'il eft digne de mort !
Il devoit mieux remplir nos vœux et notre attente,
Faire voir fur fes nefs la victoire flotante ;

Il

* Act 1. fc. 1.

Il n'eût ici trouvé que joye et que feſtins ;
Mais puiſqu'il eſt vaincu qu'il s'en prenne aux deſtins,
J'en veux à ſa diſgrace et non à ſa perſonne,
J'exécute à regret ce que le ciel ordonne,
Et du même poignard, pour Céſar deſtiné,
Je perce en ſoùpirant ſon cœur infortuné.
Vous ne pouvez enfin qu' aux dépens de ſa tête
Mettre à l'abri la vôtre, et parer la tempête.
Laiſſez nommer ſa mort un unjuſte attentat,
La juſtice n'eſt pas une vertu d'état.
Le choix des actions, ou mauvaiſes, ou bonnes,
Ne fait qu' anéantir la force des couronnes ;
Le droit des rois conſiſte à ne rien épargner ;
La timide équité détruit l'art de regner ;
Quand on craint d'être injuſte on a toûjours à craindre ;
Et qui veut tout pouvoir doit oſer tout enfraindre,
Fuir comme un deſhonneur la vertu qui le pert,
Et voler ſans ſcrupule au crime qui lui ſert.

In the tragedy of *Eſther*,* Haman acknowledges without diſguiſe, his cruelty, inſolence, and pride. And there is another example of the ſame kind in the *Agamemnon* of Seneca.† In the tragedy of *Atha-lie*,‡ Mathan, in cool blood, relates to his friend many black crimes he had been guilty of, to ſatisfy his ambition.

In Congreve's *Double-dealer*, Maſkwell, inſtead of diſguiſing or colouring his crimes, values himſelf upon them in a ſoliloquy :

Cynthia, let thy beauty gild my crimes ; and whatſoever I commit of treachery or deceit, ſhall be imputed to me as a merit————Treachery ! what treachery ? Love cancels all the bonds of friendſhip, and ſets men right upon their firſt foundations. *Act* 2. *ſc.* 8.

In French plays, love, inſtead of being hid or diſguiſed, is treated as a ſerious concern, and of greater

_____

* Act 2. ſc. 1. † Beginning of act 2. ‡ Act 3. ſc. 3. at the ꝛ ſc.

A a 4

greater importance than fortune, family, or dignity. I
fufpect the reafon to be, that, in the capital of France,
love, by the eafinefs of intercourfe, has dwindled
down from a real paffion to be a connection that is
regulated entirely by the mode or fafhion.*   This
may in fome meafure excufe their writers, but will
never make their plays be relifhed among foreigners.

> *Maxime.*   Quoi, trahir mon ami ?
> *Euphorbe.* ————L'amour rend tout permis,
> Un véritable amant ne connoît point d'amis.
>
> Cinna, act 3.fc. 1.

> *Cefar.* Reine, tout eft plaifible, et la ville calmée,
> Qu'un trouble affez leger avoit trop allarmée,
> N'a plus à redouter le divorce inteftin
> Du foldat infolent, et du peuple mutin.
> Mais, ô Dieux ! ce moment que je vous ai quittée,
> D'un trouble bien plus grand à mon ame agitée,
> Et ces foins importuns qui m'arrachoient de vous
> Contre ma grandeur même allumoient mon courroux,
> Je lui voulois du mal de m'être fi contraire,
> De rendre ma prefence ailleurs fi neceffaire.
> Mais je lui pardonnois au fimple fouvenir
> Du bonheur qu'à ma flâme elle fait obtenir.
> C'eft elle dont je tiens cette haute efpérance,
> Qui flate mes defirs d'une illuftre apparence,
> Et fait croire à Céfar qu'il peut former de vœux,
> Qu'il n'eft pas tout-à-fait indigne de vos feux,
> Et qu'il peut en prétendre une jufte conquête,
> N'ayant plus que les Dieux au deffus de fa tête.
> Oui, Reine, fi quelqu' un dans ce vafte univers
> Pouvoit porter plus haut la gloire de vos fers ;
> S'il étoit quelque trône où vous pouiffiez paroître
> Plus dignement affife en captivant fon maître,
>
> J'irois

---

* A certain author fays humouroufly, " Les mots mêmes d'amour
et d'amant font bannis de l'intime fociété des deux fexes, et relegués
avec ceux de *chaine* et de *flame* dans les Romans qu'on ne lit plus." And
where nature is once banifhed, a fair field is open to every fantaftic imitation, even the moft extravagant.

J'irois, j'irois à lui, moins pour le lui ravir,
Que pour lui difputer le droit de vous fervir ;
Et je n'afpirerois au bonheur de vous plaire,
Qu'après avoir mis bas un fi grand adverfaire.
C'étoit pour acquerir un droit fi précieux,
Que combattoit par tout mon bras ambitieux,
Et dans Pharfale même il a tiré l'epée
Plus pour le confervir, que pour vaincre Pompée.
Je l'ai vaincu, Princeffe, et le Dieu de combats
M'y favorifoit moins que vos divins appas.
Ils conduifoient ma main, ils enfloient mon courage,
Cette pleine victoire eft leur dernier ouvrage,
C'eft l'effet des ardeurs qu'ils daignoient m'infpirer ;
Et vos beaux yeaux enfin m'ayant fait foûpirer,
Pour faire que votre ame avec gloire y réponde,
M'ont rendu le premier, et de Rome, et du monde ;
C'eft ce glorieux titre, à préfent effectif,
Que je viens ennoblir par celui de captif ;
Heureux, fi mon efprit gagne tant fur le vôtre,
Qu'il en eftime l'un, et me permette l'autre.

Pompée, act 4. fc. 3.

The laft clafs comprehends fentiments that are un-natural, as being fuited to no character nor paffion. Thefe may be fubdivided into three branches : firft, fentiments unfuitable to the conftitution of man, and to the laws of his nature ; fecond, inconfiftent fentiments ; third, fentiments that are pure rant and extravagance.

· When the fable is of human affairs, every event, every incident, and every circumftance, ought to be natural, otherwife the imitation is imperfect. But an imperfect imitation is a venial fault, compared with that of running crofs to nature. In the *Hippolytus* of Euripides,* Hippolytus, wifhing for another felf in his own fituation, How much (fays he) fhould I be touched with his misfortune! as if it were natural to grieve more for the misfortunes of another than for one's own.

Ofmyn.

* Act 4. fc. 5.

Ofmyn.   Yet I behold her—yet—and now no more.
Turn your lights inward, Eyes, and view my thought,
So fhall you ftill behold her—'twill not be.
O impotence of fight ! mechanic fenfe
Which to exterior objects ow'ft thy faculty,
Not feeing of election, but neceffity.
Thus do our eyes, as do all common mirrors,
Succeffively reflect fucceeding images.
Nor what they would, but muft ; a ftar or toad ;
Juft as the hand of chance adminifters !

Mourning Bride, act 2. *fc.* 8.

No man, in his fenfes, ever thought of applying
his eyes to difcover what paffes in his mind ; far lefs
of blaming his eyes for not feeing a thought or idea.
In Moliere's *L'Avare*,* Harpagon being robbed of
his money, feizes himfelf by the arm, miftaking it
for that of the robber.   And again he expreffes him,
felf as follows :

Je veux aller querir la juftice, et faire donner la queftion
à toute ma maifon ; à fervantes, à valets, à fils, a fille,
et a moi auffi.

This is fo abfurd as fcarce to provoke a fmile, if it
be not at the author.

Of the fecond branch the following are examples.

———————————Now bid me run,
And I will ftrive with things impoffible,
Yea get the better of them.

Julius Cæfar, act 2. *fc.* 3.

Vos mains feules ont droit de vaincre un invincible.

Le Cid, act 5. *fc. laft.*

Que fon nom foit beni.   Que fon nom foit chanté,
Que l'on celebre fes ouvrages
Au de la de l'eternité.   *Efther*, act 5. *fc. laft.*

Me

* Act 4. fc. 7.

Me miferable ! which way fhall I fly
Infinite wrath and infinite defpair ?
Which way I fly is hell : myfelf am hell ;
And in the *loweft* deep, a *lower* deep
Still threatening to devour me, opens wide ;
To which the hell I fuffer feems a heav'n.

            Paradife loft, book 4.

Of the third branch, take the following famples.

Lucan, talking of Pompey's fepulcre,

 ————————Romanum nomen, et omne
Imperium Magno eft tumuli modus.   Obruc faxa
Crimine plena deum.   Si tota eft Herculis Oetc,
Et juga tota vacant Bromio Nyfeia ; quare
Unus in Egypto Magno lapis ? Omnia Lagi
Rura tenere poteft, fi nullo cefpite nomen
Hæferit.   Erremus populi, cinerumque tuorum,
Magne, metu nullas Nili calcemus arenas.

            L. 8. l. 798.

Thus in Row's tranflation :

Where there are feas, or air, or earth, or fkies,
Where-e'er Rome's empire ftretches, Pompey lies.
Far be the vile memorial then convey'd !
Nor let this ftone the partial gods upbraid.
Shall Hercules all Oeta's heights demand,
And Nyfa's hill for Bacchus only ftand ;
While one poor pebble is the warrior's doom
That fought the caufe of liberty and Rome ?
If Fate decrees he muft in Egypt lie,
Let the whole fertile realm his grave fupply,
Yield the wide country to his awful fhade ⎤
Nor let us dare on any part to tread, ⎬
Fearful we violate the mighty dead.   ⎦

The following paffages are pure rant.   Coriolanus, fpeaking to his mother,

            What

What is this ?
Your knees to me ? to your corrected fon ?
Then let the pebbles on the hungry beach
Fillop the ftars : then let the mutinous winds
Strike the proud cedars 'gainft the fiery fun :
Murd'ring impoffibility to make
What cannot be, flight work.

Coriolanus, act 5. *fc.* 3.

Cæfar.——Danger knows full well,
That Cæfar is more dangerous than he.
We were two lions litter'd in one day,
And I the elder and more terrible.

Julius Cæfar, act 2. *fc.* 4.

Almahide.   This day——
I gave my faith to him, he his to me.
  Almanzor.   Good Heav'n, thy book of fate before
     me lay
But to tear out the journal of this day.
Or if the order of the world below,
Will not the gap of one whole day allow,   ⎫
Give me that minute when fhe made that vow. ⎬
That minute ev'n the happy from their blifs might
     give,
And thofe who live in grief a fhorter time would live,
So fmall a link if broke, th' eternal chain
Would like divided waters join again.

Conqueft of Granada, act 3.

Almanzor. ——————— I'll hold it faft
As life : and when life's gone, I'll hold this laft.
And if thou tak'ft it after I am flain,
I'll fend my ghoft to fetch it back again.

Conqueft of Granada, part 2. *act* 3.

Lyndiraxa. A crown is come, and will not fate allow,
And yet I feel fomething like death is near.
My guards, my guards——
Let not that ugly fkeleton appear.
Sure Deftiny miftakes ; this death's not mine ;
She doats; and meant to cut another line.
Tell her I am a queen—but 'tis too late ;

Dying,

Dying, I charge rebellion on my fate ;
Bow down, ye flaves——
Bow quickly down and your fubmiffion fhow ;
I'm pleas'd to tafte an empire ere I go.   [*Dies*.
     Conqueft of Granada, part 2. *act* 5.

Ventidius. But you, ere love mifled your wand'ring
  eyes,
Were. fure, the chief and beft of human race,
Fram'd in the very pride and boaft of nature,
So perfect, that the gods who form'd you wonder'd
At their own fkill, and cry'd, A lucky hit
Has mended our defign.
    Dryden, All for Love, act 1.

Not to talk of the impiety of this fentiment, it is ludicrous inftead of being lofty.

The famous epitaph on Raphael is no lefs abfurd than any of the foregoing paffages :

Raphael, timuit, quo fofpite, vinci
Rerum magna parens, et moriente mori.

Imitated by Pope in his Epitaph on Sir Godfrey Kneller :

Living, great Nature fear'd he might outvie
Her works ; and dying, fears herfelf might die.

Such is the force of imitation ; for Pope of himfelf would never have been guilty of a thought fo extravagant.

So much upon fentiments ; the language proper for expreffing them, comes next in order.

C H A P.

C H A P. XVII.

Language of Paſſion.

AMONG the particulars that compoſe the ſocial part of our nature, a propenſity to communicate our opinions, our emotions, and every thing that affects us, is remarkable. *Bad fortune and injuſtice affect us greatly; and of theſe we are ſo prone to complain, that if we have no friend nor acquaintance to take part in our ſufferings, we ſometimes utter our complaints aloud, even where there are none to liſten.

But this propenſity operates not in every ſtate of mind. A man immoderately grieved, ſeeks to afflict himſelf, rejecting all conſolation : immoderate grief accordingly is mute : complaining is ſtruggling for conſolation.

> It is the wretch's comfort ſtill to have
> Some ſmall reſerve of near and inward wo,
> Some unſuſpected hoard of inward grief,
> Which they unſeen may wail, and weep, and mourn,
> And glutton-like alone devour.
> *Mourning Bride,* act 1. ſc. 1.

When grief ſubſides, it then and no ſooner finds a tongue : we complain, becauſe complaining is an effort to diſburden the mind of its diſtreſs.*

Surpriſe

---

* This obſervation is finely illuſtrated by a ſtory which Herodotus records, b. 9. Cambyſes, when he conquerd Egypt, made Pſammenitus the King priſoner ; and for trying his conſtancy, ordered his daughter to be dreſſed in the habit of a ſlave, and to be employed in bringing water from the river ; his ſon alſo was led to execution with a halter about his neck. The Egyptians vented their ſorrow in tears and lamentations ; Pſammenitus only, with a downcaſt eye, remained ſilent. Afterward meeting one of his companions, a man advanced in years, who, being plundered

Surprife and terror are filent paffions for a different reafon : they agitate the mind fo violently as for
a time to fufpend the exercife of its faculties, and
among others the faculty of fpeech.

Love and revenge, when immoderate, are not
more loquacious than immoderate grief. But when
thefe paffions become moderate, they fet the tongue
free, and, like moderate grief, become loquacious :
moderate love, when unfuccefsful, is vented in complaints ; when fuccefsful, is full of joy expreffed by
words and geftures.

As no paffion hath any long uninterrupted exiftence,* nor beats always with an equal pulfe, the language fuggefted by paffion is not only unequal, but
frequently interrupted : and even during an uninterrupted fit of paffion, we only exprefs in words the
more capital fentiments. In familiar converfation,
one who vents every fingle thought is juftly branded
with the character of *loquacity ;* becaufe fenfible people exprefs no thoughts but what make fome figure :
in the fame manner, we are only difpofed to exprefs
the ftrongeft pulfes of paffion, efpecially when it returns with impetuofity after interruption.

I formerly had occafion to obferve,† that the fentiments ought to be tuned to the paffion, and the
language to both. Elevated fentiments require elevated language : tender fentiments ought to be cloth-
ed in words that are foft and flowing : when the
mind

___

plundered of all, was begging alms, he wept bitterly, calling him by his
name. Cambyfes, ftruck with wonder, demanded an anfwer to the following queftion : " Pfammenitus, thy mafter, Cambyfes, is defirous to
know, why, after thou hadft feen thy daughter fo ignominiofly treated,
and thy fon led to execution, without exclaiming or weeping thou
fhouldft be fo highly concerned for a poor man, no way related to
thee ?" Pfammenitus returned the following anfwer : " Son of Cyrus,
the calamities of my family are too great to leave me the power of wee-
ing; but the misfortunes of a companion, reduced in his old age to want
of bread, is a fit fubject for lamentation."

* See chap. 2. part 3.   † Chap. 16.

mind is depreffed with any paffion, the fentiments
muft be expreffed in words that are humble, not low.
Words being intimately connected with the ideas
they reprefent, the greateft harmony is required between them : to exprefs, for example, an humble
fentiment in high-founding words, is difagreeable by
a difcordant mixture of feelings ; and the difcord is
not lefs when elevated fentiments are dreffed in low
words :

> Verfibus exponi tragicis res comica non vult.
> Indignatur item privatis ac prope focco
> Dignis carminibus narrari coena Thyeftæ.
> > *Horace, Ars poet. l.* 89.

This however excludes not figurative expreffion,
which within moderate bounds, communicates to the
fentiment an agreeable elevation. We are fenfible
of an effect directly oppofite, where figurative expreffion is indulged beyond a juft meafure : the oppofition between the expreffion and the fentiment,
makes the difcord appear greater than it is in reality.*

At the fame time, figures are not equally the language of every paffion : pleafant emotions, which
elevate or fwell the mind, vent themfelves in ftrong
epithets and figurative expreffion ; but humbling and
difpiriting paffions affect to fpeak plain :

> Et tragicus plerumque dolet fermone pedeftri
> Telephus et Peleus: cum pauper et exul uterque ;
> Projicit ampullas et fefquipedalia verba,
> Si curat cor fpectantis tetigiffe querela.
> > *Horace, Ars poet l.* 95.

Figurative expreffion, being the work of an enlivened imagination, cannot be the language of anguifh
or diftrefs. Otway, fenfible of this, has painted a
fcene of diftrefs in colours finely adapted to the fubject ;

---

* See this explained more particularly in chap. 8.

ject : there is ſcarce a figure in it, except a ſhort and natural ſimile with which the ſpeech is introduced. Belvidera talking to her father of her huſband :

> Think you ſaw what paſt at our laſt parting ;
> Think you beheld him like a raging lion,
> Pacing the earth, and tearing up his ſteps,
> Fate in his eyes, and roaring with the pain
> Of burning fúry ; think you ſaw his one hand
> Fix'd on my throat, while the extended other
> Graſp'd a keen threat'ning dagger ; oh, 'twas thus
> We laſt embrac'd, when, trembling with revenge,
> He dragg'd me to the ground, and at my boſom
> Preſented horrid death ; cry'd out, My friends !
> Where are my friends ? ſwore, wept, rag'd, threat-
>   en'd, lov'd ;
> For he yet lov'd, and that dear love preſerv'd me
> To this laſt trial of a father's pity.
> I fear not death, but cannot bear a thought
> That that dear hand ſhould do th' unfriendly office :
> If I was ever then your care, now hear me ;
> Fly to the ſenate, ſave the promis'd lives
> Of his dear friends, ere mine be made the ſacrifice.
>   *Venice preſerv'd, act* 5.

To preſerve the foreſaid reſemblance between words and their meaning, the ſentiments of active and hurrying paſſions ought to be dreſſed in words where ſyllables prevail that are pronounced ſhort or faſt ; for theſe make an impreſſion of hurry and precipitation. Emotions, on the other hand, that reſt upon their objects, are beſt expreſſed by words where ſyllables prevail that are pronounced long or ſlow. A perſon affected with melancholy has a languid and ſlow train of perceptions : the expreſſion beſt ſuited to that ſtate of mind, is where words, not only of long but of many ſyllables, abound in the compoſition ; and, for that reaſon, nothing can be finer than the following paſſage.

In

In thofe deep folitudes, and awful cells,
Where heavenly-penfive Contemplation dwells,
And ever-mufing Melancholy reigns.
Pope, Eloiza to Abelard.

To preferve the fame refemblance, another circumftance is requifite, that the language, like the emotion, be rough or fmooth, broken or uniform. Calm
and fweet emotions are beft exprefled by words that
glide foftly : furprife, fear, and other turbulent
paffions, require an expreffion both rough and broken.

It cannot have efcaped any diligent inquirer into
nature, that, in the hurry of paffion, one generally
expreffes that thing firft which is moft at heart :*
which is beautifully done in the following paffage.

Me, me ; adfum qui feci : in me convertite ferrum
O Rutuli, mea fraus omnis.
Æneid, ix. 427.

Paffion has often the effect of redoubling words,
the better to make them exprefs the ftrong conception of the mind. This is finely imitated in the following examples.

——————Thou fun, faid I, fair light !
And thou enlighten'd earth, fo frefh and gay !
Ye hills and dales, ye rivers, woods, and plains !
And ye that live, and move, fair creatures ! tell,
Tell if ye faw, how came I thus, how here——
Paradife loft, book viii. 273.

——————Both have finn'd ! but thou
Againft God only ; I, 'gainft God and thee :
And to the place of judgment will return. '
There

---

* Demetrius Phalereus (of Elocution, fect. 28.) juftly obferves, that
an accurate adjuftment of the words to the thought, fo as to make them
correfpond in every particular, is only proper for fedate fubjects ; for that
paffion fpeaks plain, and rejects all refinements.

There with cries importune Heaven, that all
The ſentence, from thy head remov'd, may light
On me, ſole cauſe to thee of all this wo ;
Me ! Me ! only juſt objeċt of his ire.
Paradiſe loſt, book x. 930.

Shakeſpear is ſuperior to all other writers in de-
lineating paſſion. It is difficult to ſay in what part
he moſt excels, whether in moulding every paſſion
to peculiarity of character, in diſcovering the ſentiments that proceed from various tones of paſſion, or
in expreſſing properly every different ſentiment : he
diſguſts not his reader with general declamation and
unmeaning words, too common in other writers :
his ſentiments are adjuſted to the peculiar character
and circumſtances of the ſpeaker : and the propriety
is no leſs perfeċt between his ſentiments and his diction. That this is no exaggeration, will be evident
to every one of taſte, upon comparing Shakeſpear
with other writers in ſimilar paſſages. If upon any
occaſion he fall below himſelf, it is in thoſe ſcenes
where paſſion enters not : by endeavouring in that caſe
to raiſe his dialogue above the ſtyle of ordinary converſation, he ſometimes deviates into intricate thought
and obſcure expreſſion :* ſometimes, to throw his
language

---

* Of this take the following ſpecimen.

They clepe us drunkards, and with ſwiniſh phraſe
Soil our addition ; and, indeed it takes
From our achievements, though perform'd at height,
The pith and marrow of our attribute.
So, oft it chances in particular men,
That for ſome vicious mole of nature in them,
As in their birth, (wherein they are not guilty,
Since Nature cannot chuſe his origin,)
By the o'ergrowth of ſome complexion
Oft breaking down the pales and forts of reaſon ;
Or by ſome habit, that too much o'er leavens

The

language out of the familiar, he employs rhyme.
But may it not in ſome meaſure excuſe Shakeſpear,
I ſhall not ſay his works, that he had no pattern, in
his own or any living language, of dialogue fitted
for the theatre ? At the ſame time, it ought not to
eſcape obſervation, that the ſtream clears in its progreſs, and that in his later plays he has attained the
purity and perfection of dialogue ; an obſervation
that, with greater certainty than tradition, will direct
us to arrange his plays in the order of time. This
ought to be conſidered by thoſe who rigidly exag-
gerate every blemiſh of the fineſt genius for the
drama ever the world enjoyed : they ought alſo for
their own ſake to conſider, that it is eaſier to diſcover
his blemiſhes, which lie generally at the ſurface, than
his beauties, which cannot be truly reliſhed but by
thoſe who dive deep into human nature. One thing
muſt be evident to the meaneſt capacity, that where-
ever paſſion is to be diſplayed, Nature ſhows itſelf
mighty in him, and is conſpicuous by the moſt
delicate propriety of ſentiment and expreſſion.*

I return to my ſubject from a digreſſion I cannot
repent of. That perfect harmony which ought to
ſubſiſt

The form of plauſive manners ; that theſe men
Carrying, I ſay, the ſtamp of one defect,
(Being Nature's livery, or Fortune's ſcar,)
Their virtues elſe, be they as pure as grace,
As infinite as man can undergo,
Shall in the general cenſure take corruption
From that particular fault.   *Hamlet, act* 1. ſc. 7.

* The critics ſeem not perfectly to comprehend the genius of Shakeſpear. His plays are defective in the mechanical part ; which is leſs the
work of genius than of experience, and is not otherwiſe brought to perfection but by diligently obſerving the errors of former compoſitions.
Shakeſpear excels all the ancients and moderns in knowledge of human
nature, and in unfolding even the moſt obſcure and refined emotions.
This is a rare faculty, and of the greateſt importance in a dramatic author, and it is that faculty which makes him ſurpaſs all other writers in
the comic as well as tragic vein.

· ſubſiſt among all the conſtituent parts of a dialogue, is a beauty, no leſs rare than conſpicuous : as to exxpreſſion in particular, were I to give inſtances, where, in one or other of the reſpects above mentioned, it correſponds not preciſely to the characters, paſſions, and ſentiments, I might from different authors collect volumes. Following therefore the method laid down in the chapter of ſentiments, I ſhall confine my quotations to the groſſer errors, which every writer ought to avoid.

And, firſt, of paſſion expreſſed in words flowing in an equal courſe without interruption.

In the chapter above cited, Corneille is cenſured for the impropriety of his ſentiments ; and here, for the ſake of truth, I am obliged to attack him a ſecond time. Were I to give inſtances from that author of the fault under conſideration, I might tranſcribe whole tragedies : for he is no leſs faulty in this particular, than in paſſing upon us his own thoughts as a ſpectator, inſtead of the genuine ſentiments of paſſion. Nor would a compariſon between him and Shakeſpear, upon the preſent article, redound more to his honour, than the former upon the ſentiments. Racine is here leſs incorrect than Corneille ; and from him therefore I ſhall gather a few inſtances. The firſt ſhall be the deſcription of the ſea-monſter in his *Phædra*, given by Theramene, the companion of Hippolytus. Theramene is repreſented in terrible agitation, which appears from the following paſſage, ſo boldly figurative as not to be excuſed but by violent perturbation of mind :

> Le ciel avec horreur voit ce monſtre ſauvage,
> Le terre s'en émeut, l'air en eſt infecté,
> Le flot, qui l'apporta, recule epouvanté.

Y e.

Yet Theramene gives a long pompous connected deſcription of that event, dwelling upon every minute circumſtance, as if he had been only a cool ſpectator :

A peine nous ſortions des portes de Trézéne,
Il étoit ſur ſon char.   Ses gardes affligés
Imitoient ſon ſilence, autour de lui rangés.
Il ſuivoit tout penſif le chemin de Mycénes.
Sa main ſur les chevaux laiſſoit flotter les rênes.
Ses ſuperbs courſiers qu'on voyoit autrefois
Pleins d'une ardeur ſi noble obéir à ſa voix,
L'œil morne maintenant et la tête baiſſée,
Sembloient ſe conformer à ſa triſte penſée, &c.

Act 5. *ſc.* 6.

The laſt ſpeech of Atalide, in the tragedy of *Bajazet,* of the ſame author, is a continued diſcourſe ; and but a faint repreſentation of the violent paſſion which forced her to put an end to her own life :

Enfin, c'en eſt donc fait.   Et par mes artifices,
Mes injuſtes ſoupçons, mes funeſtes caprices,
Je ſuis donc arrivée au douloureux moment,
Où je vois, par mon crime, expirer mon amant.
N'étoit-ce pas aſſez, cruelle deſtinée,
Qu'à lui ſurvivre, hélas ! je fuſſe condamnée ?
Et falloit-il encore que, pour comble d'horreurs,
Je ne puſſe imputer ſa mort qu'à mes fureurs !
Oui, c'eſt moi, cher amant, qui t'arrache la vie ;
Roxane, ou le Sultan, ne te l'ont ravie.
Moi ſeule, j'ai tiſſu le lien malheureux
Dont tu viens d'éprouver les deteſtables nœuds.
Et je puis, ſans mourir, en ſouffrir la penſée ?
Moi, qui n'ai pû tantôt, de ta mort menacée,
Retentir mes eſprits, prompts à m'abandonner !
Ah ! n'ai-je eu de l'amour que pour t'aſſaſſiner ?
Mais c'en eſt trop.   Il faut par un prompt ſacrifice,
Que ma fidelle main te venge, et me puniſſe.
Vous, de qui j'ai troublé la gloire et le repos,
Héros, qui deviez tous revivre en ce héros,

Toi,

Toi, mere malheureuſe, et qui dès notre enfance,
Me confias ſon cœur dans une autre eſperance,
Infortuné Viſir, amis déſeſpéiés,
Roxane, venez tous contre moi conjurez,
Tourmenter à la fois une amante eperdue ; [*Elle ſe tue.*
Et prenez la vengeance enfin qui vois eſt dûe.

Act 5. *ſc.* laſt.

Though works, not authors, are the profeſſed ſubject of this critical undertaking, I am tempted by the
preſent ſpeculation to tranſgreſs once again the limits
preſcribed, and to venture a curſory reflection upon
that juſtly celebrated author, That he is always ſenſible, generally correct, never falls low, maintains a
moderate degree of dignity without reaching the ſublime, paints delicately the tender affections, but is a
ſtranger to the genuine language of enthuſiaſtic or
fervid paſſion.

If, in general, the language of violent paſſion
ought to be broken and interrupted, ſoliloquies ought
to be ſo in a peculiar manner : language is intended
by nature for ſociety ; and a man when alone, though
he always clothes his thoughts in words, ſeldom gives
his words utterance, unleſs when prompted by ſome
ſtrong emotion ; and even then by ſtarts and intervals only.*   Shakeſpear's ſoliloquies may be juſtly
eſtabliſhed as a model ; for it is not eaſy to conceive
any model more perfect : of his many incomparable
ſoliloquies, I confine myſelf to the two following, being different in their manner.

Hamlet. Oh, that this too too ſolid fleſh would melt,
Thaw, and reſolve itſelf into a dew !
Or that the Everlaſting had not fix'd
His canon 'gainſt ſelf-ſlaughter ! O God ! O God !
How weary, ſtale, flat, and unprofitable
                                                        Seem

_____

* Soliloquies accounted for, chap. 16.

Seem to me all the uſes of this world !
Fie on't ! O fie ! 'tis an unweeded garden,
That grows to feed : things rank and groſs in nature
Poſſeſs it merely.—That it ſhould come to this !
But two months dead ! nay, not ſo much ; not two ;—
So excellent a king, that was, to this,
Hyperion to a ſatyr : ſo loving to my mother,
That he permitted not the winds of heav'n
Viſit her face too roughly.   Heav'n and earth !
Muſt I remember—why, ſhe would hang on him,
As if increaſe of appetite had grown
By what it fed on ; yet, within a' month——
Let me not think—Frailty, thy name is *Woman* '
A little month ! or ere thoſe ſhoes were old,   "
With which ſhe followed my poor father's body,
Like Niobe, all tears——Why ſhe, ev'n ſhe——
(O heav'n ! a beaſt that wants diſcourſe of reaſon,
Would have mourn'd longer—) married with mine uncle,
My father's brother ; but no more like my father,
Than I to Hercules.   Within a month !
Ere yet the ſalt of moſt unrighteous tears
Had left the fluſhing in her galled eyes,
She married——Oh, moſt wicked ſpeed, to poſt -
With ſuch dexterity to inceſtuous ſheets !
It is not, nor it cannot come to good.
But break, my heart, for I muſt hold my tongue,
                   Hamlet, act 1. *ſc.* 3.

 Ford. Hum ! ha ! is this a viſion ? is this a dream ?
do I ſleep ? Mr. Ford, awake : awake Mr. Ford ; there's
a hole made in your beſt coat, Mr. Ford ! this 'tis to be
married ! this 'tis to have linen and buck baſkets ! Well, I
will proclaim myſelf what I am ; I will 'now take the
leacher ; he is at my houſe ; he cannot 'ſcape me ; 'tis
impoſſible he ſhould ; he cannot creep into a half-pen-
ny-purſe, nor into a pepper-box. But leſt the devil that
guides him ſhould aid him, I will ſearch impoſſible places,
though what I am I cannot avoid, yet to be what I would
not, ſhall not make me tame.
  Merry Wives of Windſor, act 3. *ſc. laſt.*

Theſe ſoliloquies are accurate and bold copies of na-
                                    ture :

ture : in a paffionate foliloquy one begins with thinking aloud ; and the ftrongeft feelings only, are expreffed ; as the fpeaker warms, he begins to imagine
one liftening, and gradually flides into a connected
difcourfe.

How far diftant are foliloquies generally from thefe
models ? So far, indeed, as to give difguft inftead of
pleafure. The firft fcene of *Iphigenia* in Tauris difcovers that Princefs, in a foliloquy, gravely reporting
to herfelf her own hiftory. There is the fame impropriety in the firft fcene of *Alceftes*, and in the
other introductions of Euripides, almoft without exception. Nothing can be more ridiculous : it puts
one in mind of a moft curious device in Gothic paintings, that of making every figure explain itfelf by a
written label iffuing from its mouth. The defcription which a parafite, in the *Eunuch* of Terence,[*]
gives of himfelf, makes a fprightly foliloquy : but it
is not confiftent with the rules of propriety ; for no
man, in his ordinary ftate of mind, and upon a familiar fubject, ever thinks of talking aloud to himfelf.
The fame objection lies againft a foliloquy in the
Adelphi of the fame author.[†] The foliloquy which
makes the third fcene, act third, of his *Hecyra*, is
infufferable ; for there Pamphilus, foberly and cir-
cumftantially, relates to himfelf an adventure which
had happened to him a moment before.

Corneille is not more happy in his foliloquies than
in his dialogue. Take for a fpecimen the firft fcene
of *Cinna*.

Racine alfo is extremely faulty in the fame refpect. His foliloquies are regular harrangues, a
chain completed in every link, without interruption
or interval : that of Antiochus in *Berenice*[‡] refembles a regular pleading, where the parties *pro* and *con*
difplay their arguments at full length. The following

ing ſoliloquies are equally faulty : *Bajazet*, act 3. ſc. 7. *Mithridate*, act 3. ſc. 4. & act 4. ſc. 5 ; *Iphigenia*, act 4. ſc. 8.

Soliloquies upon lively or intereſting ſubjects, but without any turbulence of paſſion, may be carried on in a continued chain of thought. If, for example, the nature and ſprightlineſs of the ſubject prompt a man to ſpeak his thoughts in the form of a dialogue, the expreſſion muſt be carried on without break or interruption, as in a dialogue between two perſons ; which juſtifies Falſtaff's ſoliloquy upon honour :

> What need I be ſo forward with Death, that calls not on me ? Well, 'tis no matter, Honour pricks me on. But how if honour prick me off, when I come on ? how then ? Can Honour ſet a leg ? No : or an arm ? No : or take away the grief of a wound ? No. Honour hath no ſkill in ſurgery then ? No. What is honour ? A word.—What is that word *honour* ? Air, a trim reckoning.——Who hath it ? He that dy'd a Wedneſday. Doth he feel it ? No. Doth he hear it ? No. Is it inſenſible then ? Yea, to the dead. But will it not live with the living ? No ? Why ? Detraction will not ſuffer it. Therefore I'll none of it ; honour is a mere ſcutcheon ; and ſo ends my catechiſm.
>
> *Firſt part, Henry* IV. *act* 5. *ſc.* 2.

And even without dialogue, a continued diſcourſe may be juſtified, where a man reaſons in a ſoliloquy upon an important ſubject ; for if in ſuch a caſe it be at all excuſable to think aloud, it is neceſſary that the reaſoning be carried on in a chain ; which juſtifies that admirable ſoliloquy in *Hamlet* upon life and immortality, being a ſerene meditation upon the moſt intereſting of all ſubjects. And the ſame conſideration will juſtify the ſoliloquy that introduces the 5th act of Addiſon's *Cato*.

The next claſs of the groſſer errors which all writers ought to avoid, ſhall be of language elevated

above

above the tone of the fentiment ; of which take the following inftances.

> *Zara.* Swift as occafion, I
> Myfelf will fly ; and earlier than the morn
> Wake thee to freedom. Now 'tis late ; and yet
> Some news few minutes paft arriv'd, which feem'd
> To fhake the temper of the King.——Who knows
> What racking cares difeafe a monarch's bed ?
> Or love, that late at night ftill lights his lamp,
> And ftrikes his rays through dufk, and folded lids,
> Forbidding reft, may ftretch his eyes awake,
> And force their balls abroad at this dead hour.
> I'll try,
>
> *Mourning Bride, act 3. fc. 4.*

The language here is undoubtedly too pompous and laboured for defcribing fo fimple a circumftance as abfence of fleep. In the following paffage, the tone of the language, warm and plaintive, is well fuited to the paffion, which is recent grief : but every one will be fenfible, that in the laft couplet fave one, the tone is changed, and the mind fuddenly elevated to be let fall as fuddenly in the laft couplet :

> Il déteft à jamais fa coupable victoire,
> Il renonce à la cour, aux humains, à la gloire ;
> Et fe furant lui même, au milieu des deferts,
> Il va cacher fa peine aut bout de l'univers ;
> *La, foit que le foleil rendît le jour au monde,*
> *Soit qu'il finît fa courfe au vafte feine de l'onde,*
> Sa voix faifoit redire aux echos attendris,
> Le nom, le trifte nom, de fon malheureux fils.
>
> *Henriade, chant. viii. 229.*

Language too artificial or too figurative for the gravity, dignity, or importance, of the occafion, may be put in a third clafs.

Chimene demanding juftice againft Rodrigue who killed her father, inftead of a plain and pathetic ex-
postulation,

postulation, makes a speech stuffed with the most artificial flowers of rhetoric :

> Sire, mon pere est mort, mes yeux ont vû son sang
> Couler à gros bouillons de son généreux flanc ;
> Ce sang qui tant de fois garantit vos murailles,
> Ce sang qui tant de fois vous gagna des battailes,
> Ce sang qui, tout sorti, fume encore de courroux
> De se voir répandu pour d'autres que pour vous,
> Qu'au milieu des hazards n'osoit verser la guerre,
> Rodrigue en votre cour vient d'en couvrir la terre.
> J'ai couru sur le lieu sans force, et sans couleur :
> Je l'ai trouvé sans vie. Excusez ma douleur,
> Sire ; la voix me manque àce recit funeste,
> Mes pleurs et mes soupirs vous diront mieux le reste.

And again,

> Son flanc étoit ouvert, et, pour mieux m'emouvoir,
> Son sang sur la poussiere écrivoit mon devoir ;
> Ou plûtôt sa valeur en cet état réduite
> Me parloit par sa plaie, et hâtoit ma pursuite,
> Et pour se faire entendre au plus juste des Rois,
> Par cette triste bouche elle empruntoit ma voix.
>
> *Act* 2. *sc.* 9.

Nothing can be contrived in language more averse to the tone of the passion than this florid speech : I should imagine it apt more to provoke laughter than to inspire concern or pity.

In a fourth class shall be given specimens of language too light or airy for a severe passion.

Imagery and figurative expression are discordant, in the highest degree, with the agony of a mother, who is deprived of two hopeful sons by a brutal murder. Therefore the following passage is undoubtedly in a bad taste.

> *Queen.* Ah, my poor princes ! ah, my tender babes !
> My unblown flow'rs, new appearing sweets !

If

If yet your gentle fouls fly in the air,
And be not fixt in doom perpetual,
Hover about me with your airy wings,
And hear your mother's lamentation.

Richard III. *act* 4. *fc.* 4.

Again,

K. Philip.   You are as fond of grief as of your child.
Conftance.   Grief fills the room up of my abfent child,
Lies in his bed, walks up and down with me,
Puts on his pretty looks, repeats his words,
Remembers me of all his gracious parts,
Stuffs out his vacant garment with his form ;
Then have I reafon to be fond of grief.

King John, *act* 3. *fc.* 6.

A thought that turns upon the expreffion inftead of the fubject, commonly called *a play of words*, being low and childifh, is unworthy of any compofition, whether gay or ferious, that pretends to any degree of elevation : thoughts of this kind make a fifth clafs.

In the *Amynta* of Taffo.* the lover falls into a mere play of words, demanding how he who had loft himfelf, could find a miftrefs.   And for the fame reafon, the following paffage in Corneille has been generally condemned :

Chimene.   Mon pere eft mort, Elvire, et la premiere
épée
Dont s'eft armée Rodrigue a fa trame coupée.
Pleurez, mes yeux, et fondez-vous en eau,
La moitié de ma vie a mis l'autre au tombeau,
Et m'oblige à venger, après ce coup funefte,
Celle que je n'ai plus, fur celle que me refte.

Cid, *act* 3. *fc.* 3.

To die is to be banifh'd from myfelf :
And fylvia is myfelf ; banifh'd from her,
Is felf from felf ; a deadly banifhment !

Two Gentlemen of Verona, *act* 3. *fc.* 3.
Counteff.

* Act 1. fc. 2.

Counteſs. I pray thee, Lady, have a better cheer :
If thou ingroſſeſt all the griefs as thine,
Thou robb'ſt me of a moiety.

All's well that ends well, act 3. *ſc.* 3.

K. Henry. O my poor kingdom, ſick with civil
blows !
When that my care could not with-hold thy riots,
What wilt thou do when riot is thy care ?
O, thou wilt be a wildernefs again.
Peopled with wolves, thy old inhabitants.

Second part Henry IV. *act* 4. *ſc.* 11.

Cruda Amarilli, che col nome ancora
D'amar, ahi, laſſo, amaramente inſegni.

Paſtor Fido, act 1. *ſc.* 2.

Antony ſpeaking of Julius Cefar :

O world ! thou waſt the foreſt of this hart :
And this, indeed, O world, the heart of thee.
How like a deer, ſtriken by many princes,
Doſt thou liere lie !

Julius Cæſar, act 3. *ſc.* 3.

Playing thus with the ſound of words, which is ſtill
worſe than a pun, is the meaneſt of all conceits. But
Shakeſpear when he defcends to a play of words, is
not always in the wrong ; for it is done ſometimes to
denote a peculiar character, as in the following paſſage :

K. Philip. What ſay'ſt thou, boy ? look in the lady's
face.
Lewis. I do, my Lord, and in her eye I find
A wonder, or a wond'rous miracle ;
The ſhadow of myſelf form'd in her eye ;
Which being but the ſhadow of your ſon,
Becomes a ſun, and makes your ſon a ſhadow.
I do proteſt, I never lov'd myſelf
'Til now infixed I beheld myſelf
Drawn in the flatt'ring table of her eye.

Faulconbridge.

Faulconbridge. Drawn in the flatt'ring table of her eye !
Hang'd in the frowning wrinkle of her biow !
And quarter'd in her heart ! he doth efpy
Himfelf Love's traitor : this is pity now,
That hang'd, and drawn, and quarter'd, there fhould be,
In fuch a love fo vile a lout as he.

King John, act 2. fc. 5.

A jingle of words is the loweft fpecies of that low
wit ; which is fcarce fufferable in any cafe, and leaft
of all in an heroic poem : and yet Milton, in fome
inftances has defcended to that puerility :

.And brought into the world a world of wo.
——begirt th' Almighty throne
Befeeching or befieging————
Which tempted our attempt————
At one flight bound high overleap'd all bound.
————————————With a fhout
Loud as from numbers without number.

One fhould think it unneceffary to enter a caveat
againft an expreffion that has no meaning, or no diftinct meaning ; and yet fomewhat of that kind may
be found even among good writers. Such make a
fixth clafs.

Sebaftian. I beg no pity for this mould'ring clay,
For if you give it burial, there it takes
Poffeffion of your earth :
If burnt and fcatter'd in the air ; the winds
That ftrow my duft, diffufe my royalty;
And fpread me o'er your clime ; for where one atom
Of mine fhall light, know there Sebaftian reigns.

Dryden, Don Sebaftian King of Portugal, act 1.

Cleopatra. Now, what news, my Charmion ?
Will he be kind ? and will he not forfake me ?
Am I to live or die ? nay, do I live ?
Or am I dead ? for when he gave his anfwer,
Fate took the word, and then I liv'd or dy'd.

Dryden, All for Love, act 2.

If

If ſhe be coy, and ſcorn my noble fire,
If her chill heart I cannot move ;
Why, I'll enjoy the very love,
And make a miſtreſs of my own deſire.
    Cowley, poem inſcribed, The Requeſt.

His whole poem, inſcribed, *My picture,* is a jargon of the ſame kind.

——————— 'Tis he, they cry, by whom
Not men, but war itſelf is overcome,
     Indian Queen.

Such empty expreſſions are finely ridiculed in the *Re-hearſal:*

Was't not unjuſt to raviſh hence her breath,
And in life's ſtead to leave us nought but death.
     Act 4. ſc. 1.